VICTORY
SQUARE

VICTORY
SQUARE

OLEN STEINHAUER

ST. MARTIN'S MINOTAUR
NEW YORK

S

This is a work of fiction. All of the characters, organizations, and events portrayed in this novel are either products of the author's imagination or are used fictitiously.

www.minotaurbooks.com

Library of Congress Cataloging-in-Publication Data

Steinhauer, Olen.
    Victory Square / Olen Steinhauer.—1st ed.
      p. cm.
    ISBN-13: 978-0-312-36971-2
    ISBN-10: 0-312-36971-9
    1. Police—Europe, Eastern—Fiction. 2. Europe, Eastern—Fiction.
  3. Psychological fiction. I. Title.

PS3619.T4764V53 2007
813'.6—dc22   2007014286

First Edition: August 2007

10 9 8 7 6 5 4 3 2 1

FOR
KATRINA AND IAN

ACKNOWLEDGMENTS

•

I want to thank my good friend John Nadler for reading an early draft of this novel and offering wise and informed suggestions. Also, my former agent, Matt Williams, was vociferous in his encouragement and faith in this series from the beginning. Without his support, I certainly wouldn't have made it this far.

More than my previous books, this one depends on research I conducted during a 1999 Fulbright grant, so I would be remiss in not thanking the Fulbright Commission for its generosity. Specifically, I want to thank Ioana Ieronim, a wonderful poet and human being, who enthusiastically assisted me during my year in Romania.

As ever, Slavica Pilić has helped me better understand my own writing, as well as myself. For both, I'm eternally grateful.

26 DECEMBER 1989

TUESDAY

·

There are things you know but forget. Truths that don't stay in your head because you're distracted by daily affairs, by the manic effort of living your life. Then, unexpectedly, the knowledge returns and changes you. It makes murder possible.

Leaning through the high stone window of the Grand Hotel Duchi D'Aosta, I looked down at tourists and pigeons vying for space on the damp marble floor of the Piazza dell'Unità d'Italia, Trieste's central square. In the cold wind blowing through from the Adriatic, a basic truth came back to me: Old men die every day.

They submit in overstuffed chairs across from blaring televisions, slip in the bathtub, sink deep into hospital beds. They tumble down the stairwells of barren apartment blocks and face heart failure in swimming pools and restaurants and crowded buses. Some, already sleeping on the street, go quietly, while others take care of it themselves, because that's the only power left to them. Their wives are dead and their friends as well; their children have fled from the stink of mortality. Sleeping pills, razors, high terraces and bridges. Usually, old men go alone.

Before that week, I'd never been to Italy, though when I was a young man I dreamed of it, and of a famous bridge in Venice that spelled out a metaphor I could understand. No longer. Metaphors help you boil down the complications and ambiguities of your too-long life into a picture book. They help you lie to yourself.

My wife, Lena—she was the one who traveled, and for a long time I didn't know why. In truth, I knew nothing about her. Only later, among whining Vespas, garlic-scented streets, and bombastic Italians, feeling every one of my sixty-four years, did I finally understand. I understood her, and I understood everything, for just a moment. To the left, beyond the square, the Adriatic glimmered.

The pedestrians below didn't notice me. Bald on top, white along the sides; my one striking feature was that I had bright eyes that should've been on a younger man. Not tall—neither in height nor stature. That was me. A normal man in all ways, with the cold sea wind flapping my gray blazer. I owned nothing; even my clothes were borrowed from Brano Sev, who, until I betrayed him, was probably the luckiest man I'd ever known. Borrowed, too, was the still-warm Walther PP I kept in the blazer's stretched pocket so the tourists below wouldn't be frightened.

I wasn't thinking of the man I'd shot, who made quiet noises in the room behind me. No, I'd thought about him far too much over the last week. I was thinking, instead, about the greatness of life. All the sensations and people and moments that, if you don't hold on to them, disappear forever. And once they're gone, they might as well never have existed. That's one reason I'm telling this story, to make them last a little longer. The other reason will explain itself.

I turned back to the room. It was one of those Italian prestige hotels filled with corroded grandeur, the most expensive in town. The old man groaned on the blood-wet bed, clutching his left knee. He wasn't even looking at me now, because he knew it made no difference.

I settled into a chair, told him I would finish this, and watched as the tremors began. He let go of his knee and seized up. His right leg shot out, then the injured one, and that movement made him scream. I didn't react.

This man, descending into epileptic spasms, had an unbelievable resilience. He'd survived so much over the last century, been near death so many times, beaten down but always rising again over eighty years, despite being crippled by the falling sickness. I even felt, briefly, a measure of respect. In comparison, my own life had been soft and simple. But old men die every day—yes, women, too—and this day was no exception.

WEDNESDAY

·

ONE

•

It started six days before. Only a week. Gavra Noukas would later fill in the details I wasn't around to see, and he's checked what I've written to verify it all, at great cost to himself. Despite everything, I stand behind his version of events. The young spy has always been straightforward with me, and if anyone in this new world wants to prosecute him for what he did in the old, he can call on me to speak in his defense. But I don't think he needs my help anymore.

He'd been traveling a long time. First, a TisAir flight to Zagreb, where a cramped JAT jumbo jet brought him to JFK Airport. On that long flight he'd distracted himself by flirting with the Croat stewardess who, after bringing him vodka on the sly, told him her name was Radmila. He gave her the name on the passport he'd switched to after leaving, but before reentering, Zagreb International, and her head popped back. "You're kidding."

"I'm not."

"That's my father's name."

His passport, like all those issued by the Ministry for State Security, was worn and authentic-looking. Lieutenant General Kolev had chosen the name Viktor Lukacs, which just happened to be the name of this stewardess's father. With that name, Gavra cleared New York passport control and took a 3:00 A.M. taxi to LaGuardia. While waiting for a Delta flight to Virginia, he bought a baseball cap emblazoned with the letters *N* and *Y*.

Though he was nearly forty-five, this was only Gavra's second time in the United States. It felt loud and foreign to him, but by the time he rented a blue Toyota Tercel in Richmond and was driving westward toward Midlothian, that fish-out-of-water feeling started to fade. He cranked up the heater and yawned into his fist, merging onto the highway. After twenty-seven long hours, he was getting his second wind, but his arms and legs still ached. Sleep, though, would have to wait until he'd made his preparations for the capture of Lubov Shevchenko.

The travel and fatigue would have been more bearable had he known *why* Yuri Kolev insisted he find this Shevchenko. The Lieutenant General simply appeared unannounced at his apartment Monday evening with two assistants, clutching a lumpy manila envelope.

"May we come in?"

"Of—of course," said Gavra.

Perhaps it was more than luck that they'd shown up just after Gavra's roommate, Karel, had left. Perhaps they'd been waiting in their car.

Lieutenant General Yuri Kolev untied the belt of his thick, fur-lined trench coat, letting one of his assistants, a huge, broad-shouldered thug, take it off his back. The old man settled on Gavra's sofa and examined the room with approval, sniffing and scratching his thick gray beard.

"Nice place. We got it for you?"

"Through a friend."

"Not bad at all," the Lieutenant General said, though in fact it was just another third-floor block apartment, not worth the appreciation.

"Something to drink?"

"Thought you'd never ask."

Gavra collected four glasses and a bottle of plum brandy from the kitchen.

"Just two," said Kolev.

His assistants shifted, just slightly, in disappointment.

This was the first time Gavra had spoken to the Lieutenant General outside the confines of state security headquarters on Yalta Boulevard since the retirement party for Brano Sev, his mentor, three years before. Brano, still sturdy at sixty-nine years, and more than a little drunk, had whispered a few final words of advice to his old pupil: "Keep your eye on all these men—you hear? But listen to Kolev. He's the only one I'd want watching my back." The next day, Gavra went to Brano's apartment, if only to get him to elaborate on the warning, but Brano Sev was gone, his apartment completely empty. Without telling anyone, the old cold warrior had disappeared, and Gavra hadn't seen or heard from him in the three years since.

It was common knowledge that Lieutenant General Kolev sometimes visited people whose careers were shaky. He would walk in and share a drink, then deliver a warning, leaving before the cushions got warm. But the old Lieutenant General, peering at a small, obligatory portrait of General Secretary and President Tomiak Pankov to the right of the television, seemed in no hurry to leave. He peered up at his guards. "Balínt. Vasili." Then he nodded at the door. The two men went into the corridor and closed the door behind themselves.

Kolev tugged a photograph from the envelope and handed it over. "I want you to go to Virginia, USA, and find this man. Lubov Shevchenko."

Shevchenko was in his late fifties; he had thick black Ukrainian eyebrows below a mane of white hair, and deep-set eyes above a fat drinker's nose.

"You make sure he stays alive. That's most important. Then you call me."

"I just track him down and call you."

"Exactly. He's in Midlothian, Virginia. Working at a high school, probably in administration."

"What's it called?"

"What's what called?"

"The school."

Kolev rubbed the side of his nose and sniffed again. "Our information's sketchy. We don't have his home address either, but we do know he lives in a housing project called Brandermill. You're smart, though. You can do this with your eyes shut."

Kolev liked to ply his subordinates with outrageous compliments.

"When you're set up, call me directly. *Don't* go through anyone else. Understand?" Gavra did. "Then call again when you've got him. If anything goes wrong, return to Zagreb and switch back to your passport. As if you never left."

Gavra refilled their brandies and waited, but Kolev didn't continue. "You're not telling me more?"

"I don't think it's necessary."

"I'd like to at least know who he is. Know what to expect."

Kolev threw back his shot. Clear spirit spilled into his beard, but he didn't notice. "He's a defector. Went to the Americans in eighty-one. Shevchenko is the name they gave him."

"And his real name?"

The Lieutenant General wiped his big nose with his fingertips, then shook his head.

"If you don't know who he is," said Gavra, "then the order's coming from someone else. Who?"

The Lieutenant General went back to his nose. "I do know Shevchenko's real name, but it's not necessary you know it."

"Sure it is."

"No," said Kolev. "And you're right, there is someone else giving the order, and he agrees you should only be told what you need to know."

"Then tell me who's giving the orders."

"No."

"Why not?"

"Because he asked me to keep his name out of it."

It was infuriating, but this really wasn't such a strange thing—in the Ministry, ignorance was a common companion. "And me?" said Gavra.

"You?"

"I keep a desk at the Militia station. You've certainly got more qualified people to send."

Kolev pursed his lips. "You were specifically requested."

"By the person giving the orders?"

A nod, and nothing more.

Gavra pressed, but the Lieutenant General's reticence didn't falter. He would only admit that they were getting their sketchy information on Shevchenko, even the photograph, from a contact in American Central Intelligence. "Some low-level mole." Then he tired of Gavra's questions and handed over the envelope.

"Passport, tickets, and dollars. Your flight leaves in two hours." He stood, patting his thighs. "Remember, you call me when you're set up. Direct to my office."

Gavra helped him back into his trench coat, and they shook hands at the door. Balínt and Vasili, in the corridor, looked as if they were freezing.

Dawn glimmered over the Midlothian Turnpike, empty except the occasional blue-and-white police car. Off to the right, he noticed a green sign with clearly printed words ahead of a two-story building surrounded by pine trees:

STOP & DROP MOTEL
NEXT RIGHT

The bearded man at the check-in desk looked more exhausted than Gavra, kept awake only by the staticky voices coming from a

black-and-white television. *Dallas*. One of the few American programs shown in the Eastern Bloc—a pristine example, the information minister once told him at a party, of the decadence of the
American ruling classes. *And it says something that the American
working classes take these cretins as heroes.* Gavra didn't bother mentioning that their own classless society did the same thing.

"Wanna room?" the man said with a thick southern drawl.

When Gavra told him yes, he'd like a room, the man cocked his
head. "You Russian or something?"

"Something like that." Gavra didn't feel up to a geography lesson.
He counted out crisp American dollars from Kolev's envelope.

The man squinted. "Say . . ."

"What?"

"You guys got television over there?"

"Of course we do." Gavra nodded at the screen. "*Dallas* is very
popular."

"You don't say! Remember who shot J. R.?"

"Sue Ellen's sister, Kristin, of course. And she was right to shoot
the bastard."

The bearded man laughed. "You really do watch it! Hey, if you got
some time on your hands, I'll buy you a beer. How about that?"

"Maybe later. Thanks."

"Freddy," he said, sticking out a damp hand. "I'm right here all
day."

They shook. "I'm Viktor."

The room was better than he expected. It was warm and had its
own bathroom, a working color television, and a view through trees
of the turnpike. The water was hot immediately, unlike his apartment
back home. To wake himself, though, he took a cold shower, then
turned on a twenty-four-hour news station as he toweled off. A mustached black man, sitting in front of a superimposed banner that said
FREEDOM IN EASTERN EUROPE, introduced a series of brief seg-
ments where reporters—some British, some American—reported on

what had been an eventful year in our part of the world. Everyone focused on Berlin, and the Wall, but the other nations had been even more surprising.

In Bulgaria, President Todor Zhivkov had resigned on the tenth of November, after thirty-five years in power. Czechoslovakia, following a half-million-strong demonstration, changed hands with a series of signatures and press conferences. Since June, the previously illegal Solidarity Party had had a majority in the Polish parliament. Some of these changes had terribly poetic names: the Velvet Revolution in Prague and the slow-moving Singing Revolution in Estonia. All were triggered by those new words coming from that youthful USSR general secretary, Mikhail Gorbachev. *Glasnost* and *perestroika*—or, in the words of one Soviet economist, *catastroika*—catastrophe.

When a new correspondent came on, Gavra sat naked on the bed, watching dark, grainy footage from a town he knew well—Sárospatak, or, as it was called by locals, Patak, along the western border with Hungary, straddling the Bodrog River. An hour and a half from the Capital. A large crowd filled 25 August Square, faces lit by handheld candles. A panicked-sounding commentator said that this was the third night of anti-Pankov demonstrations, which began on the president's return, Sunday night, from a diplomatic trip to Libya, "one of this Stalinist's few remaining allies." While the Sárospatak side streets were filled with soldiers from the "hated Ministry for State Security," there had been no shots . . . *yet*. (He emphasized that last word.)

"For the last three years, this country has been under a literal cloud of *darkness*. In an effort to pay off the national foreign debt, Tomiak Pankov has rationed everything: electricity, petrol, food. He's *starving* the country, and the continual power outages leave even a city of seventeen *thousand* in complete darkness at night."

He turned off the television, because seeing it from the outside made him ill. Like most people—like myself, for instance—Gavra could not dispute the facts. Like everyone else, he knew that the

Party newspaper, *The Spark,* would call the demonstrators "imperialist-financed counterrevolutionary agitators" and never report the reason for their gathering—to protest the recent arrest of a priest, Father Eduard Meyr. But also like the rest of ours, Gavra's time was strained enough with his job, his friends, and himself. All he could do, sitting on an American motel bed, was focus on what he'd come to do: find a man and make a telephone call.

He found a fat telephone directory under the bedside table and flipped through it looking for "firearms." There they were, amazingly, five gun stores. The closest was Bob Moates Gun Shop, on Hull Street. He marked it on his rental car map.

He dressed as he knew the Americans dressed: casually. A pair of Levi's he'd picked up in a private Ministry store last year and a black polo shirt. He took out the NY baseball cap from La Guardia but was already too appalled by his outfit to add it.

The turnpike was busy with morning traffic. It took twenty minutes to find the windowless brick building with a steel door. The inside was lined with glass cases full of armaments. A fat man with a T-shirt and tattoos up his arms ate Ruffles potato chips behind the cases. "Morning."

"Morning," said Gavra.

"What can I do you for?"

"I'm looking for a gun."

"Well, I'd say you came to the right place."

"I suppose I did."

"Rifle, maybe? Just got in two AK-47s. Russian, you know."

"A little smaller, I think."

In the end he settled for a Polish P-83 with twenty rounds of 9mm cartridges, then bought three rolls of quarters. The clerk placed the pistol and ammunition into a paper sack and wished him a good day.

One more thing to do, then he could sleep.

He drove back, past the motel, to where, on the right, a ring of

stores spread. At the entrance, a large wooden sign proclaimed BRAN-
DERMILL, and beyond it were more trees—it was more like a forest
than the "housing project" he'd imagined. Another right placed him
inside the paved ring of parked cars and shops. A plaza, they called it.

At the far end was a massive Safeway grocery store. Its windows
were decorated with fake white snow and a cardboard Santa Claus
leading twelve reindeer into the sky. Near its front door was a telephone booth. At this hour—noon—he had to avoid running over
brightly dressed shoppers while searching for a parking spot.

He shoved coins into the pay phone, shivering as he dialed the
long number. After ten rings he gave up, cupping his hand to catch
the money the phone returned.

It was six in the evening back home, so the Lieutenant General
had probably left for the day. He shoved in the coins again and tried
the Ministry switchboard's international access line. An operator
picked up. "Welcome to Eastern Expressions, the world through the
beauty of icon paintings."

The cover always made Gavra smile, but he cleared his throat and
gave his ten-digit identification number, then his real name, and
asked for Lieutenant General Yuri Kolev's home number. The operator paused, her voice wavering as she said, "You *do* know about
Comrade Kolev, right?"

"What about him?"

"He's dead."

The line wasn't so clear that he could believe he'd heard her right,
so he made her repeat it. "He had a heart attack this morning, right
in the office. We're all in shock."

"Who's taking care of it?"

"What?"

"Who's doing the paperwork on his death?"

"It's been handed to the Militia," she told him. "I think Emil
Brod's working it personally."

"Why the Militia?"

"You think anyone explained it to me?"

When he hung up, the Virginia cold seemed a little harsher, the colors on the American shoppers that much more intense. He returned to his Toyota, which felt stuffy. He'd been sent here with no information, knowing only that he should capture a particular man and then get in touch with Kolev. And now . . .

He didn't like it, but Kolev had spelled it out for him: *If anything goes wrong, return to Zagreb.*

TWO

•

When the call came in, I was at my desk, having just popped two twenty-five-milligram tablets of Captopril. Hypertension. It's one of the innumerable annoyances that come with getting old. I was also wrapped in a wool coat (the heating had been out for a week), going through a box of old files I'd had shipped over from the Eleventh District Militia Archives. Why had I asked for it? I'm not sure. Maybe it was just nostalgia, because being three days from retirement makes an old man sentimental.

That's when the phone rang and a calloused voice said, "Comrade Chief Brod?"

"Yes."

"We met at Brano Sev's retirement party. Romek," said the caller. "Colonel Nikolai Romek."

All I remembered was a painfully dull party at the Grunwald Restaurant three years ago. Brano Sev surrounded by a general contingency of state security elders who only talked about sex. I'd been drunk and angry that night. "Sorry, but I don't recall."

"No matter," said Romek. "This is official business anyway. Seems one of our officers is dead. Lieutenant General Yuri Kolev. He was at the party, too."

I didn't remember the Lieutenant General either. Later, I could ask

Lena, because despite being seventy-two—eight years older than me—she had a crisp, clean memory for details I never caught. I grabbed a ballpoint and wrote down the dead officer's name. "How did it happen?"

"Fell over at his desk. Heart attack."

"Why call us?"

"Why *not* call you?"

"We're the Murder Squad, Comrade Colonel. As much as we'd like to, we don't bother with natural deaths."

Romek cleared his throat. "As you may know, Emil, we've got demonstrations in Sárospatak. What you may not know is that other counties are also making noise. We simply don't have the manpower to process this."

It was true that, over the last week, citizens in that western town had been pouring into the streets each night to protest the incarceration of Father Eduard Meyr. But it was also common knowledge that one out of five people in the country worked for the Ministry for State Security in some capacity. They had plenty of men to fill out a lousy form, while I had only two homicide inspectors.

"Just send someone over," he said. "It'll take five minutes."

I looked at the dusty, yellowed file I'd been leafing through, then closed it. "We'll be right there." After hanging up, I called down to our coroner, Markus Feder. He sounded pleased—overall, it had been a slow month for corpses.

In those days, murder in the Capital was a rare enough occurrence, and we could make do in the First District with my two detectives, Katja Drdova and Bernard Kovář. We were supposed to have three, but after the death of Captain Imre Papp four years ago, and the subsequent replacements who burned out so quickly, I gave up. When necessary, I went out with Katja or Bernard to visit crime scenes, but they usually insisted on leaving me to my desk. I don't think they liked having the boss look over their shoulders.

This time, I would insist. I didn't want either of my detectives going up to Yalta Boulevard without me there to back them up.

This morning, the homicide office was empty. Katja was investigating the murder of a retired judge, Dušan Volan, who'd been shot three days ago while wandering the grounds of his extensive Thirteenth District estate. Bernard had stayed behind, but he wasn't at his desk. I knew where I'd find him.

In the corridor, some uniforms winked at me knowingly, and others made jokes about me not getting killed before my last day. I told them I'd make a solid effort. For the last two weeks, Katja had been making arrangements for my retirement party Friday; she thought it was a secret, but she'd made the mistake of bringing Bernard in on the deception, and I'd seen the guest list he'd left on his desk.

As expected, he was in the lounge, sipping acorn coffee with one of the receptionists, a pretty girl from Vranov named Margit. "Bernard."

The big captain was surprised to see me. Surprised and embarrassed. Embarrassment looked funny on a man his size. He stood up, mustache twitching. "Chief."

"Come on," I said. "We've got a corpse to look at."

"Oh!" said Margit.

I led Bernard down a pea-colored stairwell to the second underground level, where I signed out an unmarked Militia Karpat and took the wheel. Once we'd turned onto Lenin Avenue, I broke the silence by asking about his wife: "How's Agí?"

"Good."

"The portrait's today, isn't it?"

All he did was nod at that, which annoyed me. Today was the most important commission of Agota's career—a large-format photograph of our Great Leader. He said, "She's taking Sanja to Tisakarad this afternoon. Doesn't want to wait for me."

"Surprising," I said, without a hint of surprise.

Bernard Kovář was married to, and had a baby with, Agota, the daughter of my oldest friend, Ferenc Kolyeszar. Famous Ferenc. For the last thirty years, due largely to his literary career, Ferenc had been living in internal exile, first in Pócspetri, then in Tisakarad, forty-five minutes from Sárospatak. By now Ferenc was internationally famous; even the French had praised his "dissident" works.

Agota moved to the Capital five years ago and, as her symbolic guardians, neither Lena nor I really approved when Bernard and she became an item. To us, he was still too young, at thirty-seven, to have an adult relationship with a woman ten years his senior. Despite that, they married, and nearly every day I found him flirting with another receptionist.

We turned onto the roundabout at Victory Square. To the right, the high columns of the Central Committee Building rose up. In front of it, a bronze Vladimir Ilyich, jacket raised in a permanent breeze, pointed to the gray sky.

I suppose Vladimir's gone by now.

"You've got a nice family," I told him.

"Christ, Emil. Can't a man flirt?"

I turned up Yalta Boulevard, then passed the high glass tower of the Hotel Metropol. Ahead, at number 36, two uniformed Ministry guards stood on the right side of the road, outside Ministry headquarters, waving pedestrians to the opposite sidewalk. "Just watch out," I said. "It's not only me you'll have to answer to."

"No?"

"Lena will have your balls."

Bernard groaned.

When we climbed out, a guard waved at us, saying, "Nothing to see."

I flashed my Militia certificate. "Comrade Colonel Romek called me." I said it as if the colonel and I were very old friends, then noticed the corpse. It was lying on the cracked sidewalk, covered by a simple white sheet. "Why's the body out here?"

The guard shrugged. "Orders."

Unbelievable. I approached Yuri Kolev's body; his shroud rippled in the frigid breeze. "Go ahead," I said to Bernard. "Let's see him."

He crouched and pulled back the sheet, and when I saw the dead, gray-bearded face it came back to me: a loud, drunken old man from Brano Sev's retirement party, who ogled Agota all night. I even remembered the man's bitterness when Agota walked over to Bernard Kovář and asked him to dance.

"Do I know this guy?" said Bernard, crossing his arms over his chest. "I think I know him."

"I hope you do," said a calloused voice. We turned to find a small man in his fifties, with a thin gray mustache and brown suit, smiling. He stuck out a hand. "Nikolai Romek. Remember now?"

I did. Yet another Agota-admirer from that party. Lena and I had had our hands busy keeping these men off of her, only to fail with Bernard. "Good to see you again, Comrade Romek. Meet Captain Bernard Kovář."

Romek smiled but didn't offer his hand. "Of course. I remember."

"You going to explain this?" I said.

"Explain what?"

"You've taken Kolev out of his office and left him here. My forensics man is going to explode."

"*Forensics?*" said Romek, smiling involuntarily. "Emil, the man died of a heart attack. I'm just dumping the paperwork on you."

"Because your men are too busy to fill out a three-page form."

Romek nodded—he didn't care whether I believed him or not.

I said, "Could this be related to his work?"

"Why are you obsessed with making this into a murder?"

"I meant stress, Comrade Colonel."

He paused, then shook his head. "No. We weren't burdening him with anything tougher than photocopying. He was retiring soon." Romek looked down at Kolev's flaccid, pale face. "A damned shame."

"When?"

"When, what?"

"His retirement."

"Next month."

"Medical records?"

"Send a request to Pasha Medical if you like."

I knew about file requests sent to the Ministry's private hospital. I'd be retired by the time it showed up. "We should at least have a look at his office."

"Why do you think we brought out the body?" He squinted at me. "It's a hectic time. We don't want militiamen crawling about."

Bernard, silent, watched the two of us stare at each another and exhale clouds of condensation.

"Look," said Romek, as if he were preparing to do me a great service against his better judgment, "I've already sent someone to clear out his home of classified documents. And just for you, I'll have my people go through his office. We'll let you know if there's anything suspicious. All right?"

"Don't have a choice, do I?"

Romek grunted a half-laugh and stuck his hands into his pockets.

"Was he married?" I asked.

"We're all married, Comrade Chief. To the Ministry." Romek nodded at Kolev's body. "He did have himself a pretty Saxon girl for a while, but that ended long ago."

"No one now?"

He shook his head again and began to step away. "I've got a desk full of work. Are we done?"

"For now," I said, and Bernard and I watched Romek climb the steps to where another uniformed guard opened the door of Yalta 36 for him.

Markus Feder arrived in a white Karpat hearse with spots of rust along its edges. He climbed out slowly, brushing his white lab coat straight, then his white hair, which still held on to a few flakes of red. After looking at the body for five seconds, he said, "Don't know why you need me on this, Emil. Look at those eyes—the man's had a coronary." He opened a pale hand. "That'll be eight hundred thousand korona."

I wasn't in the mood for his jokes. "Take him back with you. Do a full exam."

"Suspect something more devious?"

"Just do it, will you?"

Feder lowered his voice. "What's the story?"

"Just what you see."

"But why us?"

"They say they've got manpower problems."

He didn't believe it either. "I'll get you something in a few hours."

"Thanks, Markus."

Bernard was standing over by a kolach shop, answering a pretty shopkeeper's questions, but I ignored him and went to the Ministry guard. Now that the body was being loaded onto a gurney, he was sneaking a cigarette in the next doorway. "Can I get one?"

He tapped one out and lit it for me. "It's not murder, is it?"

I shook my head. "Doesn't look like it. Was the Lieutenant General on any medication?"

"I don't know," said the guard, peering over at Bernard, who had somehow made the shopkeeper laugh. "I wonder what'll happen to his car now."

"What?"

"The Lieutenant General's." He nodded up the street to where a shining white BMW 7 Series was parked by the curb.

"He parked out in the open?"

"Didn't trust the garage attendants. Besides, no one's going to touch a car sitting here."

I thanked him for the smoke, then hurried across the street to Feder's hearse. He was just getting behind the wheel. "Let me see the body again."

"You're getting creepy in your old age." He walked with me around the back and opened it so I could climb in to where Kolev was sealed inside a translucent body bag. I unzipped it halfway and reached in. Behind me, Feder made lewd jokes. He said, "Hmm," when I pulled out Kolev's car keys.

Bernard had finally tired of pestering the local women, and as he walked back I turned him around and guided him up the street to the BMW. "Quick search," I said.

"What're we looking for?"

"Anything. Maybe medication."

Bernard inhaled audibly when I unlocked the car. Across the way, the guard tossed his cigarette and stared. I took the front seat, rummaging around the floorboards and in the glove compartment, while Bernard crouched in the back. "Hey," he said.

He held up a narrow sheet of paper—a poorly printed flyer—that said

It was the same slogan they used in Czechoslovakia just before everything changed there. Student radicals and underground workers had used the question-and-answer to identify compatriots. The activists of our own country had borrowed the phrase.

I took the flyer and stared at it.

"What's wrong?" he said.

I looked at him a second, then past him, through the rear windshield. The guard had returned to the steps of Yalta 36 and was speaking with the other guard. I lowered my voice, though it wasn't necessary.

"*This,*" I told him. "We're called in to process the death of a Ministry lieutenant general. Forty years, and I've never seen this happen. We're being brought in for a reason."

Bernard waited for me to complete my thought, but I couldn't, not yet. I locked up the BMW, pocketed the keys and thanked the guard again for the cigarette.

Markus Feder was quicker than expected; when we stepped into the homicide office, my phone was ringing. "Emil, I've got something."

"Be right down," I said, then went out to Bernard, who was settling into his chair. He groaned as he got up again.

We went back down the stairwell to the first underground level and Markus Feder's "body shop." Feder had been assigned to the First District Militia in the fifties, and since then he'd gradually built a reputation as the most astute coroner in the country. He was the one who tracked down a rare Nigerian poison used to kill a television broadcaster in 1978. Two years later, he identified not only the weapon—a wrench—that killed the wife of a Ukrainian diplomat, but the manufacturer, the year produced, and the shop where it was purchased. He'd conjured many small miracles in his cold, stainless steel lab, and today was no exception.

"Poisoned," he said, leaning against the gurney that held Yuri Kolev's large, naked body aloft. This, for some reason, wasn't a surprise to me. He raised a finger. "Guess how."

That, I didn't know. I shrugged.

"Ever heard of an eight-ball?"

"Billiards?"

Bernard said, "Crack cocaine and heroin."

Feder wagged the finger at him. "The young man wins. He's been watching American movies. Anyway, what you've got is the same thing but without the crack. Colombian cocaine mixed with heroin."

"Injected?" I offered.

"Not at all. This man's been snorting for years. His nasal cavity's like the Postojna Caves." Feder propped his gloved finger on the tip of Kolev's nose to demonstrate. "But this time, it was mixed with uncut heroin. It was pure poison. If his heart hadn't killed him first, he would've suffocated as his body shut down."

I looked down at Kolev's pale body and noticed his freshly shaved genitals, which were unusually red. "Could he have done it by accident?"

"Emil, you don't get hold of pure heroin by accident, and you certainly don't snort it by accident."

"What's wrong with his privates?" said Bernard.

"Herpes," Feder told him. He wagged his finger again. "A visual lesson for you, son. Oh!"

"What?"

Feder stepped back to the sink and picked up a plastic bag filled with slips of paper, some change, a wallet, and two identification booklets. "His effects."

I held up the bag and peered through it. "So if it wasn't an accident, someone spiked his cocaine."

Feder nodded. "Someone who could get hold of the pure stuff."

"There you are!" said a woman's voice. "There's Daddy!"

Feder brightened, looking past us to where Agota stood in the doorway, clutching two-year-old Sanja wrapped in a purple hooded coat. Agota was beautiful in the way her mother, Magda, had once been, with pale blue eyes and dark hair.

She came in slowly. "We're interrupting?"

"Absolutely not, dear," said Feder, a massive grin filling his face.

Bernard waved for her to leave. "I'll be right out."

"Yes," I said, trying to step in front of the corpse. "Go."

"Oh," said Agota. She'd just caught sight of Yuri Kolev's white body. She clutched Sanja tighter, one hand covering the child's face. "I—"

"Wait outside," said Bernard.

We watched her retreat and close the door behind herself, then heard coughing from the corridor, and Sanja's low whine.

"Nice one," said Feder, a gloved finger on Yuri Kolev's navel. "I've always said your wife was a nice one."

"Yeah," Bernard said without interest.

"If I was you, I'd keep a tight rein on myself. A woman like that doesn't come along every day."

Bernard looked at Feder, then at me. He blinked and muttered, "Shut up," before marching out of the lab.

Using Feder's lamps, I examined Kolev's effects. He had two ID booklets: a Ministry for State Security certificate with his name, and a general citizen's pass under the name LIPMANN, ULRICH. He'd used the false one to travel to Sárospatak three times in the last week. It didn't look like the travel habits of someone who was only making photocopies for the office.

The slips of paper were receipts for four meals at the Hotel Metropol. Large bills, at least three people at the table.

I thanked Feder and found Bernard and Agota whispering in the stairwell, Sanja on her mother's knee.

"Hey, old man," said Agota.

Since moving to the Capital in 1984, Agota had gone from disconsolate textile-factory worker to weekend photographer. Then, after one successful commission shooting a Ministry general's son's wedding, she started getting calls. She applied for permission to leave her factory just after the birth of her daughter two years ago and had been photographing full-time ever since, sharing a studio co-op on Lenin Avenue, not far from the Militia station. Her life showed us that change was never impossible. She'd married a man ten years younger than herself and then became pregnant at the age of forty-five—Katja often spoke of this as if it were a miracle—and then she'd made a complete career change. These things gave the rest of us hope.

I kissed her cheeks, then Sanja's soft white forehead. "You know better than to walk into that room."

"I needed to find Berni." She wrinkled her nose. "But the smell. What *is* that smell?"

"Chemicals," Bernard guessed. He reached down to take Sanja.

"So how was it?" I asked.

"How was what?"

"Don't be funny. It doesn't suit you."

People say a lot of things about Tomiak Pankov now, most of them true, but back then you could think what you wanted; it didn't change the fact that his very name frightened you. So none of us said it aloud.

She'd done his portrait in the newly finished Workers' Palace, that Third District monstrosity fronted by the long, cobblestone Workers' Boulevard, which *The Spark* continually reminded us was one meter wider than the Champs-Elysées.

She frowned, trying to find the words to describe the experience.

"Scary?" I offered.

She blew some air, then nodded. "Terrifying. I got some nice shots, though."

"That's good."

"They searched me."

"What?" said Bernard, bouncing Sanja on his hip.

"On my way out. They searched me. As if I were a thief."

Neither of us knew how to answer that. Agota reached for her purse as she stood. "I've gotta go. Train leaves in a half hour."

"Wait a minute," I told her as we started up the stairs. "Let's call your father—I might drive you halfway. He can take you the rest."

Bernard groaned loudly. He and his father-in-law spoke only at family gatherings in the Tisakarad farmhouse. Even then, conversation was strained. He smiled, pressing his nose against Sanja's. "If you can get him to speak about something other than how much the French love him, you'll have done a great service to humanity."

"Ber*nard*," warned Agota.

Back in the office, I closed the door and pulled the blinds shut before dialing. After three rings Magda Kolyeszar picked up. We hadn't talked in a month, and it surprised me how old she sounded. "Emil, that you?"

"How's the easy life, Magda?"

"Speak for yourself. I've been assigned the job of archivist."

"Archivist?"

"For the dissident. It's amazing how much bad writing you can accumulate over a lifetime."

"You should read my case reports."

She gave a polite chuckle. "You hear about Agí's commission? Scares me to death."

"She's here now. Made it out without a scratch. Is the farmer in?"

"You're in luck," she told me. "He's decided to stay in today. You'll put Agí on afterward?"

"Sure."

She called for her husband, and after a moment that deep voice came on the line. "Emil?"

"Ferenc." I leaned into the receiver. "How's the farming?"

"The land doesn't like me."

"Can we meet today?"

"Important?"

"I've got a dead Ministry officer, and I'd like to know what all's possible."

"Who?"

"Yuri Kolev. Lieutenant general. You know him?"

"I know them all, but . . ." Ferenc trailed off. "The usual spot? I'll have to get back for tonight's rally."

"Should you say that over the phone?"

He made a *harruph* noise. "Trust me, Emil. They know already."

"What time?" I said, looking up as Agota opened my door and smiled. I waved her in.

"Say, three o'clock."

By the dusty clock on my wall, it was a little after one. "Perfect. Hold on. I've got someone who wants to talk to you."

THREE

•

It was one by the time Gavra reached the Stop & Drop office. The next flight from Richmond to New York wouldn't leave until late that night, so in the meantime he could at least catch up on his sleep.

Yuri Kolev's death surprised and disturbed him, but it couldn't be called a shock. Gavra had long heard Ministry rumors about the Lieutenant General's cocaine addiction, and so a sudden heart attack wasn't out of the question. He even began to wonder if this whole job had been some drug-fueled fantasy.

But no. Brano Sev had made such a particular point of trusting the Lieutenant General that Gavra had no choice but to feel the same. That's how much General Brano Sev's judgment meant to the younger man, even though he hadn't spoken to or heard of Brano in the last three years.

Brano Sev's postretirement vanishing act had only deepened his near-legendary reputation among Ministry agents, as well as those of us in homicide who had worked with him. He'd fought the Germans in the Patriotic War, tracked down ex-Nazis after it, and had quietly, meticulously, made the country safe for socialism. His name evoked both admiration and fear. For me, though, his name provoked feelings of revulsion.

But if the now-absent Brano Sev had said that Lieutenant General Yuri Kolev was to be trusted, that was all Gavra needed to know.

He found Freddy behind the desk, feet propped up, wearing an Orioles cap. Freddy raised the brim with a knuckle. "Well, hey there, Viktor! Decide to take me up on that beer?"

"I need to pay my bill. I'll be leaving tonight."

"As you like, man. But as for the beer, I'm insisting."

"I'm a little tired, Freddy."

"Trust me. You'll sleep like a baby."

Gavra rubbed his eyes for effect. "Okay, but just one."

Freddy leveled a finger-pistol at him and shot. "You got it, buddy." He took two cans of Budweiser—not the Czech Budweiser Budvar but something else entirely—out of a tiny refrigerator and passed one over. Gavra tried to appear pleased with the taste—like a half-can of beer topped off with stale water—but it was difficult.

Freddy began their fraternity by complaining. About his *old woman*. Which Gavra took to mean his wife, Tracey. "I mean, don't get me wrong. She's a good woman. Puts out like a goddamned machine and makes a massive pot roast. But that mouth on her . . . wow! Sometimes I'm like to take a swing at her."

"You hit her?"

"Not yet, brother. But someday it's gonna happen. Got yourself a wife?"

Gavra shook his head.

"No problem. How old are you? Fifty?"

"Forty-four."

"Well, don't hurry into it. That's a tip from the top. Might as well track down all the pussy you can before buying the cow. Can't imagine it's any different in Russia."

"It's the same all over."

"Who you visiting with?"

Gavra rubbed his eyes. He wished he could get through this

terrible can and to bed. "My cousin, Lubov. I haven't seen him in a long time."

"Lubov Shevchenko?"

Gavra thought he'd heard wrong. Not merely that Freddy knew Lubov Shevchenko but that he'd pronounced the name correctly. "You *know* him?"

"Course I do! My kid, Jeremy, he's got Shevchenko for math. He's a tough bastard, doesn't stand for no bullshit in his class." He raised his beer in a kind of salute. "Country needs more teachers like him."

"He teaches?"

"I kid you not. Didn't Lubov tell you?"

Gavra was speechless a moment. "You know Lubov. He's secretive."

"Tell me about it," said Freddy. He scratched his beard. "I figured it was all Russians, but meeting you, I see it's just Lubov. School's just a little farther up the turnpike. Clover Hill High. Done all right by himself, your cousin."

"I'm glad he's happy."

"Land of the free, and all."

He didn't have to do this. No one knew that, at the last minute, he'd been handed Lubov Shevchenko's location. But opportunity changes how you look at the world. With Shevchenko just "up the turnpike," Gavra could see that nothing really added up. A defector-turned-schoolteacher who needed to be kept alive. Why? A now-dead lieutenant general who wouldn't share the man's real name, who was in fact getting his orders from someone else who wanted to remain anonymous. He was starting to believe that the timing of Kolev's heart attack was too much of a coincidence.

So he thanked Freddy for the beer and conversation, then stepped out into the bright, cold sunlight. Behind the wheel of the Toyota, he looked around to be sure no one was watching. He reached under his seat, took the P-83 from the paper bag, then filled the clip with eight rounds. He wouldn't be sleeping anytime soon.

By two, he was on the turnpike again. Thick forests lined the road, and that somehow made the discomfort of all of this more bearable.

Over the next hill he spotted the high school. Clover Hill. It was a low, flat-topped building that spread back into a deep field checkered with a baseball diamond and an American football field and a running track. It was impressive. His own village school had been a small house. All their sports were done in the public park, or for special events they went to the Palace of Physical Culture in nearby Satu Mare.

He parked near the front door, between a Subaru and a Ford pickup, and slipped the pistol into the glove compartment. He wouldn't need it yet. Inside, crowds of teenagers clutched books and shouted at one another, ignoring him. They were on their way to classes, and the corridor soon thinned until only a few were left when the grating bell sounded. He nodded at a brunette. "Excuse me, where is the main office?"

"*There*," she said, exasperated.

Directly behind him was a door labeled OFFICE. He let himself inside.

A heavy woman sat at a wide desk, talking into a telephone. Behind her were two doors, PRINCIPAL and VICE-PRINCIPAL. To Gavra's right was a line of four chairs, and in two of them sat a boy and a girl, teenagers. The boy was pale with prematurely thinning red hair he'd foolishly chosen to grow long. The girl gripped the boy's hand, looking like a stunned model, with long blond hair and eager eyes that locked on to him. He smiled.

"Need some help?" It was the woman at the desk. She covered the telephone mouthpiece with her palm.

"Uh, yes. I'm looking for my cousin. Lubov Shevchenko. He teaches math."

He heard a gasp and turned to see the girl whispering to the boy, who nodded.

"Cousin, huh?" said the clerk. "What's your name?"

"Viktor Lukacs."

"Well, Mr. Shevchenko has a class right now."

"I don't want to interrupt him," Gavra said quickly. "When will he be finished?"

The woman thought a moment, wrinkling her nose. "I think Mr. Shevchenko's running detention today. Is that right, Jennifer?"

The girl nodded. "Last detention of the year."

"Yes, so he'll get out around five thirty. Want to leave a message for him?"

"He's not expecting me until next week. I want to surprise him."

The boy said, "I don't think Mr. Shevchenko likes surprises."

"Yeah," said Jennifer.

"Mind your own business, you two," said the clerk. "You're in enough trouble as it is."

Gavra picked up Marlboros and a ham-and-cheese sandwich from the Brandermill Plaza and learned from the pimply cashier that the name Brandermill referred to not just the plaza but the whole wooded area that bordered it. "It's a housing de*velop*ment," she told him between smacks of her chewing gum. "Ain't no *project.* Got its own lake, restaurants, sports club, and all these shops here. Ain't no reason to leave. It's just like a town."

On the drive back, Gavra was struck by the similarity—in theory, at least—between the Brandermill development and Tomiak Pankov's New Towns, those vast concrete estates where reassigned farmers were moved in order to man newly constructed factories. The difference, of course, was that people chose to move to Brandermill.

He parked in the same spot again, ate the sandwich (which was delicious), and waited in the car, smoking. Occasional adults emerged from the front doors, found their cars, and drove away. A woman with horn-rimmed glasses frowned at him when he tossed a butt out the window, but he ignored her. Later, two teenage boys came out, throwing punches at one another and laughing, then raced at full speed through the lot.

His plan was simple: find Shevchenko and then follow him home. There, he could take control of the man in privacy and get the answers Kolev had been unwilling, or unable, to share.

At four thirty, the grating bell sounded again. Students poured out. Older ones tossed bookbags into pickup trucks and small Japanese cars. Teachers patiently shouted at students to slow down, wished them a Merry Christmas, or reminded them to do this or that over the holiday. The Subaru beside Gavra's window was owned—or at least used—by a tall kid who dribbled a basketball on his way to his car, stopping as he unlocked it to glare at Gavra.

"The fuck *you* looking at, faggot?"

Gavra considered pulling the gun on him. He could use a laugh. Instead he gave the kid the same cold look he'd once given a pedophilic murderer in 1982 just before he plunged the guy's head into a toilet.

By five, the last of the buses were turning onto the road, and the parking lot had emptied of all but ten cars. In a half hour, Lubov Shevchenko would finish with his detention class.

Gavra slipped the P-83 into his coat pocket.

The corridors were empty but littered with spare pens and flakes from spiral notebooks. Just past the office, he took a left and began walking slowly past doors, each with a tall, narrow window. He paused at one where an old woman helped a black teenager with his writing, then at another where three students sat on a table, looking at notes a fourth was marking on the chalkboard. Whatever he'd written had upset a girl, who was shouting at him.

Gavra followed the corridor to the end, where it turned right, past a woman running a vacuum cleaner, and then up another right until he was back at the corridor where he'd begun. In the center of the floor was a large glassed-in library where a librarian was directing her student-workers as they shelved returned books. On the opposite side of the building, he followed another U-shaped corridor past more empty rooms until, on the last leg, he stopped at room 161.

Looking through the narrow window at an angle, he saw Lubov Shevchenko, a little fatter and older than his picture, with spectacles, seated at a desk, reading a disorderly stack of papers. He'd mark one, then go to the next, read, and write something else. He was grading students' work.

Gavra stepped to the other side and saw from that angle seven students at desks, serving their time. Some were working as well, hunched and scribbling, while the pretty girl he'd seen earlier—Jennifer—was passing a slip of paper to the balding redhead and glancing warily in Shevchenko's direction.

The scene brought on a pang of empathy. As a boy, Gavra had considered it his patriotic duty to make trouble. He'd succeeded often enough to be very familiar with the experience of staying after school.

His smile disappeared—Jennifer was looking directly at him. She touched her boyfriend's hand, and then he, too, was staring at Gavra. Jennifer smiled, and Gavra brought a finger to his lips for silence.

But Jennifer, like the young Gavra, was deaf to the pleas of adults. Through the door he could hear what she said: "Mr. Shevchenko, your cousin's here."

Gavra stepped back out of view. He almost fled as Lubov Shevchenko's accented voice said, "*Cousin?*"

"See for yourself if you think I'm a liar," said Jennifer.

Gavra only wanted to follow Shevchenko. Confronting him in the middle of a schoolhouse was not what he'd had in mind.

The door opened, and Lubov Shevchenko's spectacled face peered out. He cocked his head and spoke in their shared accent. "Can I help you?"

All reasonable plans were now figments of Gavra's imagination. He answered in our language. "Please close the door. I'd like to speak with you a moment."

Shevchenko's expression, at first confused, shifted. It was in the edges of his nose and the way his heavy eyes seemed to stretch just slightly. Fear, or repugnance. "How did you find me?"

"I'm not here to bother you."

"You are."

"No."

"Then why are you here?"

"To talk. Please come out and close the door."

Shevchenko looked back into the classroom and said in English, "I'll be right back. Everyone, quiet." Then he stepped into the corridor and shut the door. Something occurred to him, and he raised a finger. "Tell them you can't find me. Tell them I died."

"Tell who?"

Shevchenko said nothing at first. Then: "What do you want to talk about?"

That was the question for which Gavra had no real answer. So he said, "These kids are in trouble?"

Shevchenko frowned; he nodded.

"American kids, are they any worse than we were?"

"Much, much worse. But you didn't cross the Atlantic to ask me that." Behind his glasses, a dew of sweat formed in Shevchenko's thick eyebrow and rolled down his cheek. "You're going to kill me, aren't you."

"I'm not going to kill you. I just want to talk."

"You're a liar."

"Come on," said Gavra. "We're going."

"I have a job here."

"They can take care of themselves."

Shevchenko shook his head and tried to speak with conviction. "I'm not going anywhere with you."

Gavra looked past the math teacher, down the empty corridor, then behind himself. Control. He had to keep in control. This was something that, more than a decade before, Brano had hammered again and again to into his pupil. *Stay in control. Act, but never react. Once you start reacting, you've already lost.*

He took the P-83 from his pocket and shoved it into Lubov Shevchenko's stomach, whispering, "Please don't make me shoot you, comrade. I just want to talk. Walk with me."

"*Comrade.*" Shevchenko shook his head, but the fear was evident. "Never thought I'd hear that word again."

Gavra moved the pistol to the small of Shevchenko's back and gripped the man's elbow as they walked ahead, then turned left. Just before the exit stood the heavyset clerk he'd spoken to a couple hours before. She smiled brightly. "So you found him!" She winked at Shevchenko. "Lubov, your cousin wanted it to be a surprise!"

Gavra dug the barrel into Shevchenko's back, forcing a smile into the teacher's face. "Yes . . ."

"My cousin is always flustered by surprises," Gavra told the woman as they passed. "The bad girl, Jennifer—she was right!"

"Tell me about it," the clerk said, laughing as she disappeared around the next corner.

On the turnpike, Lubov Shevchenko began to weep. There was nothing gradual about it. One moment a frightened calm held him mute; the next, he covered his face with his hands and moaned, rocking back and forth. It was an unnerving sound.

"Cut that out," said Gavra, accelerating.

Lubov wouldn't stop. When he tried to speak, the tears flowed, glistening in the late afternoon sun; he coughed wetly.

"I told you, I'm not here to kill you."

"I don't care what you say," Lubov managed. "You wouldn't tell me, would you?"

"You live alone?"

The math teacher nodded.

"Where?"

"What?"

"We're going to your house."

Lubov, between fits, pointed him around a U-turn and then through a secluded side entrance to the woods of Brandermill. They looped around a flat-faced medical center, then took a left onto a tree-shaded street lined with the kinds of houses one saw in Hollywood films. Thornridge Lane. Each house had a paved driveway leading from the road, and along the curb five-digit numbers had been stenciled in green.

"What's your number?"

"What?"

"House number!"

"Three five two-oh-six."

The house was barely visible through its wooded front yard. Gavra turned down the steep driveway and stopped in front of a bark-colored bi-level.

"Teaching pays well?" said Gavra.

"In Brandermill, this is part of the slums."

"Let's not start our relationship with lies."

The math teacher swallowed. "It's the truth."

Gavra opened the car door for him, the pistol always in sight, and took him to the front door, where Lubov fumbled with keys.

Holding him by the elbow, Gavra walked through the house, trying to hide his amazement. From the landing they went upstairs into a high-ceilinged living room that opened onto a terrace with a view of the pine forest Lubov humbly called a backyard. The kitchen, too, was large, the tall, full refrigerator humming. A master bedroom, sparsely furnished, was four times the size of the bedroom Gavra shared with his roommate, Karel, and a smaller bedroom had been converted into an office.

They returned to the landing and continued to the half-underground lower floor, with two more bedrooms, a long den, and an empty utility room with a door leading into the jungle of backyard.

Convinced of their solitude, Gavra placed Lubov on the den sofa across from a massive television. "Don't tell me you live alone in this place."

He shrugged, the fear apparently waning. "It's what they gave me."

"Who?"

Lubov stiffened, then mumbled something.

"What?"

"I said, you *know* who gave it to me."

"Pretend I don't."

This seemed to confuse the man. He opened his mouth, closed it, then said, "Who *are* you?"

Gavra showed him the pistol again. "Right now, you talk. Afterward, I'll speak. Okay?"

"The Americans," said Lubov. "CIA."

"They gave you this house?"

"And the name."

"Why?"

"It was part of the deal. I answer their questions; they give me a new life. How did you *find* me?"

"From the beginning," said Gavra, pulling up a chair. "Your real name."

"Lebed Putonski."

"That's a good start. Where did you make the deal with the Americans?"

"Stockholm."

"Why were you in Stockholm?"

"You really don't know, do you?"

"I want your version of the story. Why were you in Stockholm?"

Lebed Putonski pressed his fingertips together, as if praying. "This was almost a decade ago. I was there to oversee things."

"You were the Stockholm resident?"

Putonski shrugged. "Of course. There's a reason the Ministry keeps watch on its own residents. We start to enjoy life. We start thinking maybe we'd have a better time somewhere else. And then we do."

"Why not just stay in Stockholm?"

"I was recalled. I guess the Ministry wasn't happy with my work, or maybe they suspected what I was thinking. Fair enough." He shrugged again. "I was a desk man, been one all my life. Can't say I really understood half of what I was doing. So . . ." He squinted at the pistol. "So I contacted the Americans, spent some weeks at Langley, and then I moved here. Now, eight years later, you're pointing a gun at me. Why?"

Gavra didn't understand it either. This was just another old man who'd gotten tired of the intrigues and breadlines. He wasn't an ideological turncoat, and the information he, after prodding, admitted to giving the Americans was hardly explosive: the Central Committee's position on its fraternal relations with Sweden, in-country troop sizes and distribution, and some real gross domestic product numbers. All Putonski had wanted was an easier life, and here he'd gotten it.

The telephone rang.

"You expecting someone?"

Putonski shook his head. "Maybe it's my girlfriend."

"Girlfriend?"

"Maureen." He paused. "Everyone gets lonely."

"She'll expect you at home, yes?"

Another shrug, then a nod. "Detention was almost finished."

"Okay. Come on."

He walked Putonski back up the stairs to the kitchen and took the telephone on the seventh ring, holding it to Putonski's ear and keeping his head close so he could hear as well.

"Mr. Shevchenko?" said a man's voice. American.

"Yes?" said Putonski.

"Mr. Shevchenko, there's a matter I'd like to discuss with you. Your friends from the west need some information."

Putonski's eyes went wide, and Gavra nodded at him to continue. "What's this about?"

"Let's talk in person. You'll stay at home?"

Putonski interpreted Gavra's second nod. "Yes."

"I'll be there in an hour," said the man. "We should be alone, understand?"

"Of course," said Putonski, then the line went dead. "I'll bet it's about you," he told Gavra. "You better get out of here."

"Who was it?"

"Who do you think? CIA. I haven't heard from them in five years, then you show up, and suddenly they want to discuss something."

"You don't know this man?"

"Five years is a long time. They change personnel."

Gavra stared at Putonski a moment, thinking this through. His real purpose here, as he understood it, was to protect this math teacher. Yuri Kolev wouldn't have spent the money and effort to send him to the other side of the world if the threat to Putonski weren't real. Now an unidentified voice wanted to meet Putonski alone.

"Come on," said Gavra. "We're leaving."

FOUR

•

While Agota told Magda and Ferenc about her adventures photographing Tomiak Pankov, I sat with Bernard at his desk, Sanja on his knee. He fumbled with his daughter's wispy blond hair and said, "Why are you driving her?"

"What?"

"Agí can take the train. You don't need to bother."

"It'll be nice to get out of the city."

"And go see Ferenc?"

I shrugged in a pretense of stupidity, but I think he knew what I was up to. He also knew why I wasn't going to discuss it with him. A couple of months after he and Agota married, a man from the Ministry for State Security arrived in the office. He was one of those small, petty clerk-types who sweat a lot. I was on the phone at the time and watched him go to Gavra's desk, introduce himself, and then ask for Bernard Kovář. Gavra took him over to Bernard's desk, where the little man congratulated him on his marriage. Bernard, unsure, thanked the man and then acquiesced to a coffee. The three of them were gone for an hour.

I cornered Bernard that evening. He was scared but wouldn't tell me what had happened, finally getting angry and telling me to keep to my own business. So, the next day, I cornered Gavra, who was more open. The Ministry was making a deal with Bernard. His father-in-law, Ferenc Kolyeszar, was of particular interest to the security of our socialist utopia. Perhaps Bernard could share some of his insider knowledge with them, now and then.

"He said no, right?" I asked Gavra.

Gavra rocked his head from side to side. "They've offered passports for both him and Agota."

"So?"

I was being naive, I know, because they weren't just offering Bernard and his new wife the freedom to visit other countries; they were also promising not to harass them in the future. So, inevitably, Bernard made the occasional report to Yalta Boulevard. I knew it, Gavra knew it, and even Ferenc knew it, because I told him. Ferenc assured me that he and his son-in-law, despite their mutual annoyance, had come to an agreement. Ferenc wrote Bernard's reports for him. In exchange, Ferenc promised never to tell Agota what her husband was up to.

Despite this, I wasn't going to burden Bernard with information he didn't need to know.

"Yeah," I told him. "It'll be nice to see Ferenc again."

"You think he can help on this case? I mean, the 'Time for a change' part." He sounded very earnest.

I took one of his cigarettes. "No. He won't know a thing."

He knew I was lying, but didn't press the issue.

When his wife finished with my telephone, I had Bernard carry my box of old files to where I'd parked on Lenin Avenue. I followed with Agota and Sanja, wondering if she really knew nothing about her husband's Ministry collaborations. At my Mercedes—bought, like everything, with Lena's family money—Bernard kissed his family good-bye, promising to see them by the weekend.

We soon reached Victory Square; then a side road put us on Mihai Boulevard, which followed the banks of the Tisa River—"Lifeblood of the Nation," we liked to call it. The water reflected the gray winter sky, lapping stone ramparts. Recent storms had raised the water level enough to frighten those who lived near the river. Lena and I lived higher up in the Second District and had no fear.

Many of the Habsburg buildings I remembered from my youth, which had lined the riverbank, had been demolished in the last decade. Tomiak Pankov, a great believer in the shape and look of socialism, returned from a 1978 visit to North Korea with a new vision for the Capital. Some said he was embarrassed by the provinciality of our city and raged whenever he came back from trips to Paris or London, but I'm not sure about that. I think he had a fastidious side to him, something that served him well under our first Great Leader, Mihai, when he was just a simple government bureaucrat in love with efficiency. Once he saw Kim Il Sung's rigid and clean society, and Pyongyang's long, broad avenues and crowds in perfect, military formation, he felt he'd found paradise.

Now, everything that smelled of the past was being erased. Churches were demolished, or moved brick by brick to hide behind modern towers, and the outer rings of the city were replanned to accommodate the influx of farmers reassigned as factory workers.

We got on the Georgian Bridge, heading south, and on our left lay the ruptured skyline of the Canal District, full of cranes and half-finished block towers. Even the Canal District, that symbol of everything seedy and chaotic in the country, once home to prostitutes and drug dealers, was being turned into a New Town.

When we reached the southern bank, also full of new towers, Agota said, "I spent all yesterday in a line. You know that? Trying to get an extra ration book for Sanja. Four hours, just to have the bitch behind the window tell me Sanja was missing her A-32 form."

"What's an A-32?"

"Far as I can tell, it's to prove she exists. But there she was, crying on my hip. I don't need a goddamned A-32. It's a real laugh, isn't it?

First, the maternity laws say I can't have an abortion, then they make sure I'm barely able to feed the kids I end up with."

"Want me to make a call?" I asked. I'd done this enough times before. As soon as the dietary laws started going through three years ago, specifying the forms required to get your food ticket booklets, the flaws became apparent. If you were missing a stamp on one of the four forms required—or on one of the sixteen forms needed to get those four primary forms—it meant you had to fall back on bartering with your neighbors or visiting the black market.

"Taken care of," she said.

I wondered if this was why she was rushing off to Tisakarad. The farther you got from the Capital—and Tisakarad was forty miles away—the less the ration system was followed. Local farmers had long ago realized the benefit of skimming off their Capital-bound shipments and bringing their pigs into the markets, where the city folk would trade anything for a bit of pork. I said, "I'm surprised Bernard let you go. Patak's not safe, and I'll bet Ferenc will drag you there with him."

"Think he has a say in it?" She turned Sanja to face her, switching to baby talk: "*No*, no! Daddy doesn't have any say!" Sanja didn't seem to have an opinion one way or the other.

We'd just passed the last of the towers when the roadblock appeared. Two Militia cars were parked in the grass, and a makeshift gate—a long tangle of razor wire—had been stretched across the road. As I slowed to a stop, a big militiaman in a regulation blue overcoat tossed away a cigarette and came over to my window. I rolled it down, letting in the cold. He had fat sideburns growing from under his cap, and half his face was sunburned. "Where you going?"

"Tisavar. What's this?"

"Turn around and head back. Traffic's stopped today."

I handed over my Militia certificate. He cocked his head as he read it, then pushed back his cap with a knuckle. "Sorry about that, Comrade Chief." He didn't seem very sorry. "Orders from the top."

"What does that mean?"

He squinted and rocked on his heels. "You know. Central Committee."

"To keep everyone in the Capital?"

He nodded, then noticed Agota and Sanja. He gave them a smile. "Trains are down, too?"

"Most," he said. "First train they cut was the twelve thirty to Patak." He tapped the side of his nose. "I think we all know what it's about."

"But I can go through."

"*Sure,*" he said. "You're not going to Patak, right?"

"I told you. Tisavar."

He touched the brim of his cap, then stepped back and waved us on. Two younger militiamen with thick gloves dragged the razor wire aside so we could pass.

We didn't talk about the roadblock, or the fact that suddenly the Capital had become a prison. It had happened before, when the Central Committee overreacted to a bomb that destroyed a fertilizer plant in Krosno, back on November fifth—the thirty-second anniversary of the short-lived 1956 general strike that, in the end, led to Agota's father's internal exile.

After two days, though, the roadblocks had been removed, and the government never spoke of it again. Perhaps Tomiak Pankov thought we would forget.

We reached Tisavar a little before three. Ferenc and I, whenever something required a private meeting, always came here, to a point just within the ring of his allowed movement, an hour south of the Capital, just before Kisvárda. Before the Great Patriotic War, Tisavar had been a tiny Jewish-Slav enclave that had survived and even prospered under the Austro-Hungarian government as a market town for the farmers in the nearby region. In the thirties, the mayor decided it was time for a change, and he began lobbying the between-wars government for subsidies to start building cooperative granaries. The government agreed, but before the money could make it there, the Germans marched in. Then Tisavar disappeared.

The Wehrmacht appeared in May 1939, having quickly overrun our little army. My father died in those short battles and was soon followed by my mother. At the time, I was living in the south, in Ruscova, with my grandparents, who had fled the soldiers in the Capital. The Occupation, for me, was largely about boredom. I was an anxious, too ambitious boy surrounded by dull farmers. Up around Tisavar, though, the Nazi presence was felt strongly. Soldiers patrolled the streets, and officers took over the administrative house, controlling the flow of money and property and Jews.

The region was governed by Major General Karloff Messerstein, a delinquent from Thüringen who had joined the Nazi Party during its beer-hall days. He administered the region as if it were his private fiefdom, and, perhaps inevitably, some of the headstrong Tisavar boys used munitions left over from our short-lived war to blow up Messerstein's car in 1942.

The major general survived with burns and a broken leg, and from his hospital bed directed the retribution.

Early on in the Occupation, the Germans had enlisted the help of malcontents from our Ukrainian population. These young men had been promised that, once the war was won, the eastern half of our country (including the Capital) would be returned to the Ukraine as a state within the greater German Reich. The fools believed it, because they wanted to. Messerstein decided that, given their local knowledge and natural animosity for these westerners, his Ukrainian recruits would be ideal for the job.

They first emptied the houses and led the townsfolk to what would later be called Anti-Fascism Hill, on the north side of town. There, over the space of two days, the entire population was executed and buried. Then, using a tank borrowed from a nearby

Panzer division, they destroyed the stone administration buildings, then systematically burned every house. As an added touch, Major General Karloff Messerstein arrived on crutches to personally supervise the delivery of two truckloads of Hungarian salt, which were spread over the embers.

All of this was in our history books, and people in the region never forgave the Ukrainian minority its role in the event. The irony, which the textbooks never mentioned, was that a week after the massacre, Messerstein died naturally of a cerebral hemorrhage.

Now, all that was left was a memorial in the middle of a swath of barren earth. It was placed here by Mihai during a 1951 ceremony, filmed by camera crews from all over the world. A statement on a bronze plaque attached to a stone pedestal, followed by a few lines from our national poet, Rikard Pasha:

HERE MARKS THE SPOT WHERE TISAVAR WAS
DESTROYED BY THE FASCIST MENACE
ON 8 OCTOBER 1942.

A world like leaves of the impossible creation from God's mind.
All we can hope for is a dream made clear before we die.

No one, not even Ferenc, had ever been able to tell me what those two lines of verse were supposed to mean.

He was waiting for us in front of the plaque, gloved hands clasped behind his big form, gazing down. Ferenc was just as huge as he'd always been, and though he'd recently turned seventy, he still didn't look like a writer; he looked like a retired thug. When we parked, he turned to face us, and I noticed his lumpy nose was a little bigger and redder than before. When he saw his daughter and granddaughter get out of the car, he lumbered over to hug them, grinning madly.

Perhaps unconsciously, Agota had chosen in Bernard a man who was just like her father—huge, moody, and surprisingly astute at times—and this was perhaps why the two men couldn't get along. They hated to see themselves reflected.

When we shook hands, I smelled palinka on him and wondered if he was drunk. "Still trying to figure that out?"

"Mihai," he said, nodding at the plaque. "He was a mysterious man."

"Let's walk."

Ferenc handed his keys to Agota and asked her to wait in his beat-up Russian flatbed truck. We walked across the salt-dead ground through the cold wind from Anti-Fascism Hill, which was dotted with crosses and bundles of dead flowers. "So you've got a lieutenant general's corpse," he said.

"Poisoned. Someone laced his cocaine with pure heroin."

"Ballsy."

I agreed. "By now, Feder has filed his autopsy, so it's official. I don't have much choice—I'll have to press on with the investigation. I just need to figure out how I'm going to do it."

"And you think I can help?"

I looked at him, hands deep in my pockets. The wind was making my eyes water. "You're at the center of things these days. You'd know if someone wanted Kolev dead."

"We don't want people dead," he said. "Those are the kinds of people we're fighting."

"Remember fifty-six?" I said.

He frowned. "What about it?"

"You may not want to execute anyone, but that doesn't mean someone on the fringe hasn't decided to go that route."

"And you think I'd know."

"I'd ask Father Meyr instead, but I don't know where he is."

Ferenc scratched his rough cheek, then turned to look back at the truck. We couldn't see his family through the dirty windshield. "You're right—it's possible some angry kid got it into his head to kill Kolev. Though I imagine he'd use a gun instead. If so, I don't know about it. But I think you're looking in the wrong direction."

"Am I?"

He nodded, then sniffed; he sounded congested. "End of last week, your dead lieutenant general came to Patak."

"How do you know?"

"How wouldn't I know?" he said, smiling. "When you're preparing to march against the government, you become as paranoid as you can. You notice everything. And we noticed Yuri Kolev."

"He came three times over the last week," I told him. "Under a fake name."

"Yeah. Ulrich Lipmann."

"What was he doing?"

"Not what you'd think." He switched to the professorial tone he'd gotten accustomed to among his wide-eyed student revolutionaries. "Kolev *didn't* go to the regional Ministry HQ. Instead, he went to the other side of town, to a bar where some of our guys hang out. He met with a Russian."

"Russian?" I said dumbly. I do that sometimes.

My surprise pleased him. "Now, *this* was something I didn't know about until after it happened. A couple of our worker bees watched this going on, saw Kolev leave again, get into his pretty BMW and drive back to the Capital. But the Russian stayed to finish his vodka. They followed him into town to a small one-room apartment. Then they jumped him."

"Jesus."

Ferenc shrugged. "What can I do? They're brash kids. But that's how they learned he was Russian. They questioned him, but not too roughly. Best they got was a name off his passport—Fyodor Malevich. Then they looked around. Guess what he had in a box in the wardrobe."

"Tell me."

"A colonel's uniform. Not Russian, but *our* army."

"Why?"

"We don't know. The boys called a friend of mine, but by the time he arrived, old Fyodor had escaped. He knew what he was doing. He took on the boys one at a time, knocked them out, and fled—with the uniform. The kids're fine; they just got headaches."

I didn't know what to make of a Russian masquerading as one of our colonels, but it was all Ferenc had to offer. At least, it was all he was willing to offer me. We had a long-standing friendship, but he'd been a militiaman during some of the darkest years and knew how, despite a man's desires, it was easy to be cornered, or blackmailed, and made to give up what you knew. His son-in-law was a textbook example. Ferenc's reticence protected both of us.

It was also disappointing. I'd hoped that Ferenc might be able to shed light on Kolev's murder. If it had turned out to be committed by one of his friends, my job would have been, ironically, very simple. I would have whitewashed it. Pin the murder on the next corpse that came in, or start asking for access to files the Ministry wasn't willing to give me; then I could throw up my hands and admit defeat. There were many ways to get rid of work you didn't want to do.

Walking back to his truck, he told me to keep my eye on the news. "Change is in the air." He reminded me—as if I'd just come back from the moon—that all around us democracy had defeated totalitarianism, and he said that there was nothing Tomiak Pankov could do. Change was inevitable. "You should get involved, Emil. You've got a responsibility to the next generation. We're bringing Democracy for *them*."

I grimaced.

When people use those capitalized abstracts—Democracy, Freedom, Totalitarianism—with such conviction, I'm always left unnerved. It reminds me too much of life just after the war, when everyone was encouraged to speak like that. I said, "I'm just trying to survive long enough to get my pension."

"You're the last one who needs a pension," he said, thinking of Lena's family money. "Besides, that's the kind of thinking Pankov depends on."

He was right, of course. I told him to keep safe and make sure Agota and Sanja made it through the changes unscathed. He smiled and, unexpectedly, kissed both my cheeks. I, too, had been right; he was drunk.

By the time I reached the Capital again, it was dark. Sensing a blood-pressure headache coming my way, I took two more Captopril. I found a new, fresh militiaman at the roadblock. He was sterner than the first had been, so I was sterner with him. I showed my Militia certificate, emphasizing my rank, and told him that if he didn't let me through, Colonel Nikolai Romek of the Ministry for State Security would have a chat with him. It worked.

I could hardly see the block towers because in this section of the Capital the power had been switched off again. It was a regular occurrence. In the Second District, the streetlamps were off, but the windows glowed.

I parked on Friendship Street, outside our apartment, and carried the box of old files to the elevator. It was out of order again. So I lugged it up the three floors, stopping often to catch my breath. I've never been a man of formidable strength; all I've ever had is persistence. I reached the apartment huffing crazily.

Lena wasn't amused by my lateness. She didn't answer my greeting, only stared at a rerun of *Family Popa* on television. She referred me to the oven, where a cold platter of boiled pork and cabbage waited. I scooped some onto a plate, ate half of it in the kitchen, and threw the rest away. "You going to wash that plate?" she called from the living room, just before a laugh track erupted.

"No," I said and let it drop into the sink. "I need to keep you busy."

It was an old, tired joke, but enough for her to shout back that if I wasn't nice to her, she'd down a bottle of vodka. Then she reminded me—for the tenth time, according to her—that I still hadn't talked to the mechanic about her Mercedes, which wasn't starting. For the tenth time I told her I'd do it in the morning.

She finally took her eyes off the TV when I sat next to her and pulled up the box of old files. "What have *you* got?"

I took one out at random, blew off the dust, and opened it up. "Revisiting the past."

"Which one's that?"

I checked the label, then frowned. "Imre's."

"Oh."

It was from 1985 and labeled "unsolved"—but that was a lie. His was the second "unsolved" case surrounding a dead militiaman, the first being the death of my oldest friend, Libarid Terzian, during a botched airplane hijacking in 1975. Terzian's case was transferred to the Ministry for State Security. Then, ten years later, we found my young Captain Imre Papp in the Canal District with five bullets in his head, lungs, and leg.

It made no sense to any of us. Imre wasn't on a case, and he had a wife and child; he wasn't the kind of man to go poking around the Canal District for whores. None of us knew why he was even there. We followed a number of leads, but they all ran cold until I got a phone call, at home, from Brano Sev.

The old man—then a general—had left the homicide department in the midseventies, moving on to an expansive office at Yalta Boulevard 36. Our friendship had always been tenuous—for plenty of good reasons, I'd never trusted him—and once he left the station we rarely saw each other. I didn't call him, and he didn't call me. And that was fine. I didn't really want to spend time with a man so devoted to protecting socialism in our country—so devoted that he had even arrested our friend Ferenc in 1956. Which is why it was a surprise, and a little unnerving, to pick up the kitchen phone and hear his voice.

"Emil?"

"Brano, is that you?"

"Yes, Emil. Can you step outside a moment? I'd like to talk with you. About Imre."

After that talk, I decided never to speak to the man again.

But there was no sense dredging up those old, difficult memories now. I put the file back.

"Find the other one," Lena said, moving closer.

"Which one?"

"Number one."

I pretended I didn't understand.

"When you fell madly in love with me?"

"Ah!" I said. "*That* one."

She tapped the remote until the Popa family was silenced. "Come on. Show me."

The files weren't in order—some clerk had stuffed them in the box haphazardly. So I pulled out half the box, a stack of thirty files, and handed it to Lena. "Look for 1948."

"I remember," she said, "even if you don't."

Of course I remembered. In 1948, I was only twenty-two, and Lena was a thirty-year-old widow with a serious drinking problem.

The case had begun with the murder of her first husband, Janos Crowder, a songwriter found bludgeoned to death. He'd been black-mailing a political figure named Jerzy Michalec with documents proving that Michalec had been a decorated Gestapo agent during the war. In the end, Michalec—amazingly vital despite being afflicted with epilepsy—kidnapped Lena, then traded her for incriminating German documents I'd gone all the way to Berlin to track down. Despite our deal, Brano Sev used the photographs to bring the man to justice.

Jerzy Michalec was first sentenced to death, and I can still remember the show trial we listened to on the Militia radio. It was 1949. We heard everything—the prosecutors and the hysterical witnesses, and even the confusion when, during a judge's tirade, Michalec suddenly shivered, frothing, taken by an epileptic seizure. Later, his punishment was commuted, and he was put to work in one of the many labor camps that filled the country during the late forties and fifties. Like a bad dream, he simply vanished. It was the way of the world back then. People vanished.

But the file wasn't here. I went through my stack twice, then took Lena's. In the front of the box, I found the order form I'd sent over, listing cases to be retrieved. Each had been checked by the archives clerk, except the one labeled "10-3282-48—MICHALEC, J," which was marked NH—*ne hár.* The file was missing.

The phone rang, and Lena went to get it. Central Archives was notoriously inefficient, but of all the files to be misplaced, I was surprised it would be this one.

"*Cher* comrade?" Lena was waving the receiver from its cord. "Comrade Kolyeszar requests your presence."

While I talked, Lena went through the cabinets, finding a glass and making me a scotch and soda. She'd picked up the ten-year-old malt on a trip earlier that year to England. Unlike in the old days, she didn't make one for herself.

Ferenc said, "Sorry to call at home." He sounded strange, distant, and spoke with an unsettling calm.

"What is it?"

"They're dead."

"Who's dead?"

Lena handed me the drink. Ferenc said, "I don't know. They . . . they *shot*, Emil."

"Who?"

A voice—Magda, I think—said something to Ferenc. Then Agota took the phone. "For fuck's sake, Emil, he's telling you the Ministry bastards shot into the crowd! We don't know how many people they killed—but there are dead people. Lots. You have to spread the word. Understand? *The Spark* will say something different, but you have to tell them. You have to make sure they *know.*"

Agota spoke to me with a voice I'd hear more and more over the next days. It was more than Ferenc's abstracts—it was the voice of the astonished and self-righteous.

I don't mean to say people weren't justified feeling this way; almost always, they were. I just mean that it was a voice I hadn't yet accustomed myself to. My heart palpitated and my hand sweated. I gulped down the scotch and soda and handed the empty glass back to Lena, who was staring wildly. I said, "Just tell me what to do, Agí."

What she wanted me to do frightened me, but I couldn't do it until the next day, so for the rest of the night I was impotent. Predictably, there was no mention of the Patak massacre on the two state television stations that evening.

I wanted to distract myself with my old files, because there was some comfort in cases that had been solved and closed, but in light of what was going on, they were like stories out of a piece of fiction. Lena, on the other hand, was empowered by the news. "Finally, this godforsaken country is going to see the light."

"What do you mean?"

"I mean, dear, that Pankov has crossed the line. He can starve us and cut off our energy, but once he starts shooting people in the streets it's over. Only a desperate man resorts to this."

I didn't share Lena's optimism. We'd both lived through the arrival of socialism, and both of us welcomed the idea of watching it leave again, but I worried—perhaps too much—about my friends. We weren't like the Czechs or Poles. We'd never been the kind of people to vent our frustration through the ballot box.

My problem, of course, was that I had no faith in people to make my country better. After forty years in the People's Militia, it's hard to maintain such faith.

Around ten thirty, Bernard called and swore angrily that if anyone touched Agota or Sanja, he was going to blow something up. I suggested he not say this over the phone, but there was no stopping him. He finally made it around to what I knew, when I first heard his voice, he was going to ask: "Do you really need me here?"

"Go," I said, hoping his Militia ID would get him through the roadblocks. "A dead Ministry officer, one way or the other, makes no difference." I said that because I was foolish enough to believe it.

The foolishness stayed with me all night, even as I sat in bed watching Lena clean makeup from her hollowed cheeks in the vanity mirror. She'd listened in on my conversation, so she asked about the dead Ministry officer, and I told her about Kolev. She showed more surprise than I would've expected, lowering her hands from her face in shock. "You're saying he was murdered?"

"That's what I'm saying."

"Why did you run the tests? That colonel told you not to bother."

"I don't trust him."

"You think he did it? Romek?"

"Maybe. But I don't really know."

She went back to her face, and I peered around for cigarettes but couldn't find any. I looked back at my wife. It wasn't just the stupidity that left me feeling calm. It was a kind of detachment. As I would a week later in Italy, I was thinking about something else, something to take me away from the moment, because the moment was frightening. I was remembering how thankful I was for the Afghan War.

All our life together, Lena had been an alcoholic. No—*drunk* is the better word. We twice separated because of her drinking, and her drinking led to two miscarriages and many, many hospital visits. Then, in 1983, Lena woke from another of her brief comas, this time triggered by a bottle of black-market *rakija* that had been mixed with methanol. The nurse smiled at her and laid a copy of the day's *Spark* on her bedside table. After a couple of hours, she was finally able to focus enough to take in the front-page story about the Soviet troops who had been killed in the mujahideen's most recent offensive in the Panjshir Valley.

Maybe it was the poison in her bloodstream, lingering even after the stomach pump of bad Serbian brandy—whatever it was, it had a lasting effect. On the third floor of Unity Medical, she cried uncontrollably.

Never the weeping sort, Lena nonetheless let forth at times with the hysterical weeping of the unbalanced; it was a sound that always troubled me. There in Unity Medical, though, it was as if someone else were crying, someone who understood exactly why she was crying, understood that if she'd had her wits about her, she would have been crying like this ever since she first picked up a bottle, sometime during her first disastrous marriage more than forty years ago.

She showed me the newspaper, and though I didn't understand, I never admitted it. I didn't want to undermine the vow she'd just made in a fit of emotion: As long as men were blown up in obscure corners of the world, she, Lena Brod, would not touch another drop of alcohol.

Now it was 1989, and she was seventy-two. A dry seventy-two. Her hands no longer shook, and when I returned home I no longer opened the door with apprehension, wondering about her unpredictable moods. In the winter of our lives she had given me something not unlike spring, and I was thankful.

Thankful for the floundering Soviet war in the deserts of Afghanistan, only recently ended, and for the cretin who added methanol to his batch so he could sell more of his black-market *rakija* to the alcoholics of our country.

Lena was staring at me, the light in the mirror shining against the large spectacles she'd slipped on to see me better. "What is it? You worried?"

"Not anymore," I said. It's amazing how the human mind can comfort itself.

FIVE

•

"She'll wonder," said Lebed Putonski.

Gavra pulled the beige Stop & Drop curtains shut, then parted them with a finger. He peered out at the parking lot and beyond the line of trees, to where headlights sped through the darkness. "Who?"

Putonski had trouble turning on the bed to face Gavra, because his arms were above his head, tied to the bedpost with a leather belt. "Maureen. She'll come over and wonder why I'm not home. She'll go to the school. She'll worry—she's that kind. Then she'll call the police."

"The school will say you're with your cousin."

"She'll panic."

"She won't."

It took Putonski a moment to realize this was true. "What're you going to do with me?"

Gavra dropped the curtains. "I'm not sure."

"Then let me go."

"I can't."

"Why?"

"Because you're in danger."

Lebed pressed his face into the motel pillow. "It's starting to drive me crazy, you know."

"What?"

"You're not telling me anything." He raised his head. "You've come all this way to find me, but you don't tell me who sent you. You tell me I'm in danger, but you won't say why. And then you tie me up. You expect me to *not* go a little crazy?"

"You hungry?"

"I'm more curious than hungry."

"Well, I'm hungry."

"Please."

In the bathroom, Gavra washed his face. The lack of sleep was showing in his eyes. Or perhaps it was just confusion. He'd been sent to get hold of Lebed, and he had done this, but now Kolev lay dead in a morgue, unable to tell him what to do next.

He dried himself and sat on the corner of the bed while Lebed stared at him. "Okay," he said. "I was sent by Lieutenant General Yuri Kolev."

Lebed's dry lips worked a moment. "*Kolev?* Jesus."

"You know him?"

"Of course. What does he want with me?"

"He's dead. He had a heart attack earlier today."

"Heart attack?"

"Yeah," said Gavra.

"So it's finished. Let me go."

"I can't."

"You think I'm the cause of his heart attack?"

"Maybe. Indirectly."

"A man like that has enemies. He's got hundreds."

"How do you know him?"

Lebed shook his head, unwilling to answer.

"Listen to me," said Gavra. "Kolev wanted me to find you and protect you. His words. And if this wasn't simple heart failure, then the people who killed him will want you next. I'm going to make sure that doesn't happen."

"Oh," said Lebed, and Gavra looked closely at him because he'd spoken with the voice of a small child. "But I don't *know* anything!"

"How do you know Kolev?"

"Long time ago. Before you were born, probably." He paused. "Can you at least free my hands?"

"Tell me first."

Putonski sighed loudly. "Okay. Just after the war, we were both on a Ministry tribunal. You know how it was—rooting out enemies of the state. Put them on trial, broadcast on radio, and get lots of people in as shouting, hysterical witnesses. That's how we met. We tried lots of cases, sent a lot of men and women to their deaths. I'm not proud of it, but that's how it was."

"And?"

"And what?"

"And what about after that?"

"We saw each other now and then at Yalta. We knew each other. But we didn't work together again. I'm surprised Kolev even cared about saving my skin. We certainly weren't friends."

"That's all?"

"Look," said Putonski. "*I'm* not the one who crossed the Atlantic. You're the one who's wasting his time."

Gavra stood again and slipped the pistol into his belt.

"So what do we do now?"

"We eat dinner," said Gavra. "What do you want?"

Lebed rolled his face back into the pillow. "I'd like my hands free."

"When I get back."

"Eggs, then. And sausage."

"It's dinnertime, Lebed."

"Breakfast helps when I'm nervous. Otherwise I'll throw up."

"Okay. From where?"

"McDonald's, of course."

Gavra considered covering Lebed's mouth before leaving, but the man seemed to understand now that he wasn't his enemy. He locked the door and drove up the busy evening turnpike to where he'd seen a McDonald's when he first arrived. Around the back were lit arrows pointing to a DRIVE-THRU, which he followed to an enormous menu board. A crackling female voice said, "Elcome to M'Onalds."

"Hello," he said, but there was no immediate answer. "Hello?"

"Uht an I it for oo?"

"Eggs and sausage, please. Two orders. And coffee."

"Arry, sir. We ont erve ekfas ow."

"Uh, what?"

She repeated herself, but he was just as baffled, so he drove around to a window where a girl with red, damp cheeks explained that McDonald's didn't serve breakfast at this hour.

"What do you suggest?"

She rubbed her cheek with her wrist, unsure. "Well, most people just get a cheeseburger and fries."

"That sounds perfect. I'll have two orders. With coffee."

She took his money and gave him his food with a smile. The car soon stank of processed meat. As he drove back to the motel he ate lengths of the oily but delicious French fries. He parked in front of the room and carried the McDonald's sack all the way to the door before noticing that the door was open, just an inch, and the wooden frame was cracked.

He set the food on the ground, taking out the pistol with his other hand. Behind him, three cars were parked by the line of pine trees. He lifted his foot, then kicked. The door bounced off the wall and hit his shoulder as he rushed in. Lebed was still tied to the bedpost. His face was in the pillow again, but the pillow, like the back of his fractured head, was the burgundy of fresh blood.

He didn't panic. Ministry training was an exceptional thing, and he'd served his apprenticeship under the best. *It all becomes mathematics,* Brano Sev had explained. *That's how you deal with the fear.*

*Spatial relations. Protective barriers. Escape paths. Turn them all into
numbers, and you can keep the panic at bay.*

He checked the bathroom, then peered through the curtains at
the parking lot. The three other cars appeared empty. He ignored
Lebed's body, the soft, greasy fries in his stomach mixing sickly with
the stink of organic matter as he collected his things, then kept close
watch on the trees as he put his bag and the McDonald's sack into
the car. Distances. Measurements. Escape paths. He hung a DO NOT
DISTURB sign on the door, then pulled it as shut as it would go.

It took fifteen minutes before Gavra knew he was being followed. A
cherry red Ford with Virginia plates that he felt sure he'd seen in the
Stop & Drop parking lot. But he'd just found a dead man in his
room—a scared, pitiful math teacher for whose life Gavra was
responsible—and that had flung him out of the safe realm of mathematics. His hands trembled on the wheel, and his stomach convulsed. Perhaps he was just being paranoid.

So when he saw the massive cartoon Big Boy in overalls holding a
plate of food aloft (for some reason reminding him of Lenin in a
similar pose), he left the turnpike and parked.

The Ford pulled in after him, but the man waited behind the
wheel until Gavra had tossed the now-cold McDonald's food into a
wastebasket and walked inside. Then the man got out. Through the
window, Gavra watched a blond young man cross the harshly lit
parking lot. Unattractive to Gavra's eye. A little slouched, as if life so
far hadn't been entirely fair.

He kept track of his shadow while he ate half of a Caesar salad
at the counter. When he got up to use the toilet, the man was in a
booth, cradling a cup of coffee, as if dreaming. Five minutes later,
Gavra returned, having been sick, and the shadow didn't even glance
at him—he was good at his job.

When Gavra paid and left, the man followed, and when he pulled back onto the turnpike, the lights of the Ford were visible in his rearview.

He tried some evasive maneuvers, driving through a residential area with big crabgrass yards and high houses, then reentered the turnpike heading back toward Midlothian. All his moves felt panicked and obvious, but he had no choice. By the time he took another U-turn, however, the Ford was behind him again. That's when he spotted the Chesterfield Towne Center, a shopping mall with a vast parking lot full of cars. It was just after eight.

Gavra parked by a high flat wall with a SEARS sign, pocketed his P-83, got out, and entered quickly. He didn't bother looking back, because he knew the man would be right behind him. The interior was cool, packed with racks of pastel women's clothes, counters, and fat shoppers. Dry music floated through the air, and then, just before he reached the entrance to the mall itself, the air became saturated with astringent smells that brought back his nausea. The perfume section. Women in faux medical smocks and feathered haircuts stood bored behind counters, some chatting, but all ignored him. Gavra held his breath until he was clear of them.

He paused beside a tiled water fountain, peering down the mall's length. It looked like an obscenely clean city street crowded with shoppers. Ahead, to the left, he saw a store called Fit-4-All, which advertised "Today's styles for today's gentlemen."

Only after he was inside the shop, among racks of gray and blue suits, did he let himself peer through the display windows for his shadow. He wasn't out there.

"Well, howdy, sir!"

He turned to find a broad-chested, very effeminate man with a yellow tie and a white name tag that said ROG. "Howdy, Rog," said Gavra.

Rog's smile didn't change as he said, "It's pronounced *Rodj*, sir. Short for Rodger."

"Oh."

"What can I do you for?"

"I'd like a suit."

Rog giggled. "Well, you came to the right place! What's your size?"

Gavra wanted a black suit, but Rog disagreed, insisting on "navy" blue. It was also more expensive. In the changing room, Gavra transferred his wallet, his money, both passports, and the P-83 to his new clothes. He left the jeans and polo shirt crumpled on the bench.

"*Very* handsome, sir. *Manly.*"

Gavra looked past the salesman through the open door—still no sign. "I'll take it."

"Excellent!"

"And I'll wear it now."

"As you wish." The salesman sank to his knees.

Gavra stepped back, disoriented, before realizing the man was using a large pair of scissors to snip off the price tags.

He paid in cash, and as he was leaving, Rog called, "Sir?"

Gavra looked back. "Yes?"

"Your clothes? The ones you came in with."

"Keep them."

That seemed to please Rog immensely.

In the center of the mall, Gavra stopped between another tiled fountain and an information desk where two white-capped girls chewed gum. It was busy here, loud with voices and Muzak. He considered leaving by another exit and stealing a car. But if the police caught him, they'd easily connect him to the body of Lebed Putonski back in the motel room registered to Viktor Lukacs. He couldn't toss the Lukacs passport, because his real one had no American visa. So he headed back to Sears.

Halfway there, he spotted his blond shadow standing beside the dark entrance to Spencer's Gifts, drinking from a large paper cup of Coca-Cola.

The shadow was staring back at him.

Despite the lessons that Brano Sev had hammered into him during his two-year apprenticeship a decade and a half ago, when he
met those eyes, the panic hit him hard. Rationally, he knew that if
this man wanted to kill him, he would have tried it back at the motel, but Gavra couldn't hold on to the numbers anymore.

An old woman bumped into him, then went around, muttering
something. The shadow lowered his drink and smiled. Then the panic
became solid, because Gavra could see his position here with complete clarity. He was in a foreign, enemy country with false papers,
and there was a dead man in his room.

Gavra turned and walked quickly away.

He followed bathroom signs into a white corridor and entered
the door marked with an abstracted male figure. He ignored the
men lined at the urinals and closed himself in a vacant stall, then
squatted, feet on the toilet seat, and tried to catch his breath. He
took out his pistol.

Fifteen minutes later, his knees felt like sacks of stone. He tensed
when an old man came in, taking the stall beside his, then again
when a father and son entered and went to pee together, but he
didn't move. He knew that, whatever orders the shadow was working under, he would inevitably have to come in here.

It was a momentary advantage, but he had trouble visualizing
how to utilize it. The numbers were a mess. All he could do was wait
for a sign that the man was out there. A voice, a cocked pistol, or
someone opening the stalls one at a time.

What he got was water running, then the explosion of a door
kicked open.

But it wasn't his door. The old man in the next stall screamed in
pain as the kicked door struck his knees.

Gavra leapt off the toilet, ripped open the door, and pressed his
pistol against the base of the shadow's neck. His hand still shook,
but he could visualize it all now. "Drop the gun and kick it away," he
said in English.

The young man did so, kicking a compact Bren Ten over to the sinks, shaking his head in disgust.

When Gavra told him to step back to the vacant urinals, the old man in the stall whimpered. Gavra picked up the Bren Ten and, through the door, told the old man to stay where he was. "This will take a few minutes. Then we'll go. Keep your door closed."

He heard a grunt as the old man pushed on his broken door.

His shadow seemed strangely unconcerned by this turn of events. Gavra switched to his own language. "Documents."

The blond man smiled, hands at shoulder height, and said, "I don't speak Swahili, partner."

It was the voice from Lebed Putonski's telephone. Possibly CIA, or a Ministry agent who did a good impersonation of an American. Gavra repeated his demand in English and watched the man reach slowly into his blazer and take out a brown leather wallet. He handed it over.

"And you were sent by . . . ?" Gavra asked as he used a thumb to open the wallet. "Well?"

The man shook his head.

Gavra found a Virginia driver's license with a picture of this man, the same passivity, beside the name. FRANK JONES.

"Tell me why you killed Putonski, Frank."

Jones blinked, as if the question were unexpected. "I'm a simple man. I follow my orders."

"Who gives the orders?"

Jones grinned. "That's rich, *Comrade* Lukacs."

At least the man didn't know Gavra's real name.

The bathroom door opened, and a fat man stepped in. They looked at him as he registered the pistol in Gavra's hand. He fled.

Gavra took Jones by the elbow and stood close behind him, the pistol in the small of the shadow's back—the same way, earlier that day, he'd walked Lebed Putonski out of Clover Hill High School.

"Let's go."

Gavra pulled open the door, and they slowly entered the white corridor. The Muzak returned, and voices from the mall rolled toward them. When they reached the packed line of stores, shoppers jostled into them. Gavra kept his pistol up under Jones's jacket.

"It's impossible," said Frank Jones.

Gavra's eyes swept the mall, watching for security guards. "It's possible."

But as he spoke, Jones raised his arms high above his head, and that's when Gavra realized he was right.

"You can't shoot me, not here. You'll be caught before you reach the doors. They run your name, and they'll find a dead man in your motel. Killed with the gun in your pocket." He turned to face Gavra, hands still up. He had the ecstatic pride of youth in his smile. "Go on, Comrade Lukacs. Get the hell out of here."

Around them, oblivious Americans cooed at shop windows.

"Look behind you," he added.

Through the crowd, by the corridor to the bathrooms, the fat man stood with the still-trembling old man and two burly security guards. The fat man was pointing directly at Gavra. The guards started to work their way through the shoppers.

"Good luck," said Jones.

Gavra ran.

21 DECEMBER 1989

THURSDAY

•

SIX

•

Lena kept me up most of the night, shifting and turning in our bed, sometimes saying, "Emil? You awake?" I played dead until the alarm buzzed at six thirty. She was finally deep in sleep, but I got up. After forty years of rising at the same hour, I doubted I'd ever be able to sleep late again. And it says something that this was the thought that first came to me that morning. I didn't want to think about revolutions, massacres, or even a dead lieutenant general. All I wanted was a little quiet, a little simplicity, and a peaceful retirement party the following night—and even that, I didn't give a damn about.

Only while waiting in vain for the hot water, then suffering through a cold shower, did I remember what I had promised Agota I would do. It would have to wait until the post office opened at eight thirty; I wasn't looking forward to it.

The roads were empty for that hour. I was used to swerving around Gypsy families who came into town to search through trash before the Militia arrived to send them away. That should have told me something, but without caffeine I still couldn't think straight. Instead, I focused on a pitiful papier-mâché St. Nicholas in a shoe store window, knowing that, behind the Christmas sculpture, the store was empty. I wondered why the shopkeeper even bothered.

The night crew at the Militia station was getting ready to leave, and when they saw me come in, they nodded their acknowledgment. "Any coffee?" I asked.

Tamas, a young recruit, was putting on his coat. "None in the station."

"None at all?"

He shook his head regretfully, then yawned.

"I've got some in my desk," I admitted. "I'm willing to share."

But Tamas didn't have time for it. He, like the others, wanted to get home to his family. I stopped him at the door. "Anything last night?"

"It's all on the form," he said, then unlatched himself from my grip and was gone.

The night form listed calls made over the previous eight hours. There were nine, ranging from simple disturbances—a neighbor's music was too loud—to someone insisting that she had heard tanks moving in the street. I scribbled down her number and took it up to the homicide office, where someone had left a couple of copies of the morning's *Spark*. I didn't read it. Not yet. Instead, I dialed the number.

A groggy male voice picked up. "*What?*"

"This is Chief Emil Brod of the People's Militia. Did you call last night?"

"My wife, comrade." He was suddenly awake. "No, it's nothing. Sorry to bother you."

"It's all right. But is it true?"

"Who knows? She said she heard it, but I didn't hear a thing."

"Okay," I said. "Thanks."

I used the percolator and my stash of acorn coffee in the empty lounge. When, a couple of years ago, the stores began replacing real coffee with this sludge, I suffered flashbacks of those desperate years just after the war. Acorn coffee, for me, was the irrefutable evidence that we were sliding in the wrong direction. Ration cards and petrol rationing were one thing, but when you couldn't get a cup of real coffee anymore, that was a sure sign that everything was collapsing.

Now, people were being shot in the streets.

As the coffee brewed, I read *The Spark*'s interpretation of last night. It was, not surprisingly, buried on page eight, under a lengthy profile of our most famous ice-skater, Ingrid Tolopov.

PATAK MOB KILLS 6

A riot broke out in Sárospatak's main square last night when a mob organized by foreign elements threw stones at members of the People's Militia.

Six hooligans were killed when militiamen were forced to defend themselves.

Comrade Mayor Natan Pankov said that he has been dealing with German, Hungarian, and Yugoslav reactionaries in Sárospatak over the previous month. "This is an attack on all of us," he said.

"It's no secret that the counterrevolutionary uprisings destroying the socialist frameworks of our fraternal countries have been making great efforts here."

A Militia corporal said, "I saw Hungarians breaking shop windows."

In an effort to protect his citizens, Comrade Mayor Pankov has instituted martial law.

There were no surprises here: no mention of why the crowd was there in the first place; blaming foreigners; and quoting Comrade Mayor Natan Pankov, Tomiak Pankov's son.

I threw the paper into a wastebasket and brought my cup back to the office, taking yesterday's day-end report from Katja's desk. I took a sip of the wretched coffee and tried to focus on the homicide investigation she'd been working on.

Dušan Volan was a seventy-year-old retired judge who had been found Sunday night by the high stone wall that encircled his

Thirteenth District estate. A photograph showed how he had fallen, a face-down lump on the grass, and that the bullet had entered his skull through the back. A 9mm.

The ballistics report told me that the bullet that killed the judge was shot from an ASP pistol. I'd never heard of it.

> ASP: 9×19 mm, 7 rounds. Length: 173 mm. Developed by American gunsmith Paris Theodore in 1970s. Designed for concealment—i.e., clandestine work. Only 300 on the open market, in USA, the rest supposedly produced for CIA.

It went on, going into the gun's special snag-proof design, which made it impossible to catch on clothing, the American company that produced it, and the fact that it was last known to be manufactured in 1983. The ballistics specialist added a handwritten side note. *Just dumb luck I know this—we've got 1 ASP, from a dead American 5 years ago.*

My phone rang, and when I picked it up the line was fuzzy, long distance. "Emil?" said a familiar voice.

"Gavra? Is that you?"

"Yes."

"Where've you been?"

"Zagreb," he lied. "How's the Kolev report coming?"

"It's not simple."

"You're sure?"

"Yes. I'm sure." I told him about the heroin and then heard some voice on his side, a woman over a loudspeaker—she was announcing a flight in English. I didn't bother asking about that.

There was a rush of static, then he said, "Take down this name: Lebed Putonski."

I wrote it down as, through my open door, I saw Katja arriving. She smiled at me but looked tired, and I nodded back. I lowered my voice to a whisper: "Who's Lebed Putonski?"

"Ex-Ministry. Also murdered. I should be home by tonight, but can you pull his file?"

"Is it connected to Kolev?"

"Yes, Emil. Undoubtedly."

As I hung up, Katja sniffed the air in my office. Her short-cropped blond hair looked disheveled, and her makeup seemed a little off. "Where's the coffee?"

"Lounge."

She grabbed her cup from her desk but paused at the door. She looked back at me. "Where's Berni?"

"Out of town," I said. "Just you and me."

"Oh." She frowned theatrically before continuing to the corridor.

I called Central Archives. A tired woman answered, saying, "Records."

"I need a file sent over. Name's Lebed Putonski."

I started to spell it out, but she interrupted. "You'll have to fill out the form, Comrade Chief. You know that."

What I knew was that going through proper channels would take a week. "I don't have time. Please, just check. I'll make it worth your trouble."

"You *will*, huh?"

"How's your coffee ration?"

She hummed into the phone. "How much've you got?"

"Two kilos," I said. "I'll give it to the courier."

When I hung up, Katja threw herself into the chair that faced my desk, placed an ankle on a knee, and sipped her steaming coffee. She was my most astute detective, as well as the first woman in homicide. Lena often accused me—not without justification—of having a crush on her.

I tapped her day-end report. "How's this coming?"

She shook her head. "Not well. The wife got hysterical when I asked her questions. I might have been wrong."

"How?"

"I thought she'd killed her husband." Katja rocked her head. "He'd been keeping two mistresses for years. But to be honest, I don't think she gave a damn. I was planning to visit her again today . . ." She trailed off. "You want to come?"

"Sure," I said. "Let's wait a while. I'm expecting a call."

"No hurry." She rubbed her ear with her buffed but unpainted fingernails. She had small hands with smooth, pale skin; they were very pretty. "Any more news from Patak?"

I blinked, then shook my head, that anxiety coming back.

"I heard sixteen dead."

I didn't bother saying I'd heard thirty. "Any family there?"

"No. You?"

"Agota and Bernard are in Tisakarad, but I'll bet Ferenc has dragged them over there by now."

We let that sit between us, because even though this was our space, neither of us knew for sure how well Gavra Noukas did his job, which was in part to keep an eye on us, and measure our political morality. It was always possible he'd bugged the place.

So she changed the subject. "What's going on with Yuri Kolev?"

"Poisoned. And I don't have any tenable leads."

Then Katja put into words something that had been nagging at me. "It seems odd, though. Two men, Volan and Kolev, one retired and the other ready to retire. Killed a few days apart."

"By that logic, I'm next," I said, smiling.

"Watch out, Chief."

My phone rang, but she made no move to leave. I picked it up. "Yes?"

"This is Records," said the woman.

"Will you be drinking coffee today?"

She sighed loudly. "Just send one kilo for my effort."

"Nothing?"

"The file on Lebed Putonski was signed out two weeks ago and not returned."

"You're joking."

"If you knew me, Comrade Chief, you'd know how unlikely that was. The file should've been returned after three days."

"If you can tell me who signed it out, you'll get both kilos."

"I'm not supposed to do that, you know."

"Three kilos." I didn't have three kilos, but I was retiring. This would be my last bribe as a militiaman. Katja stared at me over the rim of her cup.

"You win. Name's Rosta Gorski."

I asked her to spell it, then scribbled it in my notepad. "What else did he sign out?"

She hummed. "Don't tell me you have more coffee?"

"You need stockings?" I could take a couple of pairs from Lena if necessary.

"Hold on."

I heard her set down the phone. Katja mouthed, *What's going on?*

I shook my head and waved her out, but, like Lena, she wasn't the kind of woman to be shooed off. She read what I'd written. "Gorski?"

I put a finger to my lips as the clerk returned. "Got a pen?"

"Shoot."

"One Militia case file, number 10-3283-48."

As I wrote the number in my notepad, my hand went cold. I knew that case intimately. "Go on."

"And a bunch of personnel files. Names: Volan, Dušan. Sev, Brano . . . *hey.*"

My heart was palpitating, and my hand was damp. "What?"

"*You're* here. Brod, Emil."

For an instant I couldn't speak. Katja, seeing my face, stood instinctively. I wrote one word—*me*—and said, "Go on."

The clerk noticed my tone; when she continued, it was in a whisper. "Michalec, Jerzy, and Zoltenko, Tatiana. And that Putonski one. You got them all?"

I looked at the list. "Who gave Gorski the authority to walk out with all these files?"

"A minute."

She set the phone down again, and I heard papers being shifted and flipped through. Katja was in her seat again but leaning forward to read the names. *Brano Sev,* she mouthed, a look of terror on her face.

"Comrade Chief Brod?" I heard—but it wasn't the clerk. It was a man.

"Yes?"

"Comrade Chief, you know the regulations. As much as we respect your tenure, I'm afraid you'll have to go through proper channels for your information."

"Who am I speaking to?"

"Chief Administrator Zoran Aspitan."

"Comrade Aspitan," I said, making no effort to hide my annoyance, "you're obstructing a murder investigation, which comes under the direct supervision of Comrade Colonel Nikolai Romek of the Ministry for State Security. Do you understand what I'm saying?"

There was a pause as Aspitan tried to gauge my conviction. Perhaps I wasn't much of an actor, because he said, "Comrade, I seriously doubt the truth of what you say."

"Do you?"

"If you like," he said, "please have Colonel Romek contact me, and I'll discuss it with him. Or, if you prefer, I'll call him directly to sort this out."

I was astonished by the chief administrator's bravery. In those days, it was a rare virtue. "You'll hear from him," I said. "Very soon." I slammed the phone down.

Katja was surprised by my anger. "What happened?"

Because mine was empty, I took her cup and drank the last of her coffee. Then I explained why I initially called the Central Archives— Gavra's news, from Zagreb, that a man named Lebed Putonski had been killed. She said, "A Yugoslav?"

"No, one of ours. Ex-Ministry."

"What was he doing in Zagreb?"

"I don't know."

As I told the rest, she rubbed her nose, which was something she did when deep in thought. "You're telling me that a man named Rosta Gorski took out one case file and the files of six people. Two of them—Volan and Putonski—are recently killed, one of them is the first criminal you put away, one is Brano, and one is you?"

I nodded obliquely. "The last one—Tatiana Zoltenko—I don't know her."

"Kolev's not on the list."

"Gavra insists he's connected."

"But why your file? Why Brano's?"

"Because you're probably right."

"About what?"

"All us retirees are in trouble."

The stolen case file was, of course, my first one from 1948. When I fell in love with my wife; when she was kidnapped by Jerzy Michalec; when Michalec was sentenced to a life of hard labor. The case file linked Jerzy Michalec, me, and even Brano Sev, who made the final arrest.

But what about the others—Dušan Volan, Lebed Putonski, and Tatiana Zoltenko? Were they connected to the old case? I couldn't recall their names, and without the original case file, I might never know.

I told Katja to sign out a Militia Karpat and pick me up in front of the central post office. Then we'd go talk to Volan's wife. "You've got some mail to send?" she asked, puzzled.

"I've got a call to make."

She decided not to ask anything further, so I grabbed my hat and headed out, down past the understaffed front desk, and out the front door. Lenin Avenue was also underpopulated for eight thirty in the morning, and at the post office only one window was open. A woman with dyed black hair and a sleepy expression watched me enter—I was the only visitor—and cross to the four bubble-enclosed pay phones against the faux-marble wall. I stuck in a two-hundred-korona coin, peering behind myself to be sure I was still alone. I was, but my fingers had trouble dialing the six-digit number Agota had given me.

"Hello?" said a man's voice, wary.

"A message," I said.

"Yes?"

"From Patak."

"Go on."

I tried to remember the exact words. "There's no time to waste. The apples must be harvested by six o'clock."

"Really?"

"That's what I heard," I told him. I didn't know exactly what the phrase meant, nor what it would lead to, but I had to trust that Agota's friends here in the Capital wouldn't make a mess of my country.

"And why am I hearing from you, not from the farmer?"

In my nervousness I almost laughed aloud at the extended metaphor. "The farmer," I said, "is busy harvesting her own apples."

I'm sure I said it wrong—there was probably something about applesauce or barren trees that was more appropriate—but he seemed to understand. Although her family's phone was clean—they had begun checking it nightly—Agota suspected her friend's phone line was being listened to by the Ministry, and she didn't want the call to be traced back to her family's house. Further, she knew that in Sárospatak and Tisakarad, she and her family were being watched, and any visit to a pay phone would be noted. I accepted her paranoia as truth and used this phone to make sure nothing could be traced back to my own house, or to Lena.

"Thank you," said the man. His tone had changed. It was almost giddy. "Thank you very, very much."

* * *

Dušan Volan's Thirteenth District house was far to the north, beyond the Ninth and its clusters of block towers. Out here, among
large swaths of poorly managed wheat fields that had been cut from
thick forests, one could find the mansions of Politburo members
and those who were close to the Central Committee and its Grand
National Assembly. There was a time, long ago, when Lena lived out
here as well. Her father had been a coal baron before the Russians
marched in, and he'd made a deal with the new government to keep
hold of his foreign investments, and pass them on to Lena, while
they nationalized his business. But after the death of her father, and
then her husband's murder, there was nothing left for her out here,
so she sold the land to some up-and-coming Central Committee
member and moved into town with me.

One thing that surprised everyone was that her father's deal held
strong. Lena was allowed to keep her father's foreign investments—in
an English bank, Austrian land, and a Dutch shipping concern—
which paid for her frequent trips to Europe's capitals, and the various
perfumes and stockings and gourmet foods that always filled her luggage when she returned. Her money was why we both drove German
cars when everyone else drove our national excuse for an automobile,
the Karpat.

So, unlike Katja, I wasn't intimidated by the high iron gate, the long,
curving driveway lined with poplars, nor the large villa we parked in
front of. For me, being among these trappings of luxury was like revisiting that period when I was young and knew nothing—when knowing nothing made me brave.

At least, that's how I like to remember those days.

"Are you doing the talking?" she asked as she turned off the engine.

"Want me to?"

"That woman hates me."

The villa had been built in the thirties, during the regime of late

Bauhaus. While the foundation was constructed of stones, the walls were reinforced white concrete, which rose and curved to form elegant terraces on the second and third floors. From our angle, we could just make out the treetops of a roof garden and half of a small satellite dish pointing at the sky.

Since Katja wasn't going to do it, I pressed the buzzer, and instead of a buzz we heard a soft melody play from inside the house. Then footsteps, and a pause as someone peered through the door's spy hole. The door opened. A small, heavy woman around thirty looked back at us. She was dressed all in black. "Is Comrade Csilla Volan in?" I said.

Katja made a noise behind me as the woman smiled thinly. "*I* am Comrade Csilla Volan."

I hid my embarrassment by showing my Militia certificate. "Chief Emil Brod. You know Comrade Lieutenant Drdova?"

She looked past me at Katja, her face showing nothing pleasant. "Come to ask about my husband's mistresses again?" she said. "Maybe you'd like to know their sexual positions?"

I tried to get her attention: "I'd like to speak to you about your husband."

"Comrade Drdova didn't do her job well enough?"

"Comrade Drdova did a fine job. There've been new developments."

"Yes?"

"Please, can you let us in?"

She shrugged and stepped aside. "Not long, though. I've got an appointment."

I took off my hat as we entered a large foyer that was two stories high. "What kind of appointment?"

"My husband's funeral, Comrade Chief."

"Oh."

She led us past framed paintings that matched the design of the house—large geometric abstracts in primary colors. Squares, triangles, octagons. The furniture in the living room was similar—white cushions shaped in rigid cubes and rectangles. A minimalist steel chandelier lit the room. Against the far wall sat the largest television I'd ever seen. Though the sound was off, bright, clear images flickered across the screen selling breakfast cereals, and from the occasional text that popped up I saw it was a German station.

Katja and I settled on one of the two long couches as Csilla Volan sat on an aluminum chair. "Should I be offering you coffee?"

I shook my head no.

"Good," she said. "I don't want to waste my Colombian."

I began to suspect that Katja had, in fact, done her job poorly—she'd made her suspicions obvious during their first interview.

"Want me to turn it up?" said Csilla Volan.

I wondered what she meant, then saw she was talking to Katja, who was mesmerized by two dancing cartoon bears on the television. Katja shook her head but said, "How do you get this?"

"The magic of satellites," said Csilla Volan.

I took out my notepad, flipped to the last page, and leaned over the coffee table to hand it to her. "Any of those names familiar?"

She squinted at it, then reached for a pair of reading glasses on the table. "Your handwriting's atrocious," she said, putting on the glasses and tilting the pad to get better light. She blinked a few times. "Putonski. I know that name."

"Yes?"

She nodded slowly. "And—yes!" Despite herself, she was getting excited. "Jerzy Michalec. Of course I know about him." She looked at us. "That was one of Dušan's first big cases. He sentenced the man to death."

That's what I'd been waiting to hear. "It was commuted," I told her. "Sentenced to a labor camp instead."

She shrugged. "No matter."

"What about Putonski?"

"I know the name but not the man. They knew each other long ago. Not sure how. Dušan brought up Putonski's name because he heard the man had defected. To America, I think." She snorted softly. "Lebed Putonski was no fool."

"And the others?" said Katja.

She went back to the sheet, reading with her lips. "*Me*. Yes, I know me." She smiled. "And of course everyone's heard of Brano Sev. He disappeared, didn't he?" When we didn't answer, she arched a brow. "What's this about?"

"That's what we're trying to figure out."

"You think my Dušan was murdered because of these people?"

I reached out to take back the pad, but she wouldn't let it go that easily.

"Answer me, Comrade Brod. I'm not just a little fat woman who takes it lying down."

"Please," I said, waving at the pad.

She held it to her breast. "Answer me first."

I glanced at Katja, but she just shrugged. "Yes," I said. "We believe there's a connection between these people. Two people on the list, including your husband, have been killed in the last three days. We believe a third murder is also connected."

She looked again at the list. It was a different list now, because two of them were corpses. "Who." She said this quietly.

"Your husband, Lebed Putonski, and Yuri Kolev—he's not on the list. Did you know Kolev?"

She shook her head and returned the pad without a word, then peered past me at the television. She reached for a slim remote control on the coffee table and started pressing buttons. "Look."

On the screen were nighttime shots of crowds, the video grainy. I recognized a few buildings, so I didn't need the German voice to know it was Sárospatak. I listened anyway.

"This footage of last night's massacre comes from the Yugoslav news agency, Tanjug."

It looked less like footage of a massacre than pictures taken by someone who was very frightened. The camera jerked and jumped, and we heard a cacophony of voices punctuated by the low thump of gunshots. Screams, the video smear of flashlights in darkness, and a very quiet Serbo-Croatian voice reporting what was translated by a louder German voice:

"A peaceful demonstration against the wrongful imprisonment of a priest, which grew over four nights to also protest the economic and human rights policies of the Pankov government, was disrupted last night when members of the Militia, mixed with regiments of the Ministry for State Security, fired on the crowd in 25 August Square. Official estimates are that six died in the shootout, though unofficial estimates place the death toll as high as sixty. In a city where nightly blackouts are common, any hard estimate is difficult to ascertain."

It cut to a morning shot of 25 August Square. The camera was inside a building, looking out, fragments of broken glass framing the image. In the center of the square was a single old man with a broom, scrubbing a spot.

"By morning," said the German translator, "the government had cleaned the square, making sure that there was nothing left to contradict its official estimates."

The news turned then to China, something about arms treaties, and Csilla lowered the volume. It had all given me a headache, and I realized I'd forgotten to take my medication that morning. I grabbed my hat and stood. "Thank you for your help, Comrade Volan."

Katja was still sitting, dazed by the television. I squeezed her shoulder, and she looked up.

"Come on."

As we walked back to the door, Csilla Volan kept close to us. "You'll tell me? If you find out why Dušan was killed."

"Yes," I said.

She opened the door for us but stood in our way. There was a distant look in her eye. "What about everything else?"

"Everything else?" I said.

"Sárospatak. Everything."

"What about it?"

"Do you think there's some connection?"

I considered that a moment. "Was your husband a dissident?"

"Hardly."

"Then I doubt it," I said and gave her a sympathetic smile. "Our condolences for your loss."

On the drive back into town, we were silent. I knew what Katja was thinking, because I was thinking the same thing. In addition, I was wondering how we were going to find the reserves to focus on this case. Did it even matter anymore? When upwards of sixty people are killed in a single night, why care about a few old, rich men who've been murdered?

Then I remembered why it mattered: I was on the list.

"I need to call Aron," said Katja.

I wasn't sure what she meant, and said so.

"He should stay at his mother's, outside town. If there's shooting in the Capital, I don't want him in the middle of it."

"He won't want you in the middle of it either."

"Unlike Aron, I can take care of myself."

"I'll call Lena, too."

Our decisions made, we returned to the station, which was still only half-staffed, and used the phones at our desks. I tracked down my medicine bottle and swallowed two Captopril, then dialed. After a few rings, Lena picked up. "Hello?"

"It's me."

"A call from work. How privileged am I?"

"I want you to pack a bag and go stay with Georgi."

"No," she said. That was her initial response to everything, so I wasn't discouraged.

"Yes," I answered. "It looks like sixty people were killed in Patak, maybe more."

"Oh," she said.

"I have a feeling something similar's going to happen here."

"Now what makes you think that?"

"Remember what I was going to do for Agí?"

She hummed a yes.

"That's what makes me think it. I'm serious, Lena."

"But I can't go anywhere."

"What?"

"I told you, but you never listen. My car's not starting."

"Then call a taxi, come here, and take mine. I have to write you a pass for the roadblocks anyway."

"That sounds like a lot of trouble."

I fought the urge to shout at her; I could feel my blood pressure skyrocketing. She was being difficult because she thought it was cute. But it wasn't. "Do it, Lena. I have to leave, but I'll be back by . . ." The clock on the wall told me it was twelve thirty. "I'll be back by two. I'll expect you here."

"I love it when you talk like a sergeant, dear."

Despite myself, I smiled but tried not to let it come through in my voice. "You'll be here?"

"When you say it like that, how can I refuse?"

I found Katja with her feet crossed on her desk.

"You find Aron?"

She nodded. "His supervisor was incredibly annoyed, but I told him I'd send him to a work camp if he didn't give me my husband."

"He believed you?"

"Well, he found Aron pretty quickly."

"And he's going?"

"He'll stop by here after his shift's over."

"Good." I handed her a travel pass I'd stamped and filled out with her husband's name. "Now come with me."

"Where?"

"Just come, will you?"

SEVEN

·

Forty thousand feet above the Atlantic, Gavra was in the four-seat center row of a Boeing 747 headed to Frankfurt, cramned in beside a pensioner couple who, once they'd taken off, introduced themselves as Harold and Beth Atkins of Philly, Pennsylvania. He'd tried to ignore them, but Beth, an old woman who wore the bright primary colors one dressed a child in, just kept talking. When she told him their final destination, though, he gaped at them. "Don't you know what's going on there?"

Beth's smile remained fixed, but her husband leaned over her lap and whispered, "We did see on the TV about Sárospatak." (Gavra was impressed that Harold had said the city's name properly—because it was a Hungarian name, each *s* was pronounced *sh*.) "But we've had this vacation planned and paid off the last four months." He shook his head. "I'm not letting a little disturbance get in the way. We'll just stay around the capital."

Gavra tried not to sound irritated. "It could spread, you know."

"From what we're able to see," said Beth, "it looks like your president, Mr. Pankov, he's got a tight grip on things."

"How long are you staying?"

"A week," she said, then went on to explain that they'd originally planned for just three days, so they'd have time to go on to Prague, but Berta Rasković, their travel agent back in Philly—she'd been a proud American citizen only three years—convinced them that her home country deserved more than just three days. *Get to know the people,* she'd told them. *They're a wonderful people.*

Harold said, "You should've heard her. Wow! *Czechs?* she said. *They're the rudest people on Earth, after Yugoslavs.* Can you believe it? And she sold us koronas at 2,950 to the dollar. I checked on it afterward; it's a good deal."

"You know the real reason we're going?" whispered Beth.

Gavra bowed his head close. "Tell me."

"Harold's in love with our travel agent. She could sell him Florida swampland."

"Not so!" Harold said with vague indignation.

In addition to everything else, Gavra found himself worrying about this idiotic couple. They were staying at the Metropol, at least, which meant that they could barricade themselves in if things became violent. But still . . .

Luckily, a couple of hours into the flight, they started to doze, and he could work over what had happened in the last twenty-four hours.

After escaping the Chesterfield Towne Center, he'd driven nonstop back to the Richmond airport, where he dropped his P-83 and Frank Jones's Bren Ten into a wastebasket and bought a ticket on the next flight to JFK. He again wished he'd had an American visa in his own passport, because it was possible that by now Lebed Putonski had been discovered and an arrest warrant issued for Viktor Lukacs. So when he bought a ticket home, via New York and Frankfurt, he noticed the way the JFK Delta clerk stared at him. "Something wrong?" he said, giving a stiff smile.

The woman blushed and apologized. "Sorry, sir. You just look very tired."

"I am," he said, because by then it was four in the morning, and he'd been awake two full days.

He washed in the airport bathroom to make himself presentable, and despite more stares from the guards he was allowed through passport control to the international terminal without hassle. Only once he'd reached his gate did he allow himself a couple of hours' sleep on the uncomfortable chairs.

It was during his erratic nap that it occurred to him that Frank Jones and his Virginia driver's license weren't a lie. He *was* American. No one from Gavra's country could master the accent and idiomatic phrases as well as he had.

Before dying, Kolev had told him two things. One, that Lebed Putonski's life was in danger. Two, that he got his information from a contact in the CIA. Were those two facts linked? Had Central Intelligence ordered Putonski's murder?

Hours later, with Beth Atkins's head sliding dangerously close to his shoulder, Gavra went back to this slow line of reasoning.

Lebed Putonski was a defector, brought into the United States by Central Intelligence, protected for eight years, and then killed by his protectors. Why? Why now?

Beth Atkins's head touched down on Gavra's shoulder, but he didn't move.

Back up. Lebed Putonski and Yuri Kolev knew each other after the war, when they shared duties on a public tribunal, sentencing prisoners to work camps and executions. Afterward, Putonski had become a Ministry bureaucrat, working his way up to Stockholm resident, passing on information from their local agents and relaying orders from home.

He unconsciously rubbed his eyes, and that movement woke Beth Atkins. She smiled and apologized for falling on him. "Can't you sleep, dear?"

He shook his head. "I have a lot on my mind."

She gave him a self-consciously sad expression. "You worried about your country?"

"Yes," he said. "That's exactly what I'm worried about."

Beth patted his arm, whispering, "Me too," as if it were a secret. Then she closed her eyes and returned, magically, to sleep.

EIGHT

•

In the car, Katja said, "Where're we going?"

"You don't want to know."

"Oh no," she said, because she did know.

"I need to try. It'll be quick."

"*That* may not be up to us."

I turned off of Lenin Avenue and took a side street to Victory Square. "Does Aron think you're being overcautious sending him away?"

She grunted loudly. "That's a funny one."

"Oh?"

She gazed out at the vacant streets. "Aron's . . . well, he's been weird over the last half year. If you know what I mean."

"I don't."

She was silent a moment, but when she spoke it came out as if she'd been wanting to say this for a long time. "He's paranoid, Emil. Or he's seemed so for the last six months since his dad died. He thinks the world's about to end. He's gotten obsessed with the news, and every time something happens, it's just more evidence that God's hand is upon us."

"What? He's religious?"

She shook her head. "No. It's just like a . . . a premonition. I've had to listen to it every damned night." She went into an imitation of Aron's rants, citing a wide range of events: the collision on the River Thames of a pleasure boat and a barge, which killed fifty-one, the Tiananmen Square massacre that resulted in at least four hundred dead, the Loma Prieta earthquake in San Francisco that killed sixty-three, and even a report in the Soviet media that an alien spacecraft had landed in Voronezh. Last November's explosion in a Krosno fertilizer plant, which *The Spark* blamed on "Polish counter-revolutionary terrorists," disturbed him, as did the murder of Colombian presidential candidate Luis Carlos Galán in August. "He was shocked by it, as if the man were a close *friend*." And of course there were the changes occurring everywhere around us in our corner of the world. Each event became evidence for his unfocused paranoid thesis: *The world's collapsing from every corner.*

"You should've seen him in October, when the bulldozers were tearing down that old Calvinist church in our district. We could see it from the bedroom window. First he screamed about how he was going to kill Tomiak Pankov, then he just sat there for hours, watching the machines. I said to him, 'But you're not even religious, Aron.' And he gave me that look. It's a look I know. The one that says, *You callous bitch*."

That's how, her face as red as the hammer-and-sickle crest on our flag, the story ended. I didn't know what to say. What *can* you say when your friend's husband is in the midst of a personal apocalypse?

"But now," she said quietly, "now I don't know. Maybe he's been right all along."

We stopped in front of Yalta Boulevard 36. I took my hands from the wheel and turned so I could look directly at her. "Everything might change, but that doesn't mean it's going to end."

"Tell him that," she said, reaching for the door. "Not me."

I grabbed her shoulder. "I need to go in, but you don't. Just wait here."

She gave me a hard expression that wasn't uncommon for her, then she smiled. "Someone's got to watch over you, old man."

We showed our documents to the front-door guard, but he was the same one I'd talked to yesterday, so he didn't bother looking at them. He nodded down the street. "It's gone."

"What?"

"The BMW."

I found the spot where Kolev's car had been, now filled with a Karpat Z-20. "Where is it?"

"Ask the Comrade Colonel," he said. His voice was full of envy. I wondered how Romek had moved the car; the keys were still in my desk.

Remarkably, this was the first time I had ever passed through Yalta's oak double doors. I'd been at its threshold more than once, but never stepped through. We entered a cavernous, wood-paneled foyer with too little light. At its center stood a wide oak table in front of a large bronze sculpture: the national hawk, wings folded, head turned to the side. At the table, two women in gray uniforms sat in front of dusty computers. One, with a pretty face marred by a hare-lip, looked up at us.

"Yes?"

I flashed my Militia certificate. "I'm here to look at Comrade Yuri Kolev's office. Colonel Romek knows about this."

She looked at a clipboard beside her computer keyboard. "He's in a meeting. You can wait in 209."

"We don't need to see Romek," I explained. "We're just here to look at Kolev's office."

She smiled, the crease in her lip spreading. "You do need to see Romek first. He said you'd be coming. Room 209. Comrade Sas will show you the way."

Comrade Sas was another uniformed guard, a big man with a boxer's nose who materialized from the shadows. He opened a hand toward a doorway off to the left and nodded for Katja to go first. I followed, and he walked behind us.

It wasn't like the old days, when a summons to Yalta Boulevard was often a precursor to a man's disappearance. Those days had passed with the Prague Spring, which had reminded leaders throughout the socialist world that there were limits to what you could do before your citizens snapped and set fire to tanks in the streets.

Nonetheless, the Ministry for State Security still had the same powers it always had. If the Ministry had relinquished its magic acts of making holes where people once stood, it was because the Ministry had made that decision. Decisions could be reversed at any time.

The institutional green corridor was lined with doors, each marked by a number on an opaque window. Number 209 was four doors down, on the right. It was unlocked. Inside, a secretary sat at a desk under an old portrait of President Pankov, from when he still had hair. Beside her was another door. She hung up the phone and nodded at three cushioned chairs against the opposite wall. Without a word, we sat and waited. Comrade Sas left us to our fate.

From behind the closed door, Colonel Nikolai Romek spoke to someone we couldn't hear. A telephone conversation. The colonel said, "I don't care what those motherfuckers say. If they don't get their fucking journalists out of our country, Belgrade can kiss its coal shipments good-bye. See how they fucking like that!"

Silence followed, broken only by the colonel's, "Uh huh. Uh huh. Right in the ass, yes."

I looked at Katja. The one-sided conversation only deepened her terror, and it wasn't helping my blood pressure at all—my veins throbbed. I squeezed Katja's hand; she squeezed back.

We heard the phone bang down. The intercom on the secretary's desk buzzed. She smiled at us. "The Comrade Colonel will see you now."

I took Katja's elbow to help her up, and we walked through to the small office where Romek, at his desk, was frowning at a little metal box with five colored buttons and a speaker grille. He pressed buttons, cursing to himself. "Livia? Livia?"

The secretary's staticky voice came through the grille. "Yes, Comrade Colonel."

"Three Turkish coffees."

"Yes, Comrade Colonel."

Romek looked up as if just realizing we were there. "Please, please," he said, half standing and gesturing at two chairs facing his desk. As we sat down, he pointed at the intercom. "Can't ever figure this thing out."

"They're difficult," I said, then immediately regretted speaking. Perhaps it sounded like I was mocking him.

Romek didn't seem to notice. He gazed at Katja. "I see you're in better company today, Comrade Brod."

"Lieutenant Katja Drdova," I said.

"Of course I know," said Romek, touching his thin mustache. He came around the desk and took Katja's hand, bringing it to his lips. Katja's face was blank, as if she'd been drugged. He kissed her knuckles and said, "The first woman in homicide. You're an example for the whole country, Comrade Lieutenant."

When he released her hand and returned to his desk, I noticed Katja wiping her knuckles clean on the side of her pants.

"So," said Romek, sitting again. He clapped his hands together, as if in prayer. "You're here to look at Yuri Kolev's office. No?"

I nodded.

"Despite what I told you yesterday?"

Again, I nodded.

He took a long breath through his nose. "Well, I'm afraid that's going to be pointless."

"I don't understand," I said. Katja was still comatose.

"Of course you don't. You're busy working hard to save individual citizens from criminal death, and that's of course commendable. But over here we're more interested in saving the citizenry as a whole."

Despite myself, I was getting irritated. I leaned so my elbows touched my knees. "What are you telling me, Nikolai?"

"I'm *telling* you that I gave you this little task, which you've bungled mercilessly. You upset Comrade Aspitan from the Archives, and now I hear that your coroner's actually filed some ludicrous murder theory concerning *heroin*. So now I've taken back this simple job. It's done, Brod. I filed the paperwork this morning."

"*What?*" Katja had found her tongue.

Romek gave her a winning smile. "Comrade Drdova, I imagine you're aware—that you're both aware," he added, acknowledging me, "of last night's debacle in Sárospatak. I wish I could say that's the end of the story, but I can't. Just this morning, I received word that demonstrators are on the move right here, in the Capital. They haven't reached the streets yet—they're collecting in various apartments." He shrugged. "It's a smart scheme. By the time we've searched all the doors, it'll be too late."

Without warning, I'd learned what my morning's phone call had set in motion. My cheeks were hot; my heart made thumping noises.

He continued. "My point to the two of you is, whether or not you realize it, your case is going to end by tomorrow morning however things develop. Either martial law will go into effect, and the law will be taken over by divisions of the army and the Ministry, or—and this is of course extremely unlikely—the agitators will have their day, and you can be sure that a dead lieutenant general won't be their concern. There'll be many, many more corpses to take your attention."

"Katja," I said.

She looked at me, as did Romek, surprised by interruption.

I reached into my coat and handed over my key ring. "Please wait for me in the car."

"But, Chief, I—"

"*Now,*" I said, in a tone I'd never used with her before.

Flustered and embarrassed, she got out of her chair and mumbled, "Excuse me," to Romek.

He resurrected that shining smile and nodded at her.

As she left, closing the door tightly behind herself, I didn't take my eyes off of Romek. When I was a young man, I'd had trouble controlling my features, but years in the Militia, dealing with killers, had made this easier. He blinked at me. "What is it, Comrade Brod?"

"I'll drop the case if you'll be straight with me."

"I'll certainly try," he said.

I wasn't as sure of myself as I pretended to be. My head hurt, and I was certain Romek could hear my loud heartbeat from where he sat. With my next words I could receive enlightenment or a quick trip down to the barred cells in the basement of Yalta 36. "Four people. Dušan Volan, Lebed Putonski, Tatiana Zoltenko, and Jerzy Michalec." For the moment, I left out Brano Sev and myself. "What's their connection?"

Romek was also good at masking his face, but he didn't have the same kind of experience I did. There was an instant, as I rattled off the names, when pain flashed across his features. He recovered quickly, his upper teeth grazing his lower lip to get it back in line, but that instant had occurred. I knew that whatever followed would be a lie.

He shook his head slowly. "I don't know where you got those names. Tatiana Zoltenko's a Ministry colonel, like myself. Exemplary. Tania's in Sárospatak as we speak. The rest—Putonski, you said? And Dušan Vol—wait. I *do* know him, I think," he said with earnestness, correcting himself as if he were absentminded. "In *The Spark.* A judge. The man was murdered, wasn't he?"

I didn't want to give him the satisfaction of a reply, so I didn't.

"Yes," he continued after a moment. "A murdered judge— murdered, just as you claim Kolev was murdered. Is that what you're talking about? Have all these people been killed?"

He reached into an aluminum case and took out a cigarette. I still didn't answer him. I rubbed the edge of my dry lips. I waited.

He lit his cigarette. "Don't just sit there, Emil." He took a drag, and the rush of nicotine brought back his composure. He exhaled bitter smoke. "What's your game?"

Finally, I said, "Jerzy Michalec."

"What about Jerzy Michalec?"

"He's a murderer."

"You're saying he killed Kolev and Volan?"

"I'm saying all these people have a connection, and that connection is Jerzy Michalec."

"Interesting," he said without interest.

I blinked once. "Where's Brano Sev living these days?"

"Sev?" He shook his head. "I wouldn't know. Isn't he a friend of yours?"

"Brano Sev is no friend of mine."

Halfway through his cigarette, Romek seemed to remember who he was. He recalled that he didn't have to listen to anything I said. "I don't like your tone, Comrade Brod."

"Maybe not," I said, "but it doesn't change the fact that people are being killed. They'll continue to be killed, however things develop today."

"What made you put these names together in the first place? Did someone tell you something?"

"Who's Rosta Gorski?"

Showing your cards one at a time produces wonderful results. The pain returned briefly, the teeth again, and he put out his unfinished cigarette. "Listen, Brod. I don't know what you're getting at, but I've got my hands full trying to keep down an insurrection. I don't have time to bother with a bunch of senior citizens."

"I never said they were all senior citizens."

His eyelids drifted down in annoyance. He pointed at the door. "Get out of here, Brod. While you still can."

I got up and walked through the door, ignoring Romek's secretary, down the green corridor, past the front desk and its enormous

bronze hawk, and out the door. I heard nothing outside the dangerous pounding of my blood. Only on the sidewalk, crossing to reach
the car, did I let my body release its anxiety. My knees went weak, my
arms ached, and I thought I might cry. Or have a heart attack. That's
what Yalta 36 could do to a man. Particularly an old man like me.

"What's wrong?" said Katja.

I started the car and, with some effort, put it in first, but my
hands had trouble doing anything. I took a long breath, placed my
forehead on the wheel, and said, "Can you drive?"

"Yes, but—"

"Can you drive," I repeated, "and not ask me any questions?"

I'd been honest with Romek about everything, including Brano Sev.
We'd parted ways in 1985, and it was only at Lena's insistence that I
even attended his retirement party the following year. I remember
us fighting about it. She sat at her vanity mirror, putting on makeup
and explaining what a fool I was. "The man worked with you for
thirty years. Send him off with a pat on the back, for Christ's sake."

"Why?" I said, full of self-righteousness. "You think the others are
going because they like the man? No. They're afraid that if they
don't go, he'll leave a report on them with the Ministry. But I'm too
old to be scared. People are dead because of Brano. Do you understand what that means?"

She wouldn't have it. "You jump to conclusions. You always have.
You think you know what people are thinking, but you're nearly always wrong. The fact is, Imre's death wasn't Brano's fault." Then she
got up, found my tie, and threw it at me.

Our relationship had ended the night Brano Sev called me down
to discuss the murder of Captain Imre Papp. I found Brano parked
on Friendship Street, just outside our door. "Get in," he said.

"Why don't you come up?"

"Please, Emil."

He didn't want anyone seeing us together, so for the space of our conversation he drove slowly down half-deserted streets, where we were hidden by the warm July darkness. But I could see him. In the ten years since we'd worked together in homicide, he'd aged dramatically—he was Lena's age, but had the sickly expression of someone even older.

"I need to tell you a story, Emil. But you have to promise to keep it to yourself."

"Then don't tell me."

"I think I should. Gavra thinks I should."

"Gavra?"

Brano focused on the dark road. "He says Imre's murder is tearing you up. He thinks you should know the truth behind it."

I was surprised Gavra cared, but I was more surprised that Gavra, working every day with us as we tracked down futile clues, had never shared his secret knowledge. "Okay," I said. "I promise."

"This is not for your report, understand? Not even for Dora. I don't want his wife knowing anything."

I considered telling him that there was no deal. If I couldn't give some answers to Dora Papp, and their son, Gabor, then knowing the answers seemed pointless. But I was too curious. "Okay," I repeated.

So he told me, and the story, performed in his purposeful monotone, took ten miles of slow driving to get out. It had started the previous year with something Tomiak Pankov had brought up in one of his hour-long Central Committee speeches—the War on Revanchist Fiscal Counterrevolutionaries, by which he meant the war against corruption. The Ministry for State Security began investigating reports of large-scale bribes being taken by upper-echelon members of the People's Militia. The bribes were paid by a burgeoning Hungarian mafia that traded in Western cigarettes, off-season fruits not available at home, and Japanese radios. They would capture shipments in Austria and West Germany, sometimes Italy, then transport them through Hungary and then here. All along the way, they paid off militiamen and customs officials to get their goods to our black market.

"So? Imre was a homicide detective."

"Please," said Brano in his unbearable monotone. "Just wait."

The investigation was largely unsuccessful, because the agents working on it were equally susceptible to payoffs, and those very few who weren't kept turning up dead in the countryside. "We needed a new method."

"You needed a Hungarian," I said, slowly realizing what he was getting at.

"Exactly," Brano answered. "As you probably know, the Ministry has long been plagued by nationalist prejudices. Some people at the top—and I'm not one of them—feel that Hungarians can't be trusted. We fill the ranks with Slavs—Poles, Czechs, Slovaks, and Ukrainians—and the occasional Romanian. It's a stupid thing, but there it is. So I was asked to find a Hungarian we could trust to infiltrate the group and pass on information. Imre came to mind."

I didn't know what to say. "How long was this going on?"

"Six months. Imre's cover was simple enough—he was a militiaman in need of money. He kept the truth from everyone, even his wife. Even you. We didn't know who in the Militia was involved."

"Six *months*?"

He leaned into a turn but didn't bother answering.

"So they killed him," I said. "Despite the secrecy, they figured out who he was and executed him in the Canal District."

"I wish," said Brano.

"What?"

He drove another block before explaining. "He was killed by a Ministry agent who didn't know Imre's true role."

I couldn't find any air for a moment. Then: "He had five bullets in him."

"I know."

"Where is he? Where's the man who killed Imre?"

"Transferred."

"To where?"

"It's not important."

That was all I could get out of him, but by the time we returned to Friendship Street, I'd gone over it all many times. I knew where to place the blame.

"If you'd told me, this wouldn't have happened."

"Not necessarily, Emil."

"You know it's true. I would've had Bernard watch his back. He would still be alive."

"Or they'd both be dead."

"I'm telling Dora."

"No," said Brano. "That's a bad idea."

"Why? Why shouldn't she remember her husband as a hero?"

He shook his head. "Emil, listen to me. Everything I've said is only for you. Remember: Our country has no organized crime problem. Nor do we have serial killers. Those are capitalist diseases."

"Oh, Christ," I said.

"The truth doesn't matter," he said. "If Dora Papp starts telling her son about how his father died a hero, then he'll tell the story at school. Dora will tell Imre's mother; she'll tell other people. And what happens then? You've got a crowd of people slandering our workers' state. And that, last I checked, was a crime. A punishable one."

"You're a shit," I said and got out.

Next time I saw Brano was at his retirement party, a year later. Then, like all bad dreams should, he disappeared.

It was two when Katja and I reached the station, but there was no sign of Lena. I was suddenly worried about her. I didn't know why I should be; I was just worried about everything and everyone. I called home but after ten rings gave up.

Katja leaned into my doorway. "Who're we pissing off next, Chief?"

"I was thinking about searching Kolev's house."

"Fine," she said.

I rubbed my aching temples. "No, forget it. You heard him. Case closed."

"That's a load of shit." She sometimes talked that way.

"It is what it is."

She took the chair by my desk as she always did—as if she owned it. "But you have some idea why it is the way it is. Tell me."

We all have our flaws, and one of mine is that I find it difficult to keep too many things going on in my head at once. I'm at my best when I'm staring at a single thing for a long time, and only then can I figure it out. But now, I had to worry about a colonel who might or might not be a murderer. A man named Rosta Gorski had my file; he might be interested in killing me, as well as Brano Sev. Despite our relationship, I didn't want him murdered. Gavra was finding dead men in other countries. All of this connected to a forty-year-old case that had nearly meant Lena's death, and so I feared for her. Add to that a revolt bubbling under the surface of the Capital, and it was too much to keep in my poor head.

Katja was staring at me. I'd always been fond of her. So I told her. I told her that I suspected Romek was connected to the murders of Yuri Kolev, Dušan Volan, and Lebed Putonski. I told her that, based on the stolen files, I felt pretty sure that he also wanted to kill me, Brano Sev, Jerzy Michalec, and Tatiana Zoltenko.

"But why?" she said.

"That's the question. It looks like we're all connected to a forty-year-old case."

That explained nothing, though. Why would anyone care about an old Gestapo agent sentenced to hard labor? "Why," I said aloud, "would Romek call us to investigate Kolev's death, when he could've just signed off on it himself? It makes no sense."

"It might," said Katja.

I looked at her.

"Your name," she explained. "Not his. Maybe he didn't want anyone in the Ministry signing off on it, just in case there was an investigation later. Nothing to tie him to it."

That was good, and I wondered why I hadn't seen it before. "Maybe." Then something occurred to me. "I need to make a call."

Katja nodded, as if giving me permission, but didn't move.

"Alone," I said. "Please."

She was plainly dissatisfied, but she got up anyway and closed the door behind herself.

When I tried to call direct, I got a busy signal, so I talked to a local operator and demanded she put me through to Ferenc's house, and if necessary cut into his conversation. She told me she couldn't do that. The national operators had, since five that morning, been ordered to refuse all connections into the Sárospatak region. I rattled off my Militia number, then told her—by now I'd done it often enough that it made no difference—that this was business for Colonel Romek of the Ministry for State Security. It took a few minutes, but finally I heard Agota's voice. "Hello? Hello?"

"Agí, it's Emil. Where's your father?"

"I was in the middle of an important—"

"*This* is important," I told her.

"Did you do what I asked?"

"It's done."

"Thank God," she said, then called for her father.

Since the previous night, Ferenc had regained his swagger. "Welcome to the end of the world, Emil!"

"I need your help again."

"What about?"

"Tatiana Zoltenko, Ministry colonel. She's working in Patak. You know her?"

"I'll ask around. If she's running any of their units, then we can find her. What do you need?"

"I need her to stay alive."

"What? You think we want to—"

"Not that," I said. "I think someone's going to kill her, and I want you to make sure that doesn't happen."

"It's a tall order without more information."

All my information was too speculative to make any sense, so I just said, "If we don't save her, it's possible I'll be killed too. Or Brano Sev." Neither of us cared about Jerzy Michalec's life, so I didn't bother mentioning him.

Silence followed, but I could hear him breathing. "Okay," he said. "I'll see what I can do. I'll call you at home tonight."

"You won't be out in the streets?"

"I will," he said. "I'll be calling you late."

By two thirty, Lena arrived with one of the front-desk militiamen dragging her huge suitcase. The poor man's face was red and damp. "Right here," she said, pointing at the floor beside Bernard's empty desk, and gave offhand thanks when he left.

"What took you so long?" I said.

"I had to pack, Emil."

"It's just a few days."

Lena frowned at me, then turned to smile at Katja. "You hear how he talks to me?"

Katja came over from her desk. "He's a real cretin." She kissed my wife's cheeks. "But he's right. Aron's leaving, too."

Unsurprisingly, Katja's opinion carried extra weight. Lena touched my detective's arm and nodded resolutely. "You get out, too. Okay?"

"Soon," said Katja.

"You get hold of Georgi?" I asked.

Lena rocked her head from side to side. "I think he's drunk."

Georgi Radevych was an old friend of Ferenc's, a literary type we'd gotten to know over the years. He was genetically incapable of writing anything that could make it through the Culture Ministry censors, so when he finally tired of causing trouble at the Writer's Union and passing out at endless parties in the Capital, we offered him my family's dacha in Ruscova, down near the Romanian border. He'd lived there for nearly a decade by now, hammering away at an old typewriter, producing stacks of pages that no one, probably, would ever read. It wasn't only kindness: Since we rarely went there, he kept the little house in shape, fixing leaks and sometimes making improvements in exchange for a roof over his head. It also left him with enough change to buy liter bottles of cheap brandy.

"You'll be able to make the drive?" I said as I handed her the pass for the roadblocks.

"Of course."

"And you've got money?"

Lena gave me one of her looks—I was treating her like a child again. It was an old habit; those years when she drank more than even Georgi, it had been necessary. We went to my office, and I closed the door. She said, "This isn't just about the demonstrations, is it?"

I shook my head. "Remember that missing case file?"

She nodded.

"The person who took it also took six personnel files. I think that person killed Kolev and two of the people in the files. One of the files is mine."

She reddened and touched the desk. "Then you're coming with me."

"I will," I said, "but later. Trust me, I don't want to be around when everyone starts shooting."

She ran a hand down my arm and spoke softly. "Emil, you're allowed to end your career a day early. Come with me. Don't be stupid."

"And leave Katja on her own?"

"She's a big girl. She can take care of herself."

I shook my head. "Bernard's fled. I'm not doing the same thing to her."

She smiled, rubbing my bald scalp as if it still held hair. "You're a good man, Comrade Brod."

"You're a liar, Comrade Brod."

I kissed her—I remember that. Nothing dramatic, because I was used to her leaving me for her shopping trips to Western Europe. This was no different, not really.

Then she pulled back and blinked at me. "No."

"No, what?"

"You're not staying here. You're coming with me. We'll bring Katja and Aron, too." She fingered my lapels. "Okay? We'll be out of town in an hour."

I shook my head, then leaned closer. "Are you crying?"

She wiped her eyes quickly and even sniffed. "Don't be silly, Emil. I just don't wear widowhood very well—you know that."

"I'll be fine."

She brought her face close to mine, gripping my arms, so I could hear her choked whisper. "When?"

I wasn't sure why she was getting emotional over this—it was bewildering. "I just need to see a few things through. A couple of days."

"No," she said. "Tomorrow."

I considered that. By tomorrow, as Romek had said, the world might be an entirely different place. Tomorrow was a strong possibility. "Okay. Tomorrow. And if necessary, I'll drag Katja with me."

That seemed to satisfy her. She sniffed and fixed my tie and kissed me again.

On the way out, she ordered Katja to take care of "my pensioner husband," and I followed her out to Lenin Avenue, complaining the whole way about whatever she'd packed in her bag.

"I'm too old for this. I'm sixty-five!"

"Sixty-four," she corrected as we stepped outside into the cold. "Don't mark up the leather."

"How did you even get this to the taxi?"

"I asked the driver to come up." She flashed a fresh smile that outshone her mottled mascara. "He was strong. A real looker."

"I hope you tipped him well."

"Oh," she said, placing a hand over her mouth. "Was I supposed to?"

I groaned, heaving the suitcase into the trunk of my Mercedes.

"Keys?" she reminded me, and I handed them over. She gave me another peck on the cheek, then got rid of the smile. "Don't forget your medicine."

"Okay."

"And you promised, remember? Tomorrow. Early as possible."

"I remember."

"I'm serious, now. Do what you have to do, but even if it's not finished, you come down south. Don't get too involved in any of this. There's no reason anymore."

"You're worried about me?"

She made a face as she opened the door—her nose was already pink from the cold. "I just don't want to spend too long alone with Georgi. He reminds me too much of how I used to be." Then she kissed me again and shooed me away. "Don't waste time dawdling. You're on a deadline."

I returned to the Militia steps and waited for her to drive off. I could see her hunched over the wheel, looking for where to insert the key. This always gave her trouble, but only in my car. It didn't make sense, because we both had the same model Mercedes. I took a step down toward the sidewalk to help her out, but she got it.

I know this because the Mercedes exploded.

Katja was at her desk when the blast occurred. An instant beforehand, she looked up at a sound—a neighborhood dog let out a single worried bark. Then it happened. It was, she told me later, like two explosions. A low, bass thump she felt in her stomach, then, immediately after, a higher-toned pressure that hurt her ears and shattered the window behind her. Glass caught in her hair and covered the floor. But she didn't move.

I was thrown back, the corners of the front steps cutting into my back, and for an instant I, too, was frozen. I heard things inside the demolished Mercedes exploding, fire crackling. But the loudest thing was my damned heart. Black smoke billowed into the sky, then sagged, heavy, and filled the street. I rolled and caught the stink of burning gasoline. It was everywhere.

Through the smoke, I saw a flaming, twisted Mercedes, but I was trying to see past it, because this couldn't be the car that held my wife. I thought that mine was somewhere behind this one. I got up and ran toward it, limping, entering the smoke, choking and coughing. The militiamen told me later that I was shouting her name, but I don't remember that. I only remember the thumping sound and the smoke and heat that stopped me before I could get to her.

I wasn't alone. At the sound of the blast, and the sudden rain of broken glass in the station, the militiamen ran out, some standing stunned at the top of the steps, others running forward to wrestle me back. They shouted things I couldn't hear because my ears were dead as they dragged me back inside the station. They put me in a chair. I could see them but couldn't hear them. They were arguing over something. Katja broke through, bent down close to me, and said more things I couldn't hear, but there was some comfort in just seeing her face. Then she turned and shouted something that silenced the others. Someone went to make a phone call.

I realized why I couldn't hear anything—my ears were humming like an electrical generator. My eardrums had been kicked, and I wouldn't hear anything for another hour, and even days later the unnerving electric hum would pop up, sometimes at inopportune times.

When Katja returned, I grabbed her coat and pulled her close to me, screaming, "Where is Lena? Where is my wife?"

I couldn't hear her answer, and she understood this. She just shook her head.

I thought briefly of Katja's husband, Aron, who believed everything in the world was collapsing. He was right. The world was an entirely different place now. I felt as if someone had taken out all my internal organs but left me, inexplicably, alive. I wondered who could be that cruel.

NINE

•

TisAir Flight 38 from Frankfurt touched down at Pankov International a little after six in winter darkness. Gavra helped Beth with her carry-on luggage and guided them to the line for passport control, waiting a few paces back. He watched her grip Harold's arm. "You see that man?" she whispered loudly.

Harold looked up from a tourist brochure with three-toned color images of Orthodox churches and spas. "What man?"

"In the corner. The uniform. Is that a machine gun?"

Harold went back to the pictures. "Grow up, Beth. We're crossing a border. They're required to carry those things. It's communism."

"You're telling me it's communist law to carry machine guns?"

He turned the page. "That's what I'm telling you."

The bored clerk with sweaty bangs glanced at their visas, stamped their passports and sent them on to the luggage carousel. When he saw Gavra's passport—his real one, with the Ministry crest—he woke up. "Welcome home, comrade."

Gavra continued past the waiting passengers and on through customs, where more bored men in blue uniforms—"navy" blue, he remembered—leaned on a white table discussing basketball scores. In the marble-tiled arrivals lounge he passed waiting families and crossed to a pay phone, lit a cigarette, and dialed the Militia station. On the first ring a breathless man said, "*Yes?*"

"First District Militia?"

"Yes, yes." There was a cacophony of voices in the background.

"Emil Brod there?"

"Not here."

"Where is he?"

"At home. Chief Brod's at home."

"What's going on?" he said, but the line went dead.

He dialed my home number as he watched families greeting and hugging arrivals. On the eighth ring Katja answered. "Uh, hello?"

"Katja?"

"That you, Gavra?"

"Where's Emil?"

"I've got him lying down finally."

"Lying down? Is he hurt?"

"No, he—" She paused. "You don't know."

"Know what?"

"Lena. She's dead."

The cigarette stuck to his suddenly dry lips. "*How?*"

She told him everything, and he was stunned.

The crowd of waiting families had left, and Gavra still saw no sign of Harold and Beth. He found them at the customs area. They stood, exasperated, by the long white table, their suitcase open and its contents spread down the table's length. "What is this?" a young customs official said in heavily accented English, holding up Harold's electric razor.

"It's my *razor*," said Harold, his voice slow and measured. "I *shave* with it." He pantomimed shaving his cheeks.

When Gavra approached, Beth gave him a hopeful smile.

"What's going on here?" he asked in our language.

The one with the razor gave him a drowsy look. "Official business, comrade. Shove off."

Official business, in this sense, meant that they were waiting for a bribe.

Gavra took out his Ministry card and held it out for them to read.

"Oh," said the clerk. He placed the razor back in the suitcase.

"Clean this up," said Gavra. "And if anything's missing I'll have your head."

They got to it.

He turned to the old couple and switched to English. "I apologize. Some of our customs people get a little overzealous."

"It's no problem," said Beth, smiling.

Harold didn't smile. "Well, that's not the end of it."

"What?"

"They left Beth's suitcase in Frankfurt. I mean, all we did was change planes!"

"Did you talk with the TisAir people?"

He shoved a thumb over his shoulder, gesturing toward the luggage area. "She doesn't give a damn."

"Moment." Gavra marched off to deal with the luggage girl, whom he found flirting with one of the border guards. When he returned, having received a written assurance that the suitcase would be sent to the Metropol, his face was red from shouting. He was embarrassed by his loss of control. It was Lena's death, he told me later. He didn't know how much it was affecting him until he found himself shouting at all the wrong times.

The American couple didn't seem to notice. He carried their one suitcase out to the curb, where unofficial taxi drivers stood around smoking in the darkness. When they saw the couple, they rushed forward, saying, "Taxi, taxi?"

A few stern words from Gavra, and they backed up again. He

turned to Harold. "These guys will rip you off. I've got a car here. Please, let me drive you to your hotel."

"That's too much," said Harold warily.

Beth knocked his arm. "We'd be much obliged."

They sped down the M1 in the beige Citroën Gavra had bought a few years before—he was proud of it. Beth sat erect in the backseat, gazing out the window at passing fields just visible by the highway's lamps, while Harold worked up the nerve to say what was on his mind. "So, what was that back there?"

"What do you mean?"

"At customs. You showed them a card. I saw the look on their faces. They were scared." He paused. "Really scared."

"You think so?"

"I know it."

Harold was staring at him now, and Beth's voice floated up. "Don't pry, Harry."

"It's all right, Mrs. Atkins," said Gavra. "It's a fair question." He accelerated past an apple truck with Czech plates. "Fact is, I work for the Ministry for State Security."

"State security?" said Beth.

"He means the secret police," said Harold.

"Those guys at customs were hoping you'd give them a bribe."

"A bribe?" said Beth.

"That's what I thought," said Harold. "Didn't I tell you?"

"You told me," Beth said quietly.

"You *are* taking us to the Hotel Metropol, right?"

Gavra looked over at the old man, whose face was as stern as a schoolteacher's. "Of course I am. I'm just trying to help."

Beth leaned forward so her face appeared between them. "Well, I, for one, thank you for it. God knows where we'd be with those Karpat taxis. Probably stuck on the side of the road."

Harold grunted. "Karpats."

"You have them in the States?" asked Gavra.

Beth laughed, and Harold said, "You know what we call them in America?"

"What?"

"*Crap*ats."

As they entered town, the streetlamps became less frequent, and the streets themselves were empty. Gavra didn't like these indicators. Then, down Yalta Boulevard, he could just make out people in the darkness, filling the street where it ran into Victory Square. His stomach shifted when he noticed green army trucks parked at the edge of the crowd.

"That's your HQ, isn't it?" said Harold, pointing at the oak doors of number 36.

"How did you know?"

"Fodor's," he said. "They don't talk highly of it."

"I imagine not. Here." Gavra pointed at the tall, cylindrical tower at number 20. "There's the Metropol." When he made a U-turn to park in front of the flags-of-all-nations awning, an old, mustached doorman came out, rubbing his hands against the cold. Gavra wrestled Harold's suitcase from the trunk and gave it to a bellboy, then took a slip of paper from his coat pocket—it was the receipt from Bob Moates Gun Shop for the P-83. On the back, he wrote his name and the phone number at his Militia desk. He gave it to Harold. "If you run into trouble, you call me here during work hours. Okay?"

"You think we'll run into trouble?" said Harold.

Gavra shrugged. "Consider it insurance."

"Thanks." Harold offered a hand, and they shook. "And about before—well, I apologize. You're obviously one of the good ones."

Gavra winked at him. "Don't be too sure. Just try to enjoy your stay in our country."

Beth surprised him by giving him a hug. Then she squinted into the distance toward Victory Square. "What's that? Is it a party?"

Gavra followed her gaze. He could now see soldiers standing along the edge of the crowd, just past the army trucks. "I suggest you both go inside."

"Come on," said Harold.

"What is it?" she whispered as her husband pulled her through to the glassed-in lobby, which was full of foreign journalists reporting on the country's troubles from comfortable sofas.

Gavra watched until they made it to the check-in desk, then cornered the doorman. Voices from the square reached them, a tumult of shouts. "What's going on?"

The doorman wiped his mustache. "You wouldn't believe me if I told you."

"Try me."

"Pankov called it. He told the local Party leaders to get their workers out for a rally. He wants to speak to them. I guess that's them down there, but they're not alone. Once the word got out, all the students started pouring out of doors along the street here and joined the rally. Go see for yourself. I'll lay odds the workers are outnumbered two to one."

"*Pankov* called the rally?"

"Yeah. Not smart, was it?"

Gavra stared down Yalta Boulevard. "I'll leave the car here a few minutes."

"Do what you like."

"Thanks."

Gavra felt the doorman's eyes on his back as he walked down the cracked sidewalk toward Victory Square. It was a long walk, because here the blocks stretched out to accommodate more magnificent buildings, but his pace gradually increased until he was jogging. From beyond the trucks, the voices were loud, and he could make out halfhearted chants from the crowd. The strongest was *Pankov, you're starving your country*—which in our language rhymes.

Twenty yards from the edge of the crowd, a cluster of shivering foreign journalists with cameras and handheld tape recorders looked on. Gavra continued until an army captain told him to get back. He was a young officer, confused by the situation. Gavra showed his Ministry card. The captain squinted at him. "Are your men in place?"

"What men?" asked Gavra.

He paused, unsure. "On the rooftops. Comrade General Stapenov told us you guys would give us support from the rooftops. I just want to be sure."

"The Ministry put gunmen on the roofs?"

"That's what he told me."

Gavra approached the line of soldiers' backs. Like the captain, they were all young, none older than twenty, clutching Kalashnikovs to their chests. They were scared. He didn't need to show his Ministry papers for them to let him through; he only needed to tell them in a firm voice what he was. Between the soldiers and the crowd was an empty space five yards deep. A few students peered nervously at the soldiers, though most tried to ignore them, facing the far end of the vast square, where the lit columns of the Central Committee rose up. Gavra was tall enough to see over their heads.

The size of the crowd was shocking. It filled the entirety of Victory Square, swelling up against the Central Committee steps—also guarded by a line of soldiers—and bold teenagers scrambled up the two statues: the Socialist Realist couple in the center, holding up a concrete torch, and the bronze Lenin in front of the steps, reaching out for the future.

Gavra told me later that, standing in that crowd, he suffered a quick bout of amnesia. He forgot about the deaths of Yuri Kolev and Lebed Putonski, and the safety of the old American couple. Even Lena's death slipped his mind. Most importantly, he forgot who he was, and that his job was to make sure things like this didn't happen. He forgot he was supposed to be fighting all these young, enthusiastic, angry people.

Like many of the soldiers that ringed the crowd, he was aware of the magnitude of this moment. Crowds this size were never seen outside official Party holidays and Tomiak Pankov's birthday parade. But today they had come, on their own, a few days before Christmas. It was as if history had split from the hours and days that formed it. Time was snapping in half.

A roar blew out from the warm, steaming center of the crowd. Gavra pushed on, knocking past shoulders and wild, grinning faces to reach the sound. Then he looked up at the Central Committee Building and found its cause: A few men had come out onto the high balcony to peer down at the demonstration. From this distance they were hard to make out, but Gavra thought he recognized Andras Todescu, Tomiak Pankov's personal advisor. Todescu and a couple of men in blue work clothes were setting up a microphone in the center of the balcony. Another one carried a video camera with lines running inside.

It was the beginning of the end.

TEN

•

I woke without having fallen asleep. My face was buried in my pillow, wet not from tears, because it would be a while before I could manage those, but from the cold sweat of sickness. The sheets and duvet were soaked as well, and from the living room I could hear the tinny horns that always preceded official announcements on television.

I sat up feeling dizzy. I was naked but couldn't remember undressing. Katja had brought me home, so I guessed she'd done it, and I was overwhelmed by a sudden, deep embarrassment. I don't know why. I reached for the medicine bottle on my bedside table and swallowed two more Captopril.

Through my closed window came voices, so I put on a robe and opened it. Yes—chants, many streets away. Then Katja's voice from the living room: "Emil? You up?" She sounded scared.

"Yes."

"Come look at this."

I stumbled through the door and found her on the couch, face bathed in the blue glow, mesmerized. I sat next to her.

It all unfolded on television.

A camera moved across a crowd that filled Victory Square, but without sound, so we couldn't hear what they were chanting. Their fists were raised high.

"So many people," said Katja.

"Yeah."

Then the camera turned to our Great Leader, Comrade General Secretary and President Tomiak Pankov, stepping out onto the Central Committee balcony, a hand waved in salutation. The old man's heavy eyes were so familiar. Behind him appeared Ilona Pankov, his wife, the first deputy prime minister and chairwoman of the Academy of Sciences. She always stood near him. Tomiak Pankov's bald head was covered in a tall black Astrakhan hat, and his fur-lined coat was buttoned to his neck. Even with the poor-quality video feed you could see his breaths in the cold air.

He began to speak, giving comradely salutations to the Party faithful filling the square, then said, "The news is filled these days with lies coming out of Sárospatak, where hooligans and warmongers, supported by the American CIA, have been attempting to undermine our great workers' state."

It went on for a few minutes, and from the crowd we heard cheers. But then, when he said, "The anti-communist forces are betraying your heritage," something else came from the crowd—loud, with abandon: boos and catcalls.

It was the first time we'd ever heard such a sound at a Party rally.

The technicians fixed the situation by piping in some prerecorded applause, but it was too late. Across the country, at the same moment, people in their homes heard the sound of Pankov being jeered. There was no way to make them forget it.

He went on. I saw apprehension in Ilona Pankov's face, but her husband appeared oblivious, saying that he was instituting changes "to raise the monthly food rations and increase the wages of factory workers in our great land."

Then it sank in. The canned applause was turned up to cover the rising tide of resentment from the square below him that even his microphone caught, and Pankov looked down with a stunned expression. "I promise r-raises across the b-board," he stuttered.

Then his mouth fell open, and he took a step back from the microphone.

The picture disappeared, replaced by a red screen. At the bottom, in white letters, we were told that there were technical difficulties. We were asked to be patient.

ELEVEN

•

Gavra had met Tomiak Pankov only once, in 1985, when General Brano Sev brought him along to one of the Great Leader's many hunting retreats up in the Carpathians. They joined his entourage of sycophants, and the old man related jokes he'd recently heard from King Hussein of Jordan. The jokes were funny, but Pankov didn't deliver them well, so the laughter all around him was forced. The president didn't seem to notice.

Despite that, Gavra was struck by how personable the man was. He knew Gavra's name and had personally asked Brano to bring him along as a reward for some recent work he'd completed with distinction. They all dressed in brown hunting clothes shipped in from London and went out to track deer. They had little luck, the deer by now used to the marauding group of Party faithful toting shotguns, so Andras Todescu, Pankov's personal advisor, stepped away from the crowd and spoke into a radio. A few minutes later, three stout bucks went galloping past, and Pankov raised his shotgun, shouting, "This one's mine!" He shot and missed. "Damn," he muttered and started to run. Everyone followed, and Todescu again spoke into his radio.

Over the next hill they saw another deer—the woods were suddenly alive with game—and again Pankov aimed and shot wildly.

From that distance, Gavra knew he'd miss. Amazingly, though, the deer stumbled a moment and fell.

"Got that bastard!" shouted Pankov.

"Superb," said Brano, winking at Gavra.

"Magnificent," said Todescu.

Knowing what was expected of him, Gavra also offered congratulations, but he saw what had happened. The deer had fallen toward the hunters, as if shot from the opposite direction, and as they approached the shivering animal Gavra scanned the trees. Up on the high branches of a pine, hidden by camouflaged clothing, a Ministry sharpshooter lowered a long, laser-sighted sniper's rifle.

This is what he remembered as he stood in the cold, staring up at Tomiak Pankov talking to the crowd. He couldn't hear anything the old man said, because the air was saturated with angry noise. "Death to Pankov!" shouted some; others, "Patak murderer!" and "Down with the tyrant!"

That memory was the only thing he could dredge up to explain why Pankov had been stupid enough to call this rally just after the killings in Sárospatak. Tomiak Pankov had for decades allowed himself to be tricked by his subordinates. They helped him believe that he was a world-class hunter and magnificent jokester. It was no surprise they could also convince him that his people loved and feared him.

His assistants certainly knew better, though. Why would Andras Todescu advise him to speak on television? Had the years of devotion finally dulled the sycophants' wits as well?

People jostled into him, and he pushed back. The amnesia slid away, and the exhilaration of the crowd lost its effect. He instead noticed the warm stink of so many bodies in the same place, then he saw what I saw on television: Pankov stopping in midsentence. Pankov stepping back from the microphone, confused.

The crowd roared and pressed forward. Ahead, on the Central Committee steps, soldiers struggled to hold them back, but Gavra saw one, then five, then twenty people breaking through their lines. He looked up—the terrace was empty. He was suddenly very frightened.

He turned and started pushing through people. Fights broke out between burly workers still in their factory garb and students in layers of sweater. The factory workers got in a few good punches before being overwhelmed, the students swarming and bringing them down. Gavra fought only to get through the crowd that became tighter and firmer with each step. If he wanted to survive, he had to get home. Now.

When he finally reached Yalta Boulevard again, the soldiers were no longer in their perfect line. They were grouped on one side as the captain ran back and forth, yelling at them to keep their positions. But they had seen everything. And now, hundreds of people were swarming the Central Committee steps, kicking against the massive front doors. Then everyone looked up.

From the roof of the Central Committee, a fat helicopter began to rise. It was heavy, lurching in the air, but it managed to gain altitude, then swung around and started to move eastward.

The crowd saw it, too, and the cheer that went up was deafening. Singing erupted; Gavra recognized the tune—the pre-Soviet national anthem, which had been banned these last forty years.

> Look! Look! The hawk is flying low.
> From the Carpat to the steppes, he marks his territory.
> The borders are ringed with fire!

Gavra ran back to the Hotel Metropol. The doorman grabbed his arm. "What happened?"

"It's over," Gavra said, gasping. "It's all finished."

The doorman wasn't sure what he was referring to. "The demonstration?"

Gavra pushed past him and got to his Citroën. "Everything."

* * *

He sped the whole way, passing Militia cars that were too busy listening to radio reports to bother ticketing him. People began running from their televisions into the streets. Near his block, the streetlamps were out, and in his headlights people filled the road. He had to slow down. They were jubilant, patting his roof and shouting, "The tyrant is gone!" Someone threw red wine on his windshield, and he turned on the wipers. He made it to Block 183, on the edge of the Eighth District, where he shared his apartment with his close friend Karel Wollenchak. Near the front door, one of the neighborhood drunks, a hairy man named Mujo, noticed him. He stood up, clutching a bottle of *rakija,* and said to his fat friend, "Hey, Haso! Look who's here!"

Haso stood as well. There were three other drunks with them, and they all came to meet him. Mujo said, "You get the news, comrade?"

Gavra's stomach hurt, but he didn't panic—it was all about math, spatial relations, escape paths. "I saw it all, Mujo."

"You couldn't keep them down?" said Haso.

"It's over, comrade," said Mujo.

Gavra, unlike some others, had never made a secret of his employer. It was sometimes useful. Once, he'd helped an old woman living below him get a gall bladder operation at Pasha Medical, the private Ministry hospital. But at a time like this, no one would remember his generosity.

"Enjoy your drink," he said, pushing past them, but one of the drunks grabbed his shoulder.

"Hey," said a slurred voice.

Gavra snatched the hand and quickly turned, twisting the arm high so it hurt. The drunk moaned.

"Hold on," said Mujo.

"Just keep your hands off me," said Gavra. He released the man and continued into the building.

The foyer was empty, but there were more neighbors on the stairwell, all men, clutching bottles of cheap liquor. Everyone knew him, but they didn't say a word, preferring to lean back against the wall and watch him pass. When he reached the third floor, a wet dollop of spit struck the back of his neck. He didn't slow down.

Karel was peering out the window when he came in, while on the television a news commentator reported on crop yields. "Listen to that," said Karel. "This year's was the highest wheat yield in history. What do you think of that?"

"We've got to go."

Karel, he could see, was hysterical. His dark, fleshy cheeks were perspiring heavily. "We can stay, you know. They're going to show a repeat of last April's birthday parade. That's always a treat."

Gavra grabbed his friend's shoulders. "Listen, Karel. We can't stay here; it's dangerous, and it'll only get worse. Pack a bag right now, and we'll leave."

"What should I pack?"

"Clothes. Money. And your documents. Now *go.*"

While Karel went through his wardrobe, singing to himself, Gavra crouched in the bathroom, where he kept a Makarov pistol and thirty rounds of 9mm ammunition hidden under the drain, wrapped in a plastic bag. Then he went through his extensive record collection and picked out a few things to save. The Velvet Underground, Pink Floyd, and Elton John. He threw them into Karel's suitcase.

"What about my records?" said Karel.

"Do you need them?"

"Wow." Karel almost laughed. "I really don't."

The men were still in the stairwell, but they had shifted up closer to the third floor, so Gavra and Karel had to push through them. Karel, toting his suitcase, said hello a few times, but no one answered. Karel wasn't a member of the Ministry for State Security, but his guilt was by association. Someone behind them said, "The faggots are running!"

Another: "You better walk fast."

Gavra used one hand to clear the way, the other in his coat pocket, gripping the Makarov.

He didn't have to use it. Despite shoulders thrown in his path and a sore kidney from someone's knee, they reached the foyer without bloodshed. Mujo, Haso, and their friends were back beside the entrance, drinking again. "Have a nice trip," said Mujo.

Haso raised his bottle. "Drive safe!"

When Gavra and Karel reached the car, the laughter followed them, but the drunks stayed where they were—they'd had their fun. One side of the Citroën was covered in red paint that said MINISTRY FAGS.

"Who did that?" said Karel.

Gavra took off his coat and rubbed the still-wet paint until all that could be made out was the letter *M*.

TWELVE

•

I couldn't move. The red screen had been followed by a report on agricultural yields and then a replay of the 28 April parade in honor of Tomiak Pankov's seventy-first birthday. Katja finally got up to turn it off. "Use the remote," I said.

"What remote?"

"What?" My ears were humming.

"What remote?"

"The television's remote controlled."

"Tell me where it is, and I'll use it."

Of course, I didn't know. It was Lena who watched television, not me, and she'd hidden the little box somewhere only she knew. I started to cry, then stopped myself.

We heard more voices from the street. Katja opened the window and leaned out to look. She said, "Come see."

I didn't want to see anything. I pulled my robe tighter and stared at the black television screen.

She said, "The street's full of people."

"Good for them." Through the open window, I could hear their chants—*Olé, olé, the dictator has fled!*—as if they were at a soccer game.

"I hope Aron's all right."

"What?"

She'd told me this before, but I'd missed it. After Lena's murder, she called her husband again and told him to meet her at my apartment, so she could give him the pass for the roadblocks. She reminded me of this, but without annoyance. I, on the other hand, was annoyed by everything she said. It was eight—Aron's shift had ended at five—and there was still no sign of him.

I got up but didn't join her at the window. Instead, I went to the kitchen and examined the cabinet where we kept our alcohol. Where *I* kept *my* alcohol. I took down a bottle of vodka and filled a shot glass. I didn't put the bottle away. The shot went down and was followed by another. It was the only way I could think of to get rid of the pain that stiffened every muscle in me.

I heard a gunshot. A long-barreled rifle. Katja jumped back from the window and looked at me standing in my robe, the glass in my fist.

"What was that?" I said.

"It wasn't a Karpat."

Another shot, and a few screams from the street. Katja stood to the side of the window and slowly tilted her head to look out. I turned off the lights and joined her. Down in the street, the crowd was panicking, splitting down the middle and running to the sidewalks for cover. The shots came from above us, and at one point I saw a muzzle flash from a rooftop on the other side of Friendship Street.

Then silence. The marchers were squeezed into doorways, while in the darkness on the other rooftop we saw a shadow, hunched, running across to other roofs.

For just an instant, I stopped thinking about Lena. "What was that?"

"Ministry, I bet."

I couldn't believe it. "Not even they would . . ." I didn't finish the thought, because someone started banging on my door.

"*Aron,*" said Katja. She flipped on the light and hurried to the door but found Gavra standing in the corridor beside a small, heavyset man with dark skin. He looked like a Gypsy, and his battered suitcase convinced me he was. Katja was stunned to see them. "Gavra. Karel."

I'd never met Karel before, but Katja had. The two men had come over to Katja and Aron's for dinner a few times.

Gavra nodded at me as he came in. "You mind, Emil? We need a place to spend the night."

"Of course." I shook Karel Wollenchak's damp hand. "Emil," I said, and he smiled bashfully as he set down his suitcase.

It struck me, during the following minutes, that the apartment had never been so full of people. My detectives had visited on their own, often to discuss cases, but never as a group. Lena would have liked this—she liked being among people.

As I poured shots for everyone and went to dress, my mood shifted. I wondered if the last sober years of Lena's life had been full of boredom. I wondered if, because of my natural inclination toward solitude, she'd spent her last years miserable. And then I was convinced of it.

The feeling only intensified when Aron arrived a half hour later. I knew him well. He was flustered and chubby, also dragging a suitcase he'd hurried back home to fill. On the drive to my apartment he'd run into problems. "Mihai Boulevard is impassable. Completely. It's thick with people. Then the car gave out near the Georgian Bridge, and I had to walk the rest of the way."

Gavra flipped back and forth between the two television stations, which were still broadcasting prerecorded Party celebrations. Then he went to the radio and found a newscaster who was as panicked as the rest of us.

"At this moment there's a crowd—I can see them from my window—trying to break into the station. There must be, I don't know, five *hundred* people down there. They're shouting, Let us in! Let us in! It's . . . to tell the truth, I'm scared. I don't know what they want, but after what happened in Victory Square, anything's possible. I'll remain on the air as long as I can, all the way to the end."

"What happened in Victory Square?" said Aron.

Gavra told us everything he had seen.

"Pankov ran away?" said Katja.

"It was the presidential helicopter."

"We saw snipers," I said.

"Snipers?" Karel looked frightened; his euphoria had long since faded.

Gavra related what the army captain had told him, about support from the rooftops. "They're Ministry sharpshooters."

By then we'd all taken seats in the living room. I'd left out the vodka bottle, adding the scotch as well. Aron shifted in his seat; I knew what he was thinking. He was thinking about how right he'd been these last six months.

I didn't know what Gavra was thinking, but he later told me. He was working over his next steps. He knew that if he and Karel could make it to Hungary, they could go wherever they wanted—but the truth was, he wasn't finished here. He couldn't leave until he understood why he'd been sent to America to protect an old émigré.

Katja admitted to us that, despite her fear, and despite the danger of snipers, she was relieved. "I mean, we've all been waiting for this, haven't we?" She wasn't so different from Lena.

We nodded our agreement—even Gavra, whose job was to protect Pankov's government—but none of us spoke, as if my living room were bugged.

"So we should be out there," she said. "It's logical. If all of us go out—if everyone goes out on the streets—then events will go our way. But if we stay in, things could still go back to the way they were. That's why they're shooting out there. They want us to stay inside."

She was right, of course, but the fact was that I didn't give a damn about any of this. Only hours ago I'd watched my wife die. I didn't care who ran the country, or if a revolution was stomped into submission with firing squads. I didn't care about anything.

* * *

Ferenc wrote in his most famous book, *The Confession*, that all married people live a second, fantasy life in which they're no longer chained by marital ties. A make-believe world where you live alone but are never lonely. I think he was obsessed by this idea, because it became the focal point of his later book, *The Cat and the Czar*, which excited the French so much.

Though I understood what he was getting at, I'd never lived that fantasy life myself. Instead, when I thought about being without Lena, my stunted imagination made it into a homicide case. I could only imagine her being murdered, and then the rage that would follow.

I know why I did this—because I'm a man, and men want to believe in a primal, violent part of themselves. A force that, if let free, is unstoppable. A force that demands respect.

In that fantasy, it was all about me. My grief, my destitution, and my anger. So much self-righteous anger, and an unbearable desire for revenge.

The reality, at least that night, was different. All I wanted to do was crawl under my bed and shut off the world. I wanted everyone to go home.

By midnight, most of us were drunk. I know I was. I'd insisted that Katja and Aron stay, because we still heard sporadic gunfire outside. Gavra sometimes came to me and tried to whisper in my ear about what he'd learned during his travels, but I wasn't listening. I was listening, instead, to the radio. Around eleven, the frightened commentator disappeared. His voice rose to a shrill pitch as he told us the invaders had reached the studio, then his microphone cut off. We never learned what happened to him.

After five minutes' silence, a confused group of excited young men took over. They called themselves Free Radio Galicia, harking back to the old name for the largest part of our country, and they gave out information about the progress of the marchers, telling everyone to do what Katja had suggested: go out and join the struggle. *Power in numbers,* they kept saying. *You must go outside.*

Karel, who'd been nursing his scotch a long time in silence, suddenly looked up. "Gavra."

"Yeah?" He was standing by the window again, looking out into darkness.

"I forgot because of all the commotion—someone called for you. At home. Around seven or so."

"Who was it?"

"Brano Something."

The rest of us woke up and turned to stare at him. Gavra said, "Brano *Sev?*"

"Yeah. That's it." He paused, licking his lips. "Do all of you know this guy?"

Our surprise was interrupted by the radio. A deep, heavy voice, older than the voices we'd heard so far, identified himself as General Igor Stapenov of the People's Army, in charge of the Capital and its surrounding counties. "I've come here to tell you that my men are with you. We are with the Revolution. Down with the tyrant, and up with the people!" Then, with just as much urgency: "We are still looking for Tomiak and Ilona Pankov. We've issued a military arrest warrant, and the charge is crimes against humanity. If you have any information at all, please call . . ."

Katja laughed out loud. I didn't know what to do.

It was midnight. The telephone rang.

22 DECEMBER 1989

FRIDAY

•

THIRTEEN

•

Gavra was at the phone before I could get to my feet. "Hello?" he said hopefully, then dropped an octave. "Oh, yes. Moment." He leaned out of the kitchen and said, "It's for you, Emil."

Ferenc greeted me with "Was that Gavra Noukas?"

"Yes."

"Jesus, Emil. All this going on and you've got a *Ministry* agent in your house?"

Up to that point I hadn't considered how it looked having Gavra around, or whether or not he was a risk. Ferenc had never met Gavra, but over the years, the young Ministry man had become just one more associate I trusted to assist me in my work—the only caveat was that I knew to hide things from him that his job might compel him to report. I treated Bernard the same way. "Don't worry about him," I said. "Did you hear about Lena?"

"What about Lena?"

So I told him. I spoke with the same distant, unsettling calm he had first used to tell me about the shootings in Sárospatak. When I finished, he was silent a moment. "I don't know what to say," he managed. "I loved that woman."

"Not just you."

"Who the hell did it?"

"That's what I'm trying to figure out. Did you find Tatiana Zoltenko?"

That seemed to confuse him. "Well . . . *yes*. I mean, we *found* her, but she's dead."

"*What?*"

"Doesn't look suspicious, though," said Ferenc. "She ordered her unit to fire on some demonstrators, and one of the soldiers turned around and shot her. A Ministry corporal. The guy's a hero now."

I almost collapsed.

I never did find out if the hero-soldier—who I later learned was a Ukrainian named Dubravko Ilinski—shot Colonel Tatiana Zoltenko out of moral conviction, or because he'd been paid to do it. Either way, the list of endangered senior citizens had shrunk to only three: myself, Brano Sev, and Jerzy Michalec. As of seven o'clock the previous evening, at least, Brano was still alive. Alive enough to call Gavra. I had no idea about Michalec.

To fill the awkward silence, Ferenc told me that Sárospatak was nearly theirs. The army in that region had not yet turned to their side, but it wasn't confronting them either. The soldiers had retreated to their barracks on the northern side of town. Twice, he used the phrase "the Soft Revolution," and that marked my introduction to the term—but, like the mysterious quote on the memorial to Tisavar, I'd never figure out what it meant. "Fantastic," I told him.

He could hear my lack of enthusiasm. "I don't expect you to feel it now, Emil, but it really is."

By the time I hung up, Ferenc had told me five times how sorry he was about Lena, but his pity left me cold. When I came out, Gavra was slipping into his coat, which I noticed was covered with dry red paint.

"He thinks he's going to Yalta," said Katja.

"No," I said.

Gavra wasn't waiting for my permission. He took his Makarov from his pocket and checked the cartridge. "It's the only place I can get an international phone line."

Despite being a little drunk, I could register how dangerous this was. "Weren't you listening to the radio? The army's out there. They see you going into Yalta Boulevard, they'll check your papers. They'll lock you up, or kill you."

"I have to get in touch with Brano. I'll lay odds he's the one who sent me to the States."

"I thought you were in Yugoslavia."

"I lied, Emil. It's my job."

Karel crossed his arms over his chest. "It's not your job anymore."

"Then I'm going with you," I said. I wasn't sober enough to care about my own safety. Nor did I care about my fatigue. It was late, and I'd been squeezed out like a cleaning lady's sponge. A fresh headache flickered around the edges of my brain.

"No, you're not," said Gavra.

"Don't argue."

Katja broke our stalemate: "What about the files?"

We looked at her. I said, "What files?"

She looked at me as if only now, after all these years, had she recognized what a stupid man I was. "It's a straight shot up Friendship to the Eleventh District. No one's watching the Central Archives. We get in there, we can find out who authorized Rosta Gorski to take out those files. Then we follow up on it."

As usual, she made the most sense.

Aron wanted to come with us, but Katja took him aside and whispered a convincing argument against it. By the time she finished, his face had reddened; I wondered what she'd said. Karel, almost unconscious now from the half bottle of scotch he'd put away, didn't ask to come. He only grabbed Gavra's sleeve in a particularly affectionate gesture and told him to come back soon. Gavra promised he would, then gave Karel the keys to his Citroën. "Just for emergencies. Don't leave the house. Okay?"

We took the stairwell, and at the second floor a door opened. My elderly neighbor, Zorica, peered out. Her husband had been a major during the Patriotic War, surviving with a chest full of medals and scars to match, but ever since his death in 1982 she'd lived alone off his pension. She often brought us food, because it was no secret that Lena was a lousy cook. Zorica clutched her robe shut at the neck and whispered, "Emil!"

I stopped by her door as the others went on.

"What's happening?" she asked.

"I don't know. Just stay inside."

"You must know. You're a Militia chief."

"Pankov is gone."

"What do you mean, *gone?*"

I didn't really know what it meant either. A president takes a helicopter from the Central Committee Building and flies away. That only means he's left a building, not that he's gone for good. "I'm sorry, Zoka, I don't have time. Listen to the radio. It's all there." I didn't want to tell her about Lena; that could wait.

The three of us piled inside the Militia Karpat Katja had used to drive me home. I felt claustrophobic and hot in the passenger seat, wishing I'd brought along my Captopril. It was nearly one, and this section of Friendship Street was vacant, but we could still hear voices from the south, in the direction of Victory Square. We drove north, the street lit only by the car's headlights.

From the Second District, we crossed into the Sixth, where I lived just after the war with my grandparents. Back then, it had been a prestigious neighborhood, where Friends of the Liberators were given Habsburg houses cut up to accommodate many families. My grandfather, a communist since before the Russian Revolution, had been given a place with a view of Heroes' Square. In 1980, though, Pankov's massive reconstruction of the Capital started in this district, and my old home, as well as the whole block and even Heroes' Square itself, was plowed into the ground and replaced with more socialist-friendly concrete architecture.

We came across marauding groups of drunks who seemed as confused about the situation as Zorica. Unlike Zorica, they weren't kept indoors by their confusion. Some climbed through the broken window of a grocery store, stealing bags of flour and canned goods. Another group of five men tried to wave us down with dim flashlights—our blue-tinted license plates gave us away as government—and Katja swerved to get around them.

"Aron was right," she said.

"What did Aron say?" asked Gavra from the back.

She shook her head. "Nothing."

Once we reached the Eleventh, Friendship was quiet again, and we stopped at the high stone wall surrounding the Central Archives. Through the bars of the gate we saw a small, unlit pillbox with a guard inside. Our headlights woke him, and he came out squinting. I got out of the car and approached.

"I need you to open up," I said.

He shook his head. "We're closed."

I showed my Militia certificate, but that didn't change his mind. He crossed his arms over his chest and shook his head. "I'm under orders, Comrade Chief. That's all there is to it."

Gravel crunched behind me as Gavra walked up. "Any trouble?"

"Maybe. This man says we can't come in."

"Oh?" Without hesitation, Gavra took out his Makarov. "Comrade Guard, please open up."

The guard also had a sidearm, a bulky Czech CZ-75 in a leather holster, and he considered it.

"Don't," said Gavra. "I don't want to kill you, but it's really been a very long day."

Heinrich—the name he gave us when we asked—let us in, and we brought him with us across the parking lot to the high yellow-brick cube that held the archives of the People's Militia. I'd been here often over the decades, spending endless hours among stacks of yellowed files, tracking down the identities of suspects and victims.

They'd bought a roomful of IBM mainframes last year and were going through the agonizing process of shifting the records to floppy disks, but with four floors of files and a socialist work ethic, this would take forever.

Katja did a trick on the front-door lock that impressed both me and Gavra, and even Heinrich—he let out a disappointed gasp. We passed through the entryway, where a wall of punch cards was positioned beside a time clock, and quickly found the central distribution office, with small file-card drawers stacked to the ceiling.

Once we got going, I realized this wasn't going to be quick. None of us—not even Heinrich—understood the filing system, so for the first hour it was a matter of opening drawers at random, examining the cards inside, and then trying to infer what that set of cabinets was for. In each set, we looked for "Gorski," and finally found a typewritten card:

                    GORSKI, ROSTA
                        1957-
                    QPC-203-2948B

"What the hell does that mean?" said Gavra.

I looked at the guard and was pleased to see he was no longer scared. "Heinrich?"

He shrugged. "Higher mathematics."

I liked Heinrich.

After another hour, on the third floor we found a storage unit numbered 203, which contained an aisle marked C in section QP. Gavra held on to Heinrich as Katja and I walked the aisle, which was long enough so that the far end appeared very small. Toward the end, Katja said, "There," and pointed. Eight feet up was a file drawer marked 2948. She found a stepladder on wheels, and I climbed it. There was nothing between the files for GORJAN and GORSKOV. In the front of the drawer I found a single-page notice that referred the researcher to the overflow file, 2948B, in the basement.

By three thirty, we found it. Rosta Gorski's file was only a few pages long, mentioning Gorski's mother—Irina Gorski, widow—his home in Stryy, and his profession: farmer. There were two Militia sheets on him, dealing with small-time crimes. He'd stolen someone's cow in 1971 when he was fourteen and was jailed for a night. When he was nineteen, in 1976, he'd started a brawl in a local bar and spent another night in jail, charged with hooliganism and drunkenness.

The last sheet was a replica of the first one, dated February 1980. It restated his name, mother (deceased as of 1979), place of birth, and profession, but with a single additional line:

```
Stryy Militia reported the disappearance of
R. Gorski on 12 September 1979. As of 28.2.80
he has not been located.
```

"Nothing here about the files," I said, folding up the papers and slipping them into my coat pocket.

It wasn't until after five in the morning, an hour before the first archive clerks would arrive for work, that we finally tracked down what we were interested in. By then, I was exhausted, feeling the heat of overpressured blood thumping under my skin, but I kept going. It wasn't a measure of my loyalty to the job; Yuri Kolev hardly even entered my mind. It was a measure of the guilt slowly growing inside me. The explosive charges that killed Lena had been meant for me. I—in part because I'd never had her car fixed—was responsible for her murder. I couldn't take that burden. I needed to know, without a doubt, the identity of the responsible person, so I wouldn't have to carry that guilt alone.

That's how I was able to stay awake.

We again began in the central distribution office but realized after a long time that we were in the wrong place. Behind the office was another door leading to a table with two computer terminals, two pencils, and a stack of notepaper cut from used printed sheets. On the shelf were folders of perforated computer printouts that listed file numbers followed by codes. It took a while, but we found Gorski's QPC-203-2948B, which was followed by TR000293X.

By then, Katja had warmed up one of the computers and started a file-keeping program called Nutshell. She typed in the code and waited. After half a minute of hums and clicks, it gave us two names:

```
1. ROMEK, NIKOLAI
2. KOLEV, YURI
```

I was amazed; it was the first time I'd witnessed the speed of computers.

"These," she said, "are the two people who've signed out Gorski's file."

Gavra made a noise. "This is why they killed Kolev. They saw he'd been looking into Gorski's file. That made him a threat."

I touched Katja's shoulder. "Can you find out what other files Romek signed out?"

She didn't know, but she tried typing "1," followed by ENTER. After a minute and a half, we were presented with this list:

```
1. GORSKI, ROSTA
2. 10-3283-48 (AUTH)
3. VOLAN, DUŠAN (AUTH)
4. SEV, BRANO (AUTH)
5. BROD, EMIL (AUTH)
6. PUTONSKI, LEBED (AUTH)
7. MICHALEC, JERZY (AUTH)
8. ZOLTENKO, TATIANA (AUTH)
9. PREV YEARS
```

"There's your answer," said Katja, leaning back in her chair. "Romek authorized the release of all the files."

"Type four," I said.

She did, and a few lines of letter-and-number codes came back. I wasn't sure what they meant, but Katja was able to decipher the abbreviations. "Brano's file is in the building," she said.

"No. None of the files were returned."

She pressed a finger to the screen. "Right here. Taken out December eighth. Brought back yesterday, at six in the evening." She turned to Heinrich; we'd sat him down at the other terminal. "What time does the building close?"

He shrugged. "Open and close at six."

"Then it hasn't been filed yet," said Katja.

It was nearly six o'clock by now, so Gavra waited by the front door, watching for arrivals, while Katja and I went to the deposit room, a simple counter with steel shelves covering the wall, filled with returned files. We finally had some luck, because the clerk, eager to get home, had simply placed the returned stack of six personnel files—the 1948 case file hadn't been returned—behind the counter for the morning clerk to deal with.

We left Heinrich at his pillbox. I guessed he would stay quiet about his night's adventure rather than be grilled on why he hadn't shot any of us. We hadn't destroyed anything, and six missing files was probably their daily quota.

We kept stifling yawns, but all three of us knew it wasn't yet time for sleep. When your country is falling apart, time changes. Everything becomes equally urgent. Adrenaline kicks in, followed by something else, some undiscovered substance the body produces during national emergencies. Unlike Katja and Gavra, though, I was no longer young. My heart could only take so much of this before it would just give up.

I didn't have to tell them where our next stop was, because Nikolai

Romek's house was the only place left to go. Gavra, who'd been at the colonel's for a Ministry party last year, gave Katja directions.

Farther up Friendship, we saw a dead body outside an electrical shop. The woman, lying facedown, was alone on that vacant block. Katja slowed as we passed the blood-spattered body—she'd been shot in the back—then sped up, turning onto another street. None of us felt like talking about it, or even calling it in.

On Belgrade Avenue, the tower-lined road that would get us out of town, we saw an army roadblock at the intersection with Tisa Street. A jeep and a truck. Seven soldiers checking cars from each direction, Kalashnikovs strung over their shoulders.

"Can we make it?" said Gavra, leaning forward to see better.

"Pull over," I told Katja.

She did so, and we squinted through the dim morning light. They weren't bothering with the vehicles, instead asking each passenger for his papers. Katja and I would be fine, but I wasn't sure about Gavra. I turned to him. "Let me see your documents."

All he had on him were his passport, his Ministry certificate, and a driver's license—but that, too, identified him as a Ministry employee. He'd left his Viktor Lukacs papers in his paint-smeared car.

I didn't have to say what I was thinking. He saw the problem as well. "I'll get out here."

"Maybe we can get through another way," said Katja.

We couldn't. The army was fully aware of all the escape routes from the city, because it had secured the Capital for Pankov often enough.

So Gavra gave us the last of the directions; then I got out so he could leave. "Can you get back to my place?"

"If the metro's open, it'll be easy. Besides, I need to go by the station."

"Why?"

"I've got papers to destroy." He handed me his Makarov. "You'll need this more than I will."

* * *

We left Gavra on the sidewalk and made it through the roadblock without a problem. Katja flirted with the soldier checking our papers and asked how the revolution was coming along. He sighed and explained, as if to a child, that the terrorists—by that he meant the rooftop snipers—were still all over the city, shooting into crowds.

"Did you catch any yet?"

"Not that I've heard. But we know who they are."

"Ministry, right?"

He shook his head. "That's low even for the Ministry. We think they're Libyans."

Briefly, Katja glanced at me with a confused expression, then returned to him. "Libyans?"

"Yeah. Pankov made a deal with Muammar Qaddafi for his special forces to protect him in case this happened. Rumor is, when he came back on Sunday a second plane landed just afterward with about a hundred of these guys."

"Oh," said Katja. "And Pankov? Where is he?"

"Wouldn't we all like to know?"

Later, that Libyan rumor would become accepted truth, though in fact none of the snipers was ever caught, and no one could find records of a second Libyan flight landing at Pankov—now Tisa—International.

Romek's home was different from Csilla Volan's but no less magnificent. It was one of the old Habsburg residences, not unlike the house where Lena grew up. Its grounds had been neglected, trees and bushes growing wildly, pressing into the long driveway that took us to the front door.

I clutched Gavra's Makarov and rang the bell, but there was no answer. After a few more tries, I helped Katja break in through a window, and a high-pitched alarm squealed. She found the control box beside the front door and used a brass candelabra to bang at it until the plastic casing fell off and she could rip apart the wires. By the time she opened the door for me, we had silence.

It was a vast house, decorated in period furniture shipped in from France and Italy. I was particularly taken by the kitchen, which was entirely American. There was a microwave oven, something I'd only seen in films, and a fully stocked refrigerator nearly as large as my bed.

While I stood mesmerized on the tiled floor, Katja searched the house. She called me when she found Romek's office on the second floor. Unlike the rest of the house, it was entirely modern, with another IBM computer on a steel desk beside a lamp made of aluminum wires that looked like a sculpture. While the computer powered up, Katja went through the desk drawers, and I looked at the bookshelves.

"Here," she said. She was crouched beside the desk, holding out a slip of printed paper for me. It was a TisAir flight itinerary for three people: Nikolai Romek, his wife, Elena, and his son, Andrea. Three seats on a plane to Paris. The plane had left the previous night at seven.

I groaned. "He's gone."

"Just before everything went to hell. As if he knew."

I wondered about that: *Did* Romek know beforehand how Pankov's rally would go? Had he arranged his and his family's safety long beforehand? I checked the date at the top of the sheet—the ticket had been bought on Monday, the day after Tomiak Pankov returned from Libya.

The computer, Katja told me after a few minutes' frustration at the keyboard, was completely erased.

We continued searching but found nothing concerning the people on the death list, or Rosta Gorski, or that 1948 case. The most interesting thing was a photocopy that had been crumpled up and simply thrown in the wastebasket—a long-winded telegram marked TOP SECRET, sent from our Moscow embassy. It concerned a conversation between V. L. Musatov, "Deputy Director of the International Department of the Central Committee of the Communist Party of the Soviet Union," and our ambassador to the Soviet Union, Ignac Molovich. It had been received, decoded, and stamped by Yalta Boulevard at 7:30 A.M. yesterday.

V. L. MUSATOV RECEIVED ME AT MY REQUEST. THE DEPUTY DIRECTOR TOLD ME THAT DURING THE MEETING OF T. PANKOV WITH THE SOVIET CHARGÉ D'AFFAIRES IN OUR CAPITAL ON 20 DECEMBER T. PANKOV SAID THAT HE POSSESSES INFORMATION THAT THE ACTIONS IN SAROSPATAK WERE PRE-PARED AND ORGANIZED WITH THE CONSENT OF MEMBER COUNTRIES OF THE WARSAW TREATY OR-GANIZATION.

I AFFIRMED THIS AND MADE THE POINT THAT OUR INFORMATION SUGGESTED SOME KIND OF ACTION OF INTERFERENCE INTO OUR INTERNAL AFFAIRS UNDER PREPARATION IN THE SOVIET UNION.

THE DEPUTY DIRECTOR DECLARED THAT SUCH AS-SERTIONS PUZZLED HIM, AND HAD NO FOUNDATION AND DID NOT CORRESPOND WITH REALITY. FUR-THER, HE STATED THAT HIS WORDS REFLECTED THE USSR OFFICIAL POSITION WHICH POSTULATES THAT THE SOVIET UNION BUILDS ITS RELATIONS WITH ALLIED SOCIALIST STATES ON THE BASIS OF EQUAL-ITY, MUTUAL RESPECT AND STRICT NONINTERFER-ENCE INTO DOMESTIC AFFAIRS.

I ASKED IF THIS POSITION ALSO COVERED AREAS WHEREIN SOCIALISM IN ALLIED STATES WAS UN-DER THREAT. THAT IS, WOULD SOVIET ASSISTANCE BE AVAILABLE TO NORMALIZE THE SITUATION IN SAROSPATAK? HE SAID THAT THIS POSITION COV-ERED ALL DOMESTIC AFFAIRS OF ALLIED STATES, AND THAT ASSISTANCE IN SAROSPATAK WOULD NOT BE AVAILABLE.

I had to read it a few times to work my way through the language, but it was plain enough. Pankov actually believed that this uprising had been instigated by the Warsaw Pact, and that the Russians in particular were behind it. It seemed ludicrous to me, since I knew that, for more than a decade, Ferenc and his friends had been building up their underground organization without any Russian support. But Pankov couldn't imagine that his own people would have the will to rise up on their own.

Then I remembered Ferenc's story. Yuri Kolev met with a Russian named Fyodor Malevich who kept an officer's uniform in his wardrobe. Maybe Pankov wasn't so paranoid after all.

Katja was intrigued by the final line. Our ambassador had asked if the Russians would help put down the uprising, and Musatov had flatly said no.

This made her delirious with pleasure. The world, she told me, had abandoned Tomiak Pankov completely, and now our country would finally speak with its own voice.

In a sense, you can argue that she was right.

Still, despite the revolutionary promise in what we'd found, there was nothing here for me. Romek had fled the country with his family, and I was left with no explanation as to why my wife had been murdered.

We spent a few hours going through the house, ripping open cabinets and drawers and even banging the wall in vain for hollow spots. In the backyard, the last strings of my hope snapped. Romek owned a long, rusty grill that must have been put to good use for sides of lamb at many summer garden parties. Now it was full of ashes and flakes of recently burned papers. Hundreds—*thousands*—of them. He'd cleaned up completely before he left.

"What now?" said Katja.

Weakened by all this, I sat on the cold dirt and tried to regulate my breaths. "Sleep," I said, rubbing my eyes. "All I want is sleep."

FOURTEEN

•

Around nine in the morning, Gavra reached Lenin Avenue. The metro had not been open, so he'd walked from the edge of town. Like me and Katja, he was able to keep moving only because of adrenaline and that other unknown substance. On the endless walk these things left him, and he felt like a soldier on a long march, only aware of placing one foot in front of the other.

In October Square, he had finally found people. They were grouped around Max and Corina's café, a place popular with the Militia because of the discounts it offered. Today, though, there were no militiamen, just twenty students around a broken window, some sitting on chairs inside, others on the sidewalk looking in as a bearded young man lectured them on revolutionary organization. A few students turned to stare at Gavra, and he veered off to the other side of the square at about the moment the gunfire started.

A sniper on a residential rooftop shot slowly and deliberately into the crowd. Running for the shelter of a doorway, Gavra heard screams and saw two students fall as the others scrambled in through the broken window.

He made it out of October alive and a little more awake and found the Militia station abandoned except for two old sergeants manning the phones. "What're you doing here?" said one.

"Going to my office," Gavra told him. "Many calls?"

The sergeant shrugged. "Sure, but we just tell them to stay inside."

"Yeah," said the other.

"You're not investigating anything?"

The second one shrugged. "Someone's gotta hold down the fort."

The homicide office was locked, so he broke the glass to unlock it from inside, then started through the paperwork in his desk. There wasn't much to burn. His most sensitive case files were stored at Yalta. He took out the files that he kept on us, his coworkers, and put them in the metal wastebasket. He used lighter fluid he found in Bernard's desk and soaked the files, then lit them.

I later asked why he did this. Why he burned the files on us. He said it was because they contained a record of our assistance to him over the years. If the revolutionaries got hold of that, it would be a simple matter to convict us of being Ministry agents.

As he poked the embers with a metal ruler, his phone rang.

He didn't want to answer it. All he wanted was to get back and make sure Karel was all right, then go to sleep for a very long time.

But he did answer it, and that changed everything.

"Hello?"

"Gavra NOW-kass?"

He gripped the edge of his desk. "Harold." He said in English, "Yes, it's me."

"Oh, Jesus, I'm glad I finally got you. Gavra, something's gone really wrong."

"What is it? Are you in trouble?"

"Trouble's a good word for it. We're at the hotel, and people . . . well, they're *shooting* at the hotel."

"Who's shooting at the hotel?"

"Looks to me like army. Christ, Beth's scared out of her wits."

"Why are they shooting at the hotel?"

"You think I know? Oh!" He heard Beth's scream, and movement.

"Harold? Harold?"

"We're okay, we're okay. Just a scare. A bullet came through our window. Right through!"

Gavra rubbed his temples. "Look, I'll be over as soon as I can. What's your room?"

"Three-oh-five."

"Stay there. Sit behind the bed—no. Go into the hallway. You'll be safe there. But wait for me in the hallway. Don't leave. Okay?"

"We're not going anywhere, Gavra. No worries about that."

The Militia garage attendant was gone, so Gavra broke into his key rack and took a Militia Karpat. He sped down Lenin and over to Victory, which was empty except for the Central Committee Building. Along its steps, men and women were smoking and going in and out of the front door. From the wide balcony where he'd seen Tomiak Pankov fear for his life, two young men were tying up a banner that had been crudely painted with the words GALICIA REVOLUTIONARY COMMITTEE HQ.

Through his windows, he could hear the gunfire from Yalta Boulevard.

He stopped at the end of the long, wide street. Up two blocks at number 20, an army truck was parked among bullet-riddled cars. Behind the cars, soldiers crouched, their Kalashnikovs aimed up high along the Metropol's glass tower. Occasionally, he made out a form on the roof, which shot back and disappeared again. There were no pedestrians here.

Gavra approached the only way he could, by driving his Karpat up on the sidewalk that led to the Metropol and speeding the two long blocks. When he reached an intersection, his car lurched painfully and bounced, then bounced again as it jumped the next curb. From this angle, the snipers' bullets wouldn't reach him. He hoped the soldiers on the other side of the road wouldn't decide to take a shot.

He parked just short of the Metropol's glass entrance, which was now shattered, and ran, crouched, inside. The lobby was full of soldiers and journalists wearing three-day beards. Everyone gaped at him, and the journalists with cameras started taking his picture. "Who are you?" a woman asked in French, followed by an Englishman asking the same thing. He pushed past them and reached the stairwell. The soldiers never thought to ask who he was.

Just before the third floor, he stopped to catch his breath. His body didn't want to continue, so he had to grab the balustrade and pull himself the final steps. He didn't know what he was going to do with this stupid American couple; he only hoped he wouldn't get killed trying to help.

The third-floor corridor was empty, and the only sound was the muted thump of gunfire outside. He'd told them to stay out here. His anger flashed, then faded—perhaps they'd been hit by stray bullets before they could make it out of the room. He rushed to number 305 and knocked on the door.

"Come in!" shouted Harold.

Gavra opened the door and stepped inside. The first thing he noticed was that their window was completely intact. There were no cracks or holes in it.

Then he realized why. This side of the hotel faced the back alley, not Yalta Boulevard.

Harold and Beth were sitting on the bed beside each other, smiling at him. The gunshots were quieter here. "Gavra," said Beth. She clapped once. "You came!"

Gavra started to say something but couldn't. Beth hadn't spoken in English. She'd spoken our language, with the fluency of a native. He stepped forward, past the bathroom door and into the room. "What's going on?"

"Ask him," said Harold, and Gavra heard movement behind himself.

He turned. The bathroom door was open, and Nikolai Romek was standing in it, holding a Beretta. "Hello, Gavra."

As he came forward, a familiar brick of a man with a thick mustache followed him out, holding a small burlap sack. Just the right size for a head. "Balínt," said Romek.

Balínt handed the bag to Gavra. He remembered now—one of Kolev's two assistants. "You traitorous shit," said Gavra.

"Put it on," said Romek.

That's when, despite his fatigue, the panic set in. "Tell me what's going on!"

"I'm going to make you famous," said Romek.

"You'll be a *hero*," Beth said gleefully.

Harold looked at his wristwatch, stood, and said in English, "Let's get this show on the road."

"Well?" said Romek. With the Beretta, he gestured at the bag in Gavra's hand.

When Gavra shook his head no, Balínt came over to help him with it.

FIFTEEN

•

We made it back to my apartment by ten without incident. Karel and Aron, now asleep on the couch and chair, had finished off my vodka and scotch, which annoyed me, but I was too exhausted to complain. Katja woke Aron, and Karel awoke on his own, rubbing his eyes and asking where Gavra was.

"Had to go to the station," Katja told him.

"Why?"

"He thought it was important." She didn't know how much Karel knew of his best friend's work. If Karel didn't know who Brano Sev was, he might know nothing.

After a round of sullen embraces, she took Aron home in the Militia car, and Karel turned on the television. For some reason, that angered me as well. Of the two channels, one was still in government hands, playing an old Pankov biography, full of washed-out colors of his family's peasant home. On the other channel, a young man who needed a shave reported on where in the city the rooftop snipers had been spotted but urged the entire city to spend the day in the squares and celebrate "this new era of freedom. Long live the Soft Revolution!"

I gathered the files we'd taken from the archives and brought them to bed. I undressed, considering a wash, but didn't want to track through the living room and have to speak to Karel again. All I wanted was sleep. By then the shock of yesterday was fading, leaving me wrung out, and the depression was settling in. The same thing happened when Libarid died in 1975 and Imre ten years later. Shock, followed by depression, followed by anger.

But I persisted, because this was so much more devastating. I'd lost my wife; I'd lost everything. I couldn't go to sleep empty-handed. I reached for the Captopril.

According to my own thick file, my career began with my second case, looking into the murders of prostitutes in the Canal District, back when prostitutes could still make a living there. There was a small photo of me, which was updated every five years. This one was from '87, and I had the blank expression of a prisoner.

According to an inserted sheet that was thinner and whiter than the rest, I joined the First District homicide department on 23 August 1948 (which was true) but didn't actually do any work until two months later. My documented history simply skipped over the case that started my career and nearly killed Lena. As if it were a figment of my imagination.

With Dušan Volan's file, I began to understand. Volan was a soft-looking old man who in 1949 ruled over a variety of tribunals. Another page that was less yellowed and brittle than the rest mentioned that in August 1949 he sentenced one Jerzy Michalec to death for "counterrevolutionary activity." That is, actions against the communist government.

The truth was that Michalec had been sentenced for being a murderer and a Nazi war criminal.

The same case was mentioned in Lebed Putonski's file—again, "counterrevolutionary activity."

Brano Sev's file, which was always limited because of security considerations, was simply missing the year 1948. His photograph was older, from the seventies, a round, aging face with three moles on the left cheek. Tatiana Zoltenko's photo, taken last year, showed a tough colonel in her late sixties with black-dyed hair pulled back tight enough to raise her colored eyebrows in surprise. Since I didn't know her role in the prosecution of Jerzy Michalec, I didn't know what had been doctored in her file.

The pillow behind my back had grown soft, and I was slipping deeper into it. I had to rub my eyes raw to keep from passing out as I squinted at Michalec's file. He was born in Szekszárd, Austro-Hungary, 12 January 1909. By now, if he was still alive, he'd be eighty. In 1933, he married Agnes Höller in Vienna, and ten years later Agnes died in the Mauthausen concentration camp. The rest of the story—his history with the Gestapo—was not mentioned.

I found a photograph from a 1979 visa mug shot. Years in a so-cialist labor camp had put weight into his haggard eyes, and he'd lost the extra fat that living well after the war had given him. Re-markably, he was smiling in the picture. I wondered why.

I set the picture aside and found this:

```
August 1949: Sentenced to death for counter-
revolutionary activity. Charges included col-
laboration with anticommunist forces with ties
to American and British imperialists, as well
as sabotage of Soviet military communication
lines.
```

I finally closed my eyes, feeling sick. I'd been seeing it all wrong, and here was the evidence. Still, I had to go through more pages, through the rest of Jerzy Michalec's history, to be sure.

The file told me that a month after his verdict, Michalec's punish-ment was commuted to life in a labor camp. He served it until 1956, when our former leader, Mihai, bowing to the new wave of tolerance emanating from Khrushchev's Moscow, initiated a blanket amnesty for political prisoners. Jerzy was among those freed.

I hadn't known this before, but it made sense, and was probably true. A lot of marginal, embittered people were suddenly put on the streets that year, making our jobs that much more difficult. It also marked the beginning of Ferenc Kolyeszar's worst year.

Another whiter, and thus fabricated, sheet said Michalec was arrested by the First District Militia in 1968 for passing out leaflets supporting the Prague Spring, then again in 1976 for running a printing press from his basement. The arresting officer in 1968 was Lieutenant Libarid Terzian. In 1976, Captain Imre Papp.

Both of whom were now dead and couldn't dispute the lie.

I shut my eyes again, trying to control my exhausted emotions. They had doctored the memory of my militiamen to protect a man who was once called the Butcher. Because that's what Michalec was. The name had been used as a compliment, because of a single afternoon in the crumbling ruin of Berlin in 1945, when he assembled twenty-three *Hitlerjugend* boys under his command and killed them all. He presented their corpses to the Red Army and was cheered. Only a butcher could do that.

On the next page I found something even more striking. In June 1979, Jerzy Michalec applied for, and received, permission to emigrate to France. He left in September of that year.

September 1979.

I put the file aside and, in my underwear, stumbled through to the living room, where Karel was dozing in front of the muted television, the remote in his hand. I wondered where he had found that. On the screen, soldiers were crouched behind bullet-damaged cars, shooting up into the sky. I paused. It was Yalta Boulevard, and they were shooting up at the Hotel Metropol.

But I ignored it and went to my coat on the rack, searching the pockets until I found the few crumpled sheets from Rosta Gorski's file. As I walked back to the bedroom, I checked them. Yes. September 1979 was the same month that Rosta Gorski, according to the Stryy Militia, "disappeared."

By the time I made it to bed again, I knew it was true. When it came to Jerzy Michalec, coincidences did not exist. Michalec and Gorski moved to France together.

This, finally, was something.

But it only led to more questions. Why did they leave together? And how did Michalec, a labor-camp veteran, get permission to emigrate? For that, you had to go directly to Yalta 36 and suffer the rigors of an entire life study before you could even arrange your first interview. The Ministry only let you leave if it wanted you to leave.

I laid the files on the floor and slipped deeper under the covers, trying to silence my aching head. I was too tired to muddle through it all.

Despite my efforts I couldn't sleep. I was finally able to push Jerzy Michalec out of my head, but his place was taken, instantaneously, by Lena.

Ever since the guests started filling my home, I'd set her aside because it was the only way to deal with what had to be done. I've set aside grief many times in my life, only to come back and face it later. All those tragedies were nothing next to this. The day before, I'd felt as if all my organs had been stolen from my body, but now they were back, all of them, bloated and painful.

I kept seeing her face, and the extra lines she had from a lifetime of hard drinking and smoking. That was my Lena. She'd been beautiful when she was young, but when she lost that beauty she never let go of the toughness that had always given her beauty power. Even during our worst moments—and we had so many—that underlying fierceness bound me to her.

I was always just myself, Emil Brod, a normal man. Average in so many ways. But Lena was always a little more of everything. Funnier, more social, more destructive, and more loving than I could ever hope to be. That made her more tangible than anyone I'd known in my life, all the way through to that final moment when she was cursing at the key she'd stuck into the Mercedes.

That did it. That's what broke me. For the next hour, until the exhaustion finally did me in, all I could do was cry, and my ears were filled with that horrible electric hum. Somewhere in the middle of my fit I felt the real power of my discovery. Jerzy Michalec wasn't just another senior citizen who'd been targeted for murder. He was rewriting history and killing off those who knew otherwise.

I didn't know why, and I wasn't sure how. All I knew was that he'd finished what he'd tried to do forty years ago—he'd killed me. By killing Lena, he'd succeeded more effectively than if he'd broken each of my bones and then put a bullet in my brain.

23 DECEMBER 1989

SATURDAY

•

SIXTEEN

•

Gavra woke in darkness, cold and disoriented. His head was splitting, his mouth parched. He was on a cool floor, wood by the feel of it, and the wall behind him was rough concrete. He started to stand, but the dizziness hit, and he had to settle down again.

About five feet ahead, he could make out a line of light from the bottom of a door. When his ears cleared up, he heard heavy footsteps on the other side of the door. Dozens of them, moving purposefully back and forth, and quiet murmurs.

He rubbed his eyes and forehead, but nothing could get rid of the ache. He remembered the hotel room, and the sudden, nauseating confusion when he realized the old American couple were not what they had seemed. And Romek. What connected the colonel to these old people? Then Balínt, the Ministry heavy whose loyalty to Yuri Kolev was a joke. There hadn't been much of a struggle; Balínt's brute strength easily outmatched Gavra's. The bag was soon over his head, and then he felt a small, sharp pinch against his arm. That must have been it, an injection. Because soon afterward he blacked out.

And woke here.

He was scared, but not as scared as he had been in America when he found Lebed Putonski's corpse in his motel room. He knew he would be dead if Romek wanted him dead. Instead, the colonel had risked exposure transporting Gavra from the Hotel Metropol to here, wherever *here* was.

I'm going to make you famous, he'd said.

What did that mean?

It was hard to think with the headache and cottonmouth. What he now knew for certain was that Romek's game was tied to the revolt tearing through the country. Brano, too, was connected—why else would he, after three years' absence, have suddenly called?

Gavra also knew that he was here because of his own stupidity. He'd forgotten Brano's rule: *Act, but never react. Once you start reacting, you've already lost.*

To try to regain control, he went through the facts. Romek had been trying to kill off everyone associated with the 1948 criminal case against Jerzy Michalec. Gavra didn't yet realize that Michalec was also behind the killings; he still believed Michalec was a potential victim.

By that point, he took as truth his assumption that the Americans were part of the plan. They had sent Frank Jones to kill Putonski but hadn't given the assassin orders to kill Gavra as well. Perhaps his job had been to tail Gavra and find out how much he'd learned before killing him. That was something he would never know.

Despite the risks, Gavra was angry he hadn't tried to get to the Ministry. One phone call, and Brano Sev might have been able to clear everything up with a few words.

But there was an elephant in the room he was missing. He'd been working along the edges of Romek's operation. He didn't have enough information to even guess what was at its center.

He looked up at the sound of a key fitting into the door and tried again to get up. He pressed against the wall, sliding into a standing position, fighting the nausea as the door opened and light poured in. It blinded him briefly, and he squinted. A tall, backlit form stood in the doorway. Behind it, soldiers moved in a nondescript concrete corridor. He could now see that he'd been sitting inside a small closet with shelves filled with hundreds of rolls of toilet paper.

"Gavra Noukas," said the form. There was enough light for him to see it was an old man, very old, with just a few wispy strands of white crowning his head.

"Who're you?"

The man smiled—he was missing several teeth. "Please," he said, offering a hand. "Come with me."

Gavra ignored the hand as he stepped forward, using the wall for support. Once he reached the corridor, the old man, looking strange among these soldiers in his tailored gray suit and red tie, stepped back and let Balínt—now in an infantry uniform with a sidearm—help Gavra walk.

"Your head should clear soon," said the old man.

It was an army barracks. One steel door said ARMAMENTS and another said MESS. Gavra didn't ask anything, because there was no point. This old man had come to get him for a reason, and Balínt, holding him by the waist, was guiding him slowly to that reason.

They ended up at a door marked OPERATIONS V. Through its glass, he could see a long conference table. The old man led them in. The room was windowless. Balínt gently set Gavra down onto a metal folding chair, then saluted the old man and left them alone, closing the door to wait outside.

On the far wall was a blackboard that hadn't been cleaned well, and in the center of the table was a large glass ashtray, also dirty, beside a pitcher of water and two glasses. The old man filled one and slid it close to Gavra. "Here. Drink. You need to hydrate."

Gavra stared at the glass but didn't move.

The old man poured a second glass and drank half of it. "See? No ill effects. Drink. You'll feel better."

As Gavra drank the whole glass, the man pulled the ashtray to the edge of the table and lit a scented French cigarette. "You want to know who I am, yes?"

Gavra set down the empty glass and watched the old man refill it. He didn't want to admit to curiosity, but he had no other options. "Yes."

"I'm Jerzy Michalec."

That was something Gavra didn't see coming, and it told him what I'd figured out in the misery of my empty bed. He looked again at the old man's fine suit and the self-conscious way he brought the cigarette to his dry lips. Unlike most people those days, he was well shaven, and Gavra noticed a scar—faint but still visible—along his jawline. "And?" said Gavra.

Jerzy Michalec offered a cigarette, but Gavra shook his head. The old man sat a couple of seats down and scraped ash into the ashtray. "You're Brano Sev's protégé, yes?"

Gavra didn't answer.

"No need to be shy about it. In fact, you should be proud. Not everyone can claim something so prestigious."

He spoke as if they were both in an elegant drawing room, enjoying glasses of port by a fire. It annoyed Gavra.

"That's why you're here, you know."

"Because of Brano?"

Michalec nodded slowly. "It's integral to everything."

Gavra rubbed his head. "I don't know where Brano is, if that's what you're getting at."

"I gave up on trying to find him long ago," said Michalec. "But whether or not I find him, it makes no difference."

"Would you mind making sense?"

"We have to work you into this, Gavra. That's just how it has to be. Tell you everything, and your poor head won't be able to take it. We've still got time."

"Have a little faith in me. You'd be surprised how much I can take."

"I don't doubt it," Michalec said affectionately, then winked.

Gavra nearly threw himself across the table in order to rip out the man's eyes. Instead, he muttered, "Tell me where I am."

The old man was suddenly serious. "You're in the Sixteenth District Third Infantry barracks. No one knows you're here. If we want, we can get rid of you, and no one will ask us a single question. Remember that."

Gavra reached for his glass and started drinking again. Michalec was right; his head was clearing enough for him to start to make connections. "You and Nikolai Romek have been killing people who know about your Nazi associations. You're erasing your past. Even in America. Why?"

Michalec set his cigarette hand against the table and scratched his scar. "Mr. Lukacs."

Gavra nodded.

Michalec put out his cigarette. There was a studied look on his weathered face, but then the smile returned. "It's funny. Nikolai thought you were in Yugoslavia; so did I. Kolev turned out more wily than we thought. Then the Atkinses ended up on a plane with you. Rather beautiful coincidence, don't you think?" He shrugged. "It doesn't matter. Whatever you think you know about my past is beside the point. The only matter of importance is that you are here and that your country requires your help."

A series of rebuttals came to Gavra. *What do you know about my country? You have no idea what my country needs. I'd help my country best by killing you.* They were all childish taunts, so he remained silent for a moment, then said, "What kind of help?"

Michalec stood. "Can you walk now?"

With Balínt now following them, Gavra and Michalec continued down the corridor, passing soldiers Gavra could now see were all officers. Their faces were flushed, as if they were scared. Then he saw Nikolai Romek, also fitted out in an army uniform, walking past, but the Ministry colonel was involved in reading papers and didn't notice him.

They turned down another corridor, which was lined with classrooms marked by numbers. Odd on the left, even on the right. They stopped at number 6, which was open, and through the doorway he saw chairs with attached desktops, the kind children used. They had once been arranged in perfect rows when recruits attended lessons but now were disordered. The desks were occupied by old people, about fifteen of them, some talking animatedly, others sitting quietly with their thoughts. Through a far window, he saw black tree branches and faint light—it was dawn.

When Michalec stepped through the doorway, the conversation stopped abruptly and they all looked up. Among them sat Harold and Beth Atkins, both breaking into huge smiles. Harold came over, grabbed Gavra's hand, and started pumping it. "You feeling all right? Better now?"

"Don't crowd him, Harry," said Beth.

Harold returned to his wife, and Michalec continued to the wide lecturer's desk at the front of the room. On the large, dirty blackboard someone had written:

AIMS
END STREET FIGHTING
UNITE FACTIONS
CENTRAL CONTROL OF UTILITIES
INSTALL BUREAUCRACY
SECURE DEMOCRACY

Balínt urged Gavra forward until they also reached the desk at the front. Michalec said to the room, "Once again, I thank you all for traveling so far." He patted his hands together to applaud their long journeys, and they briefly applauded themselves.

One of the old men in the back called, "*Viva la revolución!*"

The others laughed, and even Michalec smiled. But Gavra didn't. He started to understand, and the understanding frightened him more than the confusion had.

"I have to be brief," Michalec said, then gestured toward Gavra. "You all know why this young man's here. But he doesn't know. Not yet. As we discussed before, we're going to take this slowly. We've got . . ." He checked his watch. "Nearly twenty hours to bring our man to our way of thinking."

"And if he doesn't?" said an elderly woman at the front. Her accent was strange; Gavra couldn't place it.

"We'll deal with that when it comes. It won't change our plans."

She nodded very seriously, as did a few others.

"But I wouldn't worry," said Michalec. He winked at Gavra. "I have great faith in Mr. Noukas."

That provoked another round of applause and brought on the nausea again. What he understood was that he was standing among émigrés who had returned home after decades away to assist the revolution. Unlike Gavra, and unlike me, they felt it was in their power to change a foul regime; they felt it was their duty. He should have been overcome by admiration for them, but he couldn't manage it. There was something wrong here. Their euphoria felt like hysteria, and he knew that hysterical revolutions were the bloodiest.

Then he considered the writing on the chalkboard. Practical reasons for whatever they were doing. There was nothing hysterical there—the list concerned the stabilization of the country. Rearranging the bureaucracy so that utilities would continue to work and people wouldn't be killed in the street.

Michalec said, "I just wanted you good people to see him, and remember his face. His face is our face."

That last line revived Gavra's panic. "No," he said aloud.

The crowd looked at him expectantly.

"No," he repeated, shaking his head. "I'm not any part of this."

"Give him time," Michalec told them.

Involuntarily, Gavra tried to run, but Balínt was prepared for that. His big hands caught Gavra's shoulders and pulled him sharply back. He stumbled but didn't fall.

Michalec said, "Now to our lessons," and the people laughed.

As he was guided back out to the corridor, some came to shake his hand again, and Gavra, bewildered, let them do it. Then the old man who had shouted *Viva la revolución* raised two fingers to Gavra's forehead and muttered a blessing in Spanish as he marked the cross on Gavra's body.

SEVENTEEN

•

Surprisingly for a man as old as myself, I slept for eighteen hours. I suppose it was my body's attempt to fight back. Keep me knocked out so I would stop putting it through so much. It was a good try.

I woke early on Saturday to Karel's swarthy features hanging over me. Shocked, I pushed back, eyes wide. "What the hell are you doing here?"

He sighed heavily and stepped back. "Sorry." He settled in a chair that Lena had bought in Bern, Switzerland. "Gavra's still not back."

I closed my eyes. "Did you try the station?"

"I called yesterday. Someone told me he'd left long ago and then told me to stay inside."

It didn't sound good, but neither he nor I could do anything about it. I forced myself into a sitting position and rubbed my temples. "Can you make some coffee?"

"Already did."

He left the bedroom without closing the door, so I hobbled over to shut it, tripping on the files scattered on the floor. Everything ached. Karel returned with a steaming cup of acorn brew and set it on the drawers, watching me pull on pants.

"Well?" I said, frustrated.

"What are we going to do?"

"Just get out of here, okay?"

He shrugged but did as I asked.

I drank the wretched coffee quickly, then went to brush my teeth. Karel was in front of the television again. On it, soldiers were stepping carefully through a destroyed room, lifting gold objects—vases, paperweights, a large golden frame around a sentimental painting of the First Family—and showing them to the camera.

"What's that?" I said.

"It's the presidential palace. They got into it late last night. Just look. Food rationing for us, and they've got a whole room made out of gold. Bastards."

I couldn't look. Seeing the luxury of the Pankov lifestyle made me sick, like everyone else in the country, but the sickness didn't fill me with Karel's self-righteousness.

One of my most vivid memories is from just after the war, along St. George Boulevard, which would later be renamed Mihai and is now called something else: a stunned, topless woman in rags walking along the Tisa. She was covered in bruises, and her head had been shaved. Across her breasts, in red paint, her self-righteous abusers had written COLLABORATOR.

I remembered her again as I brushed my teeth, staring into my own bloodshot eyes.

I filled a second cup and joined Karel on the couch. Spread across the coffee table were pages from The Spark. "Where did you find this?"

"Outside," he said without taking his eyes from the screen, where a soldier held up a gold bowl and tiny gold spoon—the commentator said it was a caviar set. "There's a stack of them on the sidewalk. The delivery guy must've gotten spooked and just left them."

I gathered the newspaper and refitted it together. I saw it was yesterday's edition before seeing the front-page story. My throat closed up. Above a grainy photograph of a burning wreck, it said MILITIA CHIEF'S WIFE SLAIN BY PATAK TERRORISTS.

I rushed to the toilet. I bent over and waited, gasping, my eyes dripping into the bowl. My intestines convulsed but produced nothing. I hadn't eaten in a long time.

The official lie behind my wife's murder would turn out to be the front-page story of *The Spark*'s final edition.

When I came out again, Karel twisted in the couch to watch me. "Hey. You all right?"

"I'm hungry."

"Sit down." He got up. "Let me cook up something."

I did as he commanded but couldn't look at the paper again. I used the remote to learn that both national television channels were now in revolutionary hands. So it was over. Across the bottom of the screen was a phone number to call if you had any information on the whereabouts of the Pankovs.

It was almost too much to grasp. A government that had taken a war to put into place and had survived for forty years had been destroyed in mere hours.

A commentator reported on yesterday's battle at the Hotel Metropol. Revolutionaries had tracked the snipers to the Metropol and informed General Stapenov, who sent a unit to protect the legions of foreign journalists camping inside. The gunfight that followed lasted four hours, ending only when the "terrorists" simply stopped shooting. Soldiers made it to the roof, which had been defended along the stairwells, and found that the terrorists had disappeared.

Cameras panned across the flat, empty roof, then the chaotic ground-floor lounge, where soldiers and journalists stood around examining the damage. A German man spoke slowly and purposefully in our language as he recounted his fear and his conviction that he was going to die. Then he smiled and pulled over a grinning young soldier. "But these man, he save my life!" He was followed by a Frenchwoman named Gisèle Sully, who had an intense, dark stare and a better command of our language. She spoke rapidly, with hard consonants, saying that her own investigations made her think that the terrorists might not be who we thought they were. "They've yet to be captured, yes? But they're everywhere, and when they shoot, everyone's looking for them. But they disappear. They must be working in collusion with a nongovernmental group."

She looked as if she were going to continue, but the camera cut to the studio, where the young man who still needed a shave reported on continued terrorist activity in the First and Fifth districts. There was also rumored activity in the Third.

Karel returned with toasted stale bread and a pile of Lena's left-over pork and cabbage. I remembered throwing my serving in the trash and teasing her about her wifely duties. I tried to find the humor in it as I forked the bland stuff into my mouth but couldn't.

So I turned to Karel. "Who's running things now?"

"Things?"

"The country. The government."

"The Galicia Revolutionary Committee."

"But who's their figurehead?"

"I don't know. Does it matter?"

With each bite, Lena's dish tasted better. It was filling that empty space in me and helping my head. I gathered the patience to explain it to him. "It does matter. What happens if the old communists claim they're the heads of the revolution?"

"Why would they? Everyone knows who they are."

Despite Karel's simple ignorance, he triggered a thought. It wasn't about facts. Politics never is. It was about rumors and opinions. Television broadcasts. Journalism.

I ate the rest of the food quickly without tasting it, wiped my hands on my pants, and went to the phone. It was dead. Karel, putting the plate in the sink, said, "It's been out since last night."

"Where are your keys?"

"What?"

"The keys to your car."

"It's Gavra's car. He said only in emergencies."

"This is an emergency."

I didn't want Karel to come along, but he wouldn't give me the keys otherwise, and he insisted on driving. "You think I like your apartment that much?" he said as I took a couple of Captopril and pocketed the bottle. "I'm going stir-crazy."

Gavra's Citroën was parked just around the corner. It would have been a beautiful car had the left side not been covered in smeared red paint and the letter *M*. "Who did that?" I asked.

"Stupid drunks."

"What did it say?"

He unlocked the door. "It said 'Ministry.'"

We got in, and he started it up. "Where to, Comrade Chief?"

"To the Metropol."

He was a careful driver, slowing for each turn and stopping at all the proper places. The traffic lights were out or blinking yellow, but Karel still stopped at each empty intersection and looked both ways before driving on. It was driving me crazy. At Victory Square he leaned close to the wheel to see up the height of the Central Committee, which a banner called the Galicia Revolutionary Committee HQ. He pointed at the people loitering on the front steps with cigarettes, shivering in the cold and chatting. "You wanted to know who's running the country. There they are. Want to talk to them?"

I didn't. I'd worry about my country later. "Metropol," I repeated.

Yalta Boulevard was a mess. Damaged cars lined the road, and on the sidewalk by the Metropol entrance was a battered white Militia Karpat. Ahead, I could see number 36, where I'd found Yuri Kolev's corpse only three—three!—days ago. Now, soldiers stood around the Ministry's entrance, smoking, and young men moved in and out of the building, loading boxes of files into an army truck.

Since the curb was full, Karel parked in the road. I didn't think it mattered. At the shattered front door of the hotel, an army sergeant looked at our papers and asked our business. "I need to speak to Gisèle Sully."

He frowned. "Who?"

"She's a French journalist. I need her help in a criminal investigation."

"What kind of criminal investigation?"

I was feeling impatient, but tried not to let it show. "A murder. She may have information about the suspect."

"Why're you so vague?" said the sergeant.

"Because," I said, breathing loudly through my nose, "the murdered woman was my wife."

He blinked a few times. "Wait." He read my name again. "Brod? You're—"

"Yes. I am."

He nodded curtly. I don't know what he knew about me or my situation. Perhaps he only felt sympathy.

Once we were inside, the other soldiers ignored us, as did the journalists draped over broken furniture, a few clutching bulky cellular telephones. There were two long lines at the lobby phones, the callers up front talking quickly in various languages as they read off of notepads. Karel and I went to the front desk, where a clerk, sweaty but well maintained, was talking on another phone. He nodded at us to wait.

"Do you know this woman?" whispered Karel.

"Who?"

"This Gisèle woman. Can you recognize her?"

"I saw her on television."

She wasn't in the lobby. The clerk, who had likely been suffering through the roughest days of his professional life, didn't bother giving us a smile. "Yes?"

I showed my Militia certificate, though I didn't know if it would help. "We're looking for Gisèle Sully. French journalist. She's staying here."

"All the journalists are staying here," the clerk said as his phone rang again. He pointed off to the right. "Mademoiselle Sully is in the bar."

We followed the path of his finger down a short, carpeted passage into a bar I'd been to a few times before. Since my last visit, it had been redecorated in black leather and glass. The effect was seedy, and nothing like the labored Habsburg elegance they previously tried and failed to achieve. There were just a few customers, all foreigners, sitting with glasses of beer and wine. A table of four erupted in laugher, but Sully wasn't there. She was alone at the mirrored bar, talking quietly to the tall bartender, who didn't bother looking at us when we approached.

"Gisèle Sully?" I said.

She swiveled on her stool, clutching a glass nearly empty of red wine. She was less attractive than she'd seemed on television, or perhaps she just looked drunk. "Who's asking?"

I again showed my Militia certificate. She took it from me, tilting it in the dim light. "A chief, huh? Congratulations." She handed it to the bartender. "Is it fake, Toman?"

Toman looked at it, rubbing a thumb over the Militia seal, then handed it back to me without a smile. "It's real enough."

She looked past me at Karel, who was staring at his reflection in the mirror behind the bar. Sully said, "What can I do for you, Chief?"

"Can I buy you another?"

"Only if you join me."

I climbed on the next stool, while Karel took the seat beside me. "Three more glasses," I told the bartender, and he uncorked a bottle of dry Tokaj red. I turned to Sully. "You speak our language well."

"Flattery and wine won't get me in your bed, Chief." She sniffed. "Certainly not before you've had a bath."

I felt myself reddening. She was right; I stank. "What I mean is, you're familiar with our country. I imagine you're also familiar with our émigrés living in France."

Sully didn't bother answering. She nodded at Toman as he set down three glasses of red wine. She lifted hers. "To getting rid of the old."

Karel and I joined her toast.

She set down her glass. "I just came off a forty-eight-hour shift, and now I'm trying to drink myself to sleep. Don't be surprised if I'm not much help."

"I understand," I said. "We've had a hard time ourselves."

"I bet you have," she said. "It's amazing the things I've seen in the last two days. I try to put them into words, but they just can't fit. You've got men shooting into crowds and other men in the army fighting demonstrators, then changing sides. The funny thing is, I've seen more dead women than anything else."

I remembered the dead woman we'd seen yesterday morning.

Sully raised her glass again. "To men."

I let her drink that toast alone, but Karel joined her. I think he just wanted the wine. I took out Michalec's 1979 visa photo. "I'm looking for information on this man, Jerzy Michalec. Do you know of him?"

She lowered her glass slowly, then sighed. "I'm beginning to doubt you're just a little policeman, Chief. What do you care about émigrés? That sounds like a question straight out of the Ministry for State Security."

"Want to see my badge again?"

"Come on," she said. "If you were Ministry, you could get one of those, no problem."

I turned to the bartender, who was leaning on the counter, listening to everything. "Do you have any copies of *The Spark*?"

That seemed to confuse him. He straightened and looked around. "I don't know."

"Yesterday's," I said. "It has to be yesterday's."

He disappeared behind the counter, going through a shelf of old newspapers. He reappeared holding crumpled pages. "Here."

I found the front page and flattened it on the bar. Rings of moisture bled through the picture of my demolished Mercedes. "There," I said. "Read."

Sully leaned closer and squinted, mouthing the words to herself. Partly to avoid looking at the picture again, I opened my certificate and placed it beside the paper. She saw my name in the article, then compared it to my certificate. She sat back.

"Hey," she said, almost tenderly. "I'm sorry about your wife."

"Thank you."

"But Michalec has nothing to do with those Patak revolutionaries. They're their own band of renegades. They don't take orders from anyone."

I shook my head and tapped the paper. "*This* is a lie. They had nothing to do with the murder. It was Jerzy Michalec and someone named Rosta Gorski."

"Gorski?" she said, surprised.

"You know him?"

"Why would Michalec and Gorski kill your wife?"

"Because they were trying to kill me." I said this with enough conviction that Karel, behind me, cleared his throat nervously. "Please," I said. "I need you to tell me about them."

Sully looked at the bartender, then grabbed her bulky leather purse and said, "Let's get a table."

We went to a U-shaped booth beside a tinted window that looked out onto Yalta Boulevard. An army truck rolled past, the one I'd seen being filled with Ministry files. Sully went into the booth first, and we sat on either side of her. She was either drunk or trusting—she didn't seem to feel trapped by us.

"I know Jerzy Michalec," she said. "I met him in Paris at one of those émigré conferences a few years ago. Eighty-six. He spoke better French than half of them, so he became an unofficial spokesman for his group, Le Comité de la Galicie. The Galicia Committee. They added 'revolutionary' to their name only recently."

"What did they do?" asked Karel.

She looked at him. "Hard to tell. Largely, they networked with other émigrés around the world. They weren't as vocal as, say, the Palestinian émigrés, but they had good contacts in the French and American governments. Their public persona was gentle. They raised money for orphans and lobbied to have Pankov cut off from the international community. And they succeeded in that. Jerzy always told me their final aim was the usual rigmarole—democracy and freedom—but gradually. Before this year, before the Berlin Wall, they never advocated revolution. I think that was Rosta's doing."

"Rosta Gorski," I said.

She nodded. "Berlin, Prague, Budapest—seeing those, he felt revolution here was inevitable. So they started smuggling people into the country last month to establish networks. Set up printing presses. That sort of thing."

I sat back and watched her a moment. "Gorski was a farmer. He was just a kid who got into trouble now and then drinking. Then he left, with Michalec, in 1979. Did they know each other?"

Sully looked surprised. "You don't know?"

"Know what?"

"Rosta Gorski is Jerzy Michalec's son."

"S-son?" I stuttered, not unlike Tomiak Pankov during his final rally.

Sully shook her head. "No, you didn't know."

The pork and cabbage in my stomach began to make noises. Far back, in 1948, trying to convince me to stop looking into his past, Michalec had said, *We don't make the rules. Others make the rules. We can only try to live by them.*

This personal logic had led him to the Gestapo, where he was awarded for his enthusiastic executions of Russians, British, and French. Then, in crumbling Berlin, he became a Soviet war hero by killing those twenty-three *Hitlerjugend* boys who'd been put under his command, boys who trusted him. After the war, it justified him killing Lena's husband, Janos, and then kidnapping Lena herself.

Michalec had learned sometime early in his miserable life that he would be best served by bending with history. He wasn't alone in this—most people are this way—but unlike others, he was willing to kill any number of people to achieve his aims.

Now, he had produced an heir.

I said, "How?"

"How, what?"

Not even I was sure what I was asking. How did he make a son? How did Gisèle Sully know this for sure? I shook my head. "They have different last names. Why?"

She sipped her wine, then shrugged, as if the world hadn't just changed again. "I never met Rosta, but he talked about this in an interview in *Le Monde*. His father was released from political prison in 1956. They opened the gate and told him to leave. No money, just the rags on his back. Jerzy went on foot and made it to some village around Stryy, where Irina Gorski, a widow, took him in. One thing led to another, and . . ." She shrugged. "But Jerzy left. He didn't know Irina was pregnant. Years later, she died, and he came to her funeral. And there was Rosta."

"She died in seventy-nine," I said. "That's more than twenty years. What was Michalec doing all that time?"

"Agitating, as they say. He worked in the underground, making pamphlets, running meetings. You know."

"But that's not true," I said. "His son doctored his files, so that it looks that way, but it's a fabrication."

She put her sharp chin in her palm. "Can you prove it?"

I thought about the files on my bedroom floor, then shook my head. "Not yet. Tell me more."

She glanced at Karel, who also had his elbow on the table, chin in his palm. He seemed mesmerized by Sully. She put down her hand. "So Jerzy and Rosta started sending in people to network. I imagine they could have contacted that group over in Sárospatak. Perhaps they even convinced them to start their protests over that priest, Meyr."

I shook my head. "I know the head of that group. He's an old friend. And he's not the type to take orders from émigrés, no matter how convincing they are."

"No matter how much money they offered? Remember, they have access to a lot."

I didn't really know. Ferenc and his friends certainly could have used some money to keep their printing presses going.

She said, "By the time the revolution started in earnest in Sárospatak, the Galicia Revolutionary Committee was in the Capital, waiting for its moment. Thursday night it came."

My stomach was bad and my headache was returning. Karel reacted before I could. "You're saying the Galicia Revolutionary Committee is run by these guys? The ones who killed Emil's wife?"

"They're running the country," I said.

Karel shook his head as if he weren't understanding. "But everyone knows the revolution came out of Patak. Everyone. They're not going to listen to a bunch of people who've spent the last ten years in Paris!"

Karel's naïveté was actually very charming, but he did have a point. I remembered the phone call I'd made from the post office. "The Committee didn't start the revolution in the Capital either." I stopped short of saying I'd started it.

Sully considered this, then spoke slowly, as if national politics were just a little beyond us. "By now, it doesn't matter who brought down Tomiak Pankov. The Galicia Revolutionary Committee has control of both your television stations and is printing half the newspapers. They don't need to prove anything to anyone. It's done."

"No," I said, but the burden of Lena's death was still making me stupid. "It's not finished."

"Have you been reading *The Telltale*?"

"What's that?"

Karel said, "It's one of the new papers. I saw it on TV."

Sully confirmed this with a nod. "Yesterday, *The Telltale* reported that on Thursday night President George Bush of the United States was the first world leader to telephone and congratulate the Galicia Committee on its success. France recognized the new government soon afterward. Same with the United Kingdom. The fight's over." She shrugged again, and I found her blasé attitude infuriating. "There's only one question now."

"What's that?" said Karel, more interested than I was.

"Where are Tomiak and Ilona Pankov?"

EIGHTEEN

•

As he was led past other classrooms, Gavra peered through an open door to where two men sat opposite one another at a table, scribbling on sheets of paper. One was fat, with a black beard, while the other was thin and very erect. That second man was Andras Todescu, Tomiak Pankov's personal advisor.

Gavra turned to Michalec. "You had Todescu all along."

The old man glanced back at the classroom. "You can't do this sort of thing without help."

"Todescu convinced Pankov to call the rally and speak at it."

Michalec shrugged.

Then Gavra's scalp went cold, because he'd just made a second, more important connection. "Todescu would've left with the Pankovs on that helicopter. If he's here, then . . ." He couldn't finish the sentence. It explained the look of fear he saw in all these officers' faces. "You've got the Pankovs."

They reached the end of the corridor, and Balínt put his hand on a set of double doors but didn't open it because Michalec had stopped and turned to face Gavra. He pursed his lips and crossed them with his left index finger, a gesture of silence.

They stepped out into the early morning cold. A wind raged across the barracks, where jeeps and trucks were parked in a disorderly fashion and freezing guards with Kalashnikovs paced along the high stone wall. Out here, the barracks seemed to be going through a regular, quiet day, but the guards were alert, peering often through small steel doors in the wall. The cold bore through Gavra's paint-stained coat.

They took a covered walkway down the edge of the building and through another door to where it was again warm, and thick with moisture. "They still haven't fixed that radiator," said Michalec.

Balínt grunted some kind of agreement.

The steel doors here were small and unlabeled, with locks on the outside and barred windows to see inside. At the far end of the narrow passageway stood two guards who stiffened as they approached. "How are they?" Michalec asked the younger of the two, a corporal.

"She's sleeping," said the corporal. The fear Gavra had sensed in the officers was all over this boy's face. "He wants his insulin."

Michalec nodded, and the two guards stepped to the opposite wall so the visitors could better reach the locked door. Michalec peered through the bars, nodded, and stepped back. "Go ahead," he said.

Even knowing what he would see couldn't prepare Gavra for the shock. He leaned close, blinking in the musty darkness of the cell, and found President Tomiak Pankov, the Astrakhan hat still on his head, sitting on a cot, wrapped in an officer's greatcoat. That famous face stared back at him with angry pink eyes.

Nearly all Gavra's life, this man had been the Great Leader. He was too young to have known the exhilaration of Pankov's predecessor, Mihai. For him, there was only Pankov and the many names he went by, titles that by now seem ludicrous but once meant something grand:

> General Secretary and President
> The Conductor
> The First Worker of the Country
> The Architect

That reliable leader and father and friend of young people

The Sweet Kiss of the Land

Our Polar Star

The Lighthouse

A man like a fir tree who is the sacred oak of our glory

The mountain that protects the country

A well of living water

Then the Great Leader spoke. "Don't look at me like I'm a fucking animal. *Cretin.*"

Gavra remembered that hunting trip in the Carpathians, and the boisterous, deluded, but in the end strangely endearing man who hunted with the aid of expert sharpshooters, perhaps the same sharpshooters who now ran across rooftops, firing into crowds.

"Well?" said Pankov. His voice was sharp and dry. "I need my diabetes medicine, and both of us need real food!"

In the other cot, covered in layers of gray army blanket, Ilona Pankov stirred at the noise. Her husband lowered his voice to a high whisper. "Find my chef—I'm on a diet prescribed by my doctor."

Gavra couldn't take it anymore. He straightened and stepped back, involuntarily wiping his eyes. The small passageway was blurry, and he was having trouble getting air.

"You'll get over it," Michalec told him.

"What are you feeding him?"

"Army rations. It's what we all eat."

"Get me out of here."

"Don't have any questions for the Sweet Kiss of the Land?"

"Please," said Gavra.

"Come on."

Outside, he couldn't feel the cold anymore. He leaned over a low shrub bordering the walkway, breathing heavily.

"You had to see that," Michalec said with a tone of sympathy. "It had to be done."

Gavra wiped his mouth but didn't rise. "Why?" Michalec didn't answer, so he turned to look up at him. "Why did I have to see them?"

"Because," said Michalec, as if the question were a surprise, "you're the one who's going to execute them."

NINETEEN

•

I don't know if Gisèle Sully believed me or if, as a good journalist, she just smelled a story, but she suddenly raised her hand, called to the bar, and asked Toman to make her a double espresso. As he worked on it, she said, "What're you planning to do?"

"All I can do. Find Rosta Gorski and Jerzy Michalec."

"Okay," she said, nodding. "I'm coming with you."

"No, you're not. I'm not getting you killed."

"The snipers are few and far between now, and no one's going to kill a foreign journalist. They need us."

Karel made a noise, and we turned to him. "What about Gavra?" he said.

I'd forgotten.

"Gavra Noukas?" said Sully.

We stared at her. "You know him?"

She shook her head. "Not really. Yesterday, he ran in here like a madman. You saw that car by the front door? That was him. He drove up during the battle with the snipers." She reached into her purse, pulled out an envelope filled with photographs, and started going through them. "Here." She handed one over. "He wouldn't talk to anyone, just ran through us, but I met a soldier who knew his name, said he was Ministry. Is that true? Is he Ministry?"

It was Gavra. He looked haggard, his eyes bruised, and he was running through journalists, toward the camera. I handed the photo to Karel. "Why was he here?"

"I don't know. A few of us waited, but we never saw him leave. And the car's still on the curb."

"Oh Jesus," muttered Karel.

"Gisèle," said Toman, raising an espresso cup.

When she went to get it, Karel gripped my wrist. "Maybe he's still in the hotel."

There were other exits from the Metropol, ones that the Militia and Ministry were familiar with, and that's what I told him. I didn't tell him my deeper worry, that Gavra was still here, in one of its three hundred rooms, dead.

From the look on his face, Karel had found that possibility on his own. "You think he's all right?"

"He can take care of himself."

"I need to look. He might need my help."

"Okay," I said. "You stay here, but I need to go. All right?"

I was pleased that he agreed to this. He handed over the car keys. I slipped them into my coat pocket, beside Gavra's Makarov. "But take care of it," he said. "Gavra will be pissed if it doesn't come back in one piece."

Sully was impressed by the Citroën. She asked about the paint on the side, but I didn't bother answering. "We going to the Central Committee Building?" she asked.

"Unless you've got a better idea."

She didn't. As I drove, she took out a handheld tape recorder, pressed RECORD, and held it between us. "You're a Militia chief, then?"

"Yes," I said, then remembered the truth. "Actually, no. Yesterday was my retirement."

"Well, congratulations," she said. "How did you originally meet Jerzy Michalec?"

"Just after the war." I turned onto Victory Square. "He'd killed a songwriter, and then more people, because he was covering up his war crimes."

"*War* crimes?"

I sensed disbelief in her tone. "He worked for the Gestapo. Then, when the Soviets arrived, he killed the soldiers under his own command. That's how he became a war hero. By killing his own men." I rubbed my lip, afraid of sounding like a fanatic. "Anyway, the songwriter was blackmailing him."

"Who was the songwriter? Would I know his name?"

"No one remembers him. Janos Crowder was my wife's first husband."

She lowered the recorder as I pulled up on the sidewalk and parked at the foot of the Central Committee steps. "You're kidding."

"Wish I was."

We got out and mounted the steps as a soldier trotted down, his rifle bouncing off his backside. Before he reached us, I told Sully not to say a word.

"You shouldn't park there," he told us.

I wasn't going to be thwarted because of illegal parking. "We'll just be a minute."

"Where are you going?"

"We need to see Rosta Gorski."

"Who?"

I spelled the name for him, then showed my Militia documents, while Gisèle pulled out her camera and took a few shots of freezing smokers standing between the columns.

The soldier turned out to be more helpful than I expected. He went with us up the steps and into the vast marble entrance that was full of activity. Young men and women in wrinkled clothes walked quickly from and into marble corridors holding stacks of papers, pencils lodged behind their ears. So unlike the old days, when I'd sometimes be brought in to join a large assembly of Militia chiefs and suffer through the lecture of some Interior Ministry bureaucrat who wanted to remind us of our political responsibilities.

The soldier took us directly ahead, to where a long folding table had been set up in front of the huge marble sculpture of our national hawk, which matched the bronze hawk in the Ministry foyer.

The soldier did the talking for us, bending down to speak with a tired-looking girl in her early twenties. "These people are looking for Rosta Gorski. Any idea who that is?"

"Who are you?" she asked me.

I didn't tell her who I was, instead motioning toward my companion. "Gisèle Sully. She's a French journalist. Gorski told her to come by for an interview." Gisèle started to open her mouth, but I cut in. "I'm her translator."

"You know French?" She looked doubtful.

I didn't—German was my language—but I said, "*Oui*," with my best accent. Luckily, she didn't speak it either.

She pulled over a folder and went through a stack of pages listing names and numbers. "Here it is. Room 214." She pointed at one of the corridors. "Down there and up the steps."

I thanked her and the soldier, then took Gisèle's elbow as we walked away.

"Why'd you say that?" she said.

"What?"

"That you were my translator." She sounded insulted. "I'm fluent."

"Because I need a reason to be here, and it's better for you if they think you don't understand."

She'd been a foreign correspondent long enough to know this was true—she could listen in on what people didn't want her to hear. At the end of the corridor, we took a circular staircase to the second floor, where it was quieter. At the opposite end of this corridor, I knew, was a second exit—a service stairwell that I and the other chiefs used when we wanted to make a quick, unnoticed escape from one of the Interior Ministry lectures.

"Where's your recorder?"

She took it out of her jacket pocket.

"Just before we go inside, turn it on. Okay? But don't take it out."

She nodded, grinning vaguely. The intrigue appealed to her.

It didn't appeal to me. My heart was thumping again, loudly, and I considered taking more Captopril, but held off—I only had ten left.

Room 214 was halfway down, on the left. We paused outside the door to listen but heard nothing. I pointed at her pocket, and she reached in to turn on the recorder. Then I opened the door.

Rosta Gorski had been given an exceptional office above the fray. It was large and marbled, with antique oak cabinets and a large desk where a thirty-two-year-old, clean-shaven man with a shock of very black hair sat reading papers through bifocals propped halfway down his nose. Behind him, from high windows, you could see the entirety of Victory Square.

"Yes?" he said, looking up. He removed his glasses and squinted at me, as if he knew me but couldn't place my name.

Rather than give his memory the leisure to work up an answer, I closed the door and brought out Gavra's Makarov.

"*Merde,*" said Gisèle.

Gorski didn't seem frightened by the gun. His memory caught up with events, and he raised a finger, wagging it at me. "Chief Emil Brod. You hardly look like your picture at all. It must be an old one."

"Gisèle," I said, switching to my labored English, "sit down."

"Who's she?" said Gorski, as she settled stiffly in a chair. "Do I know her?"

"I used her to get in here. She's French, doesn't understand a word we're saying."

"That's good," said Gorski, then smiled at Gisèle and said something in French about me being crazy—*fou.* He turned back to me. "Can I get a cigarette?" He motioned toward a shiny pine box on his desk.

I went to the edge of the desk and opened it. Inside were rows of

Marlboros. I chose one at random and threw it in front of him, then tossed over a pack of Metropol matches I'd grabbed from the bar.

His hands shook when he lit it, but that was more adrenaline than fear. He waved the match, making a long ribbon of smoke, then dropped it into a crystal ashtray. "What can I do for you, Emil Brod?"

"I think you have some idea."

"I have *no* idea."

I don't know what I expected from him—some eager admission of guilt, I suppose—but there are some people who can sense what you desire, and for that reason they give you the opposite. Rosta Gorski was one such person. I said, "Two weeks ago you went into the Ministry Archives with Nikolai Romek. You signed out six personnel files and one case file. You got rid of the case file and doctored the others so that no one would be able to prove that your father, Jerzy Michalec, had been a Gestapo agent."

He took a drag, blinking as smoke got into his eyes, then waved the smoke away. "Go on."

"But to ensure there were no accusations coming out of the woodwork, you proceeded to murder each person who was directly connected to that case."

"Obviously not everyone," said Gorski. His tone had cooled. "You're still alive."

"You tried but killed my wife by mistake."

Gorski blinked a few times. "*I* didn't kill anyone, Brod. And why do you think she was killed by mistake?"

I stared at him a moment, as the slow cogs of my brain refitted. I'd been staring at one thing for too long. Of course Lena was a target—Michalec had kidnapped her. She was a witness. They'd hoped we would be in the car together, or maybe hers was also wired with explosives. "But you didn't take her file. Why?"

Gorski rubbed his nostrils, wondering how much he should say. He glanced at Gisèle Sully and winked to comfort her. He said, "There was no file on Lena Brod."

"Of course there was. It was just misplaced."

He shook his head. "Her name's not even in the reference lists. She's only mentioned in your file, as your wife. Maybe *you* can explain that?"

I couldn't. I'd last seen her Militia file in 1948, just after the Michalec investigation. I'd never had a reason to look for it again.

But he was trying to distract me from what I'd come to do. I raised the pistol so that it pointed at his head. He swallowed. When I spoke, my throat was choked. "You killed my wife, or you ordered her murder. You and your father."

"If you believe that so strongly, then why haven't you shot me yet?"

"Because I want your father. You, Rosta Gorski, are nothing."

I'd judged correctly—my words stung him.

"Where is Jerzy?"

"It doesn't matter," said Gorski.

"It does. Tell me."

"Or you'll shoot me? Come on, Brod. You shoot me, and you'll be dead before you reach the square. Same with your journalist friend. And you'll never know where my father is."

Behind me, Gisèle coughed.

"You can't walk me out of here," Gorski continued. "You can't do anything. *You* may be suicidal, but you're not going to risk this woman's life as well."

It was a good try, but it wasn't true. I could put a bullet in his head, then walk out alone through the service stairwell. No matter what happened to me, Gisèle would simply stay in her chair until the soldiers arrived, then explain, in French, how I'd used her to get inside.

The desire for murder was strong, but I couldn't simply kill this man at his desk. I turned back to Gisèle and said in my stiff English, "You stay here. When they come, you tell. Tell everything what I did. In French is okay." She nodded, terrified. I added, "Don't worry," but that did nothing to allay her fear.

I walked around the desk to Gorski, who was finally showing a bit of fear. "You won't," he said, as much to convince himself as convince me.

With as much speed as my old body could muster, I moved behind him and wrapped my arm around his neck so he had trouble breathing. I, too, had trouble breathing. My pulse banged in my ears, then came that electric hum. I placed the barrel against his temple. His hands leapt up to my arm, but my grip was strong.

Close to his ear, I whispered, "I'm going to kill your father. Understand? When you see him, tell him that. Tell him that Emil Brod is going to murder him, and that's the only reason I've left his worthless son alive."

I said all this because I meant it.

Then I lowered the pistol from his temple, took aim, and shot him through the thigh.

His body convulsed. Both he and Gisèle Sully screamed at the same moment. I let go of his neck, ears humming, and watched him tumble to the floor. Blood pumped from the hole in his pants and spilled over the marble.

I made sure not to step in the blood. I was levelheaded enough to remember that. I walked, shivering, over to Sully and leaned close to her. She recoiled. Her face was pale, in shock. I whispered, "I used you to get here, but you don't know what we said. You know nothing. Remember that. It's for your own safety."

Her head jerked in a kind of agreement.

The corridor was empty, but I heard shouts from the stairwell. I ran the opposite way, slipping the gun into my coat. I glanced back as I reached the door to the service stairs. Soldiers were just arriving to save their revolutionary friend.

TWENTY

·

They brought Gavra back to the conference room and left him alone with a container of army rations. He ate it quickly—the last food he'd had was on the flight from America—but could understand why the Pankovs complained about having to eat the foul stuff. Afterward, he started to pace the length of the room and work through the immensity of what he'd been told.

But he couldn't, because it still didn't make sense. He'd been kidnapped from the Hotel Metropol in an elaborate scheme meant to place him here in order to execute the Pankovs—that in itself made no sense. With a building full of armed soldiers, they didn't need a gunman. Why Gavra?

He posed the question to Michalec two hours later when the old man unlocked the door and came in looking flushed and weak, slipping a cigarette between his dry lips.

"Why me?"

Michalec lit the cigarette and waved away scented smoke. "Why not you, Gavra?"

"Because I'm nobody. You don't even know me."

"Sure I do," said Michalec. He took a chair, grunting as he settled his bones. "You're Gavra Noukas, born in a little town outside Satu Mare, but you're estranged from your family. You don't talk to them.

I don't know why, I just know it's true. You joined the Ministry in 1973, and by the next year you were picked by then-Colonel Brano Oleksy Sev to succeed him in his post as First District Militia liaison for the Ministry for State Security, focused on the homicide department. You apprenticed with him for two years before being left on your own. You share an apartment with your good friend Karel Wollenchak, who is a line worker at the Galicia Textile Works. Not the best worker in the world, but not bad for a socialist economy."

Gavra stared into Michalec's clear blue eyes, going over each word he'd just heard. Then it hit him. "It's because you can't find Brano."

Michalec cocked his head. "What?"

"Brano Sev. He was on the list. You were going to kill him, but he's eluded you." He nodded, very sure now. "You're more scared of him than anyone else on that list. He's someone who could truly expose you."

The old man tapped some ash off his cigarette. "I think I'd worry less about your old mentor and more about your present situation."

Gavra started to see it now. "But that explains my situation, doesn't it?"

Michalec took a drag and looked at him but didn't answer.

"How, though?" Gavra started thinking aloud. "You can't find Brano and kill him; you need another way to get at him. Through me. You bring me here, get me to kill the Pankovs, and . . . and what?" His mind was working more quickly now. "How does me killing the Pankovs silence Brano Sev?"

Gavra closed his eyes and squeezed the bridge of his nose, concentrating.

"No, it won't silence Brano. But it will connect him to the murder. He was my mentor. And if you can prove that he was behind my trip to America, you can show that I've been working under his orders. That I killed Lebed Putonski for him. *Then* it would be simple to make it seem that I killed the Pankovs under Brano's orders." Gavra released his nose and looked at the old man. "You're trying to frame Brano for their murder, so you won't be responsible."

"I'm impressed," said Michalec, though he didn't seem so. He seemed bored by the discussion. "You have a fine imagination, but you've worked for too long in the Militia office. You think like a cop." He shook his head. "Why would I want to frame Brano for the murder of the Pankovs? I'd like to do it myself. I'd be a national hero."

"Again."

He raised his brows. "What?"

"You'd be a national hero again, just as you were for a few years after the war."

Michalec laughed. It was an honest laugh, devoid of bitterness. He wiped his eyes. "Trust me, Gavra. Being a war hero isn't all it's cracked up to be. I've had enough of public life. I just want to watch my family prosper, then I want to die easily."

Gavra didn't believe that, but in the end I think it was one of the few truthful things Jerzy Michalec said that week. Gavra said, "Maybe I do think like a cop. But you, Comrade Michalec, think like a Ministry official. You know that?"

Michalec seemed to find that funny. "You think so? Well, I guess it makes sense."

"How long?"

"What?"

"How long were you in the Ministry?"

Michalec considered his answer, then shrugged. "A few years in the sixties and seventies, just some minor surveillance work. But if you're feeling ambitious, you can forget it. As of yesterday, there is no record of my brief tenure with the Ministry for State Security. Nothing."

Gavra was feeling ambitious, but in a different way. He went back over his thoughts. "I may have gotten some details wrong, but I'm on the right track. You *are* trying to frame Brano. But it won't work, because I'll never kill the Pankovs."

"You might," said Michalec. "We've got your friend, you know. Karel."

"You're bluffing. He's safe."

Again, Michalec laughed, but quietly. "Bluffing was the plan. Honestly, it was. But I just got an interesting phone call. Some of our guys found Karel running around the Metropol, searching for you. He made no secret of it; he asked everyone he found, even our guys." He shook his head. "That man is very attached to you."

"Where is he?"

"Don't worry, he's fine. Karel thinks he's coming to see you." Michalec paused. "He will, won't he? He will live to see you?"

"That's up to you, I suppose."

"No, Gavra. It's up to you."

TWENTY-ONE

•

I worried about Gisèle Sully. If she followed my instructions and spoke only in French, then she would be safe. No one would assume she'd understood anything during those minutes before I shot Rosta Gorski. No one would assume I'd told her anything. But I didn't trust that she would keep her mouth shut, and that terrified me.

If she made it, though, the cassette in her pocket might bring something positive out of all this mess.

I also worried about myself. Sixty-four years is only as old as the life you live, and for too long I'd spent my days in a chair behind a desk. My heart slapped the inside of my chest as I galloped down the steel service steps; my lungs burned. But I reached the Citroën before anyone decided to start looking on other floors for me. I nodded at the soldier who'd let us in, and he said, "Where's the lovely Frenchie?"

"She decided to stay," I answered, gasping, but winked. He laughed.

I had to drive quickly. I took the turnoff that placed me on Mihai Boulevard, then crossed the Georgian Bridge, heading south past the Canal District. I could only guess how long it would take them to search the Central Committee Building, decide I wasn't there, then send out my name and description to the army units checking papers around the edge of the Capital.

By that hour—it was eleven thirty—cars had started to appear on the streets again, and I had to swerve around smoke-coughing Karpats and Trabants and Škodas while avoiding oncoming traffic. I reached the roadblock by noon, stopping behind four Karpats as the soldiers casually leaned over windows, checked papers, and chatted with pretty girls. I almost laid on the horn to hurry them up but decided against attracting attention.

When I reached the front of the line, I was faced with the same soldier who'd checked me and Agota on Wednesday, the one who had given Agota and Sanja a flirtatious smile. Having faced hundreds of faces since then, all of them much more memorable than mine, he didn't remember me. When he asked where I was going, I answered honestly. "Tisakarad and Sárospatak."

"The First City," he said.

"What?"

"First City of the Revolution. That's what they're calling Patak now."

I forced a smile. "First City it is."

He waved me on, and soon I was in the fields that lay to the south of the Capital. I wondered what would become of all this farmland, which in 1947 had been nationalized, chopped up, and given to farmers who owed half their yield to the State. By 1950, they were giving 95 percent to the State. I imagined some of the families who'd once owned all this land were still around, and soon they'd be filing claims to get it back. What would happen to the farmers who'd spent the last forty years working the soil?

That's when it came over me, and enveloped me. I pulled over on a barren patch and climbed out. Beneath my feet, frozen mud stood in ridges. I turned slowly, taking in all of it.

Shooting Rosta Gorski had cleared out a part of my head that I hadn't used, probably, since I was a child. My personal tragedy receded for a moment, and for the first time I saw that my country had become an entirely different place. It was as vast and beautiful as it

had always been; everything I knew and loved was inside its borders. But now it had changed. Maybe that's when I changed as well.
After forty years, I suddenly felt the need for all of this to survive. I
actually believed I could protect it.

It's the other reason I'm writing this.

I got back in the car and kept driving—carefully, because my eyes
kept tearing up, turning the landscape into mist. The afternoon sun
burned my roof as I crested the next hill, and the golden countryside
spread out for miles.

TWENTY-TWO

•

Michalec again left Gavra alone in the conference room, telling him to consider his options; he'd be back in a few hours. By now, Gavra had recovered fully from whatever drug they'd used to bring him here, and he was able to think through the mathematics of his situation. Escape paths.

There were none. The conference room was simple reinforced concrete, without even a vent that he could find. There was only one exit, through the locked door and past the large, gun-toting block of muscle named Balínt.

Somehow, Michalec had known that Karel was his weak point. He was the closest thing Gavra had to a family. He told me later that, despite the vigorous training he'd excelled at in the Ministry, no one had ever taught him how to let his loved ones die. He was only taught not to get himself in that kind of situation. Once there, he was in trouble.

His salvation perhaps lay in understanding why Michalec needed him to kill the Pankovs. Maybe the old man was telling the truth—he wasn't interested in framing Brano Sev for the murder—but he was certainly trying to tie Brano to it. What would that achieve?

He thought back to America. The CIA was involved with the whole operation, and that meant something. Why would the Americans care about protecting Michalec's past?

Gavra sat at the long table and rubbed his eyes. That answer was obvious.

Both the Soviet Empire and the American one worked through satellite nations. Moscow was more blatant in its aspirations, setting up puppet governments throughout Eastern Europe and in places like Afghanistan. When communist leaders came to power in Cuba or North Korea or Africa, no secret was made of the money sent pouring into their coffers.

The Americans were subtle. Their money, often passed on by the Central Intelligence Agency, was funneled to political figures they supported. People they believed would help American interests once they gained power. Rather than spreading their troops around the world—though they did that often enough—America used her great wealth to give her favored side an upper hand in any fight.

Americans had supported Solidarity in Poland and Charter 77 in Czechoslovakia—indirectly, perhaps, but there had been help. They'd found ways to stamp their support throughout the Bloc, in the hopes that once the Russians were kicked out they would have a united group of allies along Europe's eastern edge.

Gavra and the Ministry knew a fair amount about Ferenc Kolyeszar's activities, and not just from Bernard's compromised reports. The Ministry never really feared Ferenc's group, because they were cut off from the outside world. Despite some international attention, Ferenc never met with American spies or diplomats. Occasionally, French literary critics would arrive to talk to him, sometimes bringing along money buried in the false bottoms of their suitcases, but it was only enough to keep him afloat, not enough to truly threaten the government.

To the Americans, Ferenc and his people were nothing more than a rumor spread by the French. What the Americans wanted was someone they could see and hear and touch, someone who could convince them with charm. Only émigrés could do this, charming émigrés like Jerzy Michalec.

And if the Americans gave their support to Michalec over the years, might they protect their investment by killing someone on their own soil who would risk the millions they'd already spent?

Of course they would.

It made enough sense for him to back up again and whisper it aloud to see if it sounded crazy or not. "The Americans are funding Michalec's people and have helped erase Michalec's past to ensure he can come to power without resistance."

Gavra was suddenly desperate for a cigarette, but Michalec had taken his scented French packet with him. Instead, he poured more water and gulped it down.

The problem wasn't that it sounded crazy; it didn't. From an intelligence standpoint it was completely reasonable, an everyday occurrence. What disturbed him was the idea that Jerzy Michalec, a murderer and former Gestapo agent, would be elected as our country's first democratic president. That was what he couldn't take.

He heard a sound and looked up to see the door opening. He considered leaping from the chair to catch Michalec off guard, perhaps to kill him—that, at least, would save his country the trauma of having him as president.

It wasn't Michalec, though; it was Beth, smiling, followed by Harold.

"You look tense," said Beth.

"Of course he's tense," said Harold as Balínt shut the door behind them. "The man's about to become a national hero."

Despite the way this peculiar couple had tricked him, Gavra couldn't hate them. He had a feeling they were falling for a much bigger ruse.

So he stood up and gently shook Harold's hand, then kissed Beth's cheeks, which made her giggle. "No one's so polite in the States. I love being back home."

"Sit down," said Gavra.

"I told you he'd be fine," said Beth.

Harold pulled out a chair for her and winked at Gavra. "The woman's an optimist even when optimism's a fool's errand."

"Have you eaten?" asked Beth.

Gavra nodded. "I feel much better. But I'm still confused. How did the two of you end up here?"

So the story began. Their marriage was true—they'd wed in 1952 in Vranov under their real names, Heronim and Bronislawa Arondt. Soon they had two children, Oskar and Itka. "Beautiful children," said Beth. Harold squeezed her hand.

"We were just simple folk," said Harold. "I worked in a grain co-operative, and Beth in the textile factory. We raised our kids as best we could."

"But you left the country," said Gavra.

"We left because we had to," Beth said in a near-whisper.

"You're probably too young," said Harold. "You wouldn't remember what happened when Tomiak Pankov first took power in 1957."

"Tell me."

"Before then, we'd lived under Mihai." Harold smiled sadly when he said this. "Despite the fact that he was a complete bastard, the country loved him. We'd come out of a terrible war, and we were desperate for someone to look up to. He was all we had. Mihai sent his political competition to forced labor camps, but the rest of us found ways to ignore this. Beth and I were no different. We pretended there wasn't a plague in our country."

"It's what people do the world over," said Gavra.

Harold nodded seriously. "Well, then Pankov took over. He was younger, and we thought this might be a good thing. Maybe things could normalize. But we were wrong. See, he knew how much the people loved Mihai, how much support the old man had in the Central Committee, and how many other politicians had been hoping to take his place. So, very quickly, he started searching for enemies. It started in the Central Committee, and by 1958 a full third had disappeared, replaced by Pankov's automatons. Then he decided he hadn't secured his position well enough. He had to find enemies among the regular citizens. That's when the hell began for the rest of us. Ministry toughs started visiting the factories, quizzing the managers on who was dissatisfied with the government. And the managers, they knew that if they kept quiet, they'd be suspected of harboring criminals. So it soon became a quota system. In a factory of a hundred people, you've got to give at least five names; ten is better. And the manager of Beth's factory, he'd never liked Beth."

"He was a cretin," said Beth, reminding Gavra of what Tomiak Pankov had called him.

"Let's just say the man couldn't keep his hands to himself," said Harold. "Beth was something special in those days."

"Still am," said Beth.

Harold gave Gavra another wink. "Anyway, that led to visits by the Ministry. They, too, were working on a quota system. They never found anything, and that was their excuse to cart us off. We didn't have a single portrait of Tomiak Pankov in our house. We didn't buy those speeches of his they were just starting to bind and publish." He shook his head. "That made us enemies of the state."

Harold paused, then looked at his wife and squeezed her hand again. Gavra realized something. "Your children. Oskar and Itka. If you were sent to a labor camp, what happened to them?"

"Orphanage," said Beth, tears in her eyes. Her hand beneath Harold's trembled.

He didn't realize Harold was on the edge of tears, too, until the old man cleared his throat. "We were released in 1962. Four years of hard labor. Lucky to survive, we were." He swallowed. "First thing we did was try to find our kids, but it was no use. All we learned was they'd been adopted by different families. They'd been separated."

He rubbed his big nose with a knuckle. "Can you imagine? Seven and eight years old, living together all their lives, never to see each other again? The orphanage refused to tell us where they were."

"But we tried," said Beth.

"Yes. We tried for the next two years. By sixty-four we had to give up. See, we were still being harassed. I was sent away for another three months for no reason at all, and then, when I got back, I found Beth talking to a friend from that first camp. He and some more friends had hatched an escape plan. They wanted us to come along."

"That's how you got out," said Gavra.

"Broke our hearts," said Harold, "but it was the only thing we could do."

"How did you get to the States?"

Harold looked at Beth, who gave a noncommittal shrug. "Doesn't matter anymore."

Harold agreed. He turned to Gavra. "They were still keeping internment camps in Germany back then, for the occasional easterner who'd get out. We ended up at one in Frankfurt. That's where the Americans came to us."

Gavra had heard of this before. "CIA."

"Why not?" Beth said defensively. "They couldn't get their people into our country, and they've got this camp full of people who know the language and the lay of the land. Who know everything there is to know, without looking like an American spy."

"You were sent back in?" said Gavra.

Harold snorted a laugh. "I can't tell you how many times we came back here over the next decade. All the way up to détente, whatever the hell that was supposed to be." He put his hands on the table. "You should've seen us back then, Gavra. A sharp young man like yourself—I think we would've given you a run for your money. Ciphers, tooth caps full of cyanide, radio sets, and even a few disguises." He laughed. "It was a riot."

Beth wasn't laughing. "It wasn't a riot, Harold. It scared the hell out of you more than once."

Harold's smile faded, and he shrugged. He tapped his skull. "Nostalgia."

"What about your kids?"

The smile was completely gone now. He shook his head. "We tried. Every time we went back, we tried. But we never found them."

"Jerzy did," said Beth solemnly. "He tracked them down."

Harold sniffed. "Once this is over, we're going to make a couple of house calls."

It all made perfect sense now. "That's how he got your cooperation."

Beth shook her head. "We would've come anyway. This just makes it so much sweeter."

Gavra pushed his chair back and stood up. He walked to the door. Through its window he saw Balínt's wide back and, beyond, officers passing. He turned to the old couple. They would believe anything Jerzy fed them, simply for the hope of seeing their children again. He imagined similar deals had been made with the others; their enthusiasm was only partly for the Pankovs' demise. Their personal desperations were what made them hysterical.

They watched him return to his seat and lean forward, lowering his voice as he spoke. "This is more complicated than you know. Jerzy Michalec is not who you think he is. He's a murderer."

They blinked at him but didn't seem surprised.

"During the Second World War, he worked in the Gestapo. After the war, he killed others to protect this secret, and in 1949 he was convicted as a war criminal. Did you know that?"

They didn't answer at first, but from their expressions he could tell the information wasn't swaying them.

"We all make mistakes," said Beth. "Maybe this is how he's making up for his. Did you ever consider that?"

Harold nodded his agreement. It was what they both wanted to believe.

Gavra persisted. "Over the last week, he's also had five more people killed, because all of them knew about his past. One was the wife of a close friend of mine, a Militia chief."

"Brod?" said Harold. "That was the work of those anarchists in Patak."

Gavra shook his head. "No. They were scapegoats. Jerzy Michalec had her killed, and he's still after two more people: the chief himself and an old friend of mine, Brano Sev."

Simultaneously, Harold and Beth recoiled. "Brano Sev," Harold said with evident disgust.

"You know him?"

Beth looked at her husband, then rubbed his arm. Harold was reddening.

"What?" said Gavra.

"Of course we know him," Beth said coolly.

Harold patted her hand to show he was fine. "I met Brano Sev in 1965. The man tortured me."

Gavra rubbed his forehead, cursing his mistake. He should have considered this. It didn't matter, though, not anymore. "You're both part of this too, aren't you?"

They waited.

"You want me to kill the Pankovs so you can frame Brano for the murder."

Harold shook his head and pressed a finger into the tabletop, speaking defiantly. "We want you to kill the Pankovs because that's what they deserve. They took our children away and starved a beautiful country until it was ugly. I suppose you can't hear from inside this room, but there are still terrorists out on the rooftops. As long as the Pankovs are alive, they'll keep shooting innocent people. We're going to kill them and show their corpses to the whole country. We're going to bring back peace."

"But why *me*?" Gavra insisted.

Harold looked at Beth, so she answered. "We don't want just anyone to kill the Pankovs. We want someone who's spent his life serving that wretched man's interests. But not just anyone. Someone who has no political stake in the outcome."

"Which is why you can't hand a gun to Andras Todescu."

Harold nodded.

Beth said, "Brano Sev is the right man for this. If he's proven to be responsible for killing them, it will show that even the most dedicated servant couldn't take it anymore."

Harold grunted. "We're giving that bastard much more than he deserves."

"We're making him, and you, into heroes. Historians will talk highly of the two of you."

Gavra leaned back and tried to absorb this. It was hard. He traced back the steps that had brought him to this room: the trip to Virginia, the plane ride beside this couple, the phone call in the Militia office, his kidnapping, and then Karel's. It felt like too many variables at work to have been planned ahead of time, too many to be believable. Then again, it wasn't planned. Jerzy Michalec's brilliance lay in his ability to bend with situations, to quickly take into account what had changed and what should be done next. Michalec was a master at thinking on his feet.

Gavra was left in awe. Not only did this plan help assure the success of the revolution; it also assured Michalec's safety. If Brano was tied to the murder of the Pankovs, then Brano was tied to Michalec, who had captured the First Couple and arranged the execution. If, next week, Brano told the international press about Michalec's criminal history, he'd be accused of political backstabbing. There would be no evidence for him to cite, and he would be quickly marginalized. Brano Sev would become a nobody.

"You don't understand," said Gavra. "Jerzy is doing this—even *this*—to assure his past is ignored. He's doing it to assure he can become president. You're helping a murderer run our country."

Beth shook her head. "But he doesn't want to become president."

"He says that now," began Gavra, but Harold held up a finger to stop him.

"It's true," said Harold. "Jerzy wants his son to become president. He doesn't want it for himself at all."

Gavra stuttered just as Tomiak Pankov and I had stuttered. "S-son?"

"You didn't know?" said Beth. "Sweet Rosta."

"Rosta Gorski," managed Gavra.

Just then, the door opened and Michalec stepped in. "I think my son's ears are burning!"

The Atkinses laughed.

TWENTY-THREE

•

I reached Tisakarad a little after two. The low winter sun tried to break through gray clouds, and trees in the fields around me made bleak shadows. The Citroën's heater had started sputtering halfway through the journey, then died soon after. I'd zipped up my coat against the cold, but my fingers felt like ice. I took two Captopril, then turned off a side road before the city limits, following a bumpy path through fields and taking more turns past the cooperative offices that ruled over the farms in the northeastern quadrant outside Tisakarad. I soon reached the Kolyeszar farmhouse.

When Ferenc was shipped off to a labor camp in Vátrina in 1956, charged with treason, Magda brought little Agota out to the countryside. They waited for him in her parents' Pócspetri farmhouse.

I was the one who picked him up from Work Camp #480 upon his release early the next year, and I remember being shocked by his appearance. He was a lice-ridden skeleton, covered in sores, and seemed in a perpetual state of shock. I probably wasn't much help, as Lena had just suffered her first miscarriage, but I took him to a Vátrina hotel where he washed and ate and dressed in fresh clothes Magda had given me to bring along. By the time I got him to the Pócspetri farmhouse, he was just starting to become human again.

That was a long time ago. Since then, Magda's parents had died, and they'd been transferred to this smaller farmhouse in Tisakarad. While tending his hectares of apple orchards, Ferenc had produced a series of samizdat novels that over the years, and largely by the work of Georgi Radevych (during his sober hours), found their way westward. By the midseventies, French papers were writing about this "genius" living behind the Iron Curtain, whose books could not be published at home. That was true, but the crudely bound manuscripts still found their way into our hands. I'd read all five of his books and was always deeply impressed by my friend.

When I parked in front of the house, next to the Russian flatbed, the door opened, and Magda came out holding a Kalashnikov rifle. The sight stunned me. "Get out!" she shouted.

"It's me!" I called, rolling down the window so she could hear. "Emil!"

She lowered the rifle, confused. "Emil? Where'd you get that car?"

I climbed out and went over to hug her, but the Kalashnikov kept getting in the way, so I gave up. "Jesus, Magda. That's some firepower."

"This?" She took it off her shoulder and looked at it. "No bullets. But it's still scary, isn't it?"

"You're alone?"

"Everyone's in Patak making trouble. With the roads the way they are, it's an hour each way, but they seem to think it's worth it."

I gave a hug another try, pressing into her gray hair that had once been so dark and rich. She squeezed me tight, whispering, "I'm sorry about her." She kissed my cheek hard, then pulled back to look into my face. "How're you dealing?"

"Not well," I said, because it was true.

"It's only been a couple of days."

That was also true, but my sense of time was all wrong. It felt as if Lena had been killed just a few hours ago, but with everything that had happened since then, it seemed that a month must have passed. I think that's what happens when you go mad. Time stops agreeing.

Magda and Lena had never been particularly close, despite Fe-renc's and my efforts. We stuck them in the same room during visits, while we stepped onto the back porch to drink beer and reminisce, with plenty of lies, about the old days in the Militia. The women suffered each other, but I knew that Magda had always found Lena an unbearable snob, and Lena often told me what a prole Magda was. *But what can you expect from a farm girl?*

Despite this, I was always fond of Ferenc's wife. Like anyone else, they had their problems, and during that nasty year, 1956, they nearly divorced. I was glad they hadn't.

She boiled tea in the kitchen, whispering because Sanja was asleep in the bedroom. I watched her move instinctively between the stove and the cabinets; she'd gained weight, but on her it looked like health.

"What're they doing in Patak?"

"Getting things working again. It's a real chore."

"Isn't there help from the Capital?"

She grunted as she poured my cup. "The Galicia Committee? They've got their hands busy getting the Capital in working order. And the snipers." She paused. "Did you see any?"

"I saw some of their work."

"Oh."

She told me that after the massacre on Wednesday night, the only violent deaths in Sárospatak had been Tatiana Zoltenko and, on Thursday evening, Mayor Natan Pankov. I hadn't heard.

"It was a mob. Hundred or so people. Broke into his place up in the Castle District. Didn't touch the wife or any of his three kids, though—I suppose that's something—but they got hold of him and dragged him out into the street and beat him to death, then hung his body up on a lamppost so everyone could see." She set the cups down and settled opposite me. "Some miserable stuff. But I guess it's to be expected. No one else dead that I've heard of. And last night, the army officially announced it was with us."

"No Russians?"

She shook her head. "Ferenc was terrified they'd show up in army uniforms and start shooting, but it didn't happen. That guy they found before, Malevich—there's been no sign of him since." Magda peered into her cup. "You going to tell me?"

"Tell you what?"

"It's all over the news, you know. Rosta Gorski and that woman."

I knew there would be some report on Gorski's shooting, but I didn't know if they'd use my name. Then her words sank in. "What woman?"

"The Frenchwoman. They say you shot her."

My hand jerked, and I spilled my tea. "Gisèle Sully? Is she all right?"

"They say you killed her."

"No!" The word came out involuntarily, then I had trouble breathing. "She had nothing to do with it!"

Magda looked at the puddle of tea on the floor, then at me. She spoke calmly. "I don't know, Emil. I'm just telling you what they said. They said you kidnapped her and tried to kill Rosta Gorski. You only got him in the leg, but on the way out you shot and killed this Sully woman."

I got up. My knees weren't working right, and I nearly fell, but I used the wall to right myself and walked out the back to the screened-in porch, then through the door onto the cold, hard earth. The Captopril wasn't doing its job; I could feel every one of my stiff veins. I paced for a while in the fresh darkness, my anger building, and when Magda came out, holding my coat, I could tell she was very uncomfortable.

"I didn't shoot her," I said, "but I did trick her. I'm the reason she's dead."

Magda didn't speak, just handed me the coat and waited.

I was crying again. "I used her to get into the Central Committee Building because I wanted to kill Rosta Gorski. He and his father killed Lena." I looked at her; she was blurry through my tears. "You understand? But I couldn't do it. I couldn't just kill the man. So I made sure Gisèle was safe and I put a bullet in Gorski's leg because I had to do something. Anything. And now"—I turned away from her steady gaze—"now she's dead, too."

Lena was right—Magda was a prole. But Lena never understood what a good thing this could be. The proles of the world understand misery. They know misery because it comes to visit every day. Magda knew it had to be kicked, and kicked hard, before it would leave.

She grabbed my shoulders. "You're right, Emil. She's dead because of you. You screwed up. Right?"

I nodded like a weepy child.

"Now cry and then get over it. Figure out what you did wrong and make sure you don't do it again."

She spoke with such sternness and strength that I was almost frightened of her.

"I'm going inside to make dinner. When you've figured it out, come in and eat. But I don't want you inside until you've figured it out."

I nodded.

"Because my family's here. If you fuck up again, and someone I love is killed, I will kill you without hesitation. You understand?"

I blinked at her. She meant it, and she was right to mean it. "Okay," I said breathlessly.

She gave me a soft pat on the cheek. "I don't want to kill you, Emil Brod, because I love you, too. Don't make me do something I'll regret."

Then she went inside to make her family dinner.

An hour later I was still outside, freezing, when I heard the others arrive in the coughing Militia Karpat Bernard had stolen from the station. I'd figured out my mistake, just as Magda had ordered, but didn't come in because I had more to face. Lena's death was also my fault. While I had killed Gisèle Sully by using the poor woman to get my revenge, I had killed Lena by not taking care of Jerzy Michalec back in 1948. I could have, but the fact was that I'd never been the kind of man who could simply commit murder. It's much more difficult than pulp novels make it out to be.

That was my real mistake. Had I been a stronger man and killed him in 1948, there would have been no son to shoot in the leg, and Lena, Gisèle, and the others from that list would still be alive.

I heard the screen door open. Ferenc lumbered through the darkness toward me. He had a solemn expression on his face; I didn't know if it was because of Lena or because Magda had discussed her threat to kill me.

No. She was too much of a prole to talk about what didn't need to be said.

"Mag tells me this Rosta Gorski's responsible for Lena."

"Him and his father."

"Father?"

"Jerzy Michalec."

Ferenc frowned, then remembered. He'd been around that year, but we weren't close yet, and what he knew of that case was hearsay, much of it rehashed from our nostalgic beers on his back porch.

He put a heavy hand on my shoulder. He was going through mixed emotions—a revolt he'd put the last ten years of his life into had come to fruition, and that ecstatic joy was running head-on into Lena's death and my depression. "Well, then," he said, "let's go get the bastard." It was all he could think of to say.

I shook my head. "You're busy enough. Besides, I don't want anyone else dying."

"Take Bernard. He's a lousy son-in-law anyway."

He seemed to be smiling in the darkness, but it was hard to tell.

"Did you ever tell Magda or Agota about him?" I said. "About those Ministry reports?"

"No. We came to our agreement, and he stuck to it."

"Good." That's when I noticed my teeth were chattering.

"Come inside," said Ferenc. "It's freezing out here."

* * *

Halfway through the pork Magda had baked with apples, Ferenc shook his head at what I'd been telling him. "That's impossible. We own the town now, and the whole country looks to Patak for direction. They're not looking to the Capital anymore."

"You're being naive," said Bernard. Sanja was propped on his knee while Agota, beside him, fed the child soft apple mush. "All you've seen is Patak, day after day. There's a lot more country than that town. And they're watching television. Television comes from the Capital." He shrugged. "It just makes sense."

I didn't want to press the point, because Ferenc was already frustrated being put in his place by his son-in-law. He poked a fork around his plate. "You think it's true what they said in that paper?"

"What did they say?"

"That the Americans have recognized the Galicia Committee?"

I nodded. "Gisèle Sully believed it. I trusted her."

"Even if it's a lie," said Magda, "it makes no difference."

Ferenc glared at her. "Of course it makes a difference!"

She smiled at her husband. "You know better than that. If they announce to a whole country that President Bush is behind them, then President Bush would look like a coward if he said he never made the phone call. Particularly after the lie encouraged France and England to follow suit." She shook her head. "No, the Americans aren't going to be the last ones to congratulate the revolution they've been pushing us to make the last forty years."

"The Soviets still haven't recognized the committee," said Agota, grinning close to Sanja's face.

"Of course they haven't," said Ferenc. "They're trembling in their boots."

"They're not," I said, then told them about the secret telegram I'd found in Romek's house. "Pankov thought they were behind the revolution. They said they weren't, but they also refused to help put it down."

That earned a collective moment of silence, as each person read-justed his position in regard to Moscow.

After dinner, Agota took me to the guest bedroom and showed me endless black-and-white photographs she'd taken of the revolution in Sárospatak: candlelight vigils in 25 August Square; dark faces lit from below; men climbing on statues; lone fists in the air; young people on tanks and facing lines of soldiers; abandoned Kalash-nikovs on a sidewalk; blurry shots of panic during the massacre; women crying with bloodstained hands; a dead man surrounded by furious demonstrators; an empty 25 August Square, littered with lost hats, shirts, a shoe, and splashed with blood.

Going through them was like reading a story I hadn't been around to witness. Frozen instants from events that were defined by their very motion. They didn't seem to do the revolution justice, but what could?

"Here," she said and passed over a series of large color photo-graphs of an old, bald man in an Italian suit, sitting with one leg crossed over a knee, looking sternly, then smiling, at the camera. It was Tomiak Pankov. Those final portraits of the man are now fa-mous and have been seen in so many newspapers that they've lost their effect. But that evening, seeing them for the first time, I was in shock. Unlike the kinetic shots of the revolution, these were immo-bile, stolid. Pankov was a statue that no amount of wind or rain could damage. He was eternal.

I lost my breath just looking at them and had to turn the photo-graphs facedown against the pillows. I sat on the edge of the bed and rubbed my face. Agota settled beside me and rubbed my back, then held on to me. She could tell I needed it.

TWENTY–FOUR

•

Harold and Beth showed Gavra more smiles when they left, and Beth leaned her frail body down to kiss his cheeks. Even Michalec smiled as he followed them out and locked the door. Gavra was again alone.

Around ten in the evening, he noticed increased activity out in the corridor. His guard had been changed, and though the new one wasn't as large as Balínt, he was still a significant chunk of man. Gavra peered over his shoulder to see soldiers carrying electronic equipment in the direction of the classrooms. Microphones, video cameras, power cables. He wondered if all this was for him, for the single act of pointing a gun at an old couple and killing them.

Whether or not the Pankovs deserved it, Gavra was still unwilling to pull the trigger. But Michalec had been right—you give a man enough time, and he stops reacting instinctively to a proposition. He has hours to turn it over in his head, examine the pros and cons, and measure the repercussions of the threat to kill his best friend.

Gavra had met Karel Wollenchak in September of 1980, through one of his cases. Someone in Karel's building who wanted Karel's apartment had been meticulously fabricating evidence to suggest that he was in contact with spies from West Germany. Gavra was called in to examine the evidence and soon saw through the pitiful attempt. A year later, he had joined Karel in the apartment, which had once been owned by Karel's grandmother.

Though he never introduced me to his friend, I could tell when I first saw them together at my apartment that they were very close. When men make close friendships over the years, and particularly when they live together, the bond can be similar to that of a romantic relationship. Your friend becomes your other half; you begin to share weaknesses and strengths; you suddenly can't imagine your life without the other person.

That's what Gavra felt as he considered the possibility that Karel would be murdered if he didn't go through with the executions.

I go into all of this because it's vital that people understand why Gavra Noukas did what he did. He was not serving the interests of Jerzy Michalec, Rosta Gorski, or the Galicia Revolutionary Committee. What he ended up doing, he did for his own reasons, and for the good of others.

But he still wasn't convinced. Weighing the fate of his closest friend against the fate of the country was not enough to set his mind in any one direction. He needed to know more. He needed to see, hear, and feel more to decide what to do. Jerzy Michalec knew this.

That's why, at midnight, as the racket in the corridor reached its peak and he heard the faint beat of helicopter blades outside, the new guard opened his door, and Michalec stepped in.

"Come on, Gavra." He held out a hand, waving to lead him on. "There's something I want you to see."

24 DECEMBER 1989
SUNDAY
·

TWENTY-FIVE

•

He led Gavra down the corridor, which by now had become one-way. Everyone rushing with files, papers, and cameras followed the same path toward the classrooms.

"You only want me to *see* something?" said Gavra.

"For now, yes. By the way, you'll be happy to know Karel's doing fine. He's agitated, for sure. Keeps asking where you are. But he's safe, has a soft bed and food."

"Where? Here?"

"An apartment. Somewhere."

Gavra imagined a cramped tenement bedroom, Karel terrified, sitting on the edge of a bed, while in the living room a man cleaned his pistol and watched television, waiting for a phone call.

"But all isn't roses," said Michalec, his tone suddenly changing. "Seems your friend Emil Brod has shot my son."

Gavra stopped and stared at him. "Is he dead?"

Michalec shook his head. "Not a fatal shot. He'll be fine, though he'll probably walk with a limp the rest of his life." He paused. "Any idea where Brod is now? We're having a hell of a time tracking him down."

It pleased him that I'd put a bullet in Rosta Gorski. "I'm surprised he didn't kill your son. The man's responsible for Lena's death."

Michalec waved him on and, before they reached the room, ad-mitted that he was surprised as well. "But it turns out Brod goes in for theater. He told Rosta that the bullet was part of a message. The message is that he's going to come after me. And kill me. Think I should be scared?"

"I think you should be very scared."

"Thought you'd say that." Michalec winked and placed a hand on Gavra's shoulder. "Let's go inside."

This classroom was larger than the others, probably for meetings where the entire barracks needed to listen. The walls were yellow and hadn't been washed in some time, and on the ceiling two incan-descent bulbs flickered. There were no children's desks here, just rows of metal folding chairs where people—some in uniform, some not—were settling down and chatting in a steady murmur. The chairs faced the end of the long room where three tables were set up, each with a single microphone. The table against the back wall had three empty chairs. The one against the left wall had two chairs, and oppo-site, against the right wall, was another table with two chairs. In these chairs sat Tomiak and Ilona Pankov, a Kalashnikov-toting guard on either side.

"It's a trial," Gavra said involuntarily.

"There's a new thing called due process," whispered Michalec, guiding him to a chair in the back. "It's all the rage in America."

Ilona Pankov, wrapped in a fur coat with a white babushka over her hair, looked cold in this unheated room. Her nose was red, and she clutched a handkerchief against her hollow cheek, sometimes rubbing her nostrils. Tomiak Pankov, in the greatcoat that was a few sizes too large, didn't seem to mind the cold. He sat stiffly in his chair, arms folded over his chest, looking around. He sometimes leaned over to whisper to Ilona, who nodded vigorously and fol-lowed the finger he used to point out people he recognized. Their disgusted expressions made no attempt to hide their feelings.

Against the two side walls a few soldiers stood with wheeled metal racks holding recording equipment connected to two video cameras on tripods. The cameras each faced the side table against the opposite wall. There was no camera pointing at the table against the rear wall, presumably the bench.

The front row of chairs was filled with a mix of young people and the senior citizens he'd seen earlier. Beth and Harold were among them, whispering excitedly. Some sat straight and stared bitterly at the Pankovs.

Suddenly, Pankov stood and pointed across to the door, shouting, "Traitor!"

Gavra turned; it was Andras Todescu. The ex-presidential advisor reddened, then quickly came over to Michalec, crouching to the old man's ear. "They're ready," Todescu whispered.

"Good," said Michalec. "Send them in. I'm sick of waiting."

Todescu left again. Up front, Pankov was shaking his guard's hand off his shoulder and sitting down on his own.

Behind Gavra, three officers—two colonels and a lieutenant general—entered and walked around the edge of the chairs toward the table at the end of the room. A soldier switched on the video camera that faced the Pankovs. The couple whispered animatedly, shaking their heads, but the crowd was silent, watching the men approach the bench and stand behind their chairs. The lieutenant general, in the center, spoke, his voice sounding strained and awkward. "I call this session of the trial of Tomiak and Ilona Pankov to order." Then he patted his damp forehead with the back of his hand. The man was terrified.

Before the lieutenant general could continue, Tomiak Pankov leaned forward and spoke loudly. "I only recognize the Grand National Assembly. I will only speak in front of it." He planted his fist on the table to punctuate his statement, and Gavra could see his wife rubbing his knee under the table in encouragement.

Pankov was ignored.

A young man in the front row stood, shaking his head, and turned to look at the audience. He wore an elegant Western suit and held an open notepad. "In the same way he refused to hold a dialogue with the people," he said, glancing at his notes, "now he also refuses to speak with us."

It all sounded very rehearsed to Gavra.

"He always claimed to act and speak on behalf of the people, to be a beloved son of the people, but he only tyrannized the people all the time." This, then, was the prosecutor. He examined his notes again. "You are faced with charges that you held sumptuous celebrations on all holidays at your house. The details are known. These two defendants," he said, motioning toward them with a broad sweep of his hand, "procured the most luxurious foodstuffs and clothes from abroad. They were even worse than the king, the former king. The people received only two hundred grams per day, and only with an identity card."

"Eating," muttered Ilona Pankov, loud enough for everyone to hear. "Is that what they're accusing us of?"

The prosecutor stopped in the center of the floor—outside the reach of the camera, Gavra noticed—and pointed at them. "These two defendants have robbed the people, and not even today do they want to talk. They are cowards. We have data concerning both of them. I ask the chairman of the prosecutor's office to read the bill of indictment."

Another man in the front row—tall, lanky, with coarse cheeks and mouth—stood and read directly from his pages, without flourish or any hint of showmanship. His voice, like that of the president of the court, quivered. "Esteemed chairman of the court, today we have to pass a verdict on the defendants Tomiak Pankov and Ilona Pankov, who have committed the following offenses: crimes against the people. They carried out acts that are incompatible with human dignity and social thinking; they acted in a despotic and criminal way; they destroyed the people whose leaders they claimed to be—"

"Is this a joke?" said Ilona as Tomiak squeezed his arms tighter across his chest.

The chairman of the prosecutor's office paused, then continued. "Because of the crimes they committed against the people, I plead, on behalf of the victims of these two tyrants, for the death sentence for the two defendants. The bill of indictment contains the following points: genocide, in accordance with Article 356 of the penal code—"

Perhaps it was the mention of the death sentence that drew Tomiak Pankov's head up and made his wife briefly cover her eyes.

"Two," continued the chairman of the prosecutor's office. "Armed attack on the people and the state power, in accordance with Article 163 of the penal code. The destruction of buildings and state institutions, undermining of the national economy, in accordance with Articles 165 and 145 of the penal code. They obstructed the normal process of the economy."

"You don't even know what *normal process of the economy* means," hissed Ilona Pankov.

The prosecutor, who had remained standing, crossed his own arms over his chest and turned to them. "Did you hear the charges? Have you understood them?"

"I won't answer," said Tomiak Pankov. "I will only answer questions before the Grand National Assembly. I do not recognize this court." He leveled a stiff finger at the prosecutor. "The charges are incorrect, and I will not answer a single question here."

"Note," said the prosecutor, raising his own finger. "He does not recognize the points mentioned in the bill of indictment."

Gavra squeezed his hands between his knees to stop them trembling. He's since tried to explain it to me, but I honestly can't imagine what it was like to be in that room, watching this display. People in other countries might compare it to having their president or prime minister prosecuted and sitting in the courtroom aisle and watching, but that's nothing. In those countries average citizens speak daily about how their leaders should be put in jail. They openly say that they would be happy to turn the lock on their cell and would voluntarily keep guard. Those are entirely different places.

Tomiak Pankov was a man whose portrait graced the walls of every public building and many private homes. His volumes of collected speeches were de rigueur purchases. Four times a week, documentaries praising the life and life-works of this peacemaker and friend of the environment were aired on television. We knew everything about him, from his humble beginnings on a farm outside Uzhorod to the boxes full of medals he'd received from the queen of England, from America, from African countries only we had heard of, because by then they were our only allies.

And when the food shortages began, when the Maternity Laws came into effect, when the petrol and coffee ran out, we didn't run through the streets screaming for his blood. We stayed inside with our faulty heaters and waited for something to change for the better. Because Tomiak Pankov was like an abusive father. After all the years together, you can't help but feel some anguished love for him, but that doesn't temper the fear. One wrong word, and you'll be faced with rage you might not survive.

Gavra, who'd known only this Great Leader, felt as if he were a witness to, and participant in, patricide.

"I will not sign anything," said Pankov.

"This situation is known," the prosecutor continued, pacing comfortably as if, by his example, he could ease the tension in the room. "The catastrophic situation of the country is known all over the world. Every honest citizen who worked hard here knows that we do not have medicines, that you two have killed children and other people in this way, that there is nothing to eat, no heating, no electricity."

"What? What's he talking about?" said Ilona Pankov. Her husband didn't bother answering.

"All right, then," the prosecutor said. "Who ordered the blood-bath in Sárospatak?"

Tomiak Pankov squeezed himself tighter and shook his head.

"Who gave the order to shoot in the Capital, for instance?"

"I won't answer."

The prosecutor was at the edge of their table, but still beyond the camera's view, his voice rising to a shrill pitch. "Who ordered the shooting into the crowd? Tell us!"

Dryly, Ilona said to her husband, "Forget about them. There's no use in talking to these people."

The prosecutor feigned exasperation. "Do you not know anything about the order to shoot?"

The old couple wasn't even looking at him.

"What about the order to shoot?" he persisted. "There's still shooting going on. Fanatics, whom you are paying. They're shooting at children; they're shooting arbitrarily into apartments. Who are these fanatics? Are they *the people*, or are you paying them?"

Tomiak Pankov peered beyond his interrogator to the far wall, directly into the video camera with its red power light burning. "I will not answer. I will not answer any question." He held his head rigidly toward the lens. "Not a single shot was fired in Victory Square. Not a single shot. No one was shot."

The prosecutor shook his head and raised his finger again. "By now, in the Capital, there have been forty-four casualties."

"Look!" said Ilona. "And *that* they're calling genocide!"

The prosecutor continued, his patience beginning to wear. "In every municipal capital there is shooting going on. The people were slaves. The entire intelligentsia of the country ran away—they *escaped*. No one wanted to do anything for you anymore."

"Excuse me," said an eager voice from among the observers, but Gavra, through his blurred vision, couldn't make out who it was. Not an officer. "Mr. President, I would like to know something. The accused should tell us who the mercenaries are. Who pays them? And who brought them into the country?"

"Yes," said the prosecutor, nodding. "Accused, answer."

Tomiak Pankov restated his now-famous defense as his wife whispered into his ear. "I will not say anything more. I will only speak at the Grand National Assembly."

"Ilona has always been talkative," said the prosecutor. She halted her whispers and glared at the young man. "But otherwise she doesn't know much. I've observed that she is not even able to read correctly, but she calls herself a university graduate."

Ilona Pankov, in an instant, became all venom. She banged her small, red-knuckled fist against the table. "The intellectuals of this country should hear you—you and your colleagues!"

This was the kind of display the prosecutor wanted to provoke. He shook his head playfully. "More than her talkativeness, she's well known for all the titles she's always claimed to have. Scientist, engineer, academician—yet she doesn't know how to read. An illiterate, inadequate academician."

"The intelligentsia of the country will hear what you're accusing us of!" She threw herself back into her chair, as if the incredible force of her will could silence all further debate.

The prosecutor looked up from his notes. "Tomiak Pankov should tell us why he doesn't answer our questions. What prevents him from doing so?"

Perhaps realizing how he looked on camera, Pankov straightened. "I will answer any question, but only at the Grand National Assembly, before the representatives of the working class." He looked into the camera lens. "Tell the people that I will answer all of their questions. All the world should know what's going on here. I only recognize the working class and the Grand National Assembly—no one else."

The prosecutor smiled. "The world already knows what's happened here."

"I will not answer you putschists," he said firmly, again crossing his arms.

"The Grand National Assembly has been dissolved."

Tomiak Pankov looked caught off guard by that, as if he had been basing all his hopes on the National Assembly, which throughout his long reign had never said no to him. "This isn't possible. No one can dissolve the National Assembly."

"We now have another leading organ," said the prosecutor. "The Galicia Revolutionary Committee is now our supreme body."

The trembling continued, and Gavra felt sick. He wanted to run out of the room, because he kept being invaded by memories of this old man at the hunting lodge in the Carpathians. There was something almost charming about those memories. But the prosecutor hadn't lied: Pankov was a murderer. Indirectly, perhaps, but a murderer nonetheless. Yet the prosecutor himself, by being allied with Jerzy Michalec, who was grinning beside him, was a murderer as well. Off to the right, in the next row up, he saw Nikolai Romek gaping at the courtroom with the awe of a fan at a soccer game. The whole room stank of corruption.

Tomiak Pankov waved his hand. "No one recognizes that organ. That's why the people are fighting all over the country. This gang will be destroyed," he said, tapping a finger on the table to signify the whole room. "*They* organized the putsch."

"The people are fighting against *you*," said the prosecutor. "Not the new forum."

"No. The people are fighting for freedom and against the new forum." He shook his head. "I do not recognize the court."

The prosecutor slid back, closer to the audience and farther from the camera's reach. "Why do you think people are fighting today? What do you think?"

"As I said before," Pankov said evenly, "the people are fighting for their freedom and against this putsch, against this usurpation. And this putsch, as you know, was organized and financed from abroad, which the people will not stand."

No one in the room was able to take his eyes off the old man.

"I do not recognize this court. I will not answer anymore." He tried to return the collective gaze but looked confused suddenly. "I am now talking to you as simple citizens, and I hope you will tell the truth. I hope that all of you aren't also working for the foreigners and for the destruction of our nation."

The prosecutor threw up his hands in a maudlin expression of capitulation and turned to another young man in the front row, who had not yet spoken. "Ask him. Ask Pankov if he knows he's no longer president of the country. Does he know this? Does he know as well that Ilona Pankov has lost all her official state functions? And does he know, further, that the entire government has been dissolved?"

The small man he'd been speaking to stood slowly. He rubbed his mustache, which looked damp, but before he could pose the questions, the prosecutor pivoted on his heel and faced the president of the court, who was still sweating. "I ask this to find out on what basis this trial can be continued. It must be cleared up for everyone," he said, touching his palm with every other word, "whether Pankov wants to, should, must, or can answer at all. How are we to know how to proceed?"

The president of the court stared impotently back at the prosecutor, then settled his dull eyes on Tomiak Pankov. He checked his watch, then cleared his throat. The damp-mustached young man approached the Pankovs' table. "Do you," he said with a thin, wiry voice, "Tomiak and Ilona Pankov, know the aforementioned facts— namely, that you are no longer president, and that you have lost all your official functions?"

Pankov didn't. "I am the president of this country. I am the commander-in-chief of the army. No one," he said, emphasizing it with a loud, clear rap on the table, "can deprive me of these functions."

"But not of our army," said the prosecutor, stepping forward. "You are not commander-in-chief of our army."

"I do not recognize you." Pankov shook his head. "I am talking to you as simple citizens, and I tell you: I am the president of this country."

"What are you really?" said the prosecutor.

"I repeat: I am the president and the commander-in-chief. I am the president of the people. I will not speak with you provocateurs anymore, and I will not speak with the organizers of the putsch and with the mercenaries. I have nothing to do with them."

"Yes," said the prosecutor, "but you are paying the mercenaries."

"No. *No.*"

"It's incredible what they're inventing," Ilona Pankov said. "Incredible."

"Please, make a note," said the prosecutor, turning back to the audience. "Pankov does not recognize the new legal structures of power in the country. He still considers himself to be the country's president and the commander-in-chief of the army."

Then he spun again on his heel, pointing at the couple. He seemed to be enjoying himself now.

"Why did you ruin the country?" He moved closer. "Why did you export everything? Why did you make the farmers starve? The produce the farmers grew was exported, and farmers came from the most remote provinces to the Capital and other cities in order to buy bread. They cultivated the soil in line with your orders and had nothing to eat. Why did you starve the people?"

"I will not answer this question. As a simple citizen, I tell you the following: For the first time I guaranteed that every farmer and every worker received two hundred kilograms of wheat per person, *not* per family, and that he is entitled to more. It's a lie that I made the people starve. A lie, a lie in my face," he said, his voice rising. "This shows how little patriotism there is, how many treasonable offenses have been committed."

The prosecutor, full of himself, could easily match Pankov's pitch. "You claim to have taken measures so that every farmer is entitled to two hundred kilograms of wheat. Why do they then buy their bread in the Capital?" He reached into his pocket for the notepad, flipped to a page, and read aloud from Tomiak Pankov's own words, words that described his program for feeding the country. Then he looked up again. "We have wonderful programs." He shook the pad at Pankov. "Paper is patient. Why are your programs not implemented? You've destroyed the villages and the soil. What do you say? As a citizen?"

Pankov leaned forward, addressing the whole room. "As a citizen, as a simple citizen, I tell you the following: At no point was there such an upswing, so much construction, so much consolidation in the provinces. I guaranteed that every village had its schools, hospitals, and doctors. I have done everything to create a decent and rich life for the people in the country, like in no other country in the world."

Gavra was losing strength. The barrage of accusations thrown back and forth seemed to be hitting him in the stomach. But Pankov's last words made him squint at the old, deluded man. *A decent and rich life . . . like in no other country in the world.*

That truly was a surprise. All you had to do was walk down the street to see what a miserable place our country had become. Breadlines, ration cards, electrical shortages. He thought back to that place in Virginia called Brandermill, the enormous houses made of wood, not concrete, and the forests, and the large rooms and unbelievably large refrigerators. How could someone who had ever stepped into another country say those words?

Maybe that's what began to urge Gavra toward the path he would follow. It certainly pointed the way.

"We have always spoken of equality," said the prosecutor. "We are all equal. Everybody should be paid according to his performance. Now we finally saw your villa on television, the golden plates from which you ate, the food you had imported, the luxurious celebrations— pictures from your luxurious celebrations."

Pankov stared back at him, blank, perhaps shocked that dirty hands had been rummaging through his stuff. Ilona, though, recovered quickly.

"Incredible!" she shouted. "We live in a normal apartment, just like every other citizen. We've ensured an apartment for every citizen through corresponding laws!"

"You had palaces."

"No," said Tomiak Pankov. "*We* had no palaces. The palaces belong to the people."

"Yes, yes." The prosecutor nodded in a simulation of agreement. "This is true. But you lived in the palaces while the people suffered." He spread his hands. "Children can't even buy plain candy, and you're living in the palaces of the people."

"Is it possible we're facing such charges?" said Pankov, as if truly surprised.

"Let us now talk about the accounts in Switzerland, Mr. Pankov," said the prosecutor. "What about the accounts?"

"I'm not mister," sneered Pankov. "I'm comrade."

"Accounts in Switzerland?" asked Ilona. "Furnish proof!"

"We had no account in Switzerland," said Tomiak. "Nobody has opened an account. This shows again how false the charges are. What defamation, what provocations! This was a coup d'état."

The prosecutor was all smiles. "Well, Mr. Defendant, if you had no accounts in Switzerland, will you sign a statement confirming that the money that *may* be in Switzerland should be transferred to the state, to the State Bank?"

"We'll discuss this before the Grand National Assembly." Again he crossed his arms over his chest. "I will not say anything here. This is a vulgar provocation."

The prosecutor took some stapled papers from an assistant. His voice rose belligerently. "Will you sign the statement now or not?"

"I have no statement to make, and I will not sign one."

Stepping back, the prosecutor faced the president of the court. "Note the following: The defendant refuses to sign this statement. The defendant has not recognized us. He also refuses to recognize the new forum."

Pankov nodded, pleased to hear something, finally, that he agreed with. "I do not recognize this new forum."

The prosecutor turned back. "So. You know the new forum. You have information about it."

"Well, you told us about it."

"Yes," Ilona said. "You told us about it here."

Pankov leaned forward and explained it to them as clearly and simply as he could. "Nobody can change the state structures. This is not possible. Usurpers have been punished severely during the past centuries of our history. *Nobody* has the right to abolish the Grand National Assembly."

As if Tomiak Pankov had not spoken, the prosecutor said, "Tell us why you starved the people!"

"Nonsense. Speaking as an ordinary citizen, I can tell you that for the first time in their lives the workers had two hundred kilos of flour a year and many additional benefits. All you allege are lies. As an ordinary citizen, I can tell you that never in our history has there been such progress."

"What about the golden weighing machine your son used to weigh the meat he received from abroad?"

"It's a lie!" shouted Ilona. She rose from her chair. "He was a mayor. He had an apartment, like everyone else, *not* a villa. Nothing was brought in from abroad." She settled down and shook her head. "This is outrageous."

The prosecutor came nearer to Ilona. "You've always been wiser and more ready to talk, a scientist. You were the most important aide, the number two in the cabinet, in the government."

She shrugged.

"Did *you* know about the genocide in Sárospatak?"

"What genocide?" Then: "By the way, I won't answer any more questions."

Her husband nodded, agreeing. "She will not answer."

The prosecutor pointed with a ballpoint pen. "Did you know about the genocide, or did you, as a chemist, only deal with polymers? You, as a scientist, did not know about it?"

"Her papers were published abroad," said Tomiak. "Science *and* polymers!"

"And who wrote the papers for you, Ilona?"

Ilona Pankov, faced with more insults than she'd heard in the entire thirty-two years of her and her husband's reign, burst. "Impudence! I'm a member and the chairwoman of the Academy of Sciences!" Her lips were damp. "You cannot talk to me in that way!"

The president of the court, agitated, glanced at his watch and said to the prosecutor, "So she's an academician, and there's nothing more to say."

"By insulting us," said Pankov, "you're insulting all the learned bodies throughout the world that conferred these degrees on us." He patted his wife's arm.

The prosecutor opened his hands as if holding a large bowl. "That is to say, as a deputy prime minister you did not know about the genocide?"

"She's not *a* deputy prime minister," shouted Pankov, "but the *first* deputy prime minister of the Socialist Republic!"

Again, the prosecutor ignored him. "But who gave the order to shoot? Answer this question!"

"I will not answer," said Ilona. "I told you right at the beginning that I will not answer a single question."

Tomiak cut in. "You as officers should know that the government cannot give the order to shoot. But those who shot at the young people were the security men. The terrorists."

Ilona nodded. "The 'terrorists' "—she quoted with her fingers—"are from the Ministry."

The prosecutor's head popped back, shocked. "The terrorists are from the Ministry for State Security?"

The mustached man jerked to his feet with the same look of surprise etched across his features. "And who heads the Ministry? Another question—"

"No," said Ilona, realizing her mistake too late. "I've not given an answer. This was only information for you as citizens."

Tomiak Pankov raised a finger. "I want to tell you as citizens that in the Capital—"

"We're finished with you," the prosecutor said. "You needn't say anything else. The next question is," he said, turning back to Ilona, "how did Lieutenant General Yuri Kolev die? Was he killed? And by whom?"

"Ask the doctors and the people," said Ilona, "but not me!"

Michalec was already staring at Gavra with a broad smile, as if he knew Kolev's name would be mentioned at that moment. Gavra leaned close to his large ear. "They didn't kill Kolev."

"I know," Michalec whispered back, then returned to the scene.

"I will ask you a counterquestion," said Tomiak Pankov. "Why do you not put the question like this: Why did Lieutenant General Yuri Kolev have a heart attack?"

The prosecutor raised that finger again. "What induced him to have a heart attack? Earlier, we spoke, and you called him a traitor. This was the reason for his heart attack?"

"The traitor Kolev died naturally. His heart failed."

"Why didn't you bring him to trial as a traitor?"

"His criminal acts were only discovered after he had died."

"What were his criminal acts?"

"He was coordinating treason with representatives of the Soviet government. He was a liar and a traitor, and as a result of false hearsay about him, and because of his mistakes, we are in this state of siege—"

"You have always been more talkative than your colleague," interrupted the prosecutor, raising a hand to silence the old man. "However, *she* has always been at your side and apparently provided you with the necessary information. We should talk here openly and sincerely, as befits intellectuals. For, after all, both of you are members of the Academy of Sciences." He slipped his notepad back into his pocket. "Now tell us, please, what money was used to pay for your publications abroad—the selected historical works of Tomiak Pankov and the scientific works of the so-called academician Ilona Pankov."

Ilona, snidely: "So-called, so-called. Now they've even taken away all our titles."

The president of the court, feeling a burst of confidence, said, "We're not taking anything. Respond to the questions put forth by the court."

She let out a whimper of a laugh, a long *heeee* that ended abruptly. She shook her head.

The president of the court made a note on his paper. "She refuses to respond to the court's questions."

Tomiak rubbed the back of his neck, thinking, then said, "She should not have to answer these accusations, this misinformation about all of our work. The people ate as well as people from abroad, food available every day of the year, they had one thousand one hundred to twelve hundred calories a day of vegetables. And sixty grams a day of meat."

The mustached man, who'd returned to his seat, stood up again. "Please, ask Tomiak and Ilona Pankov whether they have ever had a mental illness."

Gavra leaned over to Michalec. "Who's that guy?"

"Their defense attorney," whispered Michalec.

"What?" said Ilona, unbelieving. "What should he ask us?"

The prosecutor was happy to clarify. "Whether you have ever had a mental illness."

"What an obscene provocation."

"This is not a provocation," said the prosecutor. "It would serve your defense. If you had a mental illness and admitted this, you wouldn't be responsible for your acts."

Ilona turned to her husband, but her voice asked the whole room, the whole country even: "How can someone tell us something like this? How can someone say something like this?"

"I do not recognize this court," said Tomiak Pankov. He looked at his wristwatch, mocking the president of the court. "Let's get this over with."

The prosecutor hiked up his pants before stepping forward, and Gavra was reminded of American westerns he'd seen in Ministry screening rooms: John Wayne, Clint Eastwood, Gary Cooper.

"You have never been able to hold a dialogue with the people," the prosecutor said. "You were not used to talking to the people. You held monologues and the people had to applaud, as in the rituals of tribal people. And today you're acting in the same megalomaniac way. Now, we're making a last attempt. Do you want to sign this statement?" He held up the typewritten sheets again.

"No," said Tomiak Pankov. "We will not sign. And I also do not recognize the counsel for the defense."

The prosecutor said, "Please, make a note: Tomiak Pankov refuses to cooperate with the court-appointed counsel for the defense."

Ilona said to everyone, "We will not sign any statement. We will speak only at the Grand National Assembly, because we've worked hard for the people all our lives. We've sacrificed our lives to the people. And we will not betray our people here."

The president of the court, nodding, rubbed his damp forehead and looked to the prosecutor. "Counsel for the prosecution?"

The young man looked at him, then turned to face the audience. "Now we will call our witnesses."

The senior citizens in the front began shifting in their seats, preparing for their final destination. A bald man in a corporal's uniform went to the second camera, which faced the empty desk, and turned it on.

TWENTY-SIX

•

I woke at eight thirty to the noise of a family performing their Sunday morning routine. Even during the heady days of the revolution, this was something that didn't change in the Kolyeszar household. Magda made sure it didn't. She'd woken first and made coffee—real coffee some black marketeer had gotten hold of over the border in Hungary—and fried slices of pork, which had always been plentiful in that region. She toasted bread in the same pan and stacked it on a plate. The Kolyeszars always ate plenty of apples from their orchards, and each meal had some version of the fruit. She spooned out apple marmalade she'd jarred last spring, and Sanja sat in a highchair eating applesauce. By then Ferenc and Bernard had also risen, tiptoeing past my sleeping form on the couch, and Ferenc had sent his son-in-law down to the cooperative offices where the new regional paper, *Liberation,* was delivered in boxes to be taken for free. I'd just finished a quick shower when Bernard came through the front door clutching two copies.

"Morning," I said drowsily. Everything ached.

He shook himself off. "Cold as hell out there."

I popped two more Captopril, then found everyone at the kitchen table, reading parts of the newspaper. Ferenc, unsurprisingly, took it upon himself to read out loud the most important articles. "Looks like the fighting's over everywhere except the Capital by now. Damned terrorists."

I nodded politely; Bernard said, "They'll only stop when they see the Pankovs' cold, dead bodies."

Bernard was like that. He could surprise you with insight you'd only be convinced of hours later.

"Dead?" said Magda. She put another slice of bread on my plate. "Let's hope it doesn't lead to that."

"Question is, where are they?" said Ferenc.

"In Libya," said Agota, who now had Sanja on her knee. I was struck by how quiet the child was; I had yet to hear her cry. "That's what everyone thinks. They're building up an army to come and take back the country."

"Let them try it," said Ferenc.

While they speculated, I half-read an article on the looting of Yalta Boulevard 36, which I'd witnessed when I was looking for Gisèle Sully. The boxes had been full of secret files where the Ministry kept track of its various informants and agents, and the whole following page was filled with names from those lists. The paper wanted to expose those who had been clandestinely working for the old regime, so that their neighbors would know what kind of people they lived near.

As I scanned the small-print list (there must've been at least five hundred names), I imagined that all across the country sudden break-ins were occurring that morning, and fathers and mothers were being dragged out into the street to be beaten and marked with signs that said COLLABORATOR.

Then I stopped on a name in the fifth column. The list wasn't alphabetical—in their eagerness to make it public, they didn't have time for such niceties. So the *B* name was in the middle column, near the bottom, and I had to squint and bring the paper close to my eyes to read it, reread it, think, and read it again.

Across the table, Ferenc gasped aloud and looked at me. He'd found it, too.

BROD, LENA. MAJOR

I met Ferenc's heavy eyes. Then, under his gaze, I set down the paper, went to the living room, found my cigarettes and coat, and walked out the front door. I sat on the stoop and began to smoke, but my lungs rejected it. I didn't care. I kept going, sucking in the poison and coughing and feeling the ache of my laboring heart. Ferenc appeared in his coat and sat beside me. He finally took the damned thing away from me and flicked it out into the crabgrass.

"Did you know?"

I shook my head. "I don't believe it."

He sighed audibly and patted my knee, then got up and lit a cigarette of his own. He waited a moment before speaking, because he didn't know what effect his words might have on me. "I believe it," he said. "She left the country twice a year. She had family money. It all adds up."

"Her father made a deal with the government," I explained, not wanting to see it.

"Yes," said Ferenc, "and then her father died. So they made a deal with her. She gets to keep the money and can leave the country whenever she likes, but only if she cooperates with them."

Later, when I had a chance to cool down, I would see that it made perfect sense, but I wasn't ready yet. I wasn't ready to concede that for forty years my wife had lied to me. "You don't understand, Ferenc. She hated Pankov. She hated the Ministry. To be honest, she hated this country. She only stayed because of me. No." I shook my head. "They can put anything in those files. Or in the paper. Someone made a mistake or pulled a trick." I pointed a finger at him. "It's Michalec. He puts out a warrant for my arrest, then slanders my wife on top of it. So no one will help me."

Ferenc looked at me. I wasn't even convincing myself.

Still, I prattled on about Michalec and how he was a conniving son of a bitch. It wasn't enough for him to kill people; he had to rub shit all over their reputations.

Ferenc told me quietly that Michalec had no control over what was printed in *Liberation*. It was a Sárospatak paper, and the list had been taken directly from the army clerks who had produced it. He wouldn't help me with my self-delusion, and I hated him for it. He rubbed my knee.

"Come on, old man. Finish breakfast, then I'll show you the operation. Show you what really matters."

TWENTY–SEVEN

•

While growing up, Gavra had seen films made just after the Second World War, grainy black-and-white show trials where ragged-looking, stiff men stood in the dock and became witnesses for their own prosecution. In carefully memorized speeches, they stated their crimes against the people of our great country and asked the people's forgiveness. These trials were notable for their consistency. A prosecutor went into a lengthy indictment, often very emotional, accusing the defendant of treason or collaboration or any number of crimes whose victim was the entire state. This was followed by the evidence, always in the form of teary-eyed men and women who had seen or heard or suffered because of the defendant's treachery. As their statements went on, they grew louder. They stuttered and wept when their emotions became too powerful; they shot accusing fingers at the dock, where the defendant stared back blankly. With recent torture still fresh in the defendants' minds, anything was preferable to returning to those dank prison cells and beatings. Even the bureaucracy that would lead to a life of labor or a firing squad was better than those cells. So they didn't interrupt the accusers. In fact, they sometimes nodded in agreement. Then, when the time came, they made their own statement, which concurred with everything that had been stated before. All they would say in their defense was that they'd been duped by foreign governments and their own insipid greed. They knew, and they expected, that the court would show no mercy, because mercy was something they did not deserve.

These films were documents of a particular time. Once Mihai, that wartime partisan and postwar hero, had annihilated or put to work everyone who might pose a threat to his administration, the show trials trickled away. They had served their purpose by cleaning the state of malcontents, and the films reminded everyone else of the dangers of too much unfettered ambition.

As he listened to the witnesses now, Gavra remembered those films. It was a different time, but they gave their statements much as their predecessors had. A few murmured nervously throughout, and the prosecutor had to ask them to speak louder, but most, including Beth and Harold Atkins, let their emotions enter the stories, and Beth cried three times as she tried to get it all out. Harold was defiant, pointing at the other side of the room while the Pankovs either stared blankly back or pretended to ignore what was going on. A few times, they tried to interrupt, and the president of the court scolded them. After a while, they saw it was no use and just let the old people rattle on and weep and shout.

The room, Gavra knew, was full of liars: the Pankovs, Michalec, Romek, and Andras Todescu (who had summoned enough courage to stand in the doorway). Even Gavra himself was a liar. The witnesses were the only ones in the room who were not liars; they were the only ones who were not despicable.

He knew the Atkinses' story, but when they told it again the emotion multiplied because they were finally faced with the villains they had spent the last thirty years hating. They had an audience with the devil, and the devil had no choice but to listen. "You broke apart a family, and you ended our lives," said Harold, pointing. "You made us subhuman."

A lone woman witnessed for herself and her now-dead husband and son, both of whom had been tortured to death in the early seventies within the walls of Yalta Boulevard number 36 around the time Gavra joined the Ministry. The story she told surprised even him, who had seen his employer do plenty of shocking things during his tenure.

Farmers arrived with stories of the effects of the "New Agro-Policy" Pankov implemented in the late seventies, leaving whole families starving while the land around them was full of wheat. The Maternity Laws of 1982 also produced witnesses, like one man whose wife, having already borne three children, was warned by her doctor to stop. An accidental pregnancy followed, and because abortion was now illegal, she died in childbirth, along with the baby. Others told of their fifth or sixth child being sent off to a state orphanage because there was no way to feed them all, and the child then disappearing. There were children dying of starvation in the Carpathian ranges and children dying of diabetes and influenza in hospitals with barren medicine cabinets. And homes. Homes had been lost endlessly as agro-policies forced fifth-generation farming families into socialist cubicles along the always-under-construction edges of the Capital, or the numerous homes that had been plowed under to make space for the Workers' Palace, which covered ten hectares of demolished land.

Some accusations were less visceral, such as the steady decline of electricity, which had turned once lively cities into morbid nighttime holes, and the fact that, during the last years, light bulbs available to the public had steadily declined in wattage. These days, the best you could get was a murky ten-watt bulb, all so that the country would use less electricity, and Pankov could pay off the foreign debt while he and his wife lived in well-lit splendor.

The witnesses included the senior citizens shipped in from other countries, as well as others who had never left, who could document what had become known as the Dark Eighties. There were stories of suicides, which Gavra knew had become more frequent in the last four years, and they asked what kind of man could do that to his people. What kind of man could make of his country a prison from which the only escape was suicide?

The Pankovs had no answer. They just shook their heads.

Gavra had no answers either. A few times he caught himself wiping tears from his eyes. No, it didn't matter that this was all theater, because half the players didn't know what kind of stage this was. They didn't know they were being used.

Each time the Ministry was brought into the stories—and this happened frequently—Gavra felt a sharp pain in his stomach. What the Ministry did, he felt responsible for. He had murdered children and forced people from their homes and into underground cells and tortured them until they couldn't remember their own names anymore. His breath became shallow as he remembered his own crimes, ones he'd actually committed himself, which were certainly many, and knew that whatever justification he'd had back then no longer applied. He was as guilty as the Pankovs, as Romek, who was smiling from his seat, and Michalec, who was now somber, arms crossed over his chest.

The stories continued. Whenever he thought they had finished, the prosecutor would motion to another person in the audience, state his name, and ask him to speak. It seemed to go on forever, and Gavra wanted to run out of the room—but couldn't. It wasn't Michalec or the big guard who kept him there; it was his own morbid curiosity. He wanted to know the stories, but more, he waited for the moment when Tomiak Pankov would cut in with a few words that would explain it all, offer up some simple evidence that would justify what had been done in his name, or express his shock and insist they knew nothing about this. But the best he ever offered was, "This should only be done in front of the Grand National Assembly."

The president of the court told him to be quiet.

When the last weeping witness was led back to her chair, the prosecutor turned to the bench and said, "The people rest."

The president of the court turned to his associate judges, whispering a moment. They ended the conversation with nods, and the president said to the room, "The court will now retire for deliberations."

The soldiers turned off the cameras.

The president stood, as did the other two judges, and the audience stood as well. Michalec tugged Gavra's sleeve until he, too, was standing. Only the Pankovs remained in their chairs as the judges walked along the wall and out into the corridor.

The prosecutor and defense attorney followed the judges out of the room.

As they settled back into their seats, Michalec said, "Well?"

Gavra peered over heads at the Pankovs, who were whispering to one another. "I want to talk to them."

"That's out of the question."

"I insist."

"Listen, Gavra. You know what we want you to do. You strike up a relationship with those bastards, and you're not going to be able to do it."

"That won't be a problem. I've done it before."

"Yes? Do tell."

Gavra wasn't going to regale this man with stories of jobs he'd prefer to forget. "The deal is this," he said. "You give me a few minutes with them, and I'll do it. You have my word."

"Is your word worth something?"

"More than yours, certainly."

Michalec peered over the crowd. Romek came over and whispered something in his ear, then left again. He patted Gavra's knee. "You've got yourself a deal. But I'm depending on you to stick to it. There's no way out."

He motioned to the big guard and told him where Gavra was going. The man, despite his size, was frightened, but by then Gavra was already walking around the edge of the chairs toward the front. The guard hurried to catch up.

As Gavra approached the couple, an officer cut ahead of him and squatted in front of the table. "Sir," the man said to Tomiak Pankov. "Major Ignac Maslov."

"What army?"

Ilona Pankov turned away with an expression of disgust.

"I wanted to know why you're not accepting the court's legality. Don't you realize you're only making things more difficult for yourself?"

"Because," said Tomiak Pankov in exasperation, "there is no legality to this court. Legality is granted by the Grand National Assembly, which these putschists ignore. None of this is legal."

Maslov nodded. "Also, why did you try to leave the Central Committee Building by helicopter?"

Pankov looked past the man's head, past Gavra, to the doorway where Andras Todescu still stood. "Because I was advised to take the helicopter by those who were plotting against me, and some of these traitors are right here in this room."

"Aha," said the major. He stood up and stepped away.

"They can't do a thing," whispered Ilona Pankov. "There's nothing they can do."

"Do I know you?" Tomiak said, looking up at Gavra.

"Lieutenant Gavra Noukas of the Ministry," Gavra said, only afterward realizing how ridiculous this sounded.

"You're with them, too?"

Gavra shook his head. "I was forced to come here. This is all a surprise."

Pankov raised a finger. Then, unexpectedly, he smiled. "I remember. A friend of General Brano Sev, correct?"

Gavra couldn't get the word out, so he just nodded.

"How is Brano? I shouldn't have let him retire. He would've taken care of this mob."

"Sev?" said Ilona, suddenly taking interest. "I never trusted him. I'll bet he's running this from Moscow."

"I can assure you," said Gavra. "He's not."

"Then where is he?" said Ilona.

"I—I don't know."

"Hunting!" Tomiak said suddenly. He wagged his finger. "I remember now. You came out to one of the lodges and we went hunting. I'm right, yes?"

Gavra nodded. "I'm pleased you remember. But, sir, we don't have much time. I wanted to know something."

"Yes?"

"Why didn't you answer the witnesses? Didn't you have some kind of explanation for them?"

The smile disappeared from Pankov's face, and his wife made a hissing sound. "You haven't listened to a thing," said the old man. "None of you. I will say everything in front of the Grand National Assembly. I won't recognize these putschists."

Gavra straightened. They didn't care, neither of them. "It's too late. They have the country, and after this no one will be around to take it from them."

"After what?" said Pankov.

"After your execution."

Ilona, eyes red along the lids, bared her teeth at him. "So they're going to do it. They're going to do to us what they did to our son. *Animals.*"

She looked away, but Tomiak held Gavra's gaze a moment. The younger man's fear had finally left. He turned on his heel, much as the flamboyant prosecutor had done so often, and returned to Michalec, the guard struggling to catch up. "I'll wait in the corridor until it's time."

Michalec nodded at the guard, who followed Gavra out. As they entered the corridor, they passed the three judges and two lawyers, who were filing somberly back inside.

TWENTY-EIGHT

•

After breakfast, we prepared to go into Sárospatak so Ferenc could show off "the operation." Magda had stared at me often during the meal, but I couldn't figure out what she was trying to tell me until I was putting on my coat. She pulled me aside. "What I said last night is true."

"I know."

"The other part, I mean. I love you. And I want to help you. I don't care if what they say about Lena is true. If she worked for them, she did it because she felt she had no choice. No one's going to convince me otherwise."

"Thanks."

Bernard decided at the last minute to join us, because he wanted to find a Christmas tree for Sanja. Squeezed between them in the truck, I realized that, whatever his flaws, Bernard loved his family. "Here," he said near a cluster of pine trees before the main road.

Ferenc didn't bother slowing. "Too small."

"Anything bigger, you won't be able to fit it in the house."

"We're not doing it half-ass this year," said Ferenc. "We'll find something on the way back."

They argued, shooting barbs back and forth past me as we bounced along the shoddy country road, but I wasn't listening.

Ferenc was right: Lena had worked for the Ministry, probably ever since we married in 1950. Four decades. For four decades, she'd maintained an enormous lie, and I never, not once, suspected.

It was humiliating. I'd lived forty years with a stranger. A liar. How could she have kept it from me during all those drunken years? The only way a drunk can keep such a secret is if she's living with a complete fool.

Yes, I was angry at my dead wife. I felt like I was the good but dull and dull-witted husband in those films about adultery. The husband who listens to classical music and sucks on a pipe in his study, while in his bedroom his wife is breaking out of her monochrome existence with the gardener or the business partner. She's filling her dead life with clandestine passion.

But adultery would've been easy. I could have walked in on her in another man's embrace, shouted and wept, and been done with it. This was something more, a parallel life, no doubt Lena's real life, and I never even noticed that it was right there, right next to me.

After forty years, I'd just learned that my life's role had been the pitiful one. I was the dumb but harmless mouse, the one who never raised a question, who never noticed that my wife was a spy.

It was really too much to take. It felt as if every few minutes my life, and my world, changed. I wished it would stop. I wished that something, anything, would remain as I remembered it.

"Emil?"

I blinked. Ferenc was frowning at me as he turned onto a main road. I said, "What?"

"You're not listening."

"Sorry. What's the topic?"

Bernard cut in. "He was telling you how much of a hero he was during the revolution."

"Not a hero," said Ferenc, shaking his head. "Just what happened."

"You're making yourself out to be a hero. Admit it."

"Shut up, Bernard."

Sárospatak traces its official history back to 1201, when it was granted town status by the Hungarian monarch King Emeric. It grew during the Middle Ages as a stop on the trading route to Poland. In the early fifteenth century, Ferenc told me, King Sigismund declared it a free royal town, and in 1460 King Matthias granted it the right to its own market. With the Reformation it became an academic center, and in the mid-1600s the famous educator Jan Comenius taught there. Ferenc told me all this as we crossed the city limits, adding that the famous Rákóczi family, which had owned the town's castle, took a major part in the revolution against the Habsburgs. "They call Patak 'the Athens on the Bodrog' because we've got a history of education and revolution here."

"In that order," said Bernard.

But on the outskirts, before reaching the muddy Bodrog River, there was no sign of the First City's glorious past. The remaining Habsburg buildings were crumbling from years of neglect, and the pedestrians bundled against the cold seemed insecure and confused under the gray sky.

By eleven thirty, we crossed Bodrog Bridge. On a hill to our left, the Red Tower of Rákóczi Castle rose high, looking out over the entire city.

Ferenc and his friends' base of operations was a small third-floor apartment in the center, just off Comenius Street. I spotted the window, because a sheet hung from it with the words NATIONAL DEMOCRATIC FORUM painted in blue. The stairwell stank of mildew—some pipes had frozen and burst a month ago and still hadn't been fixed—and Ferenc had to hit the door with his shoulder because it was bloated with moisture. I expected a little more from the cradle of our revolution.

Inside were five mismatched tables and seven mismatched chairs that had been borrowed from sympathizers. Today two young women and a young man watched a small television and manned two telephones, one of which had a lead that went out the window into a neighboring apartment. "Where the hell is everybody?" Ferenc asked them.

"It's Christmas," said one of the girls, a striking blonde. "I'm not staying here all day either."

Christmas? I thought.

Ferenc turned to me. "See? Is it any wonder those bastards in the Capital make more headway than us?" To the girl: "Aliz, you think the Galicia Committee's taking off for Christmas?"

Aliz shrugged, then looked at the television, where, from a hospital bed, Rosta Gorski told a reporter that his injuries wouldn't stop his mission to restore democracy to our beleaguered country. "It's no secret my assailant is connected to the Ministry—his wife was an agent. This only strengthens my resolve."

I found a chair and settled into it.

Ferenc sat with his workers and went through papers. Bernard put a hand on my shoulder. "That's the guy, huh?"

I nodded.

"He's calling you a Ministry agent."

I nodded again as he pulled up a chair beside me and began whispering.

"This is what we'll do," he said, as if he'd been thinking about it a long time. "We go back to the Capital together. You and me. I've got my Militia Walther. We'll find a way through the roadblocks, then I'll track down Michalec's address. He's got to be living somewhere. We'll get him to admit to everything on tape and play it on the radio from Patak." He sounded excited by the idea. He was a lot like his father-in-law.

I was about to thank him but tell him no when the young man at the other table, who had sideburns down to his jawline, looked up from some papers at the television. "Hey. Guys. Look."

All of us did as he asked and were surprised to see washed-out video footage of Tomiak and Ilona Pankov sitting at a long table, arms crossed over their chests, in a concrete-walled room.

"Turn it up," I said.

TWENTY-NINE

•

Hours before it was broadcast, before the last tapes had been recorded and edited to make sure none of the judges or lawyers would be seen in the final cut, Gavra was given a set of infantry fatigues. While the court delivered its verdict, he changed in the corridor, watched by his guard and Andras Todescu, who looked haggard and scared in his expensive suit. "So you're going to do it," said Todescu.

Gavra buttoned his pants.

"It must be done," said Todescu. "Yes. It must." Then he gazed through the open doorway. The prosecutor was listing the couple's crimes.

Gavra didn't want to see. He buttoned the jacket and walked farther down the corridor, peering into other, empty rooms. The guard didn't bother following.

His stomach still hurt, but it was the cold that bothered him. He couldn't manage Brano's mathematics in this chill. Escape paths, contingency plans, spatial relations, even past and future—they were all just beyond his reach. Then he heard the scuffle.

Todescu, pressed back against the opposite wall, stared at two soldiers dragging Ilona Pankov out of the room. Her hands were bound behind her back, but she tried to kick the soldiers, breaking the heel of her shoe. She stumbled. Tomiak Pankov followed; he didn't fight.

He walked patiently between his guards, loudly humming a song. Gavra's mind betrayed him by singing the words to the tune.

Arise ye workers from your slumbers.
Arise ye prisoners of want.
For reason in revolt now thunders,
And at last ends the age of cant.

He tried to silence his head but couldn't. The song refused to leave as they were led toward him.

Then Michalec appeared, confused. In his hand was a bulky video camera. He ran, gasping, past the couple, almost knocking into Ilona Pankov, and grabbed Gavra's arm. "You're not supposed to be here. Come on."

He rushed Gavra to the end of the corridor, then out a steel door into a freezing stone courtyard with high walls that stank of mold. Against one wall, three soldiers with Kalashnikovs stood smoking nervously. They looked up as Michalec shouted, "Now. *Now!* Other side." He waved to a corner of the courtyard; they shuffled over stiffly. "Lose the smokes." They tossed them to the ground. He set the camera on the stones, took the Kalashnikov from one of them, and handed it to Gavra, looking him in the eyes. "You're going to stand in that corner over there. No fanfare, okay? They'll come in through that door and you just do it. Okay?"

Gavra nodded dumbly, hearing:

Away with all your superstitions.
Servile masses arise, arise!
We'll change henceforth the old tradition,
And spurn the dust to win the prize.

"Those guys," said Michalec, jerking his head at the other corner, where the soldiers stood rigidly. "They'll shoot you if you try anything. So don't. Now go." He pointed at the empty corner, then picked up the video camera and walked to the wall, not far from the steel door. He propped the camera on his shoulder, looked through the eyepiece, and started shooting the courtyard, then focused on Gavra, who was gripping the Kalashnikov as if it were something he'd never seen before.

He was completely numb. It didn't occur to him to just turn the gun on Michalec, and he would later hate himself for that.

The door opened, and there they were, stepping out into the cold dawn light, stunned.

Gavra couldn't move. His hands were stuck. He couldn't raise the gun or squeeze the trigger.

He didn't have to.

The three soldiers in the opposite corner weren't looking at Gavra. They were mesmerized by the Pankovs, who had started to run. Instinctively, one of them raised his Kalashnikov and pulled the trigger. That led the second one to do the same, and the third produced a pistol, stretched out his arm, and began firing, too. Loud snapping sounds filled the cold air.

> *So comrades, come rally,*
> *And the last fight let us face!*
> *The Internationale unites the human race.*

Gavra shivered, watching the couple run along the wall, stumbling. Ilona Pankov squealed. Bloodstains erupted on the stones as they fell, and he thought for an instant that he was killing them. Then he realized he wasn't, and that troubled him more than even murder. He raised his rifle and squeezed, the recoil shaking through him. The scent of cordite was heavy as he filled the now-dead bodies with more bullets, so that they began to tremble, as if still alive. That only encouraged him to keep on shooting.

* * *

Once his Kalashnikov had run out of bullets, Gavra dropped it and watched as Michalec, breathing heavily, ran his camera over to the bullet-riddled bodies. More people poured into the courtyard, gaping, until all he could see was a wall of backs. He stepped over the rifle and walked past them, back inside.

In the corridor, he ran into the witnesses. Harold gripped his arm. "Is it done? Is it over?"

Gavra nodded, and Beth kissed his cheeks. As if a switch had been turned, the old people began to weep and hug and thank him, calling him their savior. Then they hurried on to get their own look.

Andras Todescu was crouched in the corridor, no farther than where he'd been minutes before. He looked up at Gavra with a pleading expression, but Gavra went on, past the now-empty courtroom and the other classrooms until he was outside in the cold again, near the stone walls surrounding the barracks. He got on his knees in the dirt, but his sickness stayed in him.

Sometime later, maybe hours, he saw a man get into a jeep clutching a medical bag filled with video cassettes. Then soldiers came out carrying stretchers with two bodies covered in gray army blankets. They put them in a truck and roared off. A while after that, he looked up to see Jerzy Michalec staring down at him, hands in his coat pockets, not smiling. "Hell of a thing," said the old man.

That's when Gavra noticed Michalec had blood on his coat, as if he'd hugged the corpses. "We have a deal."

"Of course, of course," said Michalec, but like someone who didn't know what he was saying.

"My friend."

He nodded. "Right. Liguria metro station. Five minutes' walk from here. He's waiting for you."

Michalec told the guards to let Gavra out. Once past the barracks walls, the gate closing behind him, Gavra started to run. His knees were wobbly, but he could just manage a straight line that took him past apartment blocks and people walking with shopping bags. They didn't know. Not yet. They had no idea.

Somewhere along that brief run, Gavra became convinced that his friend was dead. It was inevitable, the only logical conclusion to this day. So when he found Karel sitting nervously on a bench in the brown-walled station, he squeezed and kissed his friend fiercely. The three other commuters waiting for the metro turned to stare. That didn't matter. Nothing mattered anymore.

THIRTY

•

By now everyone in our country knows that tape, has memorized every nuance and impotent rebuttal from both of them. But as the edited video played on, the cameras never showed us the faces of the prosecutor, the defense attorney, the members of the tribunal, or the audience we sometimes heard gasp at statements. We saw the Pankovs, staring and accusing and pointing fingers at people we never saw. Then, after a while of this, the camera cut to another table, and we saw the witnesses, one after the other, their stories progressively more terrible and damning.

I can't say what other people felt during that first viewing of the famous tape. While Gavra was reminded of the show trials of the late forties and early fifties, I was instead reminded of the various courtrooms I'd visited during my career, where I witnessed against murderers and other criminals. Those times, I'd been able to separate my emotions from the trial. Not with this one. To each accusation, I felt myself saying, *Yes, yes.* I had no love for the Pankovs. They were worse than the murderers I put away, because their crimes were vaster, and they were untouchable. Now, finally, they were being touched. During that first viewing, I didn't think about the hypocrisy of the people who had arranged and run the trial. I didn't care who had put them in the dock. I only cared that it was being done.

We all thought we knew what it would lead to. The unseen tribunal would announce its verdict, that the Pankovs were guilty of crimes against the nation, and they would be sentenced to life in one of the rank prisons where they had sent so many others. What really happened was a shock.

Toward the end, the unseen prosecutor said, "They not only deprived the people of heating, electricity, and foodstuffs, they also tyrannized the soul of the people. They not only killed children, young people, and adults in Sárospatak and the Capital; they allowed the Ministry members to wear military uniforms to create the impression among the people that the army was against them. They wanted to separate the people from the army. They used to fetch people from orphans' homes or from abroad whom they trained in special institutions to become murderers of their own people. They were so impertinent as to cut off oxygen lines in hospitals and to shoot people in their hospital beds! The Ministry hid food reserves on which the Capital could have survived for months, the *whole* of the Capital!"

"Who are they talking about?" muttered Ilona Pankov.

"You should have stayed in Libya!" shouted the prosecutor.

Ilona laughed. Mockingly, she said, "We don't stay abroad!"

Tomiak agreed. "Of course not. This is our home."

It went on. The charges were repeated, and I even said, *"Yes,"* aloud, my hands sweaty on my knees, my heart palpitating in my chest.

The president of the court asked if they wanted to appeal the ruling, and Tomiak Pankov crossed his arms and stared into space. Ilona placed her hands on the table and stifled a yawn.

"All right," a voice said. "Proceed."

I knew that voice, or I thought I did. Even now, I'm still not sure.

Four soldiers entered the frame carrying Kalashnikovs on their shoulders and frayed cords in their hands. They twisted the Pankovs' arms behind their backs and bound their hands together.

At first, Tomiak took it quietly, as if afraid to embarrass himself. When he was pulled into a standing position, he shouted for the last time, "I do not recognize the legitimacy of this court!"

Ilona, though, struggled. She spoke in bits. "Everyone has . . . the right to die as . . . they wish." We could hear the hysteria in her voice. "Don't tie us up! My children, you're breaking my hands. It's a shame, a . . . disgrace. I brought you all up like a mother," she said, her voice sounding like what she thought their mothers might sound like. "Why are you doing this?"

"Whoever staged this coup," said Tomiak, "can shoot anyone they want. The traitors will answer for their treason. The nation will live, and learn from your treachery. It is better to fight with glory than live as a slave."

Beside his wife's hysteria, Tomiak's voice was so steady. Then the camera shifted, and in the light I could see that his eyes were wet, his cheeks as well. His wife, despite the rising pitch of her voice, had dry, hard red eyes.

The soldiers managed to move them out of the camera's frame, and as they disappeared, we were left with Ilona Pankov's choked voice. "If you want to kill us, kill us together. We will always be together."

Then blackness. It lasted a full second, and in that second we all exhaled audibly in the small apartment and throughout the country. It was over—we imagined them sitting in their cells now, awaiting the execution, which would happen tomorrow or next month. Sometime.

We were wrong. The screen brightened, and the now-handheld camera moved around a sullen courtyard in what we would later learn was the Sixteenth District Third Infantry barracks. The stone walls were dirty with bird shit, and in the corner stood a man in army fatigues, clutching a Kalashnikov. Stunned, I leaned closer to the television. "Christ, that's Gavra."

"Noukas?" said Ferenc, not taking his eyes off the screen.

"Oh Jesus," said Bernard. "You're right."

The camera jerked to the opposite corner of the courtyard, where a steel door opened up, and first Tomiak, then Ilona, stepped through, blinking in the morning light. Tomiak hummed a song I knew all too well—then stopped. Their vision cleared enough to see who else was in the courtyard, what he was carrying.

We heard Ilona Pankov's quiet voice; the air had gone out of her. "They're going to kill us like animals."

They ran along the wall, hands behind their backs. A sudden, distorted sound of automatic gunfire. They jerked and seemed to trip over themselves, then fall, Ilona on top in her fur coat. The gunfire didn't cease, and their dead bodies trembled from the impact of all the bullets.

Cut to a close-up of their faces on the ground, bodies turned over so no one could argue they weren't truly the dead Pankovs.

The air went out of all of us, and when, after two full minutes of blackness, the tape began playing again from the beginning, I got up and turned off the television. I had trouble walking. My knees made noises. My veins ached. I managed to reach my chair again. Everyone was still staring at the blank screen.

The young man with the sideburns was the first to speak. He stood and slapped the table. "They're dead! They're really dead!"

From outside, through the thin glass, we heard other young men screaming out their windows. "They're dead! They're dead! The tyrant's dead!"

So the young man ran to the window, ripped it open, and joined in. The young woman whose name I didn't know leaned over her knees and started to vomit. Aliz, beside her, rubbed her back.

Bernard stood, as if he were going to join the chorus at the window, then sat again. "It's good. Isn't it?"

Ferenc had his face in his hands, rubbing. He didn't answer. I nodded a moment. "It's good. Yes." I rubbed the cold tabletop with my palm. "This is what it had to lead to."

Ferenc took his face out of his hands. "Yes. They had to do it. To stop the terrorists."

"But *them*," said Bernard suddenly. "*They're* the ones who did it."

I didn't need him reminding me, nor did Ferenc. The kid with the sideburns tired of shouting. He left the window open, through which we heard whistles and car horns blaring in celebration, and returned to us, rubbing his stomach sickly. He went to the bathroom. The nameless girl had recovered, and Aliz went to the kitchen to find towels and water.

Ferenc was staring at me. I didn't know what he was thinking, and he didn't know what I was thinking. I was stunned, but clearheaded enough to be focused on Gavra's presence there. Had he joined Michalec's people? Had he turned on me? But why? It made no sense.

Ferenc said, "I didn't know your Ministry man had it in him. I'm impressed."

"I'm not," I said, slowly becoming angry.

Ferenc knew what I meant. He searched his pockets for a cigarette as the noise of delirious shouts and car horns filled the room. I went over to the window and looked down. People were pouring out of their homes, whistling, shouting, kissing, and even dancing. I'd never seen anything like it in my life.

When, an hour later, we drove out of town again, we had to keep stopping for the crowds. Sárospatak had changed its mood in an instant. It looked like Mardi Gras, not Christmas, but it was Christmas, and they'd been given a gift they'd never even thought to hope for.

Ferenc and Bernard tracked down the largest Christmas tree they could find. We were never able to wrestle it into the house. That didn't matter, though, because at around seven thirty a car appeared on a hill, its double headlights bouncing toward us. Magda noticed first, rising from the front steps and pointing. We let go of the tree and watched. Ferenc said, "It's a Moskvich. Russian plates. Mag, get the gun."

She ran inside; so did Bernard.

His eyes were good. It was a dark brown Moskvich 408 with Moscow plates. It parked behind the Citroën as Bernard came out clutching his Makarov. Magda followed with the Kalashnikov and handed it to her husband.

Just as I had when I first arrived, the driver rolled down his window first. "Don't shoot!" He was a flabby-faced Russian with gray around his temples. He gave us a reassuring smile as Bernard approached, waving his pistol.

"Who're you?" Ferenc called.

"Fyodor Malevich. Don't shoot, now."

"Malevich? What do you want?"

"Just to talk. To Ferenc Kolyeszar and Emil Brod."

I looked at Ferenc, who shrugged. I said, "What about?"

The Russian said, "I come with word from Brano Oleksy Sev."

"Well, *shit*," said Bernard.

THIRTY-ONE

•

On a rumbling metro train manufactured in a Leningrad factory a decade before, Karel told his story of leaving me to search the Metropol. "I was terrified. Some Frenchwoman told us you'd gone in the day before but didn't come out. I didn't know what that meant. I even let Emil take your car." He paused. "Sorry."

Karel had asked everyone he met, soldiers, journalists, and hotel clerks, until he ran across two broad-chested men in wrinkled suits on the third floor. "I must've had 'gullible' written across my forehead. Said they were Ministry, and you were somewhere safe. They'd take me to you." He shook his head as they arrived at the Moscow Square station, on the outskirts of the Twentieth District. "What a chump I am. Stuck me in a crappy apartment and we sat around watching revolutionary TV. You know how boring that gets after eight hours?"

Gavra smiled for the first time in days and pulled Karel up to leave the train.

"Hey," said Karel. "Where are we going?"

"We're leaving."

They took the escalator up to the concrete circle of Moscow Square, full of kolach shops, cigarette kiosks, and waiting buses. The square was busy at that hour, and in the setting sun they saw thin, dark faces in cheap faux-leather jackets wandering around in a daze, most of them drunk. One grabbed on to Karel, singing, "*Olé, olé, the tyrant is dead!*"

Karel looked scared, so Gavra shooed the man away. He'd thought he'd have more time before they broadcast the tape. "What's he talking about?"

"Let's just keep going."

"*Where?*"

Gavra didn't want to tell him, not yet, because he knew what Karel's reaction would be. Instead, he gave his friend silence and led him to a rickety bus on the edge of the square, number 86. The destination sign over the windshield, luckily, hadn't yet been changed. They took a seat among a few passengers and waited for the driver to arrive.

Up front, two teenaged boys were with a girl who sat on one's lap, bowing her head and kissing him lustily. The friend who wasn't being kissed stood up, grinning, and faced the passengers. He raised a finger and in a pretty good imitation said, "I'll only speak to the Grand National Assembly!"

A few nervous titters went through the passengers. Karel whispered to Gavra, "What's that about?"

"Wait," said Gavra.

The boy at the front shook violently, as if he were being filled with bullets, and fell back into the stairwell as the bus driver stepped on. The driver, a big man, caught him easily and pushed him back up. He, too, had gotten the joke, and started laughing.

Once they were under way, Gavra drew Karel close and began to whisper the story of the Pankovs' demise. He didn't reveal his own role in it, though at one point a middle-aged man two seats up began peering back at him. He tugged his wife's sleeve and whispered something, and then she, too, turned to peer at him.

Karel didn't notice. He was trying to comprehend the news. He didn't know if he should be happy or not.

The man twisted fully in his seat, an arm stretched behind his wife's head, and smiled at Gavra. "Excuse me. Are you . . . ?"

It was hard to know how to answer. To say no was to admit he knew what the man was talking about. To ask what he meant would lead to more questions. So Gavra leaned forward and said in very slow English, "I'm sorry, but I do not understand."

The man squinted, recognizing the language but not knowing it, then held up a hand, smiling, to show he'd made a mistake. He returned to his wife, shaking his head.

"What was that?" Karel whispered.

"When we get there, I'll tell you."

"Get where?"

"To the airport."

It was dark when they reached Pankov International. By that point, someone had spray-painted over PANKOV, but no one had yet renamed it. They climbed down from the bus at the far end of the parking lot and walked the half mile to the terminal. Gavra walked quickly, so the suspicious man and his wife would be left far behind.

"We picking up someone?" said Karel, jogging to catch up.

"We're leaving."

"Leaving? Why?"

"We're just going."

Karel stopped, and Gavra had to come back to fetch him. "I'm not going anywhere. I live here, you know."

"Come on," Gavra urged, dragging him along. "You don't know everything yet. You'll understand. We've got to get out of here."

"Then explain it now."

"Later."

"*No.*" Like a child, Karel dug in his heels, then dropped until he was sitting on the ground next to a rusted Trabant. He squeezed himself, partly from the cold. "I'm not moving until you tell me."

So Gavra returned, squatted in front of his friend, and told him everything. By the time he finished, Karel was trembling. "You? *You* did it?"

"They were going to kill you."

That was more responsibility than Karel could take. He swatted away Gavra's hands. By that point the other bus passengers had reached and passed them. They all seemed interested in Karel's behavior.

"If you'd been there," said Gavra, "you'd understand. Now come on."

"But why are we leaving?"

There was no way to explain it to his friend's satisfaction. The fact was that after shooting the Pankovs, he realized there was nothing left in our country for him. His job was obsolete. His apartment was surrounded by people who had been waiting years to attack him openly. His new government was awash in murderers. He'd done something that no one he knew—myself included—would ever be able to understand, so there was only one thing left: to abandon this place. All he could manage was, "I hate this country. I can't live here anymore."

"But what about me?"

Gavra settled on the cold ground next to him. "We'll go to Amsterdam. I have friends there. We'll find work, better work, and we'll be in the West. Don't you want to go west?"

They'd never discussed this before, so Gavra was surprised when his friend said, "Absolutely not. I've never even considered it."

"Give it a month. If it's not working out, we'll come back."

"But I don't even speak Dutch!"

Gavra's patience ran out. He gripped Karel's elbow and heaved him into a standing position. "Fine. I don't give a damn. Just come in to see me off. You can stay in this shit hole."

Despite what he'd said, after he exchanged the American dollars he still had left from Yuri Kolev, he bought two tickets to Budapest—the next international flight out—from a frazzled TisAir clerk. "It's like a sinking ship," she said, "but the rats are flying."

Gavra didn't know if the woman was trying to scold him for

abandoning the ship, but it didn't matter, because, as she was writing out a receipt, she looked up and squinted at him. "My God," she muttered. "It's *you*."

"I don't need a receipt." He stuffed the tickets into his pocket and walked over to Karel, who was moping by the glass doors. He glanced back to see the clerk talking with her manager, pointing in his direction.

He again grabbed Karel's arm and led him down a corridor, past the bathrooms, to a door labeled SECURITY. It was locked, so he knocked until a fat man in a guard's uniform opened up. The man blinked in the bright light of the corridor. "Gavra?"

"Hi, Toni. Let us in?"

Toni stepped back, and they entered a small, dark room lit by ten video monitors. Toni, who had the white skin of his job, took a seat, shaking his head. "It *was* you, wasn't it?"

"Yeah," said Gavra. He searched the monitors until he found the camera outside their door, where a few people in blue TisAir uniforms came smiling down the corridor, looking for him. They kept moving past the security office.

"What're you doing here?" said Toni.

"Hiding out until my plane leaves." He leaned on the simple desk. Karel stood uncomfortably with his arms around himself. "This is my friend Karel. Karel, Toni."

They shook hands. Then Toni bent under the desk and tugged out an old cardboard box. He produced plastic cups and a bottle of plum brandy. "This calls for a toast. To the man who rid us of a couple of real monsters."

Karel glared at Gavra.

Toni handed out the shots and raised his cup. "To Gavra Noukas, who's put us on the road to freedom!"

Toni threw back his drink, and Gavra followed suit, the rough homemade brew burning his throat. Karel took a small sip, then set it down. Gavra said, "You have to decide, Karel. Come with me."

Toni, clutching his third brandy, looked confused but was smart enough not to interrupt.

"Someone has to stay around," said Karel. "Someone has to vote."

"Won't make any difference. It'll be rigged."

Karel shook his head. "You don't know that, Gavra. In fact, you don't know anything for sure. You never have."

Thinking back over that eventful week, Gavra could see how right his friend was.

THIRTY—TWO

•

The Russian was as big as Ferenc and Bernard but padded with a lot of fat. Ferenc set aside the empty Kalashnikov and searched him beside his car, while Bernard kept the pistol trained on him. He wore a cheap gray suit of Soviet make and stared at me while Ferenc patted him down. "You're Emil Brod?"

"Do I look like Emil Brod?"

Fyodor Malevich cocked his head. "Brano said you'd look devastated. So, yes."

At that moment, I didn't like the Russian, nor did I like Brano.

We brought him into the kitchen and sat him down. He stank of some Moscow hair tonic. Magda served him tea. "Anything stronger?" he asked hopefully.

Magda obliged, setting out a bottle of brandy with four glasses. Agota wandered in, carrying Sanja. "Hello," she said, surprised.

Magda took Sanja from her, and that was the first time I heard the baby cry. "Come on. Let them get drunk and do their talking."

Bernard poured the drinks, and Malevich raised his glass. "*Nazdorovye!*"

We drank but didn't repeat the word. He reached into his jacket pocket and placed a train ticket envelope on the table in front of me.

"This, Comrade Brod, is for you. Second class straight through to Vienna."

I picked it up, confused. "Vienna?"

"Brano asks that you come see him. It leaves Sárospatak at one in the morning. He'll be waiting for you. Everything's arranged."

"How did Brano know I was here?"

"*I* knew," said Malevich. "You visited Comrade Kolyeszar's head-quarters. Think I'm *not* watching that place?"

"I'm not going to Vienna."

The Russian shrugged and pushed his empty glass forward, but no one chose to refill it. "That's up to you. I've done my duty and passed it on. You do as you like."

"But why?" I said.

He stared at his glass. "Brano told me nothing. He just sent a tele-gram saying it was urgent you come to him on that train. So I bought the ticket on the way here."

I stared at it. I had no desire to see Vienna, or Brano Sev.

"And now," continued Malevich, pushing his glass closer to the bottle, "Comrade Kolyeszar." He smiled at Ferenc, but Ferenc didn't smile back. "You and I must talk."

"About what?"

"About how to salvage this situation. How to save some little part of the popular revolution."

Ferenc reached for the bottle and refilled all our glasses. Malevich looked relieved. But then Ferenc clapped his hand over the Russian's glass. "Just over a week ago, some of my people captured you. You had a colonel's uniform in your wardrobe. I know this. Further, I know you and your KGB friends were trying to undermine my work. Why would you be interested in changing sides now?"

Suddenly, the big Russian laughed, echoing in the kitchen. He slapped the table. "No!" He shook his head and pointed at Ferenc. "You revolutionaries are so narrow-minded!"

Ferenc removed his hand from the glass and let him drink it down. The Russian set down the empty glass.

"Listen, Ferenc. You're letting paranoia get the best of you. What you may not know is that I've got a crackpot for a boss. Gorbachev. He starts seeing the results of his idiotic *catastroika* and realizes he's made a mistake. Everything's going down the tubes. The Poles, the Germans, the Czechs, the Hungarians." He shook his head. "Everywhere, it's turning to shit. So what does he do? He pulls in some of the head guys and talks over options. They tell him, quite reasonably, that the only real option is to send in the Red Army until all this blows over. Secure socialism, et cetera. But Gorby doesn't do that. He sends them all away and calls in *my* boss, Vladimir Aleksandrovich Kryuchkov. He says he's not worried about losing these countries. He's very philosophical. He only worries that the results won't be what the people want. He actually *says* that!"

He laughed, red-faced, but none of us was laughing with him.

He settled down. "Okay. You don't believe me. Whatever. But the fact of the matter is, we start getting our mission briefs. Go in, take a look at the situation, and do our best to make sure there's no bloodshed. If the people want to start a new government, then so be it. Just make sure there aren't any massacres, okay?"

Bernard broke in. "Not very successful, were you?"

The Russian squinted at him and spoke seriously. "You think thirty dead's a massacre? If it weren't for us, brother, there'd be three hundred dead."

"How does Brano Sev come into this?" I asked.

Malevich looked at me. "He's a friend of the people, our Comrade Sev. He's always been. Who do you think told us to support your buddy here?" he said, motioning toward Ferenc. "Who told us to watch out for the Galicia Revolutionary Committee and all its CIA money?"

I looked at Ferenc; he, too, was stunned, but he found his tongue. "So what have you been doing to stop the committee?"

Again the Russian shrugged, but this time he reached for the brandy himself and filled our glasses. "Not as much as I'd like. My boss tells me to protect your Democratic Forum but also says I can't shoot anybody. What am I supposed to do? Why do you think the glorious Bolshevik Revolution was so full of corpses? There's no other way to get rid of the foreign influence. Everyone's crazy about Gorby, but the man's about as practical as a firefly."

None of us knew whether or not to believe him. The fact that he'd used Brano Sev's name wasn't enough. Then again, what would the Russians gain by hurting Ferenc when the real threat was in the Capital, where friends of America were already in control of the country?

Malevich said, "I bet you never thought you'd have a Russian come to protect you from the Americans."

"That's why it's so hard to believe," muttered Bernard.

"It's just common sense," said the Russian. "You've got the CIA, they've been funding the Galicia Committee for years. Millions of dollars, probably, when you add it up. Then there's unrest in Patak, and a senator comes to visit the CIA director and says, *This is what we've been paying for, right?* Now, that director, he'd like to keep hold of his pretty secretary (who's probably his mistress), his fancy office, and his pension. So he says, *Yes, of course. This is exactly what you've been paying for.* Now, he's got to make sure it happens. He makes sure *his* team gets into power."

"They're funding murderers and communists," Bernard said.

"*Syn*, wake up," said Malevich.

"I'm not your son," countered Bernard.

The Russian raised his hands. "Okay. But the Americans don't care about this. They only care that the new government will owe them something. What they *want*, and what they're getting, is a group of countries who love them. Everybody needs to justify his budget, and if a million dollars buys you the friendship of a whole country, that's money well spent."

Ferenc, like me, was tired of this talk. "Okay. Say I believe all this. How are you going to help us?"

"Not much can be done anymore," he said. "There's only one option: You meet with the opposition and negotiate a settlement."

"Settlement?" said Bernard. "You don't settle with murderers!"

"We settle with murderers every day," said Malevich. He turned to Ferenc. "What you need to do is get a foot in the door. Then you can run for office. It's the only way."

Ferenc, too, was angry. He'd spent the last days filled with the naive optimism that somehow his ragged band of students could overpower the Capital by simple moral force. He refilled his own glass, threw the brandy down his throat, and lit a cigarette. He stood and stared down at the Russian. "Brano agrees with this?"

"He did when I spoke to him."

"When?"

"Couple of weeks ago. We discussed the various outcomes and what should be done in each case. He seemed to think he had information that could bring down the committee's main candidate. But not anymore. That fell through."

I closed my eyes, trying to block out all this. Brano, I realized, knew long ago what would unfold here. If he'd told me about this weeks ago, Lena might still be alive. I said to Ferenc, "I don't trust this."

"Neither do I," he said, wandering toward the sink, smoke streaming from his cigarette.

Bernard remained silent. He stared at his empty glass, turning it in his fingers.

"Okay, then," said Malevich. "If you've got a better plan, then let me know. I'll be happy to assist." He reached for the bottle again.

It was no use. For the next hour, the Russian gradually went through the bottle, and Ferenc tried to come up with alternatives. He made phone calls, discussing the Russian's plan with his young revolutionaries, and they reacted as he had, but with the self-righteousness of youth. They weren't able to think straight. I went outside with him and tried to come up with something, anything, but I was never a political thinker, and Ferenc, despite his position, wasn't much of one either. At least with this solution, Ferenc's people wouldn't be completely marginalized. They could represent the western part of the country in parliament, and even put forth their own candidate for president.

Malevich didn't gloat when Ferenc admitted he had no alternatives. Instead, the Russian cocked his head and said, "You know, Brano never thought it would come to this either. I told him from the beginning this is where it would go, but he refused to believe me. That man, he's as idealistic as the rest of you. He's an eternal optimist."

Ferenc frowned at him. "I never took Brano for an optimist."

Neither had I.

"Oh," said the Russian. "One more message from Brano Sev, then I take Comrade Brod to the train station."

"What's that?" said Ferenc.

"He wishes you all a happy Christmas."

THIRTY — THREE

•

Of course, I went. Like Gavra, I was starting to realize there was nothing for me at home anymore. The life of Militia Chief Emil Brod, at sixty-four years, had ended with an automobile explosion. And what had that life been anyway, when I'd never even known my wife? It had been an illusion. Whether my final days were eked out at home or in Austria, it made no difference. I just didn't want anyone else to die because of my stupidity.

When Magda kissed me good-bye, she was out of threats. She squeezed my face in her hands and told me to come back soon, because Austria would be too much for a simple man like me. She meant it as a compliment. As thanks, I handed her Gavra's Makarov and told her to bury it.

In the car, Fyodor Malevich became serious. For a moment I wondered if this was all a trap. Maybe Brano hadn't sent him; maybe I would be the last witness to die, quietly on a frigid evening roadside. But he just wanted to tell me, in private, how sorry he was about Lena. His own wife had been killed five years before when he was stationed in Paris, a hit-and-run. Though it was never solved, he believed the English had done it in retaliation for an agent of theirs he'd had to kill months before. As we crossed the Bodrog, entering Sárospatak, he said, "Get prepared, my friend, because you'll never get over it."

The train was packed, and though my ticket gave me rights to a window seat, I found it occupied by a pregnant woman and her baby, so I spent the hour until the Hungarian border smoking in the corridor. It occurred to me as we pulled into Szerencs that I didn't have a passport and would be turned back, but it was a different time then, fraternal borders briefly open to all newly freed peoples—my Militia card sufficed. We stopped for a couple of hours in Budapest, where the train emptied. I found a window seat and peered out at Déli Station, its platform still shrouded in predawn gloom, then dozed until a Hungarian man woke me in Tatabánya, insisting my seat was his. I had to change trains there anyway. I found my new train, tracked another empty seat, took some Captopril, and went back to sleep.

It was all catching up to me by then. The exertion of the last days had put my back out, but until that train I'd been able to ignore it. I kept waking up, my lower spine tight and burning, and no position helped. Of course, it wasn't just the physical discomfort. It was everything.

The worst thing was Lena, knowing that I'd never really known her. If she'd survived, perhaps she would have told me on her own. A deathbed confession, or something less dramatic. A quiet talk over dinner. She was dead, though, and I was left without answers. A part of me was starting to hate her, and that only made me hate myself. If I had any reservations about what I would later do, that's when they left me. When I started to hate myself.

I've had time since to think about a lot of things, and it still surprises me I'm alive. When your personal life runs so sharply into the life of your country, there's no place to rest. Not even in another country. And since you're no longer young, your body balks at the things you have to do. It even denies you the escape of physical pleasure. Wherever you turn, there's pain. It starts to drive you a little mad. Because people are not built to take this. Why should they be? Stories like mine are not supposed to happen.

The sun was up by the time we reached the Austrian border. I'd assumed that my Militia pass would get me through there as well, but the border guard, a tall, blond young man who didn't care what I'd been through, shook his head and led me out of the train at Nickelsdorf. *So it's over,* I thought, and a part of me was happy to be turned back. At least my story would end. I listened as he spoke to his supervisor, explaining what I'd offered as identification. "Let me see," said the supervisor.

From his pocket he unfolded a telegram, then compared my ID to it. He returned my Militia certificate and nodded politely. "Welcome to Austria, Herr Brod. You may return to the train."

The guard who'd taken me off was annoyed, and he argued with his supervisor as I returned to my seat and stared out at them. My success left me feeling uncomfortable. The train lurched and started forward again.

This was the first time since 1947 that I'd left the East. There was no difference outside my window—the sun wasn't brighter, the fields weren't more lush. I was soon asleep again, but my back still hurt.

It was a little before ten in the morning when we pulled into the large block of stone and glass that was Vienna's Südbahnhof, in the Favoriten district. I helped a student wrestle his bags down to the bleak concrete platform, then waited, hands on my hips. Police and departing passengers wandered by, some pushing wheeled carts loaded with suitcases. Then, at the end of the platform, by the Südbahnhof doors, I saw Brano Sev. He'd gotten fatter in retirement, but he wore the same cheap brown suit I remembered from his retirement party. I wondered if it had been refitted. He still had hair on top, but not much, and it was all white.

He didn't bother waving or showing any of the signs of excitement common to transportation hubs. He didn't even move quickly, and I didn't bother walking to meet him. As he approached, I saw those familiar three moles on his left cheek. I also saw I'd been wrong—it was a new suit, and it wasn't cheap. It just appeared that way from a distance, because of the way he wore it. His face was the surprise. Up close, there was color in his cheeks, and the chronic bags under his eyes had shrunk. When he retired, he'd looked older than his sixty-nine years; now, at seventy-two, he looked sixty-five.

"Emil," he said, and we shook hands. "Thanks for coming."

"I didn't have much of a choice."

"You always have a choice. I'm just pleased my telegram got you through the border."

"Me, too."

"Listen," he began, then coughed into his fist. "My condolences. About Lena."

"Oh. Okay."

He peered past me. "No baggage?"

I shook my head, then wondered if he meant it metaphorically.

"Here's something, then." He reached into his pocket and handed me a stiff brick-colored passport. On the cover was an eagle with a crest and the words REPUBLIK ÖSTERREICH and REISEPASS. Inside, I found my photograph and name.

"What's this?"

"What's it look like?" He patted my back to encourage me to walk. "My friend helped put it together, very quickly. I figured you wouldn't have your passport, and I don't want the Austrian police stopping you."

He led the way down steps, through an underground passage, and up an escalator to a dirty station with high windows looking out onto the busy main street, Wiener Gürtel. We stood at the curb as shining Western cars flew by in the cold; then Brano raised a hand easily, and a black BMW pulled up. He opened the back door and nodded me in.

Both of us took the rear seat, and I saw that the driver was younger than Brano, late fifties, perhaps. He was clearly no taxi driver. In his breast pocket he wore a carnation. He smiled in the rearview as he merged into the traffic. "Good morning," he said in our language, though it was awkward for him. "I'm Ludwig. A friend."

"German is fine," I said in German.

"*Gut,*" said Ludwig. He took a right at the next intersection, and we started driving out of town.

Brano was gazing contentedly out the window. "So?" I said.

He looked at me and blinked twice. "How rested are you?"

"Not very, but I'll manage."

"We can get you a change of clothes from my wardrobe. Tomorrow we'll go shopping. Want to come, Ludwig?"

The driver nodded. "Certainly."

"He makes all my fashion decisions," said Brano, smiling.

"Stop it," I said.

"Stop what?" Brano said it as if he didn't know.

"I just spent nine hours in a train, based on a KGB officer's suggestion. Now tell me what's going on."

Through the window, Habsburg buildings, so much cleaner than at home, sped by. Brano said, "We're going to make things right."

"Good luck."

"I thought you'd be pleased."

"Maybe I will be," I said, "but I need to know everything. From the beginning."

Brano said to Ludwig, "Take the long way." Then he turned back to me. "You know about Gavra's trip to America?"

"I know he went."

"Well, I sent him. I'd known for a while about Jerzy Michalec and Rosta Gorski's plan to seize power at home. The Austrians," he said, nodding at Ludwig, "were watching the émigrés here in Vienna. Gorski met with them regularly. He was gathering men to put back in the country. As you can imagine, I wasn't pleased about this."

"End of communism and all."

Brano stared blankly at me. "Yes. But more importantly, I learned that Jerzy Michalec's group—the Galicia Committee—was being funded almost entirely by the Americans. That was more troubling to me than the demise of communism."

Ludwig made a turn and sped up; soon we were on a broad highway.

"I got in touch with an old friend," said Brano. "Yuri Kolev. He worked from the inside, I from the outside. We started to gain a picture of what was happening. It was his idea to bring in the Russians. He knew someone in Moscow he thought he could trust. Sárospatak seemed to be the flashpoint, so we agreed that Russian agents would be best sent there. To let Ferenc's revolution follow its own course. We didn't want the Galicia Committee taking control, and we didn't want anyone killed unnecessarily. But the next part—" He tapped his head. "That was my stupidity."

"The files," I said.

He nodded. "Kolev didn't know Jerzy Michalec. Their paths had never crossed. But I remembered the case and asked him to gather the files on it from the archives. They could be of use; they might be able to discredit him. Yuri called back, two weeks ago, and told me they were gone. Signed out by Rosta Gorski, authorized by Nikolai Romek." He shook his head. "Romek was a surprise. I'd known him a long time ago—you might remember him from my retirement party. I thought he was better than that. Kolev and I realized they were going to doctor or destroy the files. We didn't know they'd follow up by killing the witnesses." He tapped his temple again. "My stupidity. I didn't imagine they would be so thorough. Only a week ago, on Sunday, when Dušan Volan was found killed, did it occur to me that everyone was in danger."

"You knew on Sunday," I said.

"Late Sunday night, yes. Kolev called. In a panic. We knew that the people in the files were in danger. He sent Gavra to America to protect one of them, Lebed Putonski. But Gavra failed."

I rubbed my stinging eyes as the anger bled into me. Brano knew, from Sunday, that Lena's life was in danger. "Why didn't you warn us? Lena's dead!"

Brano seemed surprised by my emotion. "I told Yuri Kolev to guard you," he said, then cleared his throat. "On Wednesday, I found out he was dead too. So I tried to get in touch with Gavra. He wasn't in; then no one answered his phone."

That started to make sense, but then it didn't. "You couldn't have just called me?"

"I did, Emil." He paused. "I called your house. I talked to Lena."

"But—" I began, then understood. Outside the window, rolling countryside eased past. "You were her handler. In the Ministry. Lena worked for you."

That, too, seemed to surprise him. He scratched the corners of his mouth. "Yes," he said quietly.

"You bastard."

In the rearview, Ludwig's eyes flashed at me, but he drove on without comment.

Brano said, "Lena told me you two were going to your place in Ruscova. I thought she was taking care of it."

I rubbed my eyes, remembering her attempts to get me to leave with her. She'd been angry, frustrated by my resolve. Now I knew why. "You should have told *me*."

"You're probably right, Emil. I'm sorry about that."

Now I was the one left surprised, because I couldn't remember when, during the three decades he worked in the Militia station, Brano had ever apologized.

The road hummed beneath us.

"What about Gavra?" I said. "You saw the tape, right?"

Brano scratched his nose and looked out the window again. "I don't know about Gavra. I imagine he was coerced."

"Why?"

"Because of me. Michalec probably thought it would shut me up." Brano let a little smile appear in the corners of his lips. "Michalec's wrong."

"But there's nothing else to do," I said. "Even your Russian friend admitted that."

Brano shook his head. "A lot of the Galicia Committee are good people, no matter who's funding them. Earnest. Interested in giving the government back to the people. The problem is at the top. Michalec, Gorski, Romek, Andras Todescu, and some other old communists who don't want to lose their influence. The rest of them, the ones doing the work, they're good people. The problem is, how do you get rid of the bad eggs?"

I said the first thing that came to me. "You kill them."

"I suppose that's one way, Emil. But it might be more effective to slander them. That's where our friend Ludwig comes in."

On cue, the driver waved his hand proudly.

Brano said, "You'll be thanking this man a lot in the next days. He's gotten Michalec to come to us."

I had to slow down. My simple militiaman's head wanted to take in each little bit and turn it over in my hands until it was familiar before moving on to the next bit. Brano, unlike me, had had plenty of time to learn, and when I told him to stop I saw the irritation in his face. This was why he'd brought me here, and I needed to listen. "Okay," I said. "Go on."

As it turned out, once the trial and execution had been broadcast, Brano's friend Ludwig got in touch with a friend in Austrian chancellor Franz Vranitzky's cabinet. The cabinet member then contacted our embassy on Ebendorferstraße to invite Michalec to Vienna.

"Why?"

Ludwig answered joyfully, "So the chancellor can congratulate him on his revolution and discuss monetary loans. No one could turn down an offer like that."

"You've got some influence," I told him.

"I've got friends all over," said Ludwig. "Even old commies."

"Of course," said Brano, "the chancellor knows nothing about this, because Michalec will never meet with him."

I still didn't understand. "Then why are you bringing him here?"

Brano paused. "When Jerzy was released from prison in 1956, after fathering Rosta Gorski, he went to work for the Ministry. He still had friends there, and they put him to work. Over time, he became a surveillance technician. He was too weak for any tough work. They sent him to bug rooms and set up cameras in a lot of cities, in particular Vienna. He came here five times during the seventies under different names. He just didn't know the Austrians were aware of it every time. His visits were all documented. So, as soon as he arrives, we'll arrest him as a Ministry spy."

Finally—something unambiguous and simple. Something I could understand. I even managed a smile. "But how did the Austrians know this? That he was a spy."

"Because I told them."

I stared at Brano. With only four words, he'd made it complicated again. I remembered that old, militant Brano Sev, who protected socialism at any cost. Who let Imre's murderer go unpunished and left Imre's wife without an explanation. "Wait," I began, then stopped. "You were working for the Ministry. You . . ." I rubbed my suddenly dry lips. "You were spying for the Austrians, too?"

Brano's smile—a rare thing—blew across his face. "Yes, Emil. I was a double agent. A traitor. But the Austrians, and Ludwig in particular, offered me something I couldn't refuse. Something even you could appreciate."

"What?"

"They watched over my family."

I started to ask how the Austrians could watch over his mother and sister, who lived in our country, but didn't. Even after a week of shocks, this one somehow topped them all.

The evidence was presented to me when we reached a maple-shaded farmhouse outside Vienna and parked beside a very clean pale-blue Volkswagen Bug. The front door opened, and a pretty, dark-haired woman stepped out with flowers in her hand, rosy-cheeked, waving at us.

"Oh Jesus," I said.

Brano patted my leg. "Come meet my wife."

Dijana Franković (Brano told me, almost embarrassed, that she had kept her maiden name) was remarkable. Somewhere in her late forties, she was a Yugoslav who'd lived in Vienna for decades but had learned to speak our language like a native. "Merry Christmas," she said. She handed the bundle of lilacs to me, then kissed my cheeks. I couldn't find my tongue. She said, very seriously, "I hope the flowers are right. It's the custom in your country, correct? When you lose a loved one."

I actually wasn't sure, but I nodded.

"Please," she said. "Welcome to my house."

Brano, standing behind her, beamed in a way I'd never seen. Ludwig said, "Dijana, you're looking ravishing."

She winked at me. "That man's been after me since 1967."

Inside, Brano called up the stairs to the second floor. "Jelena! Come meet our guests!"

A woman's voice floated back. "Be right down."

Stiffly, I settled on one of the leather sofas surrounding a large television. Against the wall a fireplace burned logs. Ludwig produced a pack of cigarettes and offered me one; I accepted. So did Brano. Soon all three of us were puffing away in this comfortable place. Dijana emerged from somewhere carrying a tray of cut meats and water. "Put out those filthy things and eat."

I was the only one who followed her command. The meats were delicious.

Then my surprise was complete. A tall, lovely young woman in her early twenties came down the steps. Brano smiled at her, and she even smiled back as she fitted an earring under her long, straight auburn hair. I stood involuntarily as she leaned over the table and offered a hand. She had wide brown eyes. "I'm Jelena," she said in our language.

"My daughter," Brano said proudly.

Her hand was soft, and her smile was full of white teeth.

As I settled down again, she disappeared into the kitchen, and Dijana sat beside me. She patted my leg. "Anything you want, just ask."

I couldn't think straight enough to ask for anything. I just stared at Brano. "Why didn't you tell anyone?"

"Like I said, I wanted to protect them. How do you think my old employers would have reacted if they knew I had a family here? They would've made sure I couldn't leave the country anymore, for one. Two: They would've figured out I was passing information to the Austrians. Thirdly, they would've hassled my family for information." He shook his head. "Almost no one knew."

"Lena?"

He took a slice of ham from the tray and delivered it to his mouth.

"Did you wash your hands?" Dijana said firmly.

He ignored her and looked at me. "Don't blame Lena. Never blame her. I made her swear not to tell you about this."

"And her work?" I said, my cheeks growing warm. "Did you tell her to hide that from me, too?"

"That was her idea," he told me. "At first, she was afraid. She didn't know how you'd take it. But the lie troubled her. It made her drinking worse. Remember that time she ended up in the hospital? When she quit?"

My face was burning up; I nodded.

"She called me from the hospital. She was very proud of herself. She was going to stop making your life hell. And she did this by quitting the drinking, and quitting the Ministry. That's the day she told me it was over. She wouldn't work for us anymore."

Whatever new understanding I'd had of my wife changed again. I wanted to cry. "What did she do?" I said. "Tell me that, at least."

"Nothing dangerous. Well, usually nothing dangerous. She was smart. She could talk to anyone, get in anywhere. Her job was simply to visit people who knew things, listen, and pass on the information to me."

"And you gave the information to the Ministry."

"And us," said Ludwig. He seemed annoyed at being left out of the conversation.

"Did she know?" I said. "Did she know she was also supplying the Austrians with information?"

"I made sure she didn't know," said Brano. "That would've put her in danger."

"What about her file? Rosta Gorski said it wasn't in the archives."

"A precaution," said Brano. "Before I retired, I went through and cleared out everything on her. I didn't want her being passed on to another controller, someone who might force her to go back to work."

Jelena came in, smiling, and noticed the silence. Her smile disappeared. She sat in a metal-framed chair clutching a glass of orange juice.

Brano finally said, "Lena was practical. That's why she agreed to work for the Ministry. It was the only way to keep her and your lifestyle. She knew you didn't want to leave the country, but she didn't blame you for it. It was more important that you remain happy. She knew you'd only be happy at home."

I'd heard enough. I didn't want to ask more, because Lena wouldn't want me to. I'd had enough information to deal with for one day. For the rest of my life, even. I took another of Ludwig's cigarettes and lit it. "Okay. Let's talk about Michalec. When does he get here?"

Brano raised his hand and looked at his silver wristwatch. "In three and a half hours. Two twenty P.M."

•

THIRTY-FOUR

Brano, as usual, understood the situation better than I did. If I'd trusted him, everything would have turned out differently, perhaps better, and I wouldn't feel the need to write all this out. The plan was simple. When Michalec's plane landed at two twenty in the afternoon, his entourage would drive him to our embassy. On the way, Ludwig's men would intercept the vehicle and arrest Michalec for espionage. "Why not arrest him when he lands?" I said.

Brano shook his head, but Ludwig answered. "We want it to be sensational. We want witnesses; we want the press to be interested. There won't be press waiting at the airport, because we can't publicize a meeting that isn't going to happen. But out in the street, screeching tires and pistols waving . . . the newspapers will be all over the story."

I still didn't quite comprehend it. "But what do you get out of this, Ludwig? How's all this in Austria's best interests?"

Ludwig looked at Brano, who shrugged. "Tell him."

"We're not entirely neutral," Ludwig said. "We've never been. How do you think the French get money into the East? They get it in through us. And when we feel like it, we supplement their money with our own. Your friend Ferenc—he and his people are beneficiaries of our generosity. Brano saw to that. Like the Americans, we don't want to see our money go to waste."

I looked at Brano, then the Austrian. "Ferenc never told me this."

"He knows better," said Ludwig.

I suppose it's true of all revolutions. When there appear to be two or three sides fighting over a country, each side is made up of infinite smaller interests, working to make their money pay off in the end. No one wants to be on the losing side.

Even sitting in a room with these power brokers explaining everything so clearly, it was still confusing. Magda was right about me. I was too simple for this world.

Jelena finished her orange juice and said, "Can you imagine what it's like growing up around this kind of stuff?"

I shook my head.

"She takes it well," said Brano.

"She takes after me," Dijana muttered as she got up to clear away the food.

After I'd showered and changed into some of Brano's clothes, which were a little loose on me, he came up to the bedroom with two glasses of Serbian *rakija*. We sat at a small table by the window, looking out over a forest of maples, and he showed me copies of some of the photographs to be used against Jerzy Michalec. There was Jerzy in a hotel room, clearly marked as the Vienna Inter-Continental by papers on the desk, crouched in a corner, installing a microphone in the overhead lamp, his open briefcase on the bed full of equipment. In another, shot from a passing car, he leaned against a doorway with a camera propped against his face. Another one was a photograph of a Hungarian 37M Femaru pistol laid flat on a table, with a card displaying a magnified thumbprint. "What this?" I asked.

"A murder weapon. Killed a well-known émigré named Filip Lutz in 1967. That's Michalec's print."

"He killed an émigré?"

Brano paused, considering what to reveal to me, and since it doesn't matter now I won't hide it either. "He didn't kill anyone. Michalec only did surveillance, but I'm framing him for this one. He was in Vienna at the time, though I didn't know it. He was taking photographs of me."

"Do you know who the murderer was?"

"Someone else pulled the trigger, but it was my fault. A chief of mine did it."

"Oh," I said. Asking a question about Brano Sev's life only provoked more questions.

"Tying him to a murder, rather than just basic surveillance, will let us hold him long enough to ruin his reputation."

It seemed like a well thought-out plan, but I was still unsure. I was unsure of Brano. So I asked him what I'd wanted to ask all day. "I don't get it. You, of all people. You've been a communist all your life. I thought you were one of the true believers."

Brano set down the glass and crossed his hands over his lap. When he talked, it was in a whisper. "Emil, I've spent my whole life defending socialism. It sounds silly, particularly now that it's falling apart, but I've never stopped believing in it. Socialism—and, yes, communism—were always more important than my own skin. Not more important than my girls, no, but more important than *me*." He picked up his glass and took a sip. "But all along the way, decade after decade, I kept running into people like Jerzy Michalec. From the bottom rungs to the top. People who think socialism's a joke. That it's only a tool for their own gain. And now," he said, grunting sourly, "*now* we're faced with what's probably the failure of everything I've worked for all my life. Why? Because socialism has been crippled the whole time by people like Jerzy Michalec." He cleared his throat. "It makes a joke of everything I've tried to do. It makes a joke out of my entire life. And that doesn't sit well with me."

He took another drink, as if the discussion were over. So I prodded: "If you've always worked for socialism, why were you helping out Ferenc and his people?"

He set down his glass again. "You have to understand that what we had in our country wasn't socialism. It was totalitarianism. I always knew that, but I believed—foolishly—that it was just the first step. Marx talked about it. The Dictatorship of the Proletariat. It's supposed to be a transitional phase. You control the economy and adjust it in preparation for pure communism. It looks good on paper," he said, smiling. "It really does. But Marx was as naive as I was. He thought that greed would lose its power when people were faced with the possibility of utopia. It took me a long time to see the mistake. People like Jerzy Michalec, Tomiak Pankov, and even Nikolai Romek—they're the reason we'll never see pure communism on this earth. They eat it up from the inside."

He shook his head and finished the shot. I brought my own glass to my lips but realized it was empty. Was Brano Sev really serious? Yes—it was all over the old agent's face. I felt sorry for him. He was the only true believer I'd ever met. I began to see my old country as if it were a church full of atheists, where the only Christian wasn't even standing at the podium but sitting in the back pews.

"You're full of surprises, Brano."

"I'm not," he said. "The problem is that no one has ever believed me."

We let that sit between us a while as we stared out at the maples. Then I asked him why I was there. "You don't need me for any of this."

He nodded. "That's true, but I wanted you to see it for yourself. I feel responsible for what's happened, and it's the only thing I can think of to help you. I want you to be there when the man who murdered your wife is taken down."

Everyone makes mistakes, even Brano Oleksy Sev.

He left me alone to get some rest, and that, too, was a mistake. It gave me too much time to think through my anger and come out the other end. It allowed me the time to betray him.

Whoever made the mistake, what followed was not Brano Sev's fault. It was mine. I can claim some temporary insanity, I suppose, but that's not right either. The truth is, I knew what I was doing every step of the way, and the blame is entirely mine. Remember that.

There was a telephone in the room, and I listened a moment for the dial tone, then called the operator. She had a heavy Vienna accent, which I found endearing, and after she'd given me the number of my embassy, she said, "*Gruß Gott*," which I liked as well. I didn't like the sound of the male secretary who picked up at the embassy. When I told him I needed to speak with the ambassador, he refused outright.

"Get him on now," I said. "I have information on a plot against Jerzy Michalec's life."

A half hour later, when Brano came up to fetch me, I made a show of rubbing my temples. "Sorry, Brano. I appreciate you bringing me here, but I can't. I can't look at that man again, not after what he did to Lena."

He sat on the edge of the bed and patted my knee affectionately. "Like I said before, Emil, you always have a choice. You can even stay if you want. In the West. Think about it."

"Thanks."

I walked with him across the hall to his study and watched him take a key from his desk and use it on a cabinet where he kept three handguns. He took out a Makarov and proceeded to load it. "It's important he not be killed," Brano told me, as if he suspected.

I nodded, as if I agreed.

"If we kill him, then we lose leverage over the son. A dead father is less threat to Gorski's political career than a living one with a corrupt past."

Again I nodded.

Brano locked the cabinet, put the key back in his desk, and slipped the Makarov into his belt.

I stood with Dijana and Jelena and shook Brano and Ludwig's hands and wished them luck. They went to the BMW. First they would meet up with Ludwig's men near the airport, then take their positions. That gave me time. They drove off, leaving the Volkswagen behind, and after they were gone Dijana said, "I'm scared. That bastard always tells me he's retired, then he pulls something like this."

"Dad's a professional liar," said Jelena. She seemed amused by that fact. "A commie pinko liar."

"He'll be fine," I said, then sighed audibly. "Listen. Do you mind if I borrow your car? I'd like to clear my head."

Dijana rubbed my arm tenderly. "Of course."

"I'll go up for my hat," I said. "Be right back."

"Take your time," said Dijana. "And let me give you some spending money."

She really was very nice. They both were. Brano was an unbelievably lucky man.

THIRTY-FIVE

•

Brano and Ludwig parked in a lot near the airstrip beside another BMW. They talked over the details of the operation with two of Ludwig's men and verified their radios were operating. The two assistants waited just outside the airport entrance; Brano and Ludwig would wait outside the arrivals gate for the blue-plated embassy car to leave. Once they were in pursuit, they'd radio ahead to the others, and everyone would go into town together, sandwiching the embassy car with Jerzy Michalec inside.

Then, on the Ring Road around the old town, the first car would screech to a stop, turning aside so Michalec couldn't pass, and Brano and Ludwig would do the same thing. Ludwig had already tipped off a journalist from *Der Standard,* who would be waiting at the intersection with a camera.

It proceeded according to plan. Brano pointed at a tall old man in a hat and sunglasses who stepped into the back of the embassy car, and then he radioed to Ludwig's men. There were a couple of points along the A4 where Brano worried they were losing the car, but Ludwig knew the roads, and he knew how to drive so that he wouldn't be noticed. The traffic thickened, but Ludwig remained on track, and when they reached the Ring Road, Ludwig even pointed

at a man standing by the crosswalk at Dr. K. Renner and Volks-
gartenstraße. "There's Jan. He's got the camera."

Brano picked up the radio and said, "Now."

The BMW in front turned sharply, screeching up on two wheels,
and stopped. Doors popped open, and Ludwig's men jumped out,
guns in view, screaming in German for the driver and passenger to
show their hands.

From behind, Ludwig and Brano did the same thing. Brano, because of his age, moved slower, but they waited for him to reach the
back door and rip it open, finding an old man in a hat and sunglasses wailing in our language for him to please not shoot. Brano
lowered his gun and took the sunglasses off the man's face. A moment of shock.

According to *Der Standard*'s evening edition, the old man's name
was Gustav Hegy, one of Michalec's personal assistants, of which he
had many.

It took a minute, Brano working back over everything that had
come before this moment. He was smart—he'd always been smart—
and even with so little information he was able to see that I'd betrayed
him. He grabbed Ludwig and shouted, "Airport!"

A half hour before that moment, I sat in the driver's seat of Brano's
Volkswagen, Brano's heavy Walther PP on the passenger's seat. I'd
stopped a few cars behind Ludwig's BMW and waited as the old
man got into the embassy car and Brano and Ludwig followed.
Then I started the engine. Ten minutes later, Jerzy Michalec appeared with his large bodyguard, looked around, and walked over to
a Mercedes taxi.

I gunned the engine and squealed around parked cars, nearly hitting a woman crossing the lane. At the sound of the tires, Michalec
looked up. He couldn't make out my features but knew the Volkswagen
was coming for him. He stepped back from the waiting taxi and
tugged his bodyguard's sleeve, and the big man reached into his jacket.

I struck the back of the taxi, knocking it a few feet, and pushed open my door. With the pistol in my left hand, I reached around the windshield. I fired twice. The recoil hurt my palm. The bodyguard, still reaching for his gun, jerked and fell on the pavement, kicking wildly.

Screams burst out, and people ran. Michalec froze, then dived behind the taxi. I got out of the car, my heart banging. The taxi driver's hairy hands were raised above his head, his eyes wide. I told him to lie down, but since I spoke in my language, he didn't understand.

My ears hurt. My hands and feet and stomach ached. I continued around the front of the taxi, the Walther low, but found only the groaning bodyguard on the concrete, his wide, enormous chest wet with blood.

I looked around—Michalec had disappeared. Somehow. Then, on the other side of the taxi, I saw him trying to run and realized my mistake. He had slipped around the crushed rear of the taxi.

I went after him, down the covered arrivals lane, and when he stepped out from a car to cross back into the airport, I stopped, raised the gun, gasping, and shot—but missed.

He made it through the glass doors as I shot again, shattering glass behind him, but it didn't slow him at all. I followed, clutching the heavy pistol, and when I got inside, passing a brightly lit gift shop empty of people, I had to stop to figure out where he'd gone. Off to my left, past a McDonald's, two uniformed guards stared at me, confused, then reached for their sidearms. So I ran right, past an unstaffed information desk, through bewildered travelers, and out a pair of glass doors to the sidewalk again. Directly in front of me, by a sign reading SÜDBAHNHOF–WESTBAHNHOF, a large, sooty yellow bus pulled away from the curb.

Its windows were tinted, but between gasps of cold air I could just make out a form collapsing into the fifth seat—an old man, also gasping, pulling at his tie.

Then the bus was gone in a roar of stinking exhaust, making a wide berth for the commotion around the mess I'd caused—the wreck of Brano's VW, the taxi, and Michalec's now-unconscious bodyguard. Policemen spoke into radios, and onlookers crowded in.

For a moment, I believed it was finished. I'd finally reached the end. My heart thumped against the inside of my chest, so painful that I expected that tingling in the arm and the sharp seizure of a heart attack. A part of me even welcomed the rest.

But there's something in human beings that, despite all the disappointments, shame, and heartbreak, keeps us ticking. I don't know what it is, but it came for me during that two-second pause. A dirty green Opel pulled up to the bus stop and let out a young woman. My legs moved me forward. The woman, a pretty brunette standing beside the open passenger door, smiled queerly at me. Then she saw the pistol in my hand. She screamed.

Behind me, a man—probably one of the security guards— shouted, *"Halt!"*

I didn't halt. I pushed the young woman aside, got into the car, pointed the pistol at the older woman behind the wheel, and told her to drive: *"Fahren!"*

As I write this now, the entire scene seems completely improbable. A pistol, a chase, two old men who would be of better use dying in front of their televisions, and a car hijacking.

But this is how I remember it, and I'm backed up by the Vienna airport's security footage, which is now on file with Ludwig's superiors in the Defense Ministry, the Bundesministerium für Landesverteidigung, at Roßauer Lände 1, Vienna. You can certainly ask to see the video; whether or not they let you is a different matter.

What you won't see on that black-and-white video feed is the face of Frau Ingrid Shappelhorn, the fifty-eight-year-old widow who had just dropped off her daughter, Christiane, to catch a flight to meet her fiancé, a Dutch journalist named Rolf. Of course, Christiane didn't make her flight, and Rolf was left standing in the Brussels airport, bewildered. Ingrid, the most unfortunate of them all, was stuck with a sixty-four-year-old madman clutching a Walther PP, screaming at her to *drive*. Which she did in a panic, tires burning against the road.

I go into all this because it's important. I won't call it a moral in this scattershot narrative, but it's something like that. The price of revenge is that everyone around you pays. Gisèle Sully, Brano and his family, even Ludwig—and a decent Austrian family I'd never even met before.

"*Schneller!*" I shouted as she swung around the wreck I'd made minutes ago.

Unlike her daughter, Frau Shappelhorn didn't scream, which impressed me. A heavy woman who'd spent the last six years without a husband, she was someone who took the punches as they came. She gunned the engine and shifted gears, and we sped down the ramp, past the short-term parking lot. Beside her I sat fidgeting, sweating, trying to get air, and inexplicably checking my watch—it was 3:07. My poor veins were ready to burst. Everything had happened so quickly, faster than my brain could work.

"Where?" she said.

I wasn't sure. Did I want her to run down the bus with this little car? No. "South train station," I said, remembering the sign at the bus stop. "Drive normally."

She let off the gas and switched gears again as a taxi pulled in front of us.

"Look," I said, "I'm sorry."

"You can put away the gun," she said. Though she was calm, there was fear in her voice. I felt ashamed.

"But you are taking me, right?"

"If the police don't stop us first."

At the time, I couldn't see just how cool Frau Shappelhorn was. Now I can. I slipped the pistol into my coat pocket and rubbed my face, trying to keep my eyes open. I couldn't take much more of this. I said, "There's going to be a ticket gate when we leave the airport."

"Yes," she said.

"You have a ticket?"

"Of course." She pointed at the dashboard, where a single orange stub lay.

"Go through like normal."

"Okay."

I'll never understand why she didn't try something. We rolled up to the ticket booth, the man inside said, *"Grüß Gott,"* and she said it back, handing over her ticket, and then the mechanical arm rose, and she drove through. When we reached the A4 heading into town, she admitted something: "I thought they'd stop us back there. They should've radioed ahead to stop us."

"Oh," I said, because that hadn't occurred to me.

I learned the answer later, also from *Der Standard*. The ticket booths were connected to the terminals by an underground communications system. That day, the system was being tested because of problems, and it failed when they tried to make contact. Because of the embarrassment over my escape, from the following day all the booths were equipped with wireless radios.

It takes twenty minutes to drive from the Vienna airport to the Südbahnhof, and in that time Frau Shappelhorn began to ask questions. "What's going on?" was her first.

I thought about telling her. I wanted to say, *I'm tracking the man who killed my wife, who's taking over my country.* Even then, overcome with so much physical pain and confusion, I knew it would sound paranoid. It would frighten her more. So I said, "I need to catch someone."

"You need a gun for that?"

"I think so."

"So you need to kill this person."

"No," I lied. "I just need to catch him."

The bus was nowhere in sight, and I wondered if we'd passed it. That would be a good thing. I could reach the bus stop at the

Südbahnhof and wait for him to exit, or go into the bus myself. If we weren't stopped beforehand.

Had I done the right thing? I didn't know. I knew how Brano felt—he must have hated me.

Anyway, it was done. I'd begun the chase because I felt I had no other option. I didn't want Jerzy Michalec enjoying the comforts of an Austrian jail cell and eventual extradition back home, or to France. Because revenge has nothing to do with due process—revenge wants to be sharp, and final.

Frau Shappelhorn drove steadily along the A4. She said, "You don't want to tell me more?"

"There's no point."

"Sure there is. Maybe I can help."

"No," I said. "The last person who helped me ended up dead."

It was the wrong thing to say, but I wasn't thinking straight. The car swerved briefly, and I reached over to steady the wheel; someone blew his horn and passed us. "So you're in trouble," she said.

I even grinned. "Can't you tell?"

That didn't make her feel any better.

I said, "Just drop me off near the Südbahnhof. A block away. Police will probably be waiting for me, and I don't want you to get in trouble."

That seemed to help a little, but I regretting having said it. I wasn't really sure what I'd do when I reached the train station, and it would have been smarter to keep the car. But I wasn't smart. I've never been smart.

I tried to imagine that I was Jerzy Michalec, a criminal who knew he'd been doubly conned. First, by the Austrians—surely he watched Brano and Ludwig follow his double's car. Second, by the person who had warned him. In the bus, he had no way of contacting the embassy, which would start looking for him at the airport. Brano and his Austrian friends would soon do the same, also posting men outside our embassy.

Michalec could get out at the Südbahnhof or go on to the final stop at the Westbahnhof and then try to contact the embassy. But if he believed the Austrian government was out to get him, that it was also watching his embassy, then he wouldn't feel safe here.

There was only one thing a man like Jerzy Michalec would do. He would flee Vienna on the first train leaving.

"Have you accepted Jesus?" said Frau Shappelhorn.

I blinked, unsure if I'd heard her right. "What?"

"Jesus Christ. Have you accepted him as your personal savior?"

"Please," I said. "I don't want to hear about that."

She nodded at the road. "Sure. But you'd be surprised. No matter how terrible your situation seems, Jesus Christ can help. He helps millions every day."

I looked out at the road, then at her. She was as serious about this as I was about Michalec. She took the exit for the Südbahnhof.

She said, "You have to pray. That's the first step. You have to ask Him to come to you, but you have to be ready to accept His Glory."

"Take this left," I said, but she was already taking it, and up ahead I saw a police car with blinking lights but no sirens. The station was a block ahead. "Let me out here."

She pulled to the curb along Wiener Gürtel, and I opened the door. Then, as an afterthought, I reached over to cover her hand on the gearshift. "I'm sorry about this. But thank you. I'll consider giving Jesus Christ a try."

I think that's what she wanted to hear. It meant that her day hadn't been an entire waste.

THIRTY—SIX

•

From the opposite side of Wiener Gürtel, peering through the busy traffic, I spotted the airport bus in front of the ugly Südbahnhof. It was parked along the road, empty, and outside its door stood four policemen talking with the bewildered driver. I didn't see Michalec among the small crowd of passengers who'd been taken off. He'd gotten away before the police arrived.

When the light changed, I crossed behind three teenagers cursing in German. They looked very strange—they wore leather jackets, and their long hair was shaved into Mohawks, like American Indians, but dyed bright green and purple. It was unnerving.

The car ride had given me back my breath, but not my strength. I worked hard to keep up with the teenagers, terrified that a policeman would recognize my face. No one stopped me. I crossed the sidewalk to the entrance, the pistol in my coat pocket feeling very bulky and conspicuous, and waved off a hustler trying to sell me a watch.

The station was airy and cavernous and full of travelers, just as when I'd arrived hours before. An escalator to my left led down, but I continued to the rear wall, where a vast board of departures and arrivals was being updated to the clicking noise of revolving numbers and city names.

I was looking for the next train leaving. There it was, at the top of the departures pane. In two minutes—at three thirty—the train on track 7 would depart for Trieste, Italy.

I hurried through travelers to the escalator. It was difficult getting past them, muttering *Entschuldigung* endlessly, but soon I reached the underground passageway. At the sign for track 7, I used the stairs, gasping, to reach the platform. A bell sounded, warning passengers that the doors to the dirty red train were about to close. I reached an open door on the last car and pulled myself inside. Shaking, I steadied myself against a window that looked out at the station.

As the train started to move, a crowd of policemen poured onto the first platform and spread out, looking for me, and for Jerzy Michalec. They were followed by two men without uniforms. One was tall—Ludwig—and he shouted at the policemen. The other, a short old man with three moles on his cheek, stood back a bit, his hands clasped behind his back. He was staring at my train with a severe expression. I didn't know if he could see me through the dirty glass, but then our eyes met. Brano Sev glared at me with what looked like hatred, but he didn't tug his friend's sleeve to point me out.

That, of course, was another of Brano's mistakes. I wondered, as we moved out of the station, if living so well, with a house and a family that loved him, had made him soft.

I suppose it had.

I didn't go after Michalec immediately. In the space of a couple of hours I'd betrayed Brano Sev, taken his car and ruined it, shot four times at a man, and hijacked a woman's day, chasing the man across town. I'd spent the last half hour acting like a young man, but I wasn't one. I stumbled into an empty compartment and collapsed, catching my breath and fumbling with my medicine bottle.

When the conductor came along and asked for my ticket, I used most of the schillings Dijana had given me to buy second-class passage to Tarvis, on the border. The conductor told me I could buy the rest of my passage from the Italian conductor, who would take his place there.

I thanked him.

Before leaving, he paused and squinted. "*Herr,* are you all right? Do you need something?"

I thanked him again but shook my head, blowing air through pursed lips. The train rumbled on.

I peered out the window at the passing countryside south of Vienna. It really did look the same as home, particularly as the sky turned gray and cloudy. I rubbed my eyes; my head buzzed. I again heard that hum in my ears left over from my wife's death. I tried to think back over the steps that had brought me here, to another country, but couldn't. There seemed to be links missing. I wondered where Ferenc was now, and if he was with that Russian. Then I heard her voice, Lena's, but I couldn't understand what she was saying. She sounded angry.

When the train stopped, I woke up without realizing I'd fallen asleep. We were at a station with bright lamps shining in on my face. I panicked. The sky was dark. I didn't know where I was. I got up and tugged down the window and pulled out the pistol. It caught on the fabric of my coat, but I got it free, holding it below the window as I craned my neck to see down the length of the train. A sign told me we were at a town called Bruck.

The lights at Austrian stations are brighter than at home, and I could see the people who climbed slowly down from the train. Old women mostly, and a few young people with backpacks. Michalec wasn't among them. I kept watching until the train closed up and we were under way again, moving into the darkness. It was 5:18 P.M.

I pushed the window shut and stepped out into the narrow corridor. The conductor squeezed past me, giving a genial nod as he went on to check tickets. I went the opposite way, to the bathroom. I tried not to look in the mirror but couldn't help it. In the flickering train light, I was completely white except for the dark rings around my eyes. I looked like death.

I straightened my collar and adjusted my jacket under my coat, then got a sudden, sharp pain in my left arm. I squeezed it, grunting. Not yet. Later, okay, but not yet. I breathed deeply until the pain subsided, then checked the pistol again. My hand on the metal grip was sweaty, so I dried everything off and looked through my pockets for something with friction. Rubber bands would have helped, but I didn't have any. The best I could do was take some toilet paper and press it between my hand and the grip, squeezing everything together in the pocket of my coat as I slowly proceeded up the train.

The cabins, as I moved forward, became fuller and louder. Austrian families fed plastic-wrapped sandwiches to children, and Italians, sipping smuggled wine, argued in voices that sounded like angry songs. Sometimes they paused to look up at the strange old man staring in through their doors, and once a fat Italian mother with a missing tooth smiled and offered me wine. I smiled back but went on.

I tried not to hurry. I tried to be methodical, but my sick body kept wanting to run. I stopped many times when I found elderly men facing their windows and waited for them to turn back. A couple of times I knocked on their doors and then waved embarrassedly when I saw their faces, as if I'd made a mistake, before continuing on.

The train was ten cars long, and at my steady, meticulous rate it took nearly an hour to reach the restaurant car, where I found a route schedule. Two more cars, and I was at the engine. I hadn't seen him.

I'd neglected to bring cigarettes, so I asked an Austrian businessman for one and smoked by the window, squinting at the schedule. We had another hour before Klagenfurt, then Villach, and then Tarvis on the border. I peered out at the black mountains, just visible in the lights of a passing town, and wondered if I'd been wrong. Perhaps Jerzy Michalec was still in Vienna.

No. I wasn't wrong. I couldn't be.

The bathrooms. There had been seven occupied bathrooms in the train, but I'd only had the patience to wait for four of them. That was the only answer.

I slowly worked my way back down the length of the train. The toilet paper wrapped around my pistol grip was so full of sweat that it had disintegrated into slippery mud, so I waited for a bathroom, replaced the paper, and continued.

I was slower this time, again giving bashful looks of confusion after staring at passengers too long, and people became suspicious. A young Italian man asked me in German what my problem was. I told him I had no problem. I was apparently scaring his mother, so I apologized and went on. When an old Austrian man complained, the conductor also asked me questions and then asked me to please return to my seat. He was kind, though. "You're sick, *Herr.* I can see that. But you cannot scare my passengers. They're my responsibility."

I tried to assure him of my good intentions, but people whose job it is to deal with strangers know better. They can tell, perhaps from the face, when someone has taken that final unimaginable step over the border that separates the rest of the world from murderers. Certainly I knew what it looked like—I'd seen it enough—but I couldn't see it in myself.

Because he insisted, I let him walk me, much too fast, back to my seat. I kept leaning back to look into cabins, but he had little patience. "*Mein Herr.* Please."

During my excursion, an American couple, backpackers, had set up house in my compartment. They looked disappointed when the conductor guided me to my seat. They pulled in the bags of potato chips and canned beer they'd spread over the seats to discourage just this situation. They warmed to me, though. Just before Klagenfurt, the girl offered a beer, and I finally took my hand off that damned pistol to accept it. "Thank you," I said in my best accent.

Halfway through the can, I opened the door and leaned out to look. The conductor was at the end of the corridor, an open book in front of him. He stared at me glumly, and I drew back in.

"Where you headed?" asked the American girl.

I blinked at her. My English wasn't very good.

"*Where are you go-wing?*" she repeated, slow and loud.

"Oh." I nodded and sipped the beer. "Trist."

"Trist?" said the boy.

"He means Trieste," she explained.

The boy nodded.

"We're go-wing to Ven-iss," she told me.

"Venicia," I said in my language and suddenly recalled my youth.

I'd worked for a while on a fishing boat up in the Barents Sea, and among the crew were men from many countries. One of them, a Croat from Split, was obsessed with Venice and the bridge that connected the courthouse to the prison, where prisoners got their last sight of freedom before descending into the their dank cells.

"Ponte dei Sospiri," I said, remembering its Italian name.

The girl smiled, showing all her big teeth, and nodded. She had no idea what I was talking about.

As we pulled into Klagenfurt, I set aside the empty beer can and checked the corridor. The conductor had stepped out to perform his station duties. I climbed down to the platform, again gripping the pistol in my pocket, and under the arc lights watched people leaving. The air was mountainous, cold and clean; it woke me. Again, no Michalec. Perhaps he'd actually found a way out of the Südbahnhof undetected and made his way to the embassy, but I still doubted it. Other people would have tried that, but Michalec wasn't the type of man to panic and run through the streets of a city where anyone could be looking for him. He would have assumed that the Austrian police who came over to his bus just after he'd disembarked were waiting to arrest him. He was on the train. I was sure of it.

I climbed onto the steps and leaned out as we started moving again. Once we'd picked up speed, I came inside. The conductor was standing outside my cabin, asking the Americans where I was. When he saw me, his sour expression returned. "Please, *Herr.* Do not make trouble."

"Of course not," I said.

* * *

Soon after, we stopped in Villach, but I was more confident now. I excused myself as I pushed between the Americans' knees and looked out the window. They gave me generous smiles and offered potato chips, which I declined. We were high up now, moving along dark mountainsides and whistling through tunnels. When we emerged, the moonlit clouds seemed close enough to touch. Sometimes snow blew against the window. The Americans cooed at all of it, and I wished I knew enough English to ask if this was their first trip to Europe. They were so full of joyful excitement.

At about eight in the evening, we stopped outside Tarvis, or, to the Italians, Tarvisio. Austrian guards walked leisurely down the corridor, coming upon us first because we were at the end of the train. The Americans grinned as a chubby guard stamped their passports, and I handed over my fresh Austrian one. He gripped the stamp in his fist and stared a moment at the passport. I didn't know if it was real or not—Brano hadn't told me either way—and when he closed it again without stamping it, I was sure it was a forgery, a lousy one. He gave me a brief, severe smile and nodded down the corridor. "Please, come with me."

The Americans gazed in confusion as I got up and followed him out.

It was snowing here, the winds from the Julian Alps bearing down on us as we crossed the platform. I started to tell him that I was a police officer working on a case but realized there was no point. By the door to a quaint-looking office building, my guard whispered to the ranking officer, a fat man with a white mustache. This, I supposed, was the man who would end my journey. He looked me over a moment as I stared through heavy, wet snowflakes at the train—no, no one was getting off. He held up my passport and told me to come inside.

The office was overheated and stank of burned coffee—but real coffee. He looked through the mess on his desk and picked up a telegram.

He noticed me sniffing. "Get yourself a cup," he told me. Then he picked up the telephone and dialed. I poured the coffee and drank it black—it was scalded, but I needed it. I almost unzipped my coat, then remembered the heavy pistol and decided against it.

After a moment, the officer said, "Hello? Yes, this is Major Karloff Brentswinger. Yes, Tarvis. I was told to call this number when an Emil Brod reached the border. Yes. *Danke.*"

He covered the mouthpiece as I sipped the dreadful coffee and said, "He's not in the office. They're transferring me."

"Who?"

He seemed surprised I didn't know this, but he was only too aware of the limitations of his job in this snowy outpost, so he didn't answer. I drank my coffee quickly.

"Yes," the major said into the phone. "Emil Brod." He nodded at my passport. "Yes. Okay." He held out the phone. "He wants to speak to you."

I set down the empty cup and took the phone. Ludwig's voice came through the line. "Brod? That you?"

"Yes."

"You *bastard*! Do you know what you've done?"

"Yes," I said, biting my lip before the word "comrade" made it out. "I have some idea."

"An international fucking incident. That's what you've done."

There was noise on the line, movement, then Brano Sev came on, returning to my language. "Emil? Tell me the situation."

"Look, Brano. I'm sorry."

"Just tell me."

So I did. As far as I knew, Michalec was on the train, headed to Italy. He might get off beforehand, but I suspected he would take it all the way to Trieste. I imagined he could find protection there. "I'm following him."

"To kill him?" said Brano.

"I think so."

"Are you sure about this?"

"Yes," I said.

There was a long pause. "And money? Dijana gave you some."

"Most of it's gone."

"Okay." He didn't say good-bye, just went silent; then I heard him speaking to Ludwig. I couldn't make out the words. The Austrian was agitated, but Brano wasn't. Ludwig came back on. He sounded disgusted. "Give me the major, Brod."

It was, inexplicably, accomplished. After hanging up, Major Karloff Brentswinger took a stamp from his drawer, adjusted the date, inked it, and pressed it into one of the pages of my passport. I tried to read it when he handed it over, but it wasn't in German. It was in Italian. Some kind of Italian visa. When I looked at him, he shook his head. "Don't ask, okay?" Then he went through another drawer and handed me a slip of cardboard—a second-class ticket the rest of the way to Trieste.

He walked me back to the train. The conductor, farther up the platform, stared angrily when he saw I wasn't being removed. The Americans, having seen me shake hands with the major on the snowy platform, offered another beer, which I declined with thanks.

When the Italian border guards saw the passport, they didn't give me any trouble, so I suppose the stamp was official enough. They only peered at the shelves around me, looking for extra bottles of liquor, but I had nothing. The Americans told the guards all about their plans to see Venice, then Florence, then Rome, and the guards wished them a happy trip.

After a while, an Italian conductor came through, selling tickets. I handed him my new ticket. He punched a hole in it and handed it back with a smile.

I couldn't understand my good fortune. Brano didn't want me to kill Michalec—he'd made that clear. Was he just too soft, as I'd suspected before? Had he become too sentimental about his old friends and decided to give me my revenge because I needed it? Or was he being what he had always been—practical? His plan to arrest Michalec had gone disastrously wrong, and Ludwig's journalist friend was at that moment writing a scathing article about the ineptitude of Austrian intelligence for *Der Standard*. Perhaps the only solution left to Brano was to let me get rid of Michalec. I still hadn't had a chance to ask him.

By ten, we had descended from the mountains and were moving toward the Adriatic. I could smell the sea.

26 DECEMBER 1989

TUESDAY

•

THIRTY—SEVEN

•

After an hour in Trieste, I still hadn't fired a shot. The Americans
followed me out to the platform, muttering about what track their
Venice train was leaving from. Then the girl grabbed my shoulder,
which made me reach toward my gun. She smiled toothily. "Well,
have a good trip, mister."

"And you." I smiled, then moved quickly away, rising to my toes
to see over heads. It was difficult. These people had the height of the
West, of protein-rich diets that had never been handicapped by rationing.

I spotted him. The same gray suit I'd seen at the Vienna airport.
Walking easily toward the exit. He had no idea he was being followed.

I kept my hand on the pistol in my coat, walking about five
people behind. My heart made noises again. We descended the steps
to the underground tunnel connecting the platforms.

I wanted to take care of it there. A public assassination was what
I'd tried in Vienna. But over the last seven and a half hours on the
train, it had occurred to me that that kind of impulsive behavior
wasn't truly what I wanted. I didn't want the shock of terrified Italians around me, or the sudden arrest to stop me before I could finish the job.

Admittedly, I also wanted what I'd wanted from his son—some kind of explanation or understanding. I wanted what Gavra would later tell me he'd wanted from the Pankovs—some measure of apology.

So I shadowed him into the Stazione Centrale and out to the cool eleven-thirty gloom of Viale Miramare. He wasn't hesitating over anything—I noticed that. His tall form moved directly to the taxi stand as if, unlike me, he was familiar with this town. In fact it was true, though he hadn't been to Trieste since Europe's last big war, when he was working for the Gestapo.

I took the next taxi. Instead of telling the driver to follow Michalec's taxi, I gave him unsure directions from the passenger seat, in German, watching the other car make turns. The driver was tired from a long night's shift and became annoyed. "Where but you are going?" he asked in labored German.

"I'll know when I get there."

He grunted to make his frustration clear but didn't put up a fight. He'd dealt with plenty of strange Germans in his life.

Michalec's taxi stopped in front of the eroded luxury of the Grand Hotel Duchi D'Aosta. By then, the taxi driver had figured out what we were doing and said, "I am bet you want stop there at end of the street so he don't see."

I tipped the driver well, but he frowned at the Austrian schillings. "Is that all right?" I said.

"You have none lire?"

I shook my head.

"Well, it must to be."

I thought a moment before getting out, then counted the last of my schillings. Thirty-two—about three U.S. dollars, or 9,000 korona. "Can you change these?"

The man just wanted to go home; maybe that's why he went ahead and bought them from me. With four thousand lire in my pocket, I got out.

I spent half the money on a pack of cheap cigarettes from an all-night kiosk and smoked one on the street. It was warmer here, the temperate Adriatic wind full of salt. I walked to a street called Riva Caduti per l'Italianità di Trieste, where, on the other side, a concrete boardwalk ran alongside the black Adriatic. There were no stars out, but I spotted occasional pairs of lovers wandering by. They were pleasant to look at; they helped calm my flailing heart. But over the sound of waves lapping the ramparts, my ears started acting up again, humming. By then, I was sure he'd made it to his room. I returned to the hotel.

The Duchi D'Aosta's lobby was spare and dimly lit. The rates were listed behind a wood-paneled desk in Italian, English, German, and Russian. The clerk, with his thin black mustache and oiled hair, looked like a cartoon Italian. He turned morosely from a small television, the screen the size of a hand, showing a muted soccer game. *"Mi dica."*

"I'd like a room," I answered in German.

He seemed as irritated as the taxi driver had been, but he passed over a form for me to fill out. I used the information in my Austrian papers. He gave me a key to the third floor, and I said, "My friend arrived just a few minutes before me. Jerzy Michalec. What room's he in?"

The clerk seemed to wake up a little. "You two travel light."

"We're funny that way."

"I can call up to his room for you."

I shook my head. "He'll be asleep. I won't knock on his door until he's rested."

"It's against the rules to give out room numbers," said the clerk, shrugging.

He was waiting for a bribe, but two thousand lire wouldn't get me anything. I couldn't even pay for the room. I leaned against the counter. "Can you at least tell me the floor?"

He sagged a little, realizing he wasn't going to get anything out of me. He glanced at the game on the television and said, "Same as yours."

I wasn't rested enough; I knew this. And despite the shower at Brano's house, I stank, and wanted another one. In the stairwell I prepared myself anyway. I took out the Walther.

After my fiasco at the Vienna airport, I was left with three rounds in the magazine, one in the breech. I paused at my door, number 312, checked to be sure the corridor was empty, and walked slowly past the other rooms, listening. Halfway down, on the left, at room 305, I heard it. My language, spoken softly into a telephone. It was loud enough for me to recognize the rhythm and inflection but too quiet to make out the words.

For a moment I stood there, inches from the door, staring. There was a small, bright spy hole in the middle of it. I wondered if he would check it before opening the door. Of course he would. I couldn't just knock and wait for him to let me in.

I looked at the handle—a simple but effective lock. In movies, you always see men enter a locked room by firing a bullet into the lock. I've never seen it work in real life.

I heard him hang up the telephone, and then there was silence.

I returned to 312 at the end of the corridor and washed my face and hands and stripped off my dirty coat, leaving on my wrinkled blazer. My pulse raced, bringing on another headache, so I took my last two Captopril and tossed the empty bottle into the wastebasket. More than the money, this was the one sure sign I couldn't go back.

The bed was alluring, but if I sat on it, I wouldn't get up again. So I paced, walking to the high window that looked out on the narrow, dark Via Mercato Vecchio, trying to figure this out.

Then it occurred to me.

It was one in the morning when I called down to the lobby. The grumpy clerk said, "Grand Hotel Duchi D'Aosta."

"Sorry to bother you," I said in German. "I was just down there. Can you connect me to my friend's room?"

The clerk didn't bother replying. I just heard the *brr brr* of the phone ringing. "*Da?*" Michalec said abruptly.

I couldn't find any air. It was the first time in forty years that I'd heard his voice, but there was something to that single syllable that reminded me of all the empty words he'd spoken to me in 1948.

"Yes?" he repeated, in English.

"Jerzy," I said, and there was silence on his end. Perhaps he recognized my voice as well. I said, "Jerzy, you're finished. I'm on the train behind you. We just stopped at Udine. I thought I'd give you fair warning. The kind of warning you never gave my wife."

Though the words came out well enough, my tongue felt bloated and my cheeks were hot. But I knew he'd believe it. He would believe that I, like most everyone in our country, wanted to show how morally superior I was.

"Mr. Brod," he said quietly. "I didn't think you had it in you. How did you find me?"

"I'm clever."

"So you are."

"The conductor's calling," I said. "See you soon." I hung up.

He didn't come out immediately. Jerzy believed he had about two hours until my arrival, so he would use that time wisely. I stood to the left of his door, where it was hinged to the frame, and listened to him making telephone calls. He was louder now, but that wasn't panic; he only needed to make himself heard and understood. "How fast can you get a plane to Trieste? Okay. Direct to the Capital. I have to leave this phone within the hour. Right . . . right."

I wondered whom he was talking to. Perhaps his son, or some Italian collaborator, or a Parisian friend. It didn't matter.

As I waited, a drunk couple appeared at the end of the hallway, laughing. I tried not to look at them, but I was a peculiar sight: a bald, disheveled-looking elderly man standing beside a door, one hand stuffed tight into his blazer pocket. The man said, "Hey," and I gave a brief smile. The girl opened her mouth, but I cut her off by crossing a finger over my lips, giving off a quiet *shh*. I pointed at the door and pantomimed surprising a good friend. The woman *ahh*'d and nodded; the man snickered. They went to their room a couple of doors away, and soon afterward I heard them having loud sex.

Then Michalec's door clicked as he unlocked it and paused to look out the spy hole. I was out of its range. I removed the Walther from my pocket as the door started to open, then threw my shoulder into it with all my weight. There was resistance as he flailed on the other side, but he fell back. I pushed through, stumbled, and fell heavily on top of him. My shoulder hurt. I kicked blindly until the door slammed shut.

This close, in the dim light streaming in from the Piazza dell' Unità d'Italia, I couldn't see the man under me. I could only smell him. He was scented heavily, probably something from France. I don't know. I never asked.

As I raised myself from his chest, I heard him gasping for breath. I got to my knees, the pistol aimed, as my eyes adjusted. He wasn't even trying to fight back. He just rubbed his face, took a long, phlegmy breath, then looked up at me, squinting. "Is that you, Brod?"

I almost couldn't get to my feet; my knees hurt that much. "Yes."

He rubbed his face again. "Wow. I never even suspected. You've changed."

The real surprise for me was that he was unarmed. I expected to have to fight a pistol out of his hand, or quick-draw him before he got a chance to kill me, but during his years in France, he'd learned to put his safety in the hands of other people. Maybe that's what living in the West did to people. Living in the East, one never felt that way.

I could see him better now, but the shadows on his face were deep. After locking the door, I turned on the overhead light. He blinked, shielding his eyes.

With age, anything can happen to a face. It can widen or narrow, showing off the skull inside; it can fatten like a plum or map out the torments of poorly lived decades. I seemed to find all those changes in Michalec's face. I saw the deep purple creases under the eyes that pointed to heavy years, and the gauntness below the cheekbones, left over from years in a work camp. But he'd fattened along the jaw and neck, evidence of rich French food and too much influence, and his high forehead, still rimmed with white stubble, was creased like a worrier's. He had the dark eyes of someone who'd seen more than anyone should have to.

All this came to me very quickly, in about a second of staring, and I suppose that all my interpretations were wrong. But again, it didn't matter. I was here, he was here, and it was time.

"Get up."

"Oh-*kay*," he said slowly, with the kind of calm you use on very stupid people who might not know what to do with the gun they're pointing at you. He propped himself up on his elbows, then rolled facedown and got up to his knees, facing away from me. As if realizing how it looked, like the executions we'd all seen in Italian and American gangster movies, he snatched at the bathroom door handle and pulled himself to his feet.

"The bed," I told him and watched him move slowly toward it; just beyond, the lights of the square poured in. All my pains were coming into focus: my shoulder, knees, head, and heart. I tried to ignore them.

"Should I sit?" asked Michalec.

That's when I heard it—the cocky tone I remembered from decades ago, the one that once plagued my dreams. He'd had plenty of years to cultivate his confidence. I wondered if he'd ever found himself in this situation before.

Since I didn't answer, he sat anyway, turning to face me again. The bed creaked beneath him; he wasn't the kind of elderly person whose body withered away.

"Just do it, Brod. I don't want to have to listen to your explanations."

"You might have to."

"Well, make it quick."

I almost smiled. He spoke as if he were holding the gun. I checked my watch—it was a little after two in the morning.

Despite having imagined this moment in the Capital, then in Tisakarad and Sárospatak, and again in Vienna, I never pictured it here, at the southern tip of Churchill's famous Curtain, with my head throbbing. I cut off the overhead light to ease my pain. Everything dimmed.

"You know, Brod, this isn't like you. I've kept up with your career from a distance. You've lived the life you were supposed to live. A Militia chief, a wife, no children—because you're busy enough fathering your militiamen. You protect the rules. You don't break them."

"I've already broken a lot of them," I said, looking at the high French windows and the wet lights outside.

He didn't fill in the silence that followed, though I'm sure his mind was working hard, thinking up ways to stop me.

I was sweating, so I opened the window. I turned back quickly when I heard movement but was disappointed to see he'd only pulled himself farther onto the bed to lean on the headboard. That's when I knew what I wanted from him. I wanted something to make this less cold-blooded. I wanted him to reach for a gun or a knife, or throw a distracting pillow, so I'd have some justification for putting a bullet in him. But Jerzy had always been able to read people. Like his son, he knew how to give them what they didn't want.

I pulled up a flimsy desk chair and arranged it at the foot of the bed. I sat down and crossed my knees in an expression of ease, the pistol steady against my thigh, but all the blood in my body was swollen and sore, making me shiver. I said, "There are some things I don't understand."

"Like what, Emil?"

He'd finally used my first name, a touch of mockery. "All this. The killings. You'd already changed the files. Did you really think that people who knew about your past would be able to prove a thing?"

He cocked his head, and for a moment I thought he wouldn't answer. Then he took a breath. "Emil, I don't know what to think, not really. In the West, I wouldn't have to worry. Every day, someone comes out of the woodwork to accuse politicians of fraud, of fathering their babies, of raping women, of snorting cocaine. Whatever. It's all just background noise there. No one takes it seriously until it's backed up by evidence. But the East is different. We've spent the last century being told lies. We all knew they were lies, so we started coming up with our own truths. We didn't have the information to back up our truths, but we believed them anyway, because that's all we had. It was a choice between official lies or unofficial rumors." He shrugged; he'd obviously explained this to someone before. "Now, we're suddenly handed democracy on a plate. How will anyone know what to believe and what not to believe? Our people have no practice separating rumors from facts."

"But *why*?" I insisted. "You had a good life in France, I'm sure. Why risk it by coming back?"

He examined his fingernails, which in the dimness he couldn't have been able to see well. "Emil, you've got to let go of the past. You're not the same man you were in forty-eight—clearly you're not—and I'm not the same man either. I was. For a long time I was. But then, things happened that changed me."

"Nineteen seventy-nine," I said. "Rosta."

He pointed at me. "Exactly. You wouldn't know this, but fatherhood changes you. Suddenly, without warning, you're no longer the center of the known universe. I'd already arranged my escape to the

West. I knew the right people, and, more importantly, I'd used my surveillance work to collect information about those people—information they'd rather keep quiet. I was still the center of my universe, with plenty of blackmail material to protect me. Then I heard that an old friend had died. I decided to stop in at her funeral. And there was Rosta." He coughed into his fist. "You may not believe it, Emil, but I actually do believe in democracy and all that stuff. But I believe in the right democracy. You can't elevate peasants to statesmen and expect a country to prosper. You have to keep those with experience in the right places, to make sure it doesn't fall apart, and you have to bring in new blood that's been educated in the West."

"Which is what you did to your peasant son."

Even in the darkness I could tell he was glaring at me. He didn't want anyone to use that word to describe his son. He didn't bother answering.

Again, I unconsciously looked at my wristwatch. Michalec laughed briefly, and I later realized why—I looked like the president of the court that sentenced the Pankovs to death. The irony got to him. I said, "Eighty years old. Didn't you think it was time to retire?"

He rubbed his nose. "We're all too old, Emil. You, me, Brano—even the young ones, like Gavra."

I laid the gun across my knee and settled back in the chair. "How's your condition?"

"What?"

"Your epilepsy."

He nodded, as if he'd forgotten his disease. "Oh, that. Medical science is a wonderful thing. In the sixties I started taking an English drug, Tegretol. Not perfect—the side effects made sure I wouldn't be making any more children—but getting rid of the seizures was worth it. Then, a few years ago, I switched to a new one, Frisium." He paused. "I guess it doesn't matter now, but Balínt was carrying my medication."

"Balínt?" I said.

"The man you shot in Vienna." He shook his head. "Balínt was a good bodyguard, too. Just dumb luck you're still alive."

I nodded. "I'm out of my medication, too."

"Oh?"

"Hypertension."

Michalec nodded. "Getting old is hell."

"You have anything to drink?"

"What?" He didn't seem to understand the question.

"Alcohol. Do you have any?"

"Need some Irish courage?"

I'd never heard that phrase before but got the gist of it. "Not that. I thought you might want a last drink."

"Or cigarette?"

I took my packet out of my pocket and tossed it onto the bed.

"No," he said. "I quit years ago. My lungs couldn't take it."

I didn't know if this was a joke or not. "You think it matters now?"

"It might. No need to defile the temple."

His blasé attitude was infuriating. So I stood up, rather stiffly, took aim, and shot him in his left knee.

The blast rang in my still-numb ears. He went rigid, shouting, reaching for the wound. I stuffed a pillow into his face to muffle him. Then I placed the barrel against the pillow. But I only wanted to keep him quiet. One gunshot would wake the other guests; with two they would realize it wasn't a car backfiring.

After a while, I removed the pillow. I could have smothered him, I suppose, but I wasn't ready yet. I felt cold from the air blowing in through the terrace, but I liked the chill. It woke up my nerve endings so I could be alert through all of this.

His purple face was covered in sweat. He wasn't able to glare at me anymore; the pain made that impossible. All he could do was squeeze his eyes shut and bite his lip, grunting out his frustration. He could hear me, though. I knew that.

"If you scream, I'll put the next one in your skull. And you never know. I might change my mind at the last minute. You should endeavor to be around for that."

Of course, that was a lie. I only wanted this to last.

I don't know about other people, but when I stepped over, sometime back in the Capital, or maybe later in Brano Sev's guest bedroom, I knew things were different because time lost its regularity. That's the best way I can describe it. An hour was no longer an hour, but I couldn't call it something else either. Sometimes it was longer, sometimes shorter; sometimes it was gone in the blink of an eye. And when time became completely unmoored from reality, it could even move backward.

That's how it felt then. Time jumped back, and I hadn't shot Michalec in the knee. I had—he was feebly clutching his thigh—but it just didn't feel like any of that had happened. When you go mad, these discrepancies no longer bother you.

Then I heard Lena's voice. I don't think it was really the madness. I think she actually was there, speaking, but standing somewhere in the darkness I couldn't find. Like a very talented spy. She said what she'd said a few days before, but by other people's clocks she'd said it four decades ago, when I first met her. She was making fun of militiamen: "When you breed *in* equality, you breed *out* manners. *That's* a scientific fact."

I started to laugh.

"Bastard," Michalec said through his teeth. "You're fucking crazy."

I wiped my damp eyes and looked at him. He had an expression I don't remember ever seeing on his face before. He was scared. He knew now that I was one step beyond manipulation. I'd been touched by too much in the last week, and there was no way for him to predict the results of his words. He couldn't endear himself to me, and he couldn't anger me into taking care of this quickly.

For the first time, I was in charge. That only made me laugh more.

When I went to the window again, it was because I'd started to see the first inklings of sunrise. I didn't want to miss that. I don't know what time it was then, because I wasn't bothering with my watch anymore. From behind me, he said, "What the hell are you *waiting* for?"

I really didn't know. Sometimes in life you're given the keys to something you've always desired, but you dawdle at the door for longer than you should. Despite the stink of his blood, I was happy to stay a while in this place. The air in Trieste is clean and fragrant, and the rooms are beautiful simply because of where they are. We don't have a coastline in my country; it's something we appreciate more than Italians.

With the sun, the sweepers appeared in the square below, shuffling along, pushing away dew-covered paper cups and broken glass and other detritus of human life. To my left, the water glimmered yellow. It was really very beautiful. I slipped the Walther into my jacket pocket.

Down below, I heard voices and saw another American couple crossing the square. Soon they weren't alone, and Italians crawled out into the light, scooters buzzed like insects, and the Yugoslav and German and French tourists, clutching guidebooks with chilled fingers, went about their business. The marble beneath their walking shoes was wet; the sun glistened off it. I smelled something being fried somewhere. The city was coming to life.

That's when I remembered what I'd known all along, that thing about old people, and that another one gone was nothing. Just like Ministry officers.

I sniffed, then realized I was weeping. All the moments started to come back to me, in a sudden burst of irresistible memory. I remembered an old war that I'd run away from, up north to the Barents Sea, a hot fishing-boat cabin full of sweaty exiles from all over the world, drinking, smoking, laughing, and fighting. Hot, red-cheeked faces and rough voices shouting over cards. Tough men stuck on a tough sea with the backbreaking work of catching and killing seals. I remembered a few years later, first walking into Lena Crowder's extravagant house after her husband had been killed and I'd been given the case, my first. How she lay on her sofa, drunk, looking like something out of a film. A femme fatale, which is what she'd always been to me. I remembered taking her back from the cretin now in the room behind me, all of us in a shattered, flooded square in the Canal District, and a gunfight that injured my friend Leonek Terzian. Leonek, who would later become proud of his Armenian ancestry and insist on his birth name, Libarid, then die on a plane taken over by Armenian terrorists. The ironies of existence are astounding. He was the first militiaman I grew to love. Ferenc would never be forgotten—I knew this—but I remembered him as well because I didn't know if I'd ever see him again. He was a man too full of love—for his country, for his family, and for himself. Only now could I understand; he and I were the same. Bernard and all his flaws, and Agota, who was as angry as her mother, Magda. Such incredible people. Enigmatic Katja and her prophetic Aron.

It didn't matter what the years had done to us, how they estranged us or crippled or killed us, because in that moment I remembered them all with such heartache that I felt I was dissolving in the breeze. I gripped the rail.

I wasn't making sense, but I had to hold on to this feeling, because it was the most beautiful thing I'd known, or would ever know. I even forgot about Jerzy Michalec. Maybe he'd escaped; I didn't really care. Then I did.

When I sat again at the foot of the bed, the room was bright with yellow sunshine. He groaned again, and the floral pattern on the bedspread was hard to see because of all the blood. I said, "Okay, Jerzy. I'll finish it now."

Maybe my words brought on the seizure. He finally left the knee to its own problems and stretched rigid, shouting out the pain. His problem right now wasn't me. It was the disease inside him. He trembled with the falling sickness, his teeth snapping shut, his flabby jaw suddenly tight.

I didn't want to sit with him through the whole thing. I got up, took the pillow from where I'd dropped it on the floor, and pressed it against his face. His hands, unable to reach me, were shaped like claws. I pressed the pistol into the pillow and pulled the trigger twice in succession.

It's true that pillows muffle the sound of gunshots, but they were still loud. I felt them in my head. His body didn't relax; it was as if he'd been overcome by rigor mortis while still alive, death catching up afterward. I pulled my hand away from the pillow, but by then the blood had soaked through and stained me. I didn't bother washing up.

I set the gun on the bedside table and dragged the chair over to the window to watch all the activity beneath me. It was breathtaking. I couldn't even feel my heart anymore; that's how beautiful it was.

THIRTY-EIGHT

·

Two hours after the *carabinieri* took me away, my extended family collected in the Seventh District cemetery back home. I heard about this later; it was Markus Feder's doing. Despite a revolution in the streets, filling his body shop with corpses, Markus kept his head and made the arrangements for Lena's funeral. He was troubled that he couldn't track me down, but that didn't discourage him. He made calls, pulled in a few favors, and spread the word through Katja.

Twenty-five mourners attended my wife's funeral. Among them were Ferenc and Magda, who'd come to the Capital for the first time in thirty years, bringing along Fyodor Malevich. The three of them were on their way to a meeting with Rosta Gorski in the old Central Committee Building but took the time to say good-bye to Lena.

Gavra and Karel were also there, because, as Gavra told me later, he finally broke. It was Karel's fault. On Sunday night, Karel's constant pestering made him want to slap his friend. He kept saying, "Someone has to stay. Someone has to make it right." Finally, if only to shut the man up, Gavra shouted, "Okay!" They snuck out of the airport, avoiding anyone who might recognize Gavra, and stole a decent-looking Karpat. Since I wasn't home, and they couldn't go back to their place, they went to Katja and Aron's in the Seventh District, where they slept on the couch.

Katja and Aron drove Imre Papp's widow, Dora, and ten-year-old son, Gabor, to the funeral; Bernard and Agota brought Sanja.

I wish I could have been there with them. The ceremony was run by a Catholic priest, because Markus Feder was Catholic. Though neither Lena nor I was religious, I don't think she would have minded. They stood in the crabgrass cemetery, bundled tightly against the cold. When the ceremony was finishing, Gavra noticed a black ZIL saloon with tinted windows and government plates parked some distance away. He broke away from the mourners to check on it. As he neared, the back window rolled down. Rosta Gorski stared back at him.

"Gavra Noukas," he said flatly.

"Yes," said Gavra. He wore Katja's Makarov in his belt and considered using it, but the car was also occupied by two large bodyguards.

"I've gotten some word about your friend."

"Yes?" He didn't need to hear my name to know who Gorski was talking about.

"He's killed my father."

That surprised Gavra. In fact, the news surprised everyone except Brano Sev and Magda Kolyeszar. "Where?"

"Italy."

Gavra took a breath of cold air and glanced back at the mourners. "Why're you telling me this?"

"I want you to recognize that it's over."

Gavra was surprised that there wasn't any real anger in the man. His father had just been killed, but there was no sense of loss. Then Gavra realized why: Jerzy Michalec's death actually protected the son. With a few bullets, I'd saved Rosta Gorski's political career. No one would go digging into a dead father's past. This was why Brano Sev had insisted the old man remain alive.

There wasn't anything Gavra could say in reply, so he said nothing. He wandered back to the funeral as it was breaking up. The ZIL drove away.

Later, the funeral party moved to Max and Corina's, which had just reopened. Cardboard covered the shattered windows, but the electricity still worked, and the brandy was cold. Gavra told the others what he'd learned, and shocked silence followed. Magda said she was only surprised I hadn't ended up dead myself. "He seemed dead when I last saw him."

Ferenc disagreed, and they argued over me.

It was then that Ferenc decided to put my case into his negotiations, which is what he did an hour later while sitting across from Rosta Gorski.

29 DECEMBER 1989-

20 MARCH 1990

●

THIRTY-NINE

•

The fact is that no one knew what to do with me. Brano had gotten my passport, through Ludwig, from the Austrian Interior Ministry, so it wasn't fake, but it wasn't quite authentic either. In his rush to put it together, Ludwig had skipped many of the required signatures. This was a favor to Brano he would always regret, because it left a black mark on his record that was hard to live down.

After two days of hospital observation, the Italians gave me a fresh supply of prescriptions and transferred me to a federal holding cell outside Venice, solely for illegal immigrants. It was a modern, concrete place with an always damp courtyard, much more comfortable than prisons back home. My cellmate was a Congolese worker named Tabu Bel, a big man with very black skin, who had been working summers in Italy and Austria, taking the money back home at the end of the season. This was his seventh year of migrant labor, and he'd finally been caught. He wasn't dismayed by his situation. In German, he said, "Life is full of decisions." He shrugged his thick shoulders. "No reason to regret them once you've made them."

I told him that was easier said than done, and he asked me why an old white man was in jail with him. I told him, and that's how the conversation ended.

On Friday, a visitor from our embassy in Rome arrived on the train and took a walk with me in the wet courtyard. Natan Jovovich was a small man, hair slicked off to the side to cover a bald patch, and he wore a fine Italian suit. I, on the other hand, wore the prison's white jumper. "Mr. Brod," he said, hands clasped behind his back as he walked. "You've put the government in a strange position."

"The government put me in a strange position."

He nodded; he'd been briefed on the story I'd given the Italian detectives. He, like them, didn't believe a word of it. "Be that as it may, you've killed a representative of our government. If we brought you back, under the current laws you'd be executed for treason. By all appearances, you're a counterrevolutionary fighting against the people's democracy."

I don't think he caught the irony in what he'd said—"people's democracy" was what Pankov had called his government. "So," I said, "what's the problem?"

"The problem, Mr. Brod, is that we don't want to start our democracy by executing people. It's the old way. Not our way."

Again, thinking of Pankov, the irony was apparent, but I didn't bother mentioning it. I said, "What you mean is, you don't want my testimony made public."

He sniffed. "Hardly."

"You've been given some instructions, I bet. From the Capital."

"We're going to set you free."

I stopped, and it took him a moment to realize I was no longer walking beside him. He looked back. I said, "What?"

"We're going to set you free. We don't want to make an issue out of this. I've got your passport—we took it from your Friendship Street apartment—a six-month Swiss visa, and a little money to get you started."

"Wait," I said, holding up a hand to silence him. "This doesn't make any sense."

He sighed, then glanced around at the high courtyard walls. I don't think Jovovich had been inside many prisons. "When you have friends in high places, these kinds of things do happen."

I started to ask who my friends might be, but the answer was obvious. "Ferenc."

Jovovich nodded. "Mr. Kolyeszar was adamant about this. It was a condition of his little revolutionaries taking part in the elections as peaceful participants." He came a step closer. "There's Italian paperwork to deal with, but you should be out in the next couple of days."

I wasn't sure what to think, or feel. I squinted at him. "Conditions?"

"Of course," he said. "We ask the same thing the Italians and the Austrians ask."

"What's that?"

"That you never set foot in our country again."

My legs stopped working, so I settled on the cold gravel and shut my eyes.

Jovovich approached. "Are you okay?"

"I can't do this."

"Why not?"

I wondered if he really was that dense.

"Listen," he said. "The alternative is that you stay here, in this prison, for the rest of your life. You'll be in legal limbo. The Italians won't try you, because we've asked them not to. We won't take you. And the Austrians refuse to accept that passport of yours." He squatted beside me, gravel crunching. "It's up to you, Mr. Brod."

FORTY

·

On the last day of the decade, a Sunday, they let me go. I wished Tabu good luck, then shook his strong hand. The warden had an envelope for me. It contained my old passport, a pocketful of Italian lire and Swiss francs, and a train ticket out of the country, to Zürich. The warden, a young, rather elegant man, said I had forty-eight hours to leave, and would I need an escort? I told him no, I wouldn't be needing one.

My train was scheduled to leave from Mestre, just outside Venice, at six in the evening. So I took a taxi to the edge of the canal-woven city and started walking.

I'd imagined this place all my life, but whatever pictures my feeble imagination might have come up with were nothing compared to the reality. In fact, I'd always imagined that it would look like our Canal District, with arched bridges and musty lanes and cats and everything crumbling.

Venice was like that—it had all the things my Canal District had before the cranes started tearing it apart—but at the same time it was utterly different. It was in the details. I found myself turning corners and then stopping in my tracks to gasp at churches so complex and ornate that I couldn't figure out how the human mind could produce them. Then, crossing a footbridge beside the Grand

Canal, I noticed some tourists taking photographs up a watery alley. I looked, and saw it—a covered bridge, high up, connecting two old buildings.

I didn't need to ask for verification, because I knew. It was the bridge connecting the courthouse to the prison. The bridge from where the condemned caught his final stolen glance of freedom before descending to his new, barred home.

Three months later, as I finish this, my life is something different than it once was. With the help of some fellow émigrés here in Zürich, I found work—I clean the floors and walls and desks in a private high school. Gavra doesn't understand why I do it, because I don't need the money. The Galicia Committee government has so far upheld the deal Lena's father once made with General Secretary Mihai's government back in 1946, and her foreign investments are now mine. I can't yet face dealing with all of Lena's papers, though. Besides, I like the children. They're the sons and daughters of diplomats from all over the world, and they laugh at me and ask why I speak German with such a funny accent. Despite this, I find myself thinking fondly of them when I'm at home in the evenings, writing this story.

There are visitors. Twice, Ferenc has come bearing gifts and stories of the steady opposition the Democratic Forum and its presidential candidate, Father Eduard Meyr, has been erecting against the Galicia Revolutionary Committee, running up to the May elections. Despite his endless enthusiasm, we both know he's failing.

The Galicia Committee newspapers are what everyone reads—they're funded by donations from various nongovernmental organizations fostering democracy. The recently inaugurated Sárospatak television station finds it hard to get an audience when the other two stations have an endless supply of subtitled Hollywood movies to distract everyone.

The Democratic Forum recently lost a fight over the renaming of Sárospatak's 25 August Square. Ferenc wanted it to return to its

precommunist name, King Béla Square, but before they could peti-
tion the change, the Galicia Committee had changed the signs to
read 23 DECEMBER 1989 SQUARE, the date of the Capital's uprising. A
tempest in a teacup, but it shows how little power the Democratic
Forum has.

So Ferenc has gone back to the basic technique of nonviolent re-
sistance: the demonstration. Over the last two weeks, the Democratic
Forum has staged demonstrations in Victory Square (now called
Revolution Square), demanding a level playing field in the elections.

But they're small affairs, attended only by the most devout. The
people of our country are by now exhausted. I can understand.

Gavra visits every couple of weeks to help me get my facts straight
in this. His life is different now, too. He and Karel moved to a de-
tached house outside the Capital. He still travels, but now he travels as
a spokesman for the Tisa Corporation, a company set up to convince
Western investors to look east for their fortunes. "It's early still," he
tells me, "but this really is the future."

"Coca-Cola and Ford," I say without enthusiasm, but also without bitterness. Gavra's a national hero, and I'm glad he's been able to
shed his past so easily. When I ask about Brano, he shakes his head.
They haven't talked.

When he visits, Gavra spends a lot of time by the curtains, peering out at the clean Zürich street. I know what he's looking for, because I've seen them myself. There are three that I know of, small
men who smell of the East. I can't imagine how bored they must be,
following me from home to school, then to the market and back
home. They're with me all the time.

"They don't know what you're writing, do they?" asks Gavra.

"I keep it hidden in the floorboards. But they'll know soon
enough. Ferenc is picking up the manuscript next Tuesday."

Gavra finds me frustrating; he's different than he was only a few
months ago. Success has changed him. "You really think it'll make a
difference?"

"I don't know," I say, because it's true.

"You better move."

"Move where?"

"Away. Somewhere no one can find you. I can help."

I shrug. "And leave all my children?"

It's time to finish. I'm expecting Ferenc at any moment; he's picking up these pages. Out on the street, not far from my door, two of my shadows are sharing a smoke. I can see through the curtains that the third is joining them; for once, they're having a party. I have a feeling they'll invite me soon.

I don't know if my story will help anyone, but it's all I've got to offer. I hope it does help. Because, despite the lessons of forty years in the People's Militia, there really is hope left in the world.

If you're reading this, it means there still is.

—*E. Brod*
Zürich, March 1990

AUTHOR'S NOTE

•

Students of the Romanian Revolution of 1989, which toppled the regime of Nicolae and Elena Ceauşescu, will notice many similarities between that reality and this fiction. It's no accident. In 1999, the U.S. Fulbright Commission generously granted me a yearlong grant to work on a novel based on that curious and ecstatic moment in Romanian history. The result, a novel called *Tzara's Monocle*, never saw publication, but the research that went into writing it inspired and helped inform this series of Eastern European novels, of which *Victory Square* is the conclusion.

That's not to say that the unnamed country in this series is Romania. Some have suggested this, while others imagine it's Hungary, where I live. Neither is the case. My piece of fictional real estate has always been the product of a Western imagination casting about for an image of the communist East, influenced by all the countries I've come in contact with and guided more by my personal obsessions than by any historical exactitude.

Still, it's an informed fiction, and in this volume the Romanian research is worn more on the sleeve. For example, the list of titles associated with Tomiak Pankov in chapter eighteen. Strange as it may seem, these are all actual terms used by sycophantic propagandists to refer to Nicolae Ceauşescu in Romania.

In chapter two, the "newly finished Workers' Palace, that Third District monstrosity fronted by the long, cobblestone Workers' Boulevard, which *The Spark* continually reminded us was one meter wider than the Champs-Elysées" is based on the Casa Poporului, or House of the People, in front of Bucharest's Boulevard to the Victory of Socialism. They are now called the Palace of Parliament and Unification Boulevard, respectively. As mentioned in chapter four, much of Tomiak Pankov's radical civil reengineering, including the Workers' Palace, was inspired by a trip to North Korea, just as Nicolae Ceauşescu's was.

Chapter eleven begins with a story of Tomiak Pankov's hunting retreats and a Ministry sharpshooter killing game when Pankov missed. This, too, is from the stories of Ceauşescu, though in reality it was not the Ministry but the Securitate, Romania's feared secret police.

In chapter thirteen, the following conversation takes place between a soldier and Katja Drdova in reference to the rooftop "terrorists" shooting into crowds:

> "Yeah. Pankov made a deal with Muammar Qaddafi for his special forces to protect him in case this happened. Rumor is, when he came back on Sunday a second plane landed just afterward with about a hundred of these guys."
>
> "Oh," said Katja. "And Pankov? Where is he?"
>
> "Wouldn't we all like to know?"
>
> Later, that Libyan rumor would become accepted truth, though in fact none of the snipers was ever caught, and no one could find records of a second Libyan flight landing at Pankov—now Tisa—International.

The same rumor, also unsubstantiated, ran through Romania during the confused days of the revolution and afterward.

Also in chapter thirteen is a lengthy telegram written by the country's ambassador to the Soviet Union, recounting a meeting with

V. L. Musatov, "Deputy Director of the International Department of the Central Committee of the Communist Party of the Soviet Union." The text of the telegram is amended from an original "Memorandum of Conversation with the Ambassador of the SRR [Socialist Republic of Romania] in the USSR, I. Bucur," dated 21 December 1989 and found online at the wonderful Cold War International History Project of the Woodrow Wilson International Center for Scholars. The original is from Musatov's perspective, whereas my fictional version is told from the ambassador's side, but in both reality and fiction, the leaders believed that the Soviet Union, or at least the Warsaw Pact, might be behind the uprisings in their countries.

The gunfight between "terrorists" and soldiers at the Hotel Metropol is also taken from reality, when the "terrorists" shooting into crowds were caught at the Hotel Inter-Continental in Bucharest. They shot from hotel windows, down to the street, and army units fired back. As in my fictional version, they were not captured.

But the most obvious parallel between this story and reality is the trial of the Pankovs in chapter twenty-five. The spoken words of the trial are taken, with few changes, from a translation of the Ceauşescus' trial that was published in many papers during late 1989 and early 1990, made available by the United States government's Foreign Broadcast Information Service. I've made adjustments for clarity, and to fit into my nameless country's story, but it's largely taken from the actual proceedings. My major change, besides the obvious, is the use of prosecution witnesses; there were none in the Ceauşescus' trial.

There are many other parallels. In Romania, it was from the western town of Timişoara that the revolution first sprang, and the dissident pastor László Tőkés was at the center of its movement. Also, the Timişoara revolution was subsumed by the more powerful machinations of ex-communists in the capital, Bucharest. The reasons and explanations I give in *Victory Square*, however, are entirely my own.

Even the story of the Russian Fyodor Malevich has a real-life parallel in the swirl of rumors during that period. In the days leading up to the

Romanian Revolution, tourist traffic from Russia, entering through the Ukraine, grew abnormally. According to an auto mechanic in the north of the country, one Russian car, carrying four men, broke down on its way to Timişoara. The Russians brought it to the mechanic, and as he worked on it the man discovered four Romanian officers' uniforms in the trunk.

But as I say, *Victory Square* is fiction.

For those interested in the true story of Romania under communism, along with its violent and sometimes awkward shifts toward democracy, you could do no better than to go to the works of Dennis Deletant, the foremost English-language scholar of Romanian culture and history. I owe a great debt to his efforts, as well as Edward Behr's breathless account of the Ceauşescus' story, *Kiss the Hand You Cannot Bite: The Rise and Fall of the Ceauşescus* (Villard, 1991).

—*O. Steinhauer*
Budapest, October 2006